Pay to Play

Pay to Play

Jerri Williams

Cover design by Elizabeth Mackey / elizabethmackey.com

Formatting by Polgarus Studio / polgarusstudio.com

Chapter 1

Stu Sebastiani tucked a C-note down the server's sequined bra and raised his voice above the pulsing music.

"Can I cop a feel for a hundred-dollar bill?"

The curvaceous blond in her glittery halter and hot pants smiled, signaling consent in Sebastiani's mind. However, when he patted her butt, she scowled and dislodged his hand from her backside with a well-placed slug to his solar plexus.

He winced and then laughed in spite of the pain. Didn't she know who he was? He was responsible for the place jumping off tonight and, as part of the compensation for his behind-the-scenes contributions, he felt entitled to a bit of bad behavior. He had spent the first half of the evening playing a one-sided game of grab-ass with the cocktail waitresses and dancers scurrying about the congested floor. His son, Arty, was a minority owner of JOLIE, Philadelphia's newest and most exclusive gentlemen's club. Tonight was the grand opening, and he planned to get his party on.

He massaged his now-bruised abdomen and surveyed the club. The crowd was so deep, no one could possibly take note of the painstakingly selected interior decor. So much fuss about the dimensions of the chandeliers, the grade of marble for the floors, and those ridiculous Grecian sculptures—they should have listened to him. The only thing the customers care about was the babes.

"Dad." Arty appeared at Sebastiani's side and leaned in close to shout into his ear. "I saw that. You know you're not supposed to touch."

1

"Can you blame me?" Sebastiani angled his head toward the luscious rear end of the cocktail waitress bending over to place an order of drinks on the next table. "I'm glad you took my advice and hired girls with a little something extra that jiggles when you smack it."

"Some of them are complaining."

"Most don't mind. How am I to know which ones do?" He pantomimed pinching the round bottom of an unsuspecting brunette scooching by but knew better than to feel up the paying customers.

"Why don't you go hang with your buddy Bill Leone?"

"Nah, he's all sour grapes tonight." Sebastiani caught a view through the crowd of his old friend parked at center stage, sipping a drink while checking out the featured entertainer, Lola or Lolly or something like that. Leone was probably scheming to book her at his club. "He did tell me earlier that I should claim partial credit for your success."

"Why?"

"'Cuz you inherited my appreciation of the female anatomy."

"I don't know about that."

"Sure, he's right." Sebastiani grinned at Arty. "You may have earned your master's in business administration from Wharton, but you earned your master's in boobs and ass by studying with your old man."

"That's so uncool, Dad." Arty let out an exaggerated sigh. "I hope you're not telling people that."

"Don't forget, I introduced you to your business partners."

"And thank God I can always count on you to remind me of that."

Arty muttered something else, but Sebastiani couldn't understand what he said. He ignored his son's reproach and looked past him, into the crowd, where he spied one of his pals from the old neighborhood. He called him over.

"Jimmy Mastracola." Sebastiani greeted him with a hearty embrace and a kiss on the cheek. "Glad you could make it."

"This place is something else." Mastracola pulled Arty into a bear hug. "You should be proud of yourself, Junior."

"Thanks, Uncle Jimmy."

"You too, Stu." Mastracola bumped fists with Sebastiani. "I'm sure you were an *unofficial* consultant on all this."

"We were just saying how he got his MBA from me." He winked at Mastracola. "Master's in boobs and ass."

Mastracola laughed and nodded. "No one knows more about strip clubs than you."

Sebastiani gave Arty a playful nudge.

A frown creased Arty's brow. "Come with me, Uncle Jimmy," he said, changing the subject. "I want to introduce you to my business associates. They had something to do with this too."

"Yeah, let's go see 'em." Sebastiani patted Arty on the back and smiled. "I got a surprise for you guys."

"What is it?"

"Just you wait."

Arty stared at him for a beat, sighed, and led them through the crush of bodies and introduced Mastracola to Lynette Hampton and Curtis Kincaid, both dressed for the occasion. She wore sequins and black silk, and so did he.

Sebastiani high-fived the partners and liked the way Lynette's breasts bounced in her low-cut dress when he slapped her hand. "Great crowd, Lynette. The house is packed."

"Should be." She stood with one hand on her hip. "We spent nearly a quarter of a million on marketing."

"Yeah, great ad campaign—billboards, flyers, and all that social media stuff." He scanned her body. Her ass was starting to look a little flat. Too bad. She used to have such a nice one. "But maybe," he continued, "everybody's here because your closest competitors are temporarily shut down."

Arty slid toward Sebastiani and leaned in, his eyes dark and questioning. "What do you mean, Dad? What did you do?"

"L and I is conducting a semiannual inspection of all the clubs in South Philly." He stepped sideways to allow more space between them. "The crackdowns are tonight. What a coincidence."

"What the hell?" Arty gripped his arm. "You can't just order up a raid to get us more business. You've got to call off your Department of Licenses and Inspections people, right now."

Sebastiani pretended to be unconcerned, but his mouth was

suddenly dry and there was a thickness in his throat. He raised an imaginary glass to his lips as a signal to a waitress standing nearby that he needed a drink. "Can't you see the beauty of it all? When my guys roll in, their customers leave and come here." He looked at each partner. How could they not understand what he had done for them?

"I can't believe you pulled such a boneheaded stunt," said Kincaid. His words and spittle were both forced through clenched teeth. "After all we've done to appear legit."

Sebastiani glanced around the room. The music seemed to have gotten louder. The thumping rhythm made his heart beat faster. He could feel the vibrations in his feet.

"Stu. I'm talking to you."

He gave Kincaid a stiff half smile. "It's all good. Trust me."

Lynette moved in closer. Her potent perfume made his eyes blink. He recalled how, after he had been with her, he'd have to scrub away her scent before he could go home.

Jabbing one of her lacquered talons in his face, she said, "You need to go."

Sebastiani flung his arms wide. "You're kicking *me* outta here? You guys *need* me." He turned to Arty. "Tell them."

"We'll talk about that later." Arty tugged on his sleeve. "Right now, you need to call off your boys."

Sebastiani yanked his arm away and inadvertently bumped into Kincaid, who flinched, immediately took a weak defensive stance, and raised his fists in the air.

"Really?" Sebastiani glared at Kincaid, daring him to make a move. "Aren't you afraid you'll mess up your outfit?"

"*Stop it.*" Arty stepped between them. "He'll stay and straighten everything out."

"You *better* fix this," said Kincaid. He wagged his finger at Sebastiani and then stomped away, sputtering obscenities. Lynette followed close behind, glaring back at him even as she greeted a guest with a warm hug and kiss.

Sebastiani stood motionless with his arms stiff against his sides. He looked at Arty, who was shaking his head. *What a clusterfuck. Say something to defend yourself.* He glanced over at Mastracola, who appeared to be embarrassed for him.

"But it worked. They came," said Sebastiani.

"But, Dad, it wasn't your place to do anything. You should have asked me." Arty pointed to the rear bar. "Go sit back there and make some calls to clean up this mess. Try to keep a low profile."

***

Two hours later, Sebastiani, still entrenched at the far side of the club where Arty had banished him, slumped on a barstool, his upper body draped over the counter. Just below his alcohol buzz, he detected his suppressed anger. How come everyone else got to have it all, but he was supposed to be satisfied with scraps? He ran the side of his hand slowly across the stubble on his cheek, tilted his glass to his lips, and guzzled down his Jameson.

"They can all suck my hairy balls," he mumbled to himself. "Lay low. Hell no."

No one had been upset when he used his connections to make sure zoning permits and construction inspections sailed through without a hitch. Now, after they had taken advantage of the courtesies his position provided, they acted like they didn't know him. So what if Arty got a small share in the business? He wanted his own payday. They owed *him*.

"Come 're for a minute." He waved the bartender over. His head was at her chest level. He wished he could bury his face in those fleshy, plump mounds. He spoke to her cleavage. "Did ya know I named this joint? Those shitheads wanted to call it Jolie Visage, like dudes would come in here to check out pretty faces. I told 'em," he said, his tongue thick and doughy, "I told 'em, 'Skip that highbrow French shhhit. Just call it Jolie, like that hot piece actress.'"

The bartender reached for the whiskey glass resting next to Sebastiani's head. As wasted as he was, he still managed to snatch it before she could take it away. While she waited, he lapped up the remaining brown liquid coating the bottom and sides of the empty glass, then wriggled his tongue at her.

"I hope you got it all," she said over her shoulder as she walked away with the tumbler, "'cuz that was your last one."

"Fuck it." Sebastiani pounded his fist on the bar. "I'm not gonna let 'em stick me in the corner like some sssmacked ass."

He whirled his finger around the wet ring left behind on the bar, collecting himself. He smiled. Tannie. He would get Tannie a job at JOLIE. She would be his spy. She would make sure he got his fair share of the business he had helped build.

Tannie would make sure he got what he deserved.

Chapter 2

Special Agent Kari Wheeler toggled the cursor between two e-mails on her computer screen. She took in and then let out a long breath. She didn't want to respond to either. The first was from Justin Fiske, an agent in the Chicago Division whom she'd met during a recent trip to the FBI Academy in Quantico, where, for the third time in less than two years, she had been asked to conduct an advanced seminar on recruiting and managing white-collar-crime informants.

She had flirted with Justin at the hotel bar for more than an hour. And, as was the rule of the game, just when she knew he thought she would be going up to his room, she excused herself "for a moment" and never returned. She always slipped away before things went too far, before it was too late. To know they wanted to be with her was all she needed. When she and Justin bumped into each other on the FBI Academy campus the next day, she had pretended not to recognize him. But now he was e-mailing her and asking when she would be returning to the Academy for another in-service class. *Was he kidding?*

She glanced at the photo of Kevin and the kids and then back at the e-mail on the computer screen, a giant placard flagging her shame.

She hit delete.

The second message, "Please see me," was from her new boss, Juanita Negron. Kari hadn't bothered to apply for the job. She didn't need to be the boss to be in charge. Her fourteen years working fraud cases had earned her a place of influence on the prestigious Public Corruption Squad, the FBI's number-one criminal priority. Juanita, on the other hand, had no problem proclaiming her authority. That woman ticked Kari off. Kari preferred to stay out of Juanita's office, where she held court and issued edicts. Kari had hoped Juanita would pop out to get coffee and when she walked through the squad area, Kari could casually ask what she wanted. But it had been almost two hours, and Juanita had not yet made a move.

Kari sighed, gathered up her notepad and a pen, and went in to see her boss. As she tapped on the open door and entered the sparsely decorated office, Juanita peered over the top of her designer glasses and gave Kari one of her insincere smiles. A midmarket TV reporter in Miami before she joined the FBI, her perfectly applied makeup accented her flawless, caramel-cream complexion. Juanita pushed aside the statistical evaluations she'd been reviewing and held up a single sheet of paper.

"I can't go back down to Quantico right now, if that's why you needed to see me."

"It wasn't, but is everything all right?"

"My mother's been ill." Juanita opened her mouth to speak and Kari waved her hand, swatting away Juanita's concerns. "She's doing much better now. She's in remission…" Kari immediately wished she hadn't shared that intimate detail. Her rule had always been *Don't ever give them anything to later use against you.*

"That's great," said Juanita, displaying another weak smile. "I was actually going to assign you a complaint that came in today. Sounds like bad timing."

"No, no. What do you got?"

"You have time to work another case?"

"Of course." Kari smiled. "You know me. If it's something good, I'll find a way."

"You sure?"

Kari nodded and took the paper from Juanita.

The information block of the one-page form contained the name Tannie Colosi, a telephone number, and a few lines of succinct narrative. "Complainant advised that she has information about the head of business licensing and inspections for the City of Philadelphia, Stuart Sebastiani, accepting cash and gifts from strip club owners.

Complainant is a stripper at a local club. Complainant requests confidentiality."

"I thought it was a perfect case for you. Your kind of thing."

Strip clubs? "What makes you say that?"

"I heard the *Inquirer* dubbed you the 'Hall Monitor' after your second city-councilman conviction. This case has the potential to be another public official busted on a bribery and kickbacks indictment. Right up your alley, right?"

Kari read the complaint again.

"Sebastiani? Isn't he that Boobgate guy?"

Juanita looked puzzled.

"Never mind," Kari said. "Go ahead and assign it to me." She scanned the name listed on the paper. "I'll go see this Tannie Colosi woman today."

Juanita motioned for her to return the complaint form. While waiting for her to scribble and initial an assignment memo at the bottom of the page with her Bulgari pen, Kari stared at the area behind the desk. Centered behind Juanita was the same signed and numbered watercolor print of an FBI seal and Thompson submachine gun that hung in the office or home of every FBI agent with vacant wall space. She had been promoted more than three months ago but had unpacked only this one item. Why were there no family photos, no mementos, no plaques or certificates?

"Can you take one of the young guys with you?" Juanita looked up for her desk. "They're hanging around the office too much."

Kari glanced out the doorway at the agents gathered in the squad area. Asking one of the beer-guzzling former frat boys to come to interview a stripper with her didn't seem prudent. Instead, she would bring along conservative family man Everett Hildebrand, just for "grins and giggles" a phrase she'd often heard him use.

"I'll get Hildebrand to help me out."

"Karolina, really? Hildebrand?"

She knew Juanita didn't like Hildebrand, but that was no reason for Juanita to use her full name, as if she were a child. The supervisor waited for her to say something, but she kept her mouth shut. *Just because he made the mistake of disrespecting your squad-car policy, doesn't mean I have to shun him too.*

Juanita handed back the form.

"One more thing. The Citizen's Crime Commission Awards luncheon?"

"I told you. Can't go. It conflicts with my kids' parent-teacher conferences."

"But you're one of the recipients."

"I appreciate the recognition, but as much time as I spend here, it's my family that deserves an award." She smiled, placed her right hand over her heart, and patted her chest. She left the room without saying another word.

Back in her cubicle, she got right to work. She googled the name Stuart Sebastiani. *Aha. He is that Boobgate guy.* Perhaps it was a quirk of fate that a complaint involving strip clubs and the Boobgate guy would come across her desk today. Just that morning, after finding a digital copy of *Muffs Illustrated* downloaded on Carter's laptop, she had told Kevin she was designating the past few days as "porn week."

Two days earlier, she had caught Carter looking at sex GIFs on his phone. A quick check of his Twitter account revealed that many of the people he followed had porn star names. She was now policing all of his devices. It was as if his thirteen-year-old hormones had roared into full throttle that very week. She chuckled. *Carter would go bananas if he knew I was going to interview a stripper.*

She called the number listed on the paper. A female voice answered.

"Hi, is this Tannie Colosi?"

"Yeah? Who's this?"

"Tannie, this is Kari Wheeler. I'm an agent with the FBI and I'm calling about the complaint you filed earlier today. I want to set up a time for us to talk."

"Oh. I don't know...I think I changed my mind," Tannie said. "I was angry when I called."

"At Stuart Sebastiani? Did he do something to upset you?"

Silence.

"Sometimes we try to talk ourselves out of stuff," Kari nudged, "even when we know it's the right thing to do."

Still no response.

"Hello? Are you there?"

Tannie let out a long groan. She was clearly irritated, but whether with herself or with the phone call, Kari couldn't tell. "You'll have to come to the club," she finally said. "I don't want you coming over to my place." She spit out the address to the PlayRoom, the South Philly strip club where she worked. "How long will it take you to get here?"

"You're open now?" Kari asked. It was not yet two o'clock.

"We open at noon. The lunch crowd has thinned out. If you come by now, we'll have a few minutes to talk."

"I'm on my way."

"I'm not saying I'm going to tell you anything. I'll see how I feel after you get here."

"I want you to be comfortable."

"Oh, do you? You might have to buy a lap dance then."

Kari paused for a beat and cleared her throat. *I hope she's joking.* "That will depend on what you tell me."

"Cool. Just make sure to ask for me when you get here, so I can make you out from all the other business types," said Tannie.

"I'm a black female, about five foot eight. I have on a dark gray suit."

"Of course you do."

Kari laughed to herself. Tannie thought she knew her already, the typical female law enforcement officer who underplayed her appearance. *Humph.* Tannie was right. Clean and presentable was her standard beauty regime.

"What about Sebastiani?"

"What about him?"

"You're not concerned that someone will see us talking and say something to him?"

"Nah. He's got no reason to worry about me."

Kari disconnected and called over to Hildebrand, who sat with his back to her, pecking away at his keyboard in a cubicle nearby. He swiveled his six-foot-three-inch, broad-shouldered frame to face her. She liked having him accompany her on interviews. People assumed with his height and large build that he was in charge. She enjoyed watching their reactions when they learned she was in command of their two-man team. She liked that, being in control.

"Hey, Ev," she said. "You wanna sit in on an interview with me?"

"Definitely. What's up?"

"Not sure yet. I'm guessing it's the usual scorned woman rats out lover."

"You need me to drive?"

"Uh, I don't think so," Kari said, laughing. She knew he was joking. His was the worst car on the squad. She jingled the keys in her jacket pocket. "We'll take my Bureau car."

Chapter 3

Everett didn't ask where they were going, and Kari didn't hand him the complaint until they were on their way.

"It says here"—Everett pointed at the form—"that she has info about Stuart Sebastiani. Isn't he that Boobgate guy?"

"Yep. He must have done something to piss her off."

"Where does she live? There's no address on the form."

"We're going to her job. She works at the PlayRoom," Kari said, casting a glance his way.

"Oh."

"It's a strip club."

"Yeah. I know," he said with no notable inflection. But Kari noticed he was blushing. Was he embarrassed to go with her?

"So, this Sebastiani guy, what else do you know about him?" Everett asked.

By the time Kari had shared with Everett the few things she had learned about Sebastiani, they were pulling into a rundown shopping center where, at the far end of the plaza, the PlayRoom was tucked away. The strip club shared its quarter-full parking lot with a dry cleaner, a Chinese restaurant, and a threadbare dollar store. From the outside, the PlayRoom appeared to be a regular seedy strip club. Above the storefront, a garish neon sign of a naked woman's silhouette beckoned visitors inside, and the double glass doors were shielded with red velvet drapes.

As they approached the club, Everett's eyes darted around the lot as if to check whether anyone was watching them. Other than a customer leaning against the building having a smoke, no one paid any attention to them. As they walked through the entrance, Kari studied the PlayRoom's decor. She immediately questioned the interior design.

The strip club was decorated as a children's playground. The stools in the club were giant building blocks and the walls were painted in primary colors with sultry Jessica Rabbit–like cartoon characters stenciled around the walls. In one corner, a dancer used finger paint to create art on a large plastic cloth spread out on the base of an elevated platform.

Wearing only a tiny G-string, the topless artist used more than just her hands to paint as she slid and rolled her body across the colorful canvas.

The dancer looked at Kari and smiled. Kari nodded and smiled back. Everett's gaze bounced around the room. Kari watched as he took in the finger-paint area and the mini-playground, with a swing and slide, and then the monkey bars.

Even in the middle of the workday, the club buzzed with activity. She chose a table at the side of the room with fewer customers but with a clear view of the center stage. With rigid posture, Everett scrutinized what was happening around him. She caught his attention and, placing her thumb and fingers together, motioned for him to close his gaping mouth.

Kari told their waitress, who identified herself as Sherry, they were there to see Tannie. Sherry wore a pair of pale blue short bib overalls and a baseball cap turned backward. Her suspenders barely covered her nipples.

"I'll let her know you're here. She's in the back." As Sherry walked away with their drink order, her high-cut shorts exposed a cheeky rear.

Kari surveyed the room. There she was, a married mother of three, hanging out at a nudie bar. She peeked toward the lounge area, where a customer was enjoying a couch dance performed by a skinny but energetic blond who grinded and bounced on his crotch like a construction worker's jackhammer. The man's goofy grin revealed his appreciation of her pistonlike determination.

Kari felt as if she was getting a free pass. She was on assignment, but except for the nearly naked women, the club's vibe was similar to the bars she visited when lonely hotel rooms became too claustrophobic. The PlayRoom provided all the pleasures of licentiousness without any of the guilt. But then again, should someone like her be in a place like this? Perhaps she should have thought the whole thing through a little more before she told Juanita she would take the case.

Kari looked over at Everett. He was still checking out the room, but his stare—which contained a look of discovery and intrigue—was intense. He was either awestruck or appalled, she couldn't tell which. After a few awkward attempts to engage him in conversation, Kari finally gave in and allowed him to watch the floor show. Her plan was to conduct a quick interview, assess the merits of the facts, and get out as quickly as possible.

When Sherry returned with their drink orders, she let them know Tannie would be out in a few minutes. In the meantime, did they want anything to eat? Kari shook her head, but Everett ordered a burger, fries, and another Pepsi.

As the minutes ticked away, Kari shifted in her seat, drummed the fingers of one hand on the table. Just as she was about to call over their waitress, a woman who must have been Tannie appeared, pulled out a chair, and sat.

Her blue eyes sparkled against her deeply spray-tanned complexion. Her brown hair was cut short and slicked back, highlighting her gorgeous bone structure. She was heavily made up, but her look was more polished than that of the other women working in the club. Less earthy. Kari scanned Tannie's outfit, a hot-pink low-cut baby-doll dress that barely contained her breasts and a matching pink bow in her hair. Her attire didn't scream out sleazy, in-your-face sex. She just looked hot.

Kari fought the urge to look down at her own outfit. It was going to be a long investigation if she made critical assessments of herself every time she interviewed a stripper.

"It's busier than I thought it would be. Sorry for the wait." Tannie spoke in a flat tone. "I was in the Show-and-Tell room."

"Where?" Kari asked.

"The Show-and-Tell room. My customers tell me what they want to see, and I show it to them." Tannie tugged down the top of her dress and exposed her perfect breasts. Slack-jawed, Everett stared at her chest and turned tomato red.

Kari wasn't amused.

"I know we're in a strip club, but we need to keep this meeting official." She directed her rebuke to both Tannie and Everett.

"What are you, like his mother?" Tannie dipped her head in Everett's direction.

"I'm…We're here because you have information we're interested in. But I'm not going to put myself in an embarrassing position. I don't think Agent Hildebrand wants that either." Kari glanced at her partner. "Am I right?"

Everett nodded. His face turned a dark shade of crimson. He looked away and coughed into his fist.

"Sure. No big deal," Tannie said. She shrugged, unaffected by Kari's reprimand. "I was just playing around."

"Let's start over." Kari raised both hands in mock surrender. "I'm Agent Karolina Wheeler. You can call me Kari. And this is Agent Everett Hildebrand—"

"You can call me Everett or Ev." He shook Tannie's hand with a weak and apparently wet grip.

Tannie wiped her hand on the seat cushion. "Don't be nervous, sweetheart. I don't bite."

Tiny beads of sweat dotted his upper lip and hairline. Kari shot him a look of *What the hell are you doing? Pull yourself together.*

"Tannie," Kari said, "you called about Stuart Sebastiani. How long have you been seeing him?"

"About two years. We have a baby together, a little girl."

As they settled into the interview Kari asked the basic questions necessary to assess whether they had a case worth pursuing, but Tannie kept returning to the topic of her baby. It appeared to be the reason she had made the call to the FBI, the reason she was so angry with Sebastiani, so Kari let her vent.

"So, this is about your daughter?"

Tannie nodded.

"When I got pregnant," she said, "everything changed. I thought Stu would be excited, but he asked me to get an abortion." Kari saw a single tear welling, but Tannie used her index finger to evict it from the corner of her eye.

"And you didn't want to do that?"

"Of course not. It's a sin." Outrage quavered in Tannie's voice and red flushed across her cheeks. "But I'm not sure if he stuck around because he cared or because he was afraid that I would call his wife."

"Does he give you any support?"

"Nothing. Nada."

Kari nodded. That's what she'd expected Tannie would say. She had this Sebastiani guy pegged as a player.

"I wanted to be home with Dia a little longer, but for financial reasons, I came back to work as soon as I could." Tannie wrinkled her nose and cringed. "A friend of mine owns this tacky dump."

"It's not so bad," Kari offered.

"Oh yeah it is. Believe me."

Kari looked around the room and shrugged. The club seemed clean. She certainly didn't feel like she would need to shower as soon as she got home.

At that moment, their waitress brought out Everett's food and refilled their soft drink orders. Once she left, Kari resumed the conversation, again focusing on the one topic she knew would keep Tannie talking.

"How old is your baby?"

"Seven weeks yesterday." Tannie lifted her dress and patted her stomach. She had unexpectedly flat and firm abdominals.

"Wow, you don't look like you just had a baby." After three kids, Kari knew her abs would never look like that again.

Tannie stood up from the table and caressed her curves, letting her hands float softly over her midsection to her thighs and, as she bent over, down her shins and behind to her calf muscles. As she watched the exhibition, Kari glanced around the room to see if anyone else was looking and noticed another dancer conducting a similar demonstration of her physique. Tannie was just marketing the merchandise. It was part of the show.

"When I talk about Stu, I get so stressed. Here," Tannie said, taking Everett's hand and guiding it up her hamstring. "Can you feel the tension?"

Everett, who had been noticeably quiet, jerked his hand away as if from hot coals.

"Tannie, can we stay focused?" Kari pointed to Tannie's chair and motioned for her to take her seat. "Let's go over why you called my office this morning."

Tannie sat down, took in a deep breath, and let it out slowly. Her tough act faltered as she slumped in her chair and placed her hands over her mouth. "I'm tired of Stu screwing over Dia and me." She fiddled with the rings on her fingers and then clenched her hands into fists. "He has no idea how I really feel about him."

"But you're still with him?"

"Yes and no. We never actually broke up," she said. "I stopped sleeping with him. And without the sex, there isn't much left to our relationship."

"It sounds like you're ready to end it. We appreciate you dialing the fraud tip line." Kari thumbed the pages of her pocket-sized spiral notebook. Tannie was almost ready to share. She would be able to start the real interview soon, to begin taking notes any moment now.

Tannie paused and studied Kari's and Everett's faces. Kari wasn't sure what Tannie was looking for, but she locked eyes with Tannie and hoped hers displayed acceptance and compassion.

"I got to tell you the truth. I don't give a damn about city corruption."

"So why'd you call?"

"Not for altruistic reasons or civic concern," she said, raising her eyebrows. "I called because Stu Sebastiani is a pig and a deadbeat dad," said Tannie. "I'm sick of his shit. You need to arrest his ass."

"What exactly would he be arrested for doing?" Kari flipped to a clean page in her notebook.

"Selling his office. He's shaking down every club owner within the city limits for money, free gifts, sex."

Finally, they were broaching the subject that had brought them together. A less experienced agent would have pushed the agenda and risked Tannie clamming up. But Kari remembered Tannie's initial reluctance during their earlier phone conversation and took the time to put her at ease, to let her feel like she was being heard. The extra time provided Kari the opportunity to see where Tannie was going with her story before narrowing in on specific areas.

"In addition to the bribes," Tannie added, "I think he has a hidden interest in JOLIE."

"JOLIE?"

"Yeah, it's a new club not far from here. Opened last month. Stu told me his son, Arty, Stuart Sebastiani Jr., is a part owner. At least that's what it says on the books, but Stu probably has a piece too."

"Why do you think that?" Kari asked.

"Because I know how Stu operates. Trust me. He'll find some way to pull cash out of there. He's a selfish ass."

"Have you thought about suing him for child support?"

"Screw him. I don't need his fucking money. I don't need him."

Kari moved off the touchy topic and returned to Sebastiani's other crimes.

"So tell me more about JOLIE."

"It's nothing like this shit hole. The PlayRoom is unlimited hot wings and beer, the Hooters of strip clubs."

"And JOLIE?"

"JOLIE is classy, top-shelf steaks and expensive wine. And talent. Gorgeous entertainers, not skanky strippers like here. They have a website."

Kari made a note to check it out.

"Do you know any of the girls working at JOLIE?" she asked Tannie. "Someone you trust who might help us find out what's going on over there?"

Tannie pointed a finger at herself. "Stu says he's gonna get me a spot there. I'm not like these girls who work in this creepy place. I'm a performer."

The dancer crossed her arms in front of her chest and pursed her lips. Kari realized her slow nod might have given off a patronizing vibe, so she nodded more enthusiastically.

"Stripping is more than just shaking your ass," Tannie said. "You wait. When you see my act, you'll see the difference." She pointed to a stripper on the stage nearest to them wiggling up against a pole and whipping her hair back and forth. "That's not talent. She's just advertising her services."

"What services?"

"In the back, in the private booths. There's all kinds of stuff going on. People getting blow jobs, getting laid, doing drugs. I'm not into that."

"Does Sebastiani know?" Kari asked.

"Ah, yeah. Toss a few big bills his way, and he can be persuaded to ignore just about anything."

"And at JOLIE, is he ignoring illegal activity there too?"

"I doubt it," Tannie said. "The girls earn good money there. None of them should need to fuck for cash. But if a few of the girls are, I'd bet they do it off site."

"And drugs? Are they doing drugs at JOLIE?"

"Look, there are all kinds of strip clubs, desperate ones like here, where anything goes, and high-profile clubs, where they try to follow the rules. At the legit clubs, they do random drug tests, and if the girls are using, they don't get to perform," Tannie said. "It's all about the clientele. Your big spenders don't want to be around nasty, spaced-out sluts. The difference in what you can earn at the PlayRoom versus at clubs like JOLIE can be as much as a thousand or more dollars a night."

Kari let out a long low whistle and tapped her pen on her notebook. That much for taking your clothes off in front of strangers, who knew?

"When are you supposed to start working at JOLIE?"

"Stu left me a message saying I should call him when I get back in shape." Tannie let out a groan. "Like I'm some damn housewife who has to work off the baby fat." In a voice that gave off heat, she turned to Everett and asked, "I think I'm ready now, don't you?"

Before he could respond, she laughed so heartily she snorted.

"I'm just joking with you, sweetie." Tannie winked at Kari. "I know

I have to behave myself if we're going to be hanging out together."

That was it. The sign Kari was waiting for, the connection that signaled Tannie's commitment to the investigation, to the team.

"Let me ask you a question," Kari said. She sat up straight in her chair and leaned in close. "When you start working at JOLIE, would you be willing to tell us what's going on over there?"

Tannie rested her chin on her hand and, looking back and forth between Kari and Everett, hesitated before answering. "Yeah, why not."

Kari dipped her head in a grateful bow to her new source. She then plucked a few french fries off of Everett's plate and stuffed them in her mouth. *And that's how you do it. Patience. Let them think they're calling the shots, while you're slowly pulling them in. Informant recruitment 101. Now to seal the deal.*

"To formalize your cooperation," she said, chewing and talking at the same time. "I'll need you to read and sign some papers spelling out the rules and regulations."

"Sure, no problem. You have them here?"

Kari nodded but hesitated to take out the paperwork. She glanced around the club. "You sure there's nobody in here who'll report back to Sebastiani?"

"Don't worry." Tannie patted the table. "I'll just tell everybody you were here to help me refinance my mortgage."

"Great," Kari said. "I'm in a club full of sexy strippers and you're saying I look like a loan broker."

"You're just as hot as any of the girls in here, but you could use some makeup."

"Thanks for the tip." Kari tucked a stray lock of her medium-length hair behind her ear.

"I'm just saying, if you want to fit in more. You know, go undercover or whatever."

"Got it." Kari pulled out the papers and laid them on the table for Tannie to read and initial.

That made it official. Tannie was now part of their team. She agreed to call Sebastiani and tell him she was ready to start dancing at JOLIE. The call would be recorded. Although no smoking gun, a conversation between Tannie and Sebastiani about employment at a club he should legally have nothing to do with would be important. Kari told Tannie they would return the next day to go over what she would say and to set up the digital recording. They could meet in the parking lot to make the call.

"Hey, we should go," said Kari, glancing at the time on her cell phone. "I don't want your boss to get mad at you."

"We've been talking on my dime. All of us girls are independent contractors. I pay the owner for the privilege of dancing here. In turn, I keep my tips and all but fifteen percent of the fees I charge my customers."

"We can pay you too, for your information."

Tannie frowned. "I don't want your cash. I'm not doing this for money." She stood facing Kari, placed her hands on the back of Kari's chair, and leaned in close for emphasis. "Unless you want to pay me for that lap dance we talked about on the phone."

Tannie's breasts pressed against Kari's, and their faces were less than an inch apart. Kari froze for a beat, taken aback by the unnerving sensation moving through her body. As a mother, she understood Tannie's desire to protect her daughter. But what she felt at that moment, as Tannie nestled her body close enough for Kari to bear her weight and be engulfed in her scent, was something more than empathy.

Kari pushed back in her chair to focus on Tannie's entire face, not just her lips, and said, "I don't think that would be a good idea."

The stripper stepped back. "I'm not even going to ask you," she said to Everett. Her smile had a hint of a smirk. "I doubt you could handle this." She hugged them both and returned to the Show-and-Tell room.

As Tannie sauntered away, Kari wondered how the stripper was able to expose herself so freely, while she, by comparison, had always held her emotions and desires tight, so others wouldn't discover things about her she couldn't bear for them to know.

Kari gathered up her purse and notebook, but when she rose to leave, Everett pointed at his mouthful of burger. He hadn't finished eating. Reluctantly, she sat back down while her temporary partner took another bite and licked catsup from the corner of his mouth. A stripper, with what must have been double G's, swung her gravity-defying way across the monkey bars. Everett's chewing slowed, and with wide-eyed wonder and his head tilted for a better view, he continued to take in all the sights and sounds the PlayRoom had to offer.

As Kari waited for him to finish, it dawned on her: during the interview, Everett hadn't asked a single question.

***

She confronted Everett as soon as they stepped out of the PlayRoom and into the parking lot.

"You seemed to have forgotten how to talk to a witness. It's like you were in a trance or something. You didn't say a word."

Everett opened his mouth to protest, but only a weak grunt emerged.

"Tannie's job is to come on to her customers," Kari said, "and you let her work her mojo on you right in the middle of my interview."

Everett offered no defense as he walked to the car, opened the passenger door, and slumped into the front seat.

Kari slid behind the wheel but sat and stared at Everett before she placed the key in the ignition. "Look, Hildebrand, I can't have you distracted by boobs like some naïve schoolboy. That can't happen again."

"You're right." Everett's face flushed hot pink. "But I think I should be, ah…commended…under the circumstances."

Kari probed Everett's peculiar expression. "Don't tell me that was your first time?" She knew the answer even before he responded.

Everett slowly nodded.

"Are you for real? How did you get through college without being dragged into a strip club once or twice?" she asked. "You've at least been to a bachelor's party with strippers, right?"

"Nope," he said. "I was trying to play cool, but I guess I didn't quite pull that off."

"Damn," Kari said. "No wonder you looked like you'd just walked in on your sister naked." She widened her eyes and peeked through her fingers. "Why didn't you say something?"

"For the record, I don't have a sister. And remember, you didn't tell me where we were going until we were halfway here," said Everett. "I was psyched that you chose me to go with you. Everyone knows you're the best."

"How can you be so...innocent and an FBI agent?" said Kari, ignoring the compliment. He couldn't brownnose his way out of this.

"This has nothing to do with innocence. It's a spiritual, religious choice."

"So I corrupted you, so to speak." She sat quietly beside him and tried to understand what he was saying.

"I wouldn't have turned you down even if I had known ahead of time where we were going. I wanted to work with you and, I mean, it was case related, part of the job. I did ask myself what my father would do in the same situation. But—"

"Your father?" Kari said. "What does he have to do with this?"

"Deputy Assistant Director Hank Hildebrand. He'd be disappointed that I didn't suggest we wait until Tannie finished work so we could meet her someplace else. Can I tell you a story?" he asked. "I'm not trying to make excuses. I just want to explain my behavior."

Kari started the car. "Go ahead. I'm listening." She placed it in drive and pulled out onto the street, wondering how this development would impact her decision to continue working with Everett.

"When my brother J. T. and I were in our early teens, we had our first introduction to sex education, courtesy of my father. He discovered a *Playboy* magazine hidden under J. T.'s mattress. My dad dragged him outside and made him sleep in the storage shed for two nights." Everett held up two fingers. "J. T. wasn't allowed in the house to use the bathroom, shower, or eat. My mom brought his meals out to him, and he had to use the wooded area behind our house for his other needs."

Kari sat back, shaking her head. She thought about Carter and porn week.

"I know the treatment sounds harsh, but dad wanted J. T., who's now an agent in the Newark division, and me to learn to respect women."

"This is all news I could have used *before* I invited you to go with me to a strip club, Hildebrand."

"Why did you?'

"Ask you to come along?" Kari shrugged off the doubt building up inside her. "I thought you were the safer bet. Now, I'm afraid you'll be forever traumatized. You know, breaking your vow of celibacy and—"

"I'm not celibate; I'm married. And I am certainly not traumatized."

Kari tilted her head and hiked a shoulder.

"Don't worry. I can do this."

"I'm not so sure." With her hands resting on the steering wheel of the idling car, her eyes locked on his. She knew he believed in what he was saying. But she was having doubts that he could readjust his mindset. He would be encountering lots of people whose spiritual choices were way different than his. "I mean, who does that?" she said. "Exiles a child to the storage shed because he was harboring a *Playboy*?"

"What's so hard to understand? My dad has no respect for guys like Sebastiani, who cheat on their wives, or women like Tannie, who exploit their bodies. Neither do I."

Kari stared at Everett, so resolute in his condemnation, his moral righteousness.

"Try not to be so judgmental." She put the car in drive and fixed her eyes on the road. "Who really knows what makes people do the things they do?"

Chapter 4

As soon as they returned to the office, Kari and Everett logged on to the Internet to check out JOLIE's website. Tannie was right. JOLIE was nothing like the PlayRoom. The site featured photos of luxurious, dark-stained wood bars, book-filled shelves, soft, brown leather couches, and masculine colors. Lustrous illumination from ornate crystal chandeliers bounced off polished marble floors. It looked like money—big money.

The website also featured profiles of the JOLIE entertainers. Many of the girls had their own Web pages filled with risqué and revealing photos advertising their particular talents. As she and Everett scanned the website, several of the guys on the squad suddenly appeared, swarming like fruit flies around Everett's desk to help them with their research.

"Hey, who's that luscious ginger-haired beauty?" asked Tommy, a fairly new agent on the squad, as he admired the dancer on the screen.

"According to her bio," said Kari, "that's Sasha."

"Sasha is sweet," concluded another agent, Shawn. As Kari moved the cursor and opened the page for the next featured dancer, Shawn added, "Oh, and so is Lexi."

"Kari, click on Jasmine's profile. I want to see more of her," said squad mate Mark.

"No, no. Let's check out Mercedes," Shawn argued. "*Me gusta* those Latina girls."

"Hey, make up your minds. Better yet, here." Kari pushed the mouse toward Shawn.

After relinquishing control, she continued to sit among her male coworkers as they scrolled through the website. Each JOLIE entertainer was stunningly beautiful and had an amazing body. Kari couldn't help but admire how gorgeous and flexible they were. Neither could the guys.

"Hot damn," Tommy said. "Check out this one with the ginormous tits."

"Hey," she said, "we're working here."

"Riiight. What kind of a case is this? 'Undercover?'" Tommy made air quotes.

"No. It's a corruption case. That *is* what we work on this squad."

In a chorus, several onlookers said, "Need any help?"

"Too late. I already asked Hildebrand."

Tommy frowned. "What a waste of a good case."

"Excuse me?" said Kari.

"You know what I mean." Tommy laughed. "As far as I can tell, Everett's vice-less and you...you're a married woman with kids. Neither of you will have as much fun on this case as any of us."

"Plus, it's not fair. You get all the good jobs," Scott said with an exaggerated pout. "Let the rest of us earn a stat or two."

"That sucks for you." Kari laughed, pushing back her chair. "But you guys can keep looking at the website if you want. Let me know if you find any evidence."

As she walked away, more curious agents pushed past her to join the group. She had just started the case, and look at the commotion it had already generated.

Kari thought about Tommy's remark. When it came to determining who was the best choice to work this assignment, she and Everett would surely have been voted least likely.

She'd barely sat down at her desk when Everett appeared.

"I thought you were checking out the website." She glanced over toward his cubicle.

"Those guys can goof off. I want to get started on the case. So what do we do next? What's the game plan?"

"What?"

"Do you want me to map out some investigative steps, maybe create a flowchart on how we should proceed?"

"Really?" she said. "You're not still using that damn 'memo to the file' FBI Academy crap, are you?"

"They showed us a method to track—"

"That's file filler. Some instructor at Quantico who never worked a damn case in his life made that up. I call it 'stuff, fluff, and puff.' That's what an agent does if he doesn't have a clue and is afraid he'll be discovered when he has his ninety-day file review. He stuffs his files with useless paper like flowcharts, fluffs it up with memos about what he *plans* to do, and then tries to blow smoke up his supervisor's butt about how hard he's been working. That's the puff part."

"But we need to have a plan, don't we?"

"When we see Tannie tomorrow, we'll figure out who to interview next. She probably knows a few other people who hate Sebastiani as much as she does. But right now, let me finish this paperwork." She turned back to her desk. "I'm determined to get out of here on time tonight."

Kari began to type her FD-302 report of interview. The time spent with Tannie at the PlayRoom was enough to get them started. She was a credible source, but the investigation would need to develop into more than just what one person knew.

In the stillness of the squad room, she allowed herself a moment to think about what she was taking on. Everett was a bit stiff and inflexible, but he would be a good partner for her. She liked the idea of having someone uncorrupted and with a solid moral compass working with her on a case that could present temptations. He would be like gates at a train grade crossing, lowering if she came too close to the danger line.

When Kari next looked up from her cubicle, she was surprised to see that it was 6:19 p.m. She powered down her computer and cleared off her desk. Everett was still there too, tucked away in the dark in his corner cubicle. The light of his computer illuminated his face as he stared at the screen.

When she was close enough to see what held his attention, she said,

"Are you looking at the website again?"

Startled, Everett made a frantic move to click the minimize button and remove the image on the screen.

"Why did you do that?" Kari asked as a nude JOLIE dancer faded from the screen and the homepage for the FBI website popped up.

Bright red flushed across Everett's neck up to the tips of his ears.

"I was checking out the website again to see if I could learn more about the club and—"

"Come on, what are you trying to find out? How big the dancers' boobs are? Where they like to do it? That website is all about marketing. They don't even list the girls' real names…or their real cup sizes for that matter."

Everett scratched his head.

She reached for the mouse, clicked on the link hidden on the taskbar, and reopened the JOLIE website.

"Ev, I know this is a first for you, but you've got to get okay with it fast or it's not going to work. Your daddy's not here, and I'm not your mamma. If you want to take a peek, take a peek."

She passed by her desk, picked up her gym bag, and went home.

Chapter 5

Kari smirked as she recalled the PlayRoom's marquee —A Gentlemen's Club. Watching naked women prance around is not an activity she would associate with the refined term *gentlemen*. Such a titillating afternoon had been unexpected. But that part of the day was over, and she was late. Again.

As she came through the back door, she found Kevin silhouetted by a roaring fire, sitting on the couch in the family room, his feet propped up on the coffee table. He was watching *Jeopardy!* and grading papers. His reading glasses rested on the tip of his nose. He peered over the rims at her before turning his attention back to the program. Apparently, her husband was pissed.

She poked her head into the dining room, where her kids were doing their homework. "Hi, guys."

"Mommy," echoed the twins. Casey and Morgan ran over and gave her a quick hug around the waist before returning to their papers.

Carter gave her a little wave.

"How was school today?"

"Good." This time, all three sang the same answer.

"And how about you?" Kari asked her son. "Any more video surprises today?"

He blushed and buried his face in a book.

She kissed the top of his head. And then, mentally preparing to exchange the wintry temperature outside with the frosty reception she was about to receive, Kari took off her coat and gloves and walked into the living room to greet Kevin.

"Guess where I was today?" she said.

He barely looked up at her. "Somewhere that made you miss dinner with your family?"

"We've talked about this. Eat. Don't wait for me."

"We wouldn't have a problem waiting for you if we had some idea when you might be home," he said. "I believe they issued you a cell phone along with that gun you carry."

"I'm sorry. I started a new case today, and I just got caught up with all the paperwork."

"Whatever."

He used to love being married to a special agent. More than that, he loved her stories, loved living through her daily intrigues. But all of the late nights had worn on them both. Now all it took was her being late for dinner for him to get upset.

Too tired to argue, Kari plopped down next to him on the couch. Several minutes went by before she moved over close enough for their thighs to touch and tentatively placed her hand on his leg. Neither of them spoke. They sat together, silently watching TV until a commercial came on.

"I fixed you a plate," Kevin finally said, pointing toward the kitchen.

Kari wasn't hungry, but rejecting the meal he had prepared would only fuel his recurring grievance, so she pushed herself up from the sofa and walked over to the adjoining kitchen. Kevin followed behind her as she went over to the stove and lifted the aluminum foil covering the plate of food—baked barbecued chicken, mac and cheese, and green beans—he had left out for her.

"This looks good. Thank you." Kari smiled as she reheated her dinner in the microwave. She didn't mention to him that she wanted to lose the ten to fifteen pounds she had put on over the past few years, a decision made while at the strip club. Eating when she wasn't even hungry was not a good way to start a diet. Feigning an appetite, she sat down at the kitchen table anyway.

"So where were you?"

"At a strip club called the PlayRoom," Kari said with a mouth full of food.

"Did you say a strip club?" He raised his eyebrows.

Kari nodded. "I was interviewing one of the dancers about her ex."

"So you were, like, in an office talking?"

"Nope. Right out on the floor, with the customers getting their lap dances."

"Did anybody try to hit on you?"

"I had on this," she said, pointing to her suit. "And there were naked women dancing around."

"Naked?

"Practically."

"What kind of case is this?"

"Corruption, of course. The PlayRoom is the first of many strip clubs we'll be checking out."

Kevin looked at Kari with apprehension.

"We go where the witnesses are."

"Great. More late evenings."

"Stop sucking the fun out of my day. I thought you'd be happy."

"About your new case?"

"The subject's Stuart Sebastiani. You know, the Boobgate guy who was in all the papers last year."

"Who?"

"Remember the stories about how that guy from Licensing and Inspections escorted some strippers to entertain at the city finance director's bachelor party? And how one of the other partygoers captured Sebastiani on video motorboating that stripper's huge breasts?"

"No."

"Yes you do. Someone leaked that video to the press, and it was everywhere for two weeks." Kari giggled just thinking about the YouTube clip. "Mayor Sheridan himself gave it the name 'Boobgate.' I guess he hoped people would laugh and then forget about it. I'll pull up the video for you later."

"Don't bother."

She was frustrated that he refused to take any interest in her work, even a case involving strip clubs. "You should watch it. It's really funny. The mayor ended up having to suspend Sebastiani for sixty days. He probably hated to have to do it. I hear Mayor Sheridan is known to appreciate the ladies too."

"You seem to know a lot about this."

"I googled Boobgate this morning. I told you, Sebastiani's my new subject."

"Humph. Sounds like Sebastiani's a boob."

"My interview today with his ex was…stimulating. Don't you want to hear about the naughty outfits, stripper poles, and sexy music?" Kari snapped her fingers and moved her shoulders to an imaginary beat.

Kevin treated her to his first smile of the night. "I see you picked up some moves while you were there."

"As a matter of fact, I did."

Just as she was about to supply more details, one of the twins called out from the dining room.

"Mommy, I need help."

"I'm eating and talking to Daddy. I'll be there when I'm done."

"No, now *pleeeeease*. I don't know how to do this stupid math."

Kari looked at Kevin and shrugged. "Let me go help Casey."

"But you were just about to tell me what you learned today."

"How about I show you later?"

"On a weeknight?" He smiled and wiggled his eyebrows.

She punched him in the arm. "You want me to show you or what?"

"*Mom*," Casey cried out from the other room.

"I'll go help her," said Kevin. "Finish your dinner."

"No, you've been dealing with the kids all evening. I got it." Kari pushed herself away from the kitchen table and carried her plate into the next room where both girls welcomed her with a chorus of complaints.

***

Several hours later, after helping the kids with their homework, throwing a couple of loads in the wash, and carving out a moment to curl up on the couch with a novel, Kari prepared for bed. She was beat but knew Kevin, who had been grinning at her all evening, would soon be skipping up the stairs to the bedroom. She'd been daydreaming all afternoon about giving Kevin a play-by-play performance of her trip to the PlayRoom, but it had been a long day. Could she recover the excitement? After a quick shower, she stood in front of the bathroom's full-length mirror and took in her naked reflection. She looked as tired as she felt. Her thirty-nine-year-old face had a hint of puffiness under her eyes, and her body, once toned and fit, was turning a little soft.

Kari ran her hands down her middle, stopping to grab and pull at the fleshy thickness around her once-trim waist. She cupped her ample breasts in her hands, lifting them up as she sucked in her tummy. She pivoted for a side view and then exhaled.

Her body no longer looked like Tannie's, but she still had her well-toned legs and arms. She flexed to admire the cuts in her biceps and triceps. On her first date with Kevin, she had bragged that she could pump out fifty military push-ups, and on his dare, she had proven it, right there in the restaurant parking lot.

She needed to get back on track. Perhaps she should take pole-dancing lessons. She heard they were good for the core.

Timidly, Kari swayed her hips to mimic the strippers. At first she giggled, but soon she moved with the music from the strip club, replaying it in her head. The sensual memories of Tannie and the other dancers lingered in her thoughts, creating a tingling warmth in her body. Maybe she wasn't as tired as she had thought.

Kari finished brushing her teeth and went into the bedroom. She walked over to the dresser where she kept her nightgowns and opened the drawer but closed it without taking anything out. Instead, she climbed into her bed and slipped under the covers, primed with anticipation. She loved Kevin. And tonight she planned to show her gorgeous, brown-skinned husband the new moves she'd learned while visiting the PlayRoom.

As she waited under the crisp, cool sheets for Kevin to join her, Kari whispered to herself, "Thank you, Tannie Colosi."

Chapter 6

Stu Sebastiani unlocked his office. He brushed his hand over the front of the door where his name and title were inscribed in large, brass letters. Last year, when he had returned from a temporary suspension, his nameplate had been missing. To replace it, he had ordered the much larger sign and had it affixed to the door with metal screws. The subtle message was delivered: he was back—to stay.

His office was a standard city-issued square box with one window, from which Sebastiani had an excellent view of city hall and the western side of Market Street. He placed his briefcase on the sturdy wooden desk he had used for the past eight years. He grinned just thinking about all the activities accomplished at that desk. A forensic swab of the surface would turn up a hell of a lot more than just ink marks and coffee spills.

Piled on the left-hand corner was a stack of regulatory applications and violations his assistant had left for him to review. Sebastiani flipped through the files and plucked one out. He gave it a cursory review before picking up his office phone.

"Mastracola, are you out of your fucking mind?" he asked as soon as the call connected.

"What? What's wrong?"

"That violation you wanted me to look into—that's what's wrong."

"Can you take care of that for my buddy?"

"No, I can't. You didn't tell me that the stripper was holding a damn used condom in her hand when the inspectors walked in. I don't have any magic tricks to make this report disappear."

"Okay, by next Thursday then. Can you get my buddy's business opened again by next Thursday night?"

"You're not listening to me, Cola." Sebastiani rested his forehead on his hand. "You said *suspicion* of illegal sexual activity. They were caught in the act. There's a picture of the condom in the file and a log showing this was the seventh violation."

"So, what am I supposed to tell the owner?"

"Thirty days."

"*Thirty days?*"

"He should receive a six-month suspension."

"Shit."

"That's the best I can do."

"Humph. Really?"

"Just make sure you see me later today. Before the hearing."

"Yeah, of course. I gotcha covered."

Sebastiani hung up the phone and massaged his temples as he looked out his office window at the city's skyline. He liked that people came to him for help, that they knew he could make things happen, but nothing was ever easy. He had more than fifty inspectors working under him, not nearly enough workers to get around to all of the businesses, restaurants, bars, and entertainment venues within the city limits.

He made sure to personally inspect places where he wanted the owners to know his name. He knew how to work the pay-to-play system where right and wrong depended entirely on whom you did it *with*, did it *to*, or did it *for*. He kept a mental account of all the favors he distributed, so he could cash them when he needed a last-minute reservation, a better table, hard-to-get tickets, or female companionship. The freebies were good, but he had admitted to himself long ago that what got him off more was the power trip. He liked being in control.

Sebastiani read a few more files and made a few more phone calls until his growling belly signaled lunchtime. He picked up the phone and made another call, this one to Johnny Bell, the owner of Slippery Tales. Perhaps Sebastiani would stop by for the strip club's signature steak-and-eggs lunch special.

"Johnny, who's in the kitchen today?" Sebastiani asked.

"That you, Stu?" said Johnny. "Let me ask your opinion about something."

"Sure. I was thinking of coming by for lunch. But that new kid never remembers that I don't like my eggs runny."

"Come on over. Omar's on the grill. But if he gets it wrong again, send it back and make him do it right."

"Okay, I'll be there in twenty." Sebastiani patted his stomach. "What did you need?"

"I got this idea I want to run by you. Something I read that a place on Long Island is doing. They have a menu just like ours, but the girls serving the food are completely nude."

"That won't work in Philly."

"Why not?"

"The health department is not going to allow naked people to walk around serving food. Plus, think about it." Sebastiani scrunched up his face with disapproval. "It's just a bad idea."

"You really think so?"

"I tell you what. When I get there, we can try it out. Have one of your girls take all her clothes off and bring my steak and eggs to me in your office." Sebastiani sniggered. "But let her know, hunger ain't the only appetite getting satisfied."

He hung up the phone and walked the stack of papers out to his administrative assistant, Jenny—fifty-six years old, homely, skinny, and with breasts that hung down like two wet loaves of bread. She was a patronage appointee he'd been forced to hire. But it all had worked out for the best; her appearance guaranteed he'd be able to do his job without distraction. Just looking at her lowered his sperm count.

"Jenny. I'm going over to Slippery Tales for lunch," he said. "If my wife calls, tell her I'm in a meeting." He tipped a finger to her and was halfway across the department, headed to the elevators, when his cell phone buzzed.

Tannie.

He sighed loudly and returned to his office. "I better take this before I go," he muttered and held up the phone, purposely giving the impression it was an important work-related call.

"What's up, babe?" Sebastiani plopped down in his sturdy swivel chair and stretched out his long legs.

"I'm ready. Is your offer still good?" Tannie asked. "Did you save a spot for me at JOLIE?"

"You ready?" he said doubtfully. "How're your boobs?"

"Good."

"How's your ass?"

"Good and firm. Remember, I came home from the hospital in the same skinny jeans I wore before I got pregnant."

"Yeah, but what about your belly?"

"Nice and flat. Stu, what do you got there, a damn checklist? I'm ready."

"Okay, come by the club any day next week between four and six. And bring your portfolio."

"Why? Are you going to make me audition?"

"I could come over and conduct a private inspection."

"I don't think so, Stu. I'll be there Tuesday. You gonna be there?"

"Of course. I wouldn't miss an opportunity to see your sweet ass, babe."

"Wow. Thanks."

"I miss it," he said. When she didn't reply, he asked, "Did you want anything else?"

"No," said Tannie. But her tone suggested she was angry about something.

"Okay then," Sebastiani said, rushing to end the call. "Call if you change your mind."

"Aren't you forgetting something?"

"Uh…like what?" he asked hesitantly.

"How about asking how your baby daughter's doing?"

Before he could recover from his oversight, Tannie ended the call. He stared at his phone for a second, shrugged, and headed out to lunch.

***

Kari watched as Tannie jammed the end call button three times in row. She and Everett sat in the front seat of the Bureau car while Tannie sprawled out in the back. They were parked at the far end of the PlayRoom's parking lot.

"Did you hear that?" Tannie yanked the earpiece from her ear and tossed the digital mini-recorder onto the seat next to her. "I told you he's a pig."

"We were hoping you would get him to say more about JOLIE," said Kari.

"Sorry. I couldn't stand to be on the phone with him one second longer. With you guys listening in, I really heard how he speaks to me." Tannie held her palms out and, squeezing them open and closed, mimicked Sebastiani. "'How's your ass? I miss it.'"

"He's something else," said Kari, offering a declaration of solidarity.

Tannie pulled up a picture of her daughter on her phone.

"I can't understand how he can ignore this little face." She kissed the screen.

"Oh, Tannie, she's adorable." Kari leaned across the front seat to get a better look. The baby's lovely, gray-green eyes appeared to radiate from her deep-olive complexion, which was framed by dark brown curls. "My God. Look at those gorgeous eyes."

"Dia has Stu's eyes. But that's all right, baby. Mommy loves you anyway," Tannie cooed to the picture. "All I would need to do is send a picture of this precious child to Stu's wife, and she would instantly know what's up."

Tannie's shrewd smirk left no doubt that she had, at one time or another, seriously considered doing just that.

"Do you two have kids?" Tannie said, her eyes still on her daughter's image.

"I have three." Kari rummaged in her leather satchel and pulled out her personal cell and passed it back to Tannie, who flipped through the photos. Kari pointed as images of her family zipped past. "Without that crew, I'm lost."

"And you?" Tannie asked Everett.

"Yeah. I have kids."

Tannie and Kari waited for him to offer more, and when he didn't, Tannie said, "Don't you think my Dia looks just like Stu?"

"I've only seen pictures of him in newspaper articles." Kari took a long look at the baby's photo. "In black and white, his eyes are nowhere near as gorgeous as Dia's, but we'll take your word for it."

"I'll show you."

Tannie scrolled through her phone's photo gallery.

"Here's Stu in full color."

Kari and Everett studied both photos. Sebastiani's hair was prematurely silvery white, but just like Dia's, his smoky-gray-green eyes were striking and seemed to glow from his deeply tanned face. He was ruggedly handsome, with a prominent nose and a strong, square jaw.

Without thinking, Kari said, "Good-looking guy."

"On the outside, maybe," Tannie snapped back. "But there's a whole lot of ugly on the inside."

At that moment, Kari understood just how deeply Sebastiani had hurt Tannie by rejecting baby Dia. Kari looked at the photo again. This time, she could see the ugly too.

Chapter 7

Everett stood in front of Juanita's desk. As soon as she held up the evidence log for the recording Tannie had made the day before, he knew why he had been summoned.

"Is this your signature?"

"Yes."

"Why are you signing in evidence on Kari's case?"

"Didn't she tell you she asked me to be her co-case agent?" Anxiety flooded over him. *Please don't pull me off this case.*

"Kari's not the supervisor. I am." Juanita waved the paper back and forth. "She said she was taking you along on the initial interview, but that doesn't give you the right to assign yourself to the case."

Everett waited for her to continue. She stared at him and he could see the irritation simmering behind her eyes.

"This is the second time you've done this."

"I'm so sorry, but it's not what it seems like. I didn't know…" How many times was he expected to apologize to this woman?

"Is this a general disregard for authority or just me?" She continued to stare at him. He had no idea why she was playing these mind games with him.

Hoping that he was displaying a contrite expression, he said, "What happened before was an inadvertent misunderstanding."

"That you promised wouldn't happen again." She threw her hands up. "And here we are."

"So you're not assigning me to the Sebastiani case?" *Don't say it.*

"I haven't decided." A strange smirk whipped across her face.

"It's a bribery case with great potential. I'd appreciate it if you'd let me team up with Kari." What did she want him to do, beg? He would if it meant he could stay on the case.

Juanita let out a deep breath. "Did I ever mention that I was in the LA division when your father was the assistant director?" Juanita looked off into the distance and didn't wait for Everett to answer. "I worked my ass off out there. On the gangs and violent crimes squad."

"He's retired now," Everett said with an upbeat tone. "The next time I talk to him I'll let him know—"

"Don't bother." She peered at him over the top of her glasses.

Everett thought he might have detected a flash of anger, but then it was gone. A feeling of dread overcame him. What was that about?

"I only brought that up to say that this doesn't even seem like the type of assignment someone like you would feel comfortable working."

"What do you mean?"

"You're a BYU graduate, aren't you? Do they have strip clubs in Utah?"

"I imagine they're just about everywhere." He nodded while noting the inference. His anxiety climbed.

Juanita stoked her chin and sat back in her chair. "You really want to work on this case?"

"I've already explained to Kari that I can handle it."

"Oh, so Agent Wheeler has her doubts about you too."

"No." He felt flustered and hoped the warmness climbing up his neck and across his cheeks wasn't displayed as a hot-pink flush on his skin. "Not anymore."

***

Dazed but relieved, Everett walked back to his cubicle and squad mates Tommy and Shawn. "You guys almost got your chance to work with Kari on the strip club bribery case."

Shawn looked up from the file he was reviewing and glanced over to Juanita's office. "What'd she say to you in there?"

"At first she threatened to take me off." He shrugged. "But she surprised me and said I could stay on it."

"She really has it out for you. Is it still about the car?" said Tommy.

Everett shook his head. "She mentioned she used to work for my father a few years back, when they were both in LA. He can be a real ball-breaker."

"That's it then. It's all about Daddy Hildebrand."

Everett was just glad that Juanita had let him stay on the case. He wanted to work on the Sebastiani investigation even more now, to prove to everyone that he was his own man, to stop being compared to his father. He especially wanted to work on this case—the kind of case his father would never have touched.

Shawn let out a slow whistle. "I bet he wasn't very nice to her when she was a new agent. You, my friend, are being served a heaping dish of payback."

"You are in trouble." Tommy pantomimed hanging from a noose and poked out his tongue. "She's got plans for you."

"Really?"

"Don't listen to him." Shawn elbowed Tommy in the arm. "Just bide your time."

"You sure?" He recalled the discrimination lawsuit filed by Hispanic agents out in LA. Juanita must have been involved. "Should I talk to her?"

"No, no, no." Shawn shook his head. "Don't do that. She'll get her ticket punched and transfer out in no time."

At that moment, Kari entered the squad area and joined the conversation. "Did I hear you saying something about someone getting their ticket punched? You must be talking about our glorious leader, Juanita. Her type is all about checking off the prerequisites for that high-paying post-Bureau retirement job."

"Her type?" asked Shawn.

"You can tell which supervisors spend their careers adding bullet points to their résumés in order to score a $250,000 corporate-security position. She already looks the part. Her personality might not be all that appealing, but the outward packaging is glamorous."

"Yeah. That's Juanita," said Everett. "She's corporate from head to toe."

"Not exactly head to toe." Kari pointed to her feet. "Next time check out her grandma shoes."

Everett burst out laughing. "Oh my God. You're right."

"Something bad is happening with those toes." Tommy raised and wiggled a foot. "Maybe she has bunions."

"What did you call them?" Everett croaked, laughing and choking at the same time. "Grandma shoes?" He wiped his eyes. "I don't know why that tickled me so much."

"'Cause she's a piece of work," said Kari. "I've always avoided girls like her."

"Did you just call her a girl?"

"You know what I meant."

"So you don't like her?"

"I don't know her well enough to dislike her, but I certainly don't trust her."

Chapter 8

Kari stepped into Sugar Lips, a strip club three grades down from the PlayRoom and at least a ten-level drop from the upscale JOLIE. She caught Everett's eye and grimaced. The club consisted of two dingy rooms connected together. It was as if the owner had planned to create one large room but learned too late that the middle section was a bearing wall and, if removed, would cause the whole building to fall down. There was no other explanation for the awkward configuration. Cheap, distorted mirrors and huge, out-of-date disco balls were strategically placed to force reflective light into the place. It didn't work. The framed magazine photos of nude women didn't add much to the ambiance either. She and Everett had already visited a half dozen clubs, and, compared to those, even Sugar Lips's dancers looked like they could benefit from a remodeling. Their costumes—naughty nurse, sassy pirate, and cheeky cheerleader—all looked like they'd been plucked off a drugstore's Halloween clearance rack.

"FBI? No shit," said Adrianne Myers after the agents flashed their credentials.

An intimidating pirate wench with peroxide-blond hair and dark, smoky eye makeup, Kari had learned that Adrianne had been working the night Sugar Lips was temporarily interrupted by L and I—the same evening of JOLIE's grand opening. Kari explained why they had stopped in to see her.

"Yeah, I remember that night." She pointed to a group of barstools nearby. "You want to sit?"

"Thanks," said Kari as she and Everett made themselves as

comfortable as they could in the seedy dive. "Can you tell us what happened?"

"The L and I inspectors came in, turned on all the lights, shut the music off, and took, like, ten to fifteen minutes to check our business privilege licenses," Adrianne said. "We all tried to keep the customers from leaving by giving them discounted drinks and free appetizers, but most left anyway, especially after some of them received tweets about a new club just down the block hosting its grand opening that night."

"Did the compliance inspectors say anything about the new club?" Kari asked.

"I don't remember. Probably." Adrianne shrugged. "Anyway, just like that, the whole thing was over."

"So that was it?"

"Yep. They only cited the club for routine stuff, like a fire code violation and something about inadequate exit signage. There were so many obvious violations. They should have closed the place down."

"And why didn't they?" Kari asked.

Adrianne playfully smacked her forehead. "Ah, come on. It wasn't a real raid. It was just a scheme to drive customers to JOLIE. Sebastiani called out his boys to help."

"What makes you think Sebastiani arranged the raid to benefit JOLIE?"

"His guys didn't just get the *customers* to go to JOLIE. *They* ended up there too," she said.

Everett spoke first. "What do you mean?"

"By the time the L and I guys left here, business was dead," Adrianne said. "So the owner closed up and I went to check out JOLIE myself. I get there, and what do I see? The same L and I crew who had been here at Sugar Lips, standing around one of the bars."

"How do you know they were the same guys?" Kari asked.

"I got a good look at the inspectors while they were here. One of them, a female inspector, was a real butch. I recognized her right away. And then I saw Stu go over and comp their drinks. It didn't take a rocket scientist to figure out what was going on."

"If it was so obvious," Kari said, "why didn't anyone call L and I about it? Why didn't anyone file a complaint?"

"They'd be crazy to do that. I mean, who's going to investigate that complaint? Someone from L and I, Sebastiani's own guys."

"So you know Stu Sebastiani?" asked Everett.

"Yeah. And I know his son, Arty, too." Adrianne giggled, piled her brassy mane on top of her head, and then let the tresses fall onto her shoulders.

"Exactly how well do you know them?" asked Kari.

Adrianne winked and giggled again.

"Just to be clear," Kari said, "are you saying you've been intimately involved with them both?"

"Not at the same time!" The stripper pretended to gag. "Gross. A father-son thing is too freaky, even for me."

"But you've had relationships with senior and junior?" Everett asked, belaboring the point. "At different times."

"I didn't say anything about having a relationship," she said, pointing her index finger at him. "But yeah, I've had *relations* with them both."

"Sorry for the confusion," Everett said.

"Hey, that's how you get by in this business. You have to give head to get ahead."

When Kari didn't respond, the stripper frowned.

"You think I'm a bimbo?"

Kari waved Adrianne's insecurities away. "Not at all. You're the expert." She poked the dancer's arm. "We don't know this business. That's why we're here talking to you."

Adrianne grinned.

"Now, we've heard that, sometimes, dancers are asked to deliver money to Sebastiani, the father, not the son. Have you ever done that?"

Adrianne told them about giving Sebastiani envelopes plump with fifty- and hundred-dollar bills and how, whether they met up in his car or his office, he expected her to give him a "little something extra" along with the cash.

***

After several more similar interviews, Kari decided to record Sebastiani in action. To verify the need for such invasive evidence-gathering methods, she prepared an affidavit, listing everything they knew so far about Sebastiani and then had the tech squad follow him around for several days, learning his routine and figuring out when and where they could break into his car to install the recording devices. Once they had court authorization, tech agents concealed surveillance cameras and microphones in it. The feed from the tiny digital cameras mounted inside the windshield visor and behind the dashboard transmitted the captured images and audio back to the Philadelphia FBI office, where it was reviewed and analyzed.

The videos captured Sebastiani entering his car with different women and receiving cash and oral sex, all while he was on the taxpayer's dime. The agents assigned to monitor the videos watched in amazement as the fiftyish target distinguished himself as being insatiable. After reviewing only a few recordings, Kari was able to categorically confirm that Tannie was right.

Sebastiani was a pig.

Chapter 9

"Did you do something to your face?"

Kari and Kevin were in the kitchen, cleaning up after dinner.

"What do you mean?" said Kari. She had wondered how long it would take her husband to notice her new look. She and Everett had been working the Sebastiani case for several weeks, interviewing club owners and dancers. Kari was experimenting with a touch of makeup.

"You look…different."

"Oh yeah? In what way?"

"Better."

"Do you mean I look pretty?"

"Yeah, that's what I meant." He smiled as he took a closer, more intimate look at her. "It's your eyes. Did you do something different to your eyes?"

"Yes, thank you," she said. "Tannie suggested I put on some makeup, to fit in."

"You mean the stripper?

"I think she prefers to be called a dancer."

"Did you go to another strip club today?"

Glancing toward the dining room, where their kids were finishing their homework, Kari said, "As a matter of fact, I did and I picked up some more dance moves. Want me to show you later?"

Kevin smiled his boyish grin, and his brown eyes twinkled. He pulled her into the pantry and out of the children's view. She giggled while he put on a private dance show, swiveling his hips and shuffling his feet.

"Maybe," Kari suggested, "we should install a pole in our bedroom."

He thrust his pelvis against her hips. "Don't worry about the pole. I have that covered."

"A bit immodest, aren't you?" She locked onto Kevin's gaze and squeezed her hand down in between their tightly pressed bodies to rub his crotch. "We don't have time right now. But I'm gonna climb on that pole tonight as soon as the kids go to sleep." Kari kissed him hard and pushed him out into the kitchen.

"Damn. I can't wait until your stripper starts rubbing off on the way you dress." Kevin glanced at Kari's standard dark trousers and white blouse. "She'll have you going to PTA meetings in a skintight top and miniskirt. All the other dads will be so jealous of me."

Kari leaned against the kitchen sink. "You have this fantasy all figured out, don't you?"

"Yep. At the next bake sale, all the guys will line up to drool over you."

Kari turned on the tap and squeezed dish soap into the slowly filling sink. "Okay," she said. "I'll talk to Tannie."

"Let her know your husband wants her to help you embrace your inner slut. She's tapping into a part of you I've never seen before."

Kari turned away as shame took hold of her. *Her inner slut.* If he ever found out the truth about her past, he would leave and take the kids with him.

She continued attacking the dirty dinner dishes and wiping down countertops, but her thoughts drifted to when she was an army brat, moving from base to base with her family. When and where they moved was completely out of Kari's control. In middle school and high school, it had been hard to make friends, to break into the cliques girls formed, but she'd discovered the boys didn't mind the class slut hanging around. She connected with those who offered companionship, no matter the cost. And later, as a young adult, that's the way she liked her relationships—quick and meaningless. Even now, when she felt alone or stressed, she fantasized about her old behaviors. She had no idea why. It was something that, as a married mother, she would never do. She loved her man, her kids, her life.

"Honey, did you hear me?" Kevin asked.

Startled, she gripped the edge of the sink. "What were you saying?"

"We're leaving for the girls' game in fifteen minutes. Are you all right? If you're too tired, stay home."

"Don't be silly," she said, turning to smile at him. "Of course I'm coming."

"Okay. Could you make sure the girls are ready? I'm going to take Auggie out." Kevin hooked a leash onto the collar of their playful golden retriever and walked out the door.

Kari went to the bottom of the stairs and called up to her daughters. "Girls, are you dressed? Daddy wants to leave in fifteen minutes."

Morgan appeared at the top landing wearing her number-12 red team jersey and holding one of her basketball shoes in her hand. "I got a knot," she said, lifting the shoe up high.

"I'll get it loose. Put the other one on."

"I don't know where it is."

"Go look. Throw that down. Hurry up."

The shoe hurtled down at Kari. She managed to catch it with one hand but broke a fingernail. Kari looked down at the cracked nail as she summoned her other daughter.

"CASEY! Where are you?"

The other twin, also sporting a red shirt, this one adorned with 11, appeared at the top of the staircase. She had both her shoes on.

"Turn around," Kari said. Casey made a quarter turn. "All the way around, young lady. They're too tight. Go take them off."

"But, Mom, it's our uniform. See," she said, pointing at her sister, who had returned to the landing with one shoe on. "Morgan has on blue shorts too. We're all supposed to wear blue shorts."

"Morgan's fit. Find some other pair."

"But, Mom—"

"You have a cute little bottom, but we don't need to advertise it to everybody in the gym. Take them off."

"But, Mom…"

"They're too tight."

"…I *have* to wear blue!"

"Casey! What did I just say? Take the shorts off!"

The young girl stood defiantly with her hands on her hips.

"Young lady, you are not leaving *this house* with *those shorts* on!"

"Hey!" Kevin walked into the foyer and held his hands up in a *T.* "Time-out. What's all the yelling about?"

"Daddy! I'm supposed to wear blue shorts."

"I don't care," said Kari. "Go take them off! They're too tight."

Kevin shot a baffled look at Kari and climbed the stairs toward his daughter. "Come on, honey. Let's take a quick look in the laundry basket. I think there's another blue pair like Morgan's in there."

In less than two minutes, Kevin and both girls were downstairs and ready to leave for the game. He placed his hands on their shoulders and steered them toward the back door.

"Go get in the car. Tell your brother too. He's playing in the yard. I want all of you in the van by the time we come outside."

After they left, he turned to Kari. "What was that about?"

"I guess I kind of lost it."

"I noticed."

"I couldn't believe she wanted to parade around in those bootylicious shorts."

"Ummm, she's eleven-years-old. I think she just wanted to wear blue shorts."

"You were okay with them?"

Kevin shook his head. "Does this have anything to do with that pole dancer friend of yours?"

"Tannie? What are you talking about?"

"Are you afraid our daughter is gonna grow up to be a stripper?"

"Of course not."

"You sure? When Tannie was a child, did she wear booty shorts?"

"Now you're making fun of me." Kari paused. "My God, Casey must think I'm crazy."

"Don't beat yourself up. I'm sure Casey thought it was about the shorts."

He put his arm around Kari and gave her a squeeze. "Let's go, sexy face. I want to show off your new look."

"Wait." Kari looked down at her hand and pulled open the kitchen junk drawer.

"Come on. Don't make the coach late."

Kari continued to rummage through the drawer.

"What are you looking for?"

"A file or a clipper. I broke a nail."

"Since when do you care about a broken nail?" With a look of horror, he pretended to muffle a scream. "Uh-oh." In his best Dr. Frankenstein accent, he said, "Has the slutty mommy transformation begun?"

Kari aborted her search, stuck her fingernail in her mouth, and peeled off the jagged piece with her teeth. "Nope, I'm good," she said, holding out her finger.

***

Later that evening, when they returned home after the game, Kari sat with her family in front of the TV. She loved her life. Carter grabbed a spot on the floor and leaned against her legs and Casey and Morgan fought over which of them was going to sit next to her. Kevin had to give up his spot to end the argument. They pestered her with questions and stories throughout the evening. Her family needed and loved her. Life was good.

By ten o'clock, the kids were in bed asleep, and by eleven so was Kevin. At 12:35 a.m., after transcribing her witness notes from an earlier interview, Kari killed the power on her laptop, prepared for bed, and slipped under the covers. Finally, it was her time to sleep, but instead, she lay still and stared at the ceiling.

She needed to get out of her head. Kari, too tense to relax, was having another one of her mind-body disconnects. Thoughts about her mother battling breast cancer, her kids, and work raided her brain. She wished she could quiet her mind.

With envy, she watched her sleeping husband next to her, and gradually, her worries were replaced with thoughts about Tannie. She allowed herself to imagine what it would have been like to go through with the lap dance Tannie had offered at their first meeting. She recalled the way Tannie's breasts had pressed against hers, their faces only inches apart. This wasn't the first time she'd fantasized about Tannie. The visualization turned her on. But she knew Kevin held the magic touch to bring her back into her body, to provide release. Hiking up her nightgown, Kari reached out for Kevin in the stillness of the night and pressed her naked belly and breasts against his shirtless back.

When she kissed his shoulders, he mumbled, "Damn, girl, I was deep asleep. It's too late. You were supposed to come up earlier." But as her nimble fingers moved from his back around to his chest and downward, he responded, "Mmmmmmm," and stopped protesting.

Chapter 10

The next morning, Kari hurried about the house, juggling the routine of the morning and helping the kids get ready for school. She felt energized. Kevin grinned when she came into the kitchen to clear away the breakfast dishes.

"That was the fourth time this week you woke me up in the middle of the night. That stripper case of yours is ruining my sleep," he said with a wink and kissed her on her forehead.

Kari shrugged and smiled. "Yeah, but you know how to do me so good."

"That's what I'm here for."

Kari ran her hands down her floral-print blouse and slim skirt. She was disappointed but not surprised when Kevin didn't notice her outfit was more colorful and formfitting than what she usually wore to the office. She would still have to cover it up with one of her boxy, shapeless jackets. A tailored one wouldn't do much to hide the 40-caliber Glock she strapped on every day.

Clueless to the effort she had made, he finished off his last drop of coffee and placed the cup in the sink. "Do you have to work tonight?"

"Yeah, I'll be late. We've been trying to catch up with this one club owner and finally got ahold of him yesterday. He asked us to stop by the club tonight." She leered at Kevin and patted him on his butt. "You know what that means, don't you?"

"Yeah, you're spending too much time in strip clubs."

Kari didn't respond, but she detected that Kevin was only half joking. When he put on his jacket to take the dog out one last time before leaving for work, Kari followed him into the mudroom. "Don't worry. I've got this under control," she said and pulled him in close for a kiss.

***

By the time he returned from outside, Kari was hanging up the phone.

"They're not coming." Kari stood with her hand still resting on the receiver. She could feel her eyes welling up.

"Who's not coming?"

"My parents."

She had been looking forward to their weekend visit, spending time with them. Lately she seemed to be running from one thing to another.

"My mother has an appointment with hospice." As she said the word, the brimming tears tumbled forward and down her cheeks.

"Hospice?"

"Oh my God. Kevin, she's…dying." Kari reached out for him and, confused and speechless, he gathered her in his arms and held her as she wept.

"I thought she was in remission?"

"Her last test results came in. The cancer's in her liver." Kari buried her face in Kevin's chest.

She hadn't been prepared for the devastating news. *Who died from breast cancer anymore?* She knew at least three women at work and was aware of even more TV and movie stars who had been diagnosed. They had chemotherapy or radiation, lost their hair, and by the time it started to grow back, they were cured. This was her mother's second turn with the disease, but Kari had never thought she would die from it.

"It's like they've given in already. Mom sounded weak, and my dad seemed so lost."

"We'll go there," Kevin said to console her. "On Friday, we'll pack up the kids and drive down to North Carolina."

"No. Not this weekend."

"You gotta be kidding." Kevin loosened his hold and stared at her with disbelief.

"What? My sisters are going down. My father thought it would be too much if we all visited. I told him we'd come the next weekend."

"Oh," said Kevin.

She detected a breath of relief in his reply. "Why did you think I didn't want to go this weekend?"

"Never mind."

"No, I want to know."

"I…I thought it was because of that damn case of yours."

"Really?" First shame, then anger flared inside her and she pushed away from his embrace. "You thought I cared more about work than my own mother? Thanks a lot."

"Kari, I'm sorry."

"You must really think I'm a coldhearted bitch."

"Let's not fight."

"I'm not the one who brought it up. *You did*."

"I said I'm sorry. You've just gotten some terrible news. I don't want to argue about this."

"I knew you thought I was an awful mother and wife. Now I'm a bad daughter too."

"I never said any of that."

"*What*? You're always saying that, always telling me I'm too wound up in my job."

"Let's not do this, now," said Kevin, reaching for her hand. "You have nothing to feel guilty about."

Kari snatched her hand away. She could feel herself losing it, but she couldn't stop.

"You're *right about that*. No guilt here. I'm doing everything I'm supposed to do. I take care of my kids, this house, and *you*."

"What? I'm one of your chores?"

"You've done okay since I started this investigation."

"What does that mean?"

"You know."

"The sex?" Kevin stood in the middle of the kitchen with his mouth agape. "I'm supposed to be grateful because I'm getting laid more? To whom? The stripper? The FBI?"

"That was one thing I didn't hear you complaining about!"

"Skip it. Let's not go there now." He reached out again and took her hands in his. "Are you going to take off work today?"

"No. Why?"

"Because you just learned your mother is dying of breast cancer. That's why."

"I have to go in. We have an interview scheduled." Upon seeing the look in Kevin's eyes, she added, "I'll be okay."

"Can't you cancel?"

"No. We need to meet with the owner now, before he changes his mind about cooperating."

Kevin rubbed the back of his neck and let out a loud breath. "Do me a favor. When you come in tonight, don't wake me."

"What?"

"Don't wake me up. Last night you had this vacant look in your eyes, like you were doing someone else, not me."

"You're kidding, right?"

Kevin plunked himself down on a chair and planted his forehead on the table.

"I don't want to argue with you, but something's not right here. I can feel it."

"What are you talking about?"

"That's the problem. You don't get it, Kari." His voice was low and muffled. He sighed deeply, raised his head, and stared at her.

Kari knew she must look a mess. Her nose was running. Her eyes were probably red.

"You gotta give yourself a break," he said.

"You started this."

"You just found out your mom is dying, but here we are, fighting about the FBI again."

"I'm confused. Why exactly are we arguing?" Kari glared at her husband. "Is it because I'm spending too much time at work or that you don't want to make love to me anymore?" Kari stiffened when he placed his hand on her hip.

"Don't twist this around," said Kevin. "Don't you see the pattern here? Every time you start a new case, you throw yourself into it, let it take over our lives, and you start to lose yourself. Sometimes, I don't even recognize you."

"I'm tired of this."

"Me too. Haven't you heard what I've been saying? You're not superwoman. No one expects you to do it all."

"*So stop fighting. Help me!*" She was angry but wasn't sure who was the villain. Certainly not her.

"You know what you are, Kari? A martyr. No one, not even your precious FBI, expects you to make all these sacrifices."

"A *martyr?* You don't understand the responsibility it is to be an agent."

"Because it's all in your head."

Kari sniffed and swabbed her eyes with her sleeve. She didn't have the strength to respond to her husband's assertion. She watched him pick up his car keys, heading off to work. He paused in the doorway and turned to her.

"How many times are you going to have to learn this lesson?" Kevin asked calmly. "The FBI is a job, not a calling, not a mission. It's just a place where you work."

Chapter 11

Kari found a voice message from Everett waiting for her when she arrived at the office. She returned the call and learned he wasn't coming in.

"Ev, did you forget we have that interview tonight over at Bustle and Booty?"

"You got to cancel," he croaked. "I have the flu. I can't make it."

Kari hung up. She had no intention of canceling the interview. If she went home right after work, Kevin would think she agreed with him that something was wrong. She was dealing with a demanding job and a busy home life. And now her mother was dying. If her healthy sex drive calmed her nerves and eased her anxiety, why should he care? Most husbands would be thrilled. How dare he threaten to cut her off?

She spent most of her day at the office, worrying and speaking to her sisters over the phone about the hospice care arranged for her mother. By the time Kari left for her interview, grief still consumed her.

***

Bustle & Booty was similar to many of the other strip clubs she and Everett had visited. Located off the Delaware River waterfront, it served a Center City business crowd. The owner, Hugh Motley, was sixtyish, with a head that looked too big for his body and a crushing handshake.

"Are you here by yourself?" Motley asked after Kari introduced herself and discreetly displayed her credentials.

Kari nodded. "I'm riding solo tonight. My partner caught a bad bug," she said. "But I'm here and very interested in what you have to say."

"Do you want to go to my office?"

"If it's all right with you, why don't we grab a table and talk out here," Kari suggested, trying to avoid being sequestered in the back alone with Motley. She glanced around the club and assessed the subdued midweek customers. "It's not too noisy."

"No, Wednesdays are slow. Thursdays and weekends are our crazy nights."

They retreated to the rear of the club, where Kari took out her notebook and, after gathering basic identifying information, began the interview.

"How long have you owned Bustle and Booty?"

"Less than two years. Before that I managed a few clubs in Northeast Philly."

"How's business?"

"Could be better," said Motley and then nervously rushed out a frank plea. "I called 'cause I heard you're investigating that Sebastiani guy. I need your help getting him off my back. He's milking me dry. I haven't even turned a profit yet, and he's demanding I pay him off to stay in business."

"You are paying him to stay in business." Kari repeated his words to ensure that he knew she was listening, that she was interested in what he was saying. Testimony like his was what she needed to make her case against Sebastiani stick. Pretty young women claiming to have willingly climbed into the back of a car to give a handsome man an envelope and a blow job don't necessarily make convincing witnesses, even if captured on camera. She nodded to convey that she wanted him to continue.

"I was open for less than a month before I had my first visit." Motley's Adam's apple bobbed as he swallowed. "Sebastiani said I had to pay him $1,000 a month as insurance that L and I wouldn't shut me down."

"Did you refuse?"

"I tried that once. He warned me if I didn't pay, I'd be closed by the end of the day. Less than three hours later, he made good on the threat. The inspectors said they had received complaints that my girls were violating the rules, that their nipples weren't covered. They shut me down for the weekend because the dancers weren't wearing the required pasties.

It was a lie, but I paid up, and since then, I've continued to pay. I have no choice but to stay on his good side by giving him whatever he wants."

Kari wrote down Motley's words in her notebook. What Sebastiani was enacting was extortion. No gun to the head, but extortion nonetheless.

"I can't keep this up. I have expenses."

"Does he expect anything else other than cash?"

Motley turned and directed Kari's attention to the dancer on the stage. "He has a thing for my Erika. She goes out with him."

"Like on a date?" Kari watched the young dancer move her hips to the slow R&B beat. She was pretty but thin and waiflike.

"No." Motley relaxed for a moment and a flicker of a smile crossed his face. "She walks him out to his car. She doesn't have a problem going. I think he peels off a hundred for a BJ. From my money, of course."

"Would she be willing to talk to me?"

"Yeah. I think so. But you're gonna have to wait a few. After her set, she'll want to get in a couple of lap and table dances. Those dollar bills they're stuffing in her G-string won't pay her bills. You want to wait at the bar?"

Kari, enshrined at the bar near the bouncer's vantage point, tried to be as inconspicuous as possible. She sipped a Diet Coke and watched Erika entertain clients, noting that she was no Tannie Colosi. Her moves were clumsy and crude, but the man Erika was grinding against didn't seem to mind. Kari felt twinges of desire stirring. She shifted in her perch and closed her eyes to collect herself. When she opened them a second later, she found herself face-to-face with a handsome white stranger. A flush of heat crept across her cheeks.

"I didn't mean to startle you," he said. "I saw you sitting alone and thought maybe I could buy you a drink." His boyish grin and gentle, brown eyes reminded her of one of the agents who worked on the cyber squad.

"No thank you." Kari held up her glass. "I have one."

"Can I sit down and talk to you until you need another?"

"I don't think so."

"Aw. Why not?"

"Because I don't know you."

"The other girls here will vouch for me. They think I'm adorable. Just ask them."

When Kari laughed a little too loud, the bouncer, who Motley must have told to look out for her, leaned over and asked, "Is he bothering you?"

"No. He's okay."

The bouncer gave them both a questioning gaze and returned to his duties, surveying the activities of the club.

"Thanks," the stranger said, pulling up a stool beside her. "I have a feeling that one word from you and the big guy would have tossed me out headfirst."

"I couldn't live with that on my conscience."

He was probably in his midforties, but with a youthful smile that produced endearing dimples. *He's cute*, she thought.

He glanced down at her notepad resting on the counter. "Do you work here?"

"Me? No," Kari said, laughing and shaking her head.

"I saw you talking to some guy and taking notes. What's a nice girl like you doing in a place like this? You're obviously not a dancer."

Kari laughed and placed her hands on her hips. "Oh, thanks."

"I didn't mean it that way. I think you're hotter than any of the girls in here." He eyed her with an approving gaze that didn't feel invasive or lewd. "So…what are you doing in a strip club?"

"I'm…selling health insurance."

"Really? Health insurance?" The handsome stranger smirked and, with exaggerated concern, pointed to Erika. "That one might need some extra coverage," he said. Erika twerked and pumped her narrow hips up and down on the lap of a satisfied customer.

"Funny you should notice that. I'm actually waiting to give her my sales pitch."

"My name's Joe Wilson."

"Joe Wilson." Kari shook his hand. "Right. That's original."

"No, really. Joe Wilson. I wouldn't lie to you."

"That's nice to know."

Wilson gave a reassuring smile. "What's yours?"

"My what?"

"Name. What's your name?"

"Oh, I don't want to lie to you either."

He let out a short laugh. "Fair enough."

Kari enjoyed Wilson's conversation as they continued to observe Erika's routine. Every now and then, Kari noticed Joe's stolen glances at her. He was checking out a glimpse of thigh exposed when she crossed her legs. Kari didn't bother to adjust the hem of her skirt. She didn't mind. She was just killing time.

"When you're finished here," Wilson said, "maybe we could go somewhere else for a drink?"

"I don't know if that's such a good idea."

"Will you at least think about it?" He placed his hand on her knee and pouted.

Just as Kari was about to answer with a definitive no, Motley came over to let her know Erika was ready to speak with her. Kari shook Joe's hand. "It was nice to meet you. Thanks for keeping me company." She walked away without a backward glance.

Fifteen minutes later, after interviewing Erika about her "dates" with Sebastiani, Kari left Bustle & Booty.

Joe Wilson waited outside, leaning against the building.

"You're not waiting for me, are you?"

"Yeah," he said cheerfully. "Come on, we were having fun. Let's hang out some more."

Kari didn't respond.

"My car's right over there," said Wilson. "The black Bimmer with the New Jersey tags."

"So you're from Jersey."

"North Jersey. I'm a visitor to your city. Aren't you supposed to be welcoming to out-of-towners?" Wilson scanned the lot. "Where's yours?"

"My what?"

"Car, silly. Where's your car? You want to follow me, don't you? Or did you want to ride with me?"

Kari looked at her cell phone screen. It wasn't yet nine o'clock.

What else was she going to do? Go home and fight with Kevin? What the hell, she thought and turned to Wilson. "I'll follow you. Where are we going?"

"There's a nice bar at the Sheraton. I was supposed to meet a friend there, but she canceled on me. It's just—"

"I know how to get there." The hotel was across the street from Tannie's Society Hill Tower condo. Kari knew the area well.

"So you're really coming?" Wilson ran his hands through his wavy, brown hair and rested them on the top of his head. He seemed harmless. And if he wasn't, Kari was confident she could take care of herself.

"Yeah. I'll meet you there." Kari placed her fists on her hips and stared into Wilson's eyes. "For a drink. Okay?"

On the way to the Sheraton, Kari was amused. Wilson turned her on. Uneasy about her recent fantasies featuring Tannie, she had found herself testing her sexuality, gauging her attraction to other women she worked with or passed on the street. So far, other than Tannie, no females pushed her buttons.

Relieved that she was not having a Sapphic midlife crisis, Kari had few reservations about having a drink with Joe Wilson. Nevertheless, her law enforcement cynicism kicked in, and "in an abundance of caution," she pulled up close to his bumper to read his license plate. She called it in to the office, fully aware she was violating a rule against record checks for personal use.

"Six-oh-two to Central. I need you to run a New Jersey tag for me," she said. While she parallel parked along Dock Street, Central came back with the info.

"That tag belongs to Joe Wilson at a residence in Teaneck, New Jersey. Ready to copy?"

"No, that's all I needed."

"Okay," said Central. "I'll route it to your file."

"Thanks."

"Wait. I'm gonna need the file number or the subject name."

"Oh. Uh. Sebastiani. Send it to the Stuart Sebastiani file."

The lounge in the Sheraton was busy with several groups of noisy business travelers, but as soon as she slipped through the double doors, she spied Joe Wilson waiting for her at the bar.

"I wasn't sure you would really come." He stood up to greet her and gave her a peck on the cheek as if they were old friends. "Let's get a booth," he said, taking her elbow and steering her to the more private, upholstered benches along the side of the room. She slid in and could feel him close behind her.

"No. You sit across from me," Kari chuckled, barring him from sliding in next to her. "This way I can keep my eyes on your hands at all times."

"Oh well," he said, wiggling his fingers. "Can we at least play footsies under the table?"

"I don't know anything about you. Why don't you tell me some more about yourself before you start asking to fool around with my feet?" Kari smiled and relaxed. There was something familiar about Wilson. She felt comfortable tucked in a bar booth with him—comfortable enough to lie to herself about what they were doing, why he thought she was there.

They both ordered the house beer on tap. He told her he was in pharmaceutical sales. "My region covers North Jersey. But I'm here once or twice a month. I usually come down on Wednesdays, spend the night, and go home before the weekend."

"Where do you stay?"

"Here, at the Sheraton." He added, almost in a whisper, "I have a room upstairs."

Kari caught Joe's gaze for a moment, before dropping her head to stare at her hands. Wilson reached across the table and touched them with the tips of his fingers. He looked down at her wedding band, turned the diamond away from view, and lightly stroked her palms. His hands traveled along her forearms. "You have beautiful, soft, brown skin," he said.

Kari didn't ask him to stop.

"And you're easy to talk to."

"I'm an army brat. We moved a lot—six different countries, thirteen different cities, and as many schools. I learned how to make friends quickly and often." *Yeah,* thought Kari, *the boys really liked being my friend,* as long as she first met them behind the school stairwell or in their bedrooms before their parents came home from work. And when she got older, she made new friends by picking up men in hotel bars like this one. But that was all before she'd met and married Kevin.

"That must have been hard."

"What?"

"Moving around all the time." He waved his hands about as if navigating a highway. "Having to get to know the kids at school each time."

Kari shrugged. "I was a decent athlete—basketball, cross-country, track—so I latched on to the jocks."

"With all that moving, you must have friends all around the world."

Kari tilted her head and smiled. She knew Wilson would think she was reminiscing about those old acquaintances. But the truth was, she had no idea where any of her former schoolmates were. Once she'd moved away, she never thought about them again. She was skilled at making friends but didn't value friendship. She recalled a TV show she once watched about decluttering closets, where the organization expert said that for every new outfit you bring home, you should discard an old one. That's what she did with people. But she never shared that with anyone. It was none of Wilson's business. She changed the subject.

They chatted about superficial things—the weather, the economy, the Eagles, and the Giants. All the while, Kari focused on his bright hazel-brown eyes. She found them reassuring.

"I'm ready to go upstairs. Are you?" Wilson stared into her eyes and smiled.

Kari nodded. But when Wilson stood and reached for her hand, she didn't take it.

"You go up first," she said. "What's your room number?"

"Eight sixteen. You'll come right behind me?" Suddenly, he seemed desperate. "Promise?"

She smiled and again nodded, knowing that as soon as he left, she would slip away, never to be seen again. That was the rule of the game.

"Okay. I'll see you in a few." He got up to leave. "Are you ever going to tell me your name?"

She shook her head. "Tonight, I don't know who I am."

He left the bar and entered one of the elevators across from the lounge. She laughed as he blew her a kiss and waved just as the doors glided shut. Kari gathered up her coat and purse, but instead of heading toward the exit, she found herself among a noisy group of corporate types and a lovely older couple waiting for the next elevator. When the doors opened, Kari hesitated and let them enter first. What was she doing?

"Going up?" asked the elderly man, holding the door open for her. He sported a giant foam Liberty Bell headpiece and a wide grin, his arm draped around the shoulders of his cheerful wife.

"That's okay," said Kari. "I'll get the next one."

"Don't be ridiculous. Me and the little lady can squeeze in tighter to make room for you," he said with a twinkle in his eye.

As the elevator climbed, Kari beheld the reflection of the happy loving couple standing beside her in the stainless steel doors. He wrapped both of his arms around his wife, and they giggled as they huddled close in an exaggerated effort to conserve space for Kari. When the doors opened to deposit her on the eighth floor, she hesitated again and glanced at the old couple. They waved a cheerful good-bye, and she stepped off the elevator.

The doors closed behind her.

As she stood in the narrow hallway, a familiar carnal urge nurtured by a sick soup of detachment, denial, and loneliness radiated deep inside her. This time, the sickness had taken over while she was within miles of her home and family—and while she had been on the job. She knew she should resist, but something inexplicable propelled her forward and soon she found herself knocking on the door of room 816.

Once inside, neither Kari nor Wilson said a word. When he grabbed her hand to lead her to the bed, she shook her head and pointed to a chair. Wilson, following her lead, slid the chair from under the writing desk and placed it in the center of the room. While she watched, he unzipped his pants, lowered them down to his feet and waited for her next command. She pushed him onto the seat, hiked her skirt up, and, placing her hands on her knees, slowly rotated and gyrated backward onto his lap. An erotic, silent lap dance.

She spoke to him breathlessly over her shoulder. "I tried to take good notes tonight. Am I doing this right?"

He nodded and, gripping her by the waist, yanked aside the crotch of her panties to thrust himself inside her.

"Wait, wait," she said, twisting to the side and reaching down to the floor to rummage through the pockets of his pants still crumpled around his ankles. She looked up at him from her bent-over angle. "Don't you have any condoms?"

"Damn, of course," he said. "Can you get up for a quick second?" He patted her playfully on her bottom. "I have some in my wallet on the nightstand."

By the time Wilson, laughing and shuffling around with his pants around his ankles, had retrieved his wallet and had turned to triumphantly wave the condom packet in the air, Kari had taken a moment to assess the situation.

She gave him a fabricated smile; she was numb inside.

But she didn't say no; she didn't say stop.

This time, she had taken the game too far. This time, she had broken the rules.

***

During the twenty-minute ride home, Kari brushed away tears that kept coming. Only a few cars were on the highway, but the drivers seemed to stare into her window as they passed by, as if they knew where she had been, what she had done.

In that moment, the saddest details of her life came flooding back to haunt her. She had cheated on her husband and her mother was dying. A repulsive diversion played out in her mind. What if Kevin had cancer too? Brain cancer, lung cancer, colon cancer—any of the big C's could rip him from her. The morbid vision caused more tears to flow.

And then it hit her. She was no better than Sebastiani. If he was a pig, then she was one too. All the screwed-up defects inside him urging him to cheat lived inside her too. It was that revelation that finally broke her. After fifteen years of fidelity, she had reverted to her old ways. Taking on this strip club case was turning out to be one of the biggest mistakes of her life.

By the time she arrived home, it was well after ten o'clock. She made sure the kids were in bed with the lights off but barely spoke to Kevin as she hurried to change into her running clothes and headed out the door to take a couple laps around the block. She needed an excuse to take a shower and wash Wilson's nasty handprints off her body.

When she returned from her run, she fled to the bathroom. Kevin was waiting in the bedroom and followed her in disbelief.

"What are you doing?"

"I went for a run, and now I'm taking a shower."

"It's nearly midnight." Kevin stepped between her and the shower. She reached into the stall to turn the handle and let the water flow.

"It's like you're in a damn cult, you know."

"It's not the FBI. Don't blame my shortcomings on the FBI."

His eyes searched her face. "How else can you explain your fanatic devotion?"

"Let's not start this again. Not now." She was determined to cleanse herself. She stripped off her clothes and moved to squeeze past him.

He blocked her way again. "Something's wrong," Kevin said. He stared at her in a way that as much as said he knew she was worthy of suspicion. "Are you feeling guilty?"

Kari held her breath. She stood before him naked, exposed and vulnerable and prepared to tell him the truth, to deal with the consequences.

"Let's go ahead and visit her this weekend anyway," he continued. "If we tag-team the driving, we can go down for the day and turn around and come right back, if you want."

Kari didn't know what to say. Kevin thought she was feeling guilty about visiting her mother. He trusted her. Now she really felt like a selfish slut. If she didn't get her act together, sooner or later, her behavior would cost her, her relationships with Kevin, her parents, and her kids. She was determined to change.

"Thank you. That would be nice," said Kari in a weak, sad voice. She gazed softly at Kevin for a moment before retreating into the protective sanctuary of the steam-filled shower.

Chapter 12

"Turn here," said Kari. "The club should be up the street, on the left."

Tannie had suggested that Kari and Everett reach out to Bill Leone, a childhood friend of Sebastiani's who was not feeling the love for his old buddy. She thought Leone might be angry enough to talk to the agents. "If you can convince him to cooperate, this will be an easy breezy investigation for you," she'd said. "He knows all of Stu's dirt."

Leone was the owner of a popular strip club with two locations, Club Friskee in South Philly and Club Friskee II in Manayunk, a newly gentrified section of Philly known for its microbreweries, which was quite appropriate since the English translation of the Native American word Manayunk literally meant "where we go to drink." *Funny*, Kari thought, *the Lenape Indians were referring to the river water. I wonder what they'd think about the young and hip who flock to the area to guzzle beer.*

They were about to drive right past the building when Everett pointed out the discreet signage. "Slow up. There it is."

No flashing neon marquee, no brazen I. Only a coy sign, simple and nondescript, announced Club Friskee II. They pulled the car into the closest metered spot and walked a block back to the club.

"Where's the 'Live Nude Girls' sign?" Everett wondered. "This one's different than those other clubs you dragged me inside."

"Yeah right, kicking and screaming," Kari half whispered to Everett as they stepped through the doors of Club Friskee II, where they were greeted by a hostess.

"We're here to see Bill Leone," Kari said. "Is he in?"

"He's expecting you?"

"Tell him we're here about his buddy Stuart Sebastiani."

"Oh, did Stu send you?" The hostess took a long look at Kari. "Are you here to audition?"

Kari suppressed a smile. "No. But thanks for asking."

"Yeah," Everett laughed. "She's gonna note that in her journal tonight."

The hostess asked them to wait and walked toward an office to the left side of the entrance. After she went through the doorway, Kari punched Everett in his arm. "What's so funny?"

"Ouch." Everett rubbed his arm and grinned. "The hostess was just being nice. We both know you're far from looking like a stripper."

Kari scrunched up her nose and, while peeking at her reflection in the entry's mirrored half wall, she adjusted her muddy-brown pantsuit. She had always thought of herself as a *natural* beauty but managed to dab on a little makeup, a touch of lipstick, and a couple of flicks of mascara on her eyelashes. She had returned to her slacks-and-boxy-jacket wardrobe. Joe Wilson's face flashed through her thoughts as she recalled the last time she had put on a skirt. Never again.

"You two looking for me?"

Kari heard him speak before she saw the good-looking man in his late fifties. He was about Everett's height and wore a crisp, white shirt and faded jeans. The tailored shirt suggested rock-hard pecs and a taut middle. It was unbuttoned at the neck, revealing a few salt-and-pepper chest hairs that matched the full set of curls on his head. He wore soft leather moccasins, no socks. An attractive man, but his orange, tanning-bed glow ruined the package.

"Bill Leone?" Kari said, extending her hand. "I'm Kari Wheeler and this is—"

"Everett Hildebrand."

"Honey told me Stu sent you." Leone's eyes scanned Kari and Everett. "Are you selling something? My business manager handles sales."

"We'd like to ask you a few questions about Mr. Sebastiani," Kari said. "We heard he's a friend of yours and thought you might be able to help us."

Leone stroked his clean-shaven chin with his thumb and forefinger. "Friend?" he said. "Let's talk in my office."

The agents followed Leone as he led them toward the music. Soon they were in a familiar setting—the floor-to-ceiling mirrors behind the main stage made the room appear larger than it actually was. Plum-colored leather banquettes along the sides and, closer to the stage area, velvet upholstered booths seemed to go on forever. Most of the seating was occupied by an after-lunch crowd.

Speaking above the pumping beat, Kari motioned toward the strippers dancing on a multileveled stage, and said, "When you're in the other room, you can't even tell that this is a strip club."

"Gentlemen's club," Leone politely corrected her. "We had to make a number of concessions for the neighborhood association to accept us, and the discreet marquee and the front receiving room were two of them. But it all works. People find us. The name Club Friskee communicates who we are."

The party of three made their way across the room, passing several conservatively attired female guests and dozens of men in business suits with loosened ties or golf shirts and dress slacks, some with strippers perched on their laps, others with welcoming dancers hovering nearby. When they reached the mirrors, Leone led them down a short hallway to his office. It was a large, masculine space, with a plasma screen hugging the wall opposite a massive and rich-looking mahogany desk that anchored the room. Just as doctors and lawyers displayed their diplomas, Leone also flaunted his credentials. A wall unit full of photos showed Leone embracing barely clothed or nude women. Kari recognized Sebastiani in a few of them. He posed brazenly, fully clothed, but with practically nude women in almost pornographic shots.

"Have a seat."

Leone directed them to two chairs. Leone took a seat on the leather couch.

"So…go ahead talk. Who are you, and what do you need from me?"

"We're with the FBI," Kari said, flashing her badge and credentials. Everett held his out too.

"FBI. Isn't that something?" Leone arched an eyebrow but didn't seem surprised.

Kari spied a hint of anticipatory glee in his eyes.

"My back has been killing me, an old golf injury. I hope you don't mind if I lie down." As Leone spoke, he gingerly lowered his torso, raised his legs, and rested his feet on a thick pillow. "This helps." Leone turned his head in her direction and nodded for them to continue.

"We've been made aware of some, uh, allegations about Stuart Sebastiani," said Kari.

"Allegations?" Leone raised his eyebrows. "That son of a bitch is the most corrupt person I know. The only chance you got at stopping that bastard from taking bribes is to force him to wear pants without pockets for the rest of his life."

She and Everett laughed.

"So you know about him accepting cash—"

"He had his hand out the first time I met him," Leone interrupted. "And he was only twelve."

"We understand you two had a falling out," Everett said.

"Sort of. I was just trying to expand my business, and the self-absorbed asshole took offense. Did you hear what that bastard did to me? It's probably another crime you could add to whatever else you've got on him."

Tannie had been right; Leone needed no prompting.

"What happened?"

"It's simple. I wanted to build this place"—Leone motioned around the room—"and Stu wanted me to redo my South Philly location so he could continue to sponge off me in luxury. He was a pain in my ass until I saw things his way." Leone flipped a bird at an imaginary Sebastiani standing in front of him. "What a fucking baby!"

"And he was supposed to be your friend," said Kari, nudging him to continue talking. She nodded as Everett pulled out his spiral notepad.

Over the last few years, Leone explained, the South Philly site had been losing business. A significant number of adult clubs had sprung up on Spring Garden Street, along Columbus Boulevard and down toward the sports stadiums off of Packer Avenue. It was worse now that JOLIE was also located around the corner from the original Club Friskee. The newer clubs were stand-alone structures offering free parking, unlike the inconvenient metered and permit parking available at Club Friskee. Onsite parking was a premium amenity.

"In spite of Stu's wishes, I was determined to put my money in a less competitive market, and I began building Club Friskee II, here in Manayunk."

"And was that okay with Sebastiani?" said Kari.

"At first, I had no problem getting the necessary building and zoning permits. But immediately after we broke ground, we started having serious setbacks. Time after time, construction was red-tagged or halted due to some building issues or damn code violation. And I began to suspect that Stu was behind all the delays."

"I thought Sebastiani's department just handled regulatory issues, not new construction?" Kari said.

"Yeah, but the inspectors in compliance and construction take care of each other. I asked Stu to tell them to ease up a little, and do you know what he tried to get me to swallow? That he didn't want to interfere, that he was being cautious."

Everett looked up from his note-taking. "Cautious about what?"

"He told me some bullshit about everyone knowing we were friends and that he was concerned that his enemies were just waiting for him to pull strings for me. So instead, he left me hanging out on a limb, savaged by overrun charges and costly revisions. No one else wanted anything to do with me. Even stuffing a couple of C-notes between the pages of the damn permit application didn't help."

"That doesn't sound like something a friend would do," Kari said.

"Exactly. He was pissed off about the South Philly spot," said Leone. "I couldn't afford to hold out any longer. So…I did what I had to do. I caved and ate shit." Leone's face contorted as if he could taste the apology. "Had to. The clock was ticking. When you get a liquor license, they give you six months to pour your first drink or they yank it."

"So you fixed up both places?" asked Kari.

"Yeah. And once I gave in, he didn't give a damn about anyone keeping book on him. Both projects moved along without a blip or a snag. Stu even wanted to give me tips on what colors and fabrics I should use to reupholster the booths and barstools. What a joke! I hate that motherfucker. A boatload of dough later, and where the fuck is he? His ass is hanging out at JOLIE. Now ain't that a bitch!"

In obvious pain, Leone sat up and swung his feet around to the floor. "What do I have to do to help you guys send his lying ass to jail?"

Kari was pleased, very pleased. But she didn't show it. She glanced over at Everett. *Good. Poker face.*

"Do you have documentation of all the issues you had while building this place?" Kari asked.

"Yeah, my attorney has all my files and records." After his free-flow ranting, the agents were surprised when Leone added, "But I'm going to need a subpoena first."

"A subpoena?" repeated Everett.

"Hey, I'm not some snitch meeting you in a dark alley. I'm a businessman. If you're asking me to produce records, I'm going to need a subpoena. I know how this works."

"Are you willing to provide grand jury testimony about the things you're telling us?" Kari asked.

"Doesn't testimony work the same way? If you give me a subpoena, I'm required to appear. Right?"

"Yes, but I was getting the impression that you were willing to cooperate without us having to compel you," Kari said.

"A subpoena will help me feel less dirty, you know, like a rat," Leone said with a wry smile.

"How far are you willing to go?" Everett asked, jumping in. "Are you willing to wear a wire?"

Kari cringed. He was pushing too soon.

"Hell no. I'm not doing anything sneaky like that. I'll tell you what I know, what I heard, but wearing a wire and setting up people…I ain't doing that."

"No problem, Bill. We don't need you to wear a wire. We're talking to a lot of people," she said.

Leone stared suspiciously at them both.

"Why don't you tell us about your current relationship with Sebastiani and what you know about his involvement in JOLIE?"

Leone relaxed. He stretched out on the couch and began telling tales about Sebastiani. "That's a sweet deal he has there at JOLIE."

"Did he tell you he has a piece of the club?"

"Nah, but come on. His son does. Who do you think is behind that? Stu's the expert when it comes to operating a strip club. His ass has been hanging out in titty bars for as long as I've known him."

"How long is that?" Everett asked.

"Shit. Stu and me went to junior high together and he was going to strip clubs with his old man then. He considers himself to be a boob man, the bigger the better. He doesn't care if they are real or fake, as long as they are big, round, and high." Leone grabbed at his own chest, fondling imaginary breasts.

"But I've been out with him," Leone said with a wink, "and I question if he is, in actuality, an ass man." Leone rambled on.

Everett had stopped taking notes, which was fine with her. Leone was giving them nothing of value or substance. But she wondered if that was the reason Everett ceased writing or if he was just too enthralled with the topic.

The one-way conversation gravitated to Leone's likes and dislikes. It soon became apparent that Bill Leone was quite impressed with himself. Kari had only known him for a few minutes, and she already found him annoying.

From his horizontal position on the couch, he told the agents about how much money he had and how many cars and boats he owned. He also proclaimed that he had slept with every one of the beautiful girls working in his clubs. Leone bragged about his bedroom conquests more than about the expensive things he owned, although one could argue he probably saw the women among the expensive things that belonged to him.

When Kari guided the conversation back to Sebastiani, Leone only wanted to talk about the early days when Sebastiani was working in the field as an L&I inspector. He told the agents how Sebastiani learned to "shake hands" with business owners and palm a few extra dollars. When he was pressed for more current and relevant activities, Leone said Sebastiani was too powerful now to settle for mere pocket change. For the last few years, Sebastiani had developed an inner circle of strip club and restaurant owners who wanted to stay on his good side and took care of him with personal "loans" he was never expected to pay back, in addition to those who had no choice.

"When he visits their places of business, you might catch him accepting a free meal or lap dance, but he would be suspicious of anyone he didn't know trying to hand him money. Stu has his own well-established, uh, routine."

"A routine?" asked Kari.

"Yeah, when it's time for him to leave, he sometimes asks the business owners to send a girl to walk him to his car. She's the one who gives him whatever it is the owner wants him to have."

"Do you ever send someone out to his car?"

"Occasionally, when we're on speaking terms."

"Would we be able to send an undercover agent to give him his envelope?" Kari thought about Becca Benner, a new squad agent, for the role.

"Sure, if she gives good head," said Leone. "Stu usually expects more than just an envelope once they reach his car."

Kari returned his lewd grin with a weak smile. She expected him to simulate a hand job or a blow job and was grateful when he didn't.

"One thing you should know about Stu is," Leone said, seeming to pause for maximum effect, "he's a pussy chaser spring-loaded for action. He's always on the hunt for cunt."

Kari felt her face harden.

He laughed.

She didn't.

"Sorry," he said. "I didn't mean to offend you."

"I'm sure you didn't." She folded her arms and shot him a reprimanding look. She wasn't about to continue down that path.

The standoff was broken when Leone called for Honey to bring him something for the pain in his back. As soon as she left the room, Leone proclaimed with a wink, "I did her too."

Kari stood. "I think we're finished for now."

Leone remained where he lay. "I'd show you out, but—"

"No. No. Don't get up." Kari waved her hands.

"I wasn't joking, you know. I want to help you guys get Stu."

"Great. We'll be in touch," Everett said, pointing to a small tray of business cards on Leone's desk. "Can I take one?"

"Sure. You're gonna leave me yours?"

She and Everett placed their cards on Leone's desk and let themselves out.

Chapter 13

"If Leone is getting as much sex as he claims, no wonder his back is killing him," said Kari as she and Everett walked to the car.

"He was so cool. I couldn't believe some of things he was saying."

"You liked him?"

"Yeah. Didn't you?"

Kari stopped and placed her hand on Everett's shoulder. "Don't tell me you have a man-crush on him. Trust me. Don't fall in love with that one. He's not good enough for you."

"It wasn't like that."

"Hey, I'm teasing you."

"You really didn't think he was cool?"

"Not at all. I think he's an ass."

"We're still going to open him as an informant, aren't we?"

"Sure. I don't have to like him to work with him."

"What if I make Leone my source?"

"I don't know if that's such a good idea," said Kari. "I think Bill Leone is a live wire, and I'm not sure you're going to be able to control him."

"What do you mean?"

Kari could see that she had insulted Everett. She attempted to explain. "He's unpredictable, and I'm not ready to trust him."

"But he was willing to speak to us without any assurances."

"Yeah, that's the problem," Kari said. "He was playing a game with us in there. What did we learn that we didn't already know?"

"Leone told us stuff." Everett held up his notebook.

"Like what? Stu Sebastiani is an ass man." Kari snatched the notebook from Everett and flipped through the pages. "Riveting intelligence," she said. "I hope you wrote it all down."

Kari noted Everett's frown when she handed back his pad. She had worked with many informants over the years. She collected them like cards in Old Maid, and now she could add the Strip Club Owner and the Stripper cards to the deck. *What does he know at this stage of his career?* His hand was empty.

"He reminds me of one of those guys who used to hang around the football team or the cool kids in high school. Not in the same league, but allowed in because he was always doing something wild and outrageous to entertain the group. Do you know what I mean?"

"No," Everett said. "I wasn't in either of those groups."

"He makes me uncomfortable."

Against her better judgment, when they reached the car, Kari told Everett to go ahead and complete the informant registration. She warned him that she or another agent should always accompany him to his meetings with Leone. She didn't think he would ever fully cooperate and provide them with something of real value. But if having his own informant made Everett feel more confident, why should she say no?

"I know his type," Kari said, cautioning Everett. "Remember, Bill Leone will never be your friend. He's not talking to us because he likes us."

***

As soon as they returned to the office, Everett filled out the necessary documents to officially register Bill Leone with the office's Human Intelligence Unit. After dropping off a request for the NCIC operator to run Leone's criminal history, Everett sat at his desk with his feet resting on his trash can. He felt great. He was the co-case agent of what could turn into one of the biggest corruption cases in the office, and he now had a high-caliber informant working for him.

Everett wasn't worried about handling Bill Leone. Maybe he would have been when they first opened the case, but not now. After their visit to the PlayRoom, he'd had to admit his sexual naïveté. He had always been proud, almost self-righteous, that he and Brenda had been virgins when they'd married. However, on this assignment, his inexperience was a problem. So he'd designed and implemented his own rapid desensitization program.

The first thing Everett had done was search the Internet for everything about strip clubs. He reviewed hundreds of websites and thousands of photos of strippers so he wouldn't be so noticeably uncomfortable around them. His research had worked. After several days of practice, he was now able to sit in front of his computer in his home office while his family was in the next room. He could view videos and images without his face registering what he was seeing.

He hadn't planned to enter any porn sites. An innocent mouse click linked him to the explicit Web pages. He certainly did not consider his viewing habits as an issue to share or discuss with Brenda. She wouldn't understand. He wasn't the type of person who

watched porn for pleasure. He wasn't one of those guys. This was part of his job.

Chapter 14

Sebastiani blew smoke from his first cigarette of the day out the partially opened kitchen window. Anna, who was still asleep, would kill him if she knew he was smoking in the house.

Since he had ended his relationship with Tannie, he felt as if a heavy burden had been lifted from his shoulders. It had always been just about the sex. The first time he saw her dancing on stage he, like everyone else in the club, wanted her. Well, he got her, and for a while, it was good.

Until she got knocked up.

Jesus, Joseph, and Mary. A fucking baby? Why hadn't Tannie been more careful? If his wife found out, she would leave him for sure, especially if she found out Tannie named the baby Dia. Tannie claimed it was a family name, but she knew his daughter's name was Mia. Tannie did it out of spite. The bitch thought she was being clever.

"Goddamn you, Tannie," he said in an angry whisper. He already had a wife. He already had a family. The last thing he needed was another one.

Married for almost thirty years, he had been unfaithful throughout. From the beginning of each affair, he told his girlfriends he would never leave his wife. He always watched for warning signs that any of the women might be a bunny boiler, like the chick in *Fatal Attraction*. Despite his honesty, two or three of his lovers claimed to have called his home and spoken to Anna. But she never said a word, never confronted him.

Sebastiani looked out of the window, taking long pulls on his cigarette. As if on cue, his twenty-year-old next-door neighbor, his newest side thing, appeared. Gina walked across her yard and sat down on the rubber seat of her childhood swing set. With her legs too long and the seat too low for her to push off and swing high, she just gently swayed. Her limbs poked out at odd angles, and her knees were practically in her chest as she moved side to side, then back and forth. She held on awkwardly, quickly releasing one hand to light and take a quick drag on her cigarette before grabbing for the chain just before the swing started to dip and twist around. Sebastiani laughed when she miscalculated, took too long of a puff, and barely caught hold of the chain in time. One second slower and she would have been tipped out of the seat, onto the mulch bed underneath.

He grabbed his coat from the rack in the mudroom and stepped out onto the porch. The brisk late March morning air felt good. He turned slightly toward Gina's yard and, without making eye contact, glanced over to make sure she had seen him come outside. He strolled through the backyard, smoking and pulling weeds, until he had made his way to the rear of the property, where he dumped the handful of cold, limp leaves and dead, dry stalks into the compost pile.

Stalling with delicious anticipation, he stooped down as if tending to his dormant garden and waited for Gina to signal him from the tall evergreens between the two yards. When he heard her cough, he hurried around behind the storage shed.

"My oh my, what do we have here?" he whispered, as soon as he saw her standing among the bushes with her hands in the tight pockets of her low-cut jeans.

She came over to him and, unzipping her puffy parka, rubbed up against him and hugged his neck. She was so young, so pretty. Why did she want to be with him? He even asked her once and she told him, "Because you remind me of Mr. Big on *Sex and the City*."

He had no idea who Mr. Big was, but he liked the character's name.

Gina had been hanging around, trying to get him to pay attention to her since she was sixteen years old, just about the time her crazy, screwed-up mother divorced Gina's father, and a steady stream of potential new husbands began to move in and out of their house. Gina would come into the garage while he was working on his car, telling him she wanted to learn about car maintenance. She offered to help him rake leaves or wash the dog, anything to be alone with him. He told her to go away. If he needed any help, he had a daughter her age to assist him. She had frightened him. He had been a grown man afraid of a teenage girl with a ponytail. But he'd known that if he'd been caught with her, he'd lose more than just his marriage and family— he'd also lose his freedom. So he spent four years hiding and running from her.

Now, everything was different. Gina was twenty and legal. The first time he and Gina had gotten together was when Tannie was about seven months pregnant. Although with her clothes on he could hardly tell, the change in Tannie's body when she was naked was disturbingly apparent. The truth was he had had trouble getting aroused as soon as she told him about the baby.

So when Gina had approached him and asked him to meet her behind the shed, he had. Ever since, they had gotten together on a regular basis. He didn't have to fear that she thought their relationship was going anywhere. Gina had known his family for most of her life. She used to play with his daughter and son. His wife was like an aunt to her. Unlike Tannie, Gina understood their relationship.

As she kneeled down in front of him, Sebastiani caressed the top of Gina's head and tangled his fingers in her hair. Damn. She was worth the wait.

Chapter 15

As soon as they entered the restaurant, Kari's appetite revved up. The aromas wafting from kitchens made her stomach dance and her mouth water.

They were at McKenna's, a small but popular Center City restaurant. Among the boxes of subpoenaed L&I records, Kari and Everett had found three citations issued after the restaurant underwent renovations without the required permits. Allegedly, the violations had been corrected and the proper fines were collected, all certified by Sebastiani. She scanned the dining room. The tablecloths were starched white, and the place settings were out. The lunch-hour rush was just about to begin, but no one came to the front of the empty restaurant to greet them.

"We're here to see the owner. Is that you?" she called out to a Hispanic man wiping his hands on a white apron. He shook his head and slipped through a door in the rear of the bistro. Shortly after, someone dressed in a black shirt and black dress pants appeared.

"Are you the owner?"

"Yeah, Bobby McKenna. How ya doing?"

Kari and Everett introduced themselves and handed McKenna some documents to review, citations issued for expanding his dining area without permits.

"Yeah, I remember this," he said, returning the papers to Kari. "I took care of everything I needed to take care of. What's the problem?"

"I don't know if there is a problem," Kari said. "We're just conducting a general review of the Department of Licenses and

Inspections and pulled a few files. Yours just happened to be one of those pulled.

"Am I being investigated for something?"

"We don't have any issues with you. This is a simple review of the city's business compliance process. Do you recall the circumstances involving your violations?" she asked.

"Yeah, some guy came in, said he was with L and I, looked around the place, and by the time he left, he'd cited me for three code violations. I was afraid they were going to close me down until I fixed them." McKenna told them he had operated the expanded service area for almost two years before drawing the attention of the compliance inspector.

"And did they close you down?" Everett asked.

"I called a friend who called a friend, and he arranged for me to stay open while I made the corrections."

"Who was the friend of your friend?" Kari and Everett asked at almost the same time.

McKenna looked at them both and smiled. "Stu Sebastiani. He really took care of me, and he didn't know me from Adam. He was great."

"And what did you have to do for Mr. Sebastiani in exchange?"

"If you're asking if I had to pay him a bribe, absolutely not. He didn't ask for a dime."

"Sebastiani took care of all of this for you," Everett said as he held up the paperwork, "and he didn't ask for anything?"

"Yeah, that's right."

"The friend who introduced you to Sebastiani, did you pay him?"

"Yeah, $2,500. He's an expediter. Jimmy Mastracola. He helps people navigate through the permit system. I paid him for his services."

"Why'd you need his assistance?" Kari asked.

"Look, everybody knows L and I is mismanaged and inefficient. And slow as hell. You wait in a line for over an hour, and when you get to the front, you find out it's the wrong line. You call, and they say they're gonna call you back, and they never do. You're supposed to get something in the mail, and it never comes." McKenna threw his hands up. "I mean, if there's a way to avoid all that running around, wouldn't you pay someone to help you?"

"Do you know if your expeditor, Mr. Mastracola, shared his fee with Sebastiani?" Kari asked.

"Don't know, don't care." McKenna shook his head. "The work was approved. Sebastiani came in once or twice during the renovations to check on the progress. I told him I appreciated his help and invited him to dine here as my guest. Now you can't tell me there's anything wrong with that."

McKenna further explained that, a week or two later, Sebastiani took him up on his offer and came in for dinner with his wife. McKenna had the chef prepare the house specialty for his important guests and served them one of the restaurant's best bottles of wine. He did not present Sebastiani with a bill and refused Sebastiani's offer to pay for the meal. Over the last year or two since, Sebastiani had dropped in for dinner four or five more times, at least one more time with his wife and probably three other times with different female companions. McKenna said he refused payment for those meals as well, but Sebastiani always made sure to leave a generous tip for his server.

"Yeah so…I've known Stu Sebastiani about two years. There's nothing funny going on here. He's a prince."

At the end of the interview, McKenna offered to have his chef whip something up for the agents. They declined. Kari, noticing a stack of menus resting near the door, picked one up and turned to McKenna.

"I'll take one of these though," she said, holding the menu high. "Perhaps we can come back another day to eat. It smells so good in here."

***

As soon as they reached the car, Kari handed Everett the menu.

"Put this in the evidence envelope with your notes. We can tally up an estimate of how much each of those meals was worth to Sebastiani."

"Can we really charge him with eating free food?"

"Isn't an expensive meal something of value?"

"Yeah, but—"

"Gift or bribe, we'll let the jury decide."

That little rhyme soon became a mantra Kari and Everett recited after interviewing witnesses with similar stories. Bobby McKenna's gratitude illustrated how easy it was for Sebastiani to enjoy the perks of his position.

Kari had learned from her prior interviews that there was nothing more embarrassing to a business owner than having an inspector place a big orange violation sticker on the front wall or window of his establishment or, worse yet, having the business shuttered. To get rid of the ugly noncompliance notice as quickly as possible, the owners hired an expediter with connections to Sebastiani or, if they were one of his boys, they would contact him directly for "clarification." For as little as $500, Sebastiani would take care of the problem by arranging for the "right" inspector to do the next inspection.

"I wish there were some way we could introduce Sebastiani to an undercover agent posing as a club owner and record him accepting bribes directly from the UCA," said Everett as they were on their way to interview yet another witness. "You know, like the sting operation run last year by the guys working cultural property crimes. They operated their own high-end pawn shop."

"Wouldn't that be wild? It would be a G-string sting," Kari said and laughed. "But HQ would never approve us running our own strip club. The concept's too complicated and too expensive."

"How 'bout we use it as our case name?" suggested Everett.

"Operation G-String Sting." Kari nodded in agreement. "Yeah, I like that."

Chapter 16

"Mr. Sebastiani, thank you for coming," said the councilwoman, ushering him into her office. "I'm in need of your expertise pertaining to business regulations and compliance in the adult entertainment industry."

"How can I help?"

He already had an inkling why Councilwoman Frances Finney, a powerful legislator with more than twenty years on the City Council, had summoned him. The rumor was her husband had visited a local strip club and run up a significant tab. When Finney had discovered the credit card charges and what he had gotten for his money, she vowed to clean up the industry. Sebastiani wondered what, exactly, Finney wanted him to do about it.

"As you are well aware, several such adult clubs exist in my South Philadelphia district," Finney said. "Recently, I have received numerous complaints from my constituents regarding some of the lewd activities in which these clubs are engaged."

"My staff conducts regular inspections of strip clubs in South Philly and throughout the city," Sebastiani said. "Any club that doesn't abide by section 14-1605 of the zoning and planning regulated-use laws receives a notice of violation and is fined."

"That nasty, filthy behavior must be stopped."

He willed himself to maintain eye contact with the horse-faced woman. Finney was one dried-up, old black bitch. With her wiry, gray hair sculpted into a severe helmet, a boxy, two-piece skirted suit that hid any hint of curves, and her wire-rimmed glasses perched on her thick nose, Sebastiani understood why her husband sought the companionship of a real woman.

"You don't need to worry," he said. "My guys monitor all activity."

When Finney appeared unsatisfied, he added, "Which of the clubs are you getting reports about? Maybe we can double up on our inspections at those clubs."

"JOLIE."

Sebastiani hid his concern. Of all the clubs in town Mr. Finney could have visited, he had chosen JOLIE. *Ain't that a bitch?*

"Councilwoman Finney, I'm surprised that you've received a complaint about JOLIE. I know of that particular venue, and it is one of the most legitimately operated clubs in the city. Are you sure the calls weren't in reference to some other club down that way? There are a few I could have my guys close down immediately." Sebastiani held up his cell phone to illustrate his willingness to cooperate. "But," he declared, "we don't have any issues with JOLIE."

"I'm told that the dancers allow men to touch their naked bodies. Is that true?"

"Not exactly. The dancers may be partially nude and they may make...uh...have limited physical contact with their customers, but the customers are not allowed to touch them."

"And that's legal at JOLIE? Rubbing up against people like that?"

"You're talking about lap dances, right? They're not against the law."

"They should be."

"There are loopholes that allow club owners to get around some of the regulations, but we crack down on the clubs who blatantly refuse to obey the law."

"I know all about those loopholes. I met with the police commissioner before I asked to see you."

"Oh, I wasn't aware of that," said Sebastiani. "What did Commissioner Samuels say?"

"The same thing you're telling me, that giving a lap dance isn't a crime." Finney's wide nostrils flared as if she smelled something unpleasant.

"There you have it," Sebastiani said with a shrug of resignation.

"I disagree. It's a public safety issue. I heard all about those private booths. What goes on in those little rooms is unsafe and leads to prostitution and sexual diseases."

"I'm not sure where you're getting your information from, but it's wrong. There are no such booths at JOLIE." Recognizing how defensive he sounded, Sebastiani added, "The bottom line is, if the club has a cabaret license, there's nothing we can do."

"Yes, there is." She gave him a stern look. "I think what the second district needs is a new zoning *no-touch* code for cabarets."

That's when she told him of her plan to enact "councilmanic prerogative," a Philadelphia City Council custom wherein members were allowed to autonomously rule over their districts—even make major zoning changes—and the rest of the council would give its rubber-stamp approval, knowing that the same courtesy would be extended to each of them when they had a project up for vote. It was a "father knows best"—or in this case "mother knows best"—edict.

He folded his arms across his chest and cocked his head. "Are you saying you want to keep customers and strippers from having any contact whatsoever?"

"Yes, and ban full nudity." Finney clapped her hands together and leaned closer to him. "Perhaps make the dancers stay at least ten feet away from customers and behind a high railing, like a good, old-fashioned burlesque show. Doesn't that sound better?"

Sebastiani didn't know what to say. A wave of dread grew inside him. If Finney had her way and the rezoning were to pass, in three months or less, lap dancing would be banned in South Philly.

***

As soon as he left Finney's office, he sped over to JOLIE to warn Arty and his partners of the imminent demise of the ever-so-popular lap dance. Sebastiani knew that, along with selling overpriced liquor, industry income was made from providing private one-on-one entertainment.

"But JOLIE won't survive without lap dances," said Lynette

Hampton after Sebastiani recounted his meeting with Councilwoman Finney.

"We'll need to act fast then," Sebastiani said. "Unless we can convince at least one city council member to vote against it, the rezoning could go through before anyone knows what's happening."

"How's that possible?" asked Curtis Kincaid. "Don't they have to hold public hearings?"

"Not for council rezonings. They're not even required to post a notice."

"So what are we supposed to do?" said Arty.

"Look, the other council members won't share Finney's concerns about strip clubs. But then again, none of them will want to go on record as being *for* nudity and touching." Sebastiani took a moment to chew over the dilemma.

"We obviously need your assistance, but…" Kincaid shook his head. "I remember what happened the last time you helped us. You know, at the grand opening. You can't muck this thing up."

"Jesus Christ, man. Why you gotta bring that up?" Sebastiani recalled how they had humiliated him that night and, with his fists pressed against his hip bones, he defiantly struck a superhero pose. "Face it. I'm your only hope."

Sebastiani, in his self-appointed role as the savior of the South Philadelphia strip club, knew from past experiences that most people could be persuaded to do just about anything if their reputations and dignity were bargaining chips. They would need to compromise a councilman by recording him getting a lap dance or worse, and then threaten to send the video to the *Inquirer* or *Daily News* unless the guy agreed to help them.

"Are you sure, Dad?" Arty's face twitched as he spoke. "That seems sort of drastic…and illegal. Shouldn't we first try to appeal to him based on the revenue the clubs bring to the city?"

"And you think that's a strong enough argument to convince him to defy Finney? Really?"

"There has to be another way."

"Okay. So what's your suggestion?" Sebastiani waited for a response, allowing the silence to dominate the room before he spoke again. "That's what I thought."

Sebastiani recommended their target be Councilman Barry Yhost.

"He's a real perv. Every time he sees me, he's whining that his wife never gives him any and asking about the babes I've been with."

"Cool. Get him down here, and we'll make him a video star." Hampton clapped her hands together.

"Yhost is not coming to JOLIE or any other club. He'll be worried that someone will see him," Sebastiani stated.

Hampton, Kincaid, and Arty gave him puzzled looks.

"How's this supposed to work then?" said Hampton.

"If you can't bring the dirty old bastard to the nookie, you got to bring the nookie to him."

Sebastiani, excited to be needed and trusted by the partners, devised a scenario to entrap Councilman Yhost. The first thing he did was obtain the assistance of good "friend," Natalia Hall. Sebastiani called her whenever high-profile associates needed to be entertained. She was very expensive but worth every penny.

A significant sum was paid for Natalia to seduce and videotape Yhost in bed with her or, at the least, with his pants down around his ankles. Natalia followed the script and staged two "accidental" meetings at Yhost's favorite Sunday breakfast spot, where he always went alone while his wife was at church. She made earnest attempts to convince him to come back to her hotel room. The plan was abandoned when Yhost turned her down. Twice.

But after the botched attempts to compromise Yhost, Arty discovered an old college acquaintance, Craig Snyder, worked for the councilman. Arty knew Snyder from the University of Penn, where they had had several classes together. After running into him at a local bar, Arty deduced that Snyder, with staggering credit card balances and student loans in forbearance, would be an easy mark.

So less than a month after learning of Finney's rezoning plans, a new countereffort had come together. Arty offered to help Snyder with a "loan" to mitigate his nagging financial problems. His collateral? A promise to persuade his boss to vote down Finney's bill.

"We want him to do things for us; he wants money," Sebastiani said. "That's how the game works."

Snyder was invited to an all-expenses paid evening at JOLIE so Hampton and Kincaid could meet him and finalize the deal.

***

Nursing his last drink of the evening, Sebastiani watched Tannie perform her final set. *Damn, she's good.* Plus, she was smart. He guessed that was why they broke up. She was too smart to put up with his shit. He took another swallow of whiskey and wiped his moist lips with the back of his hand. Sebastiani would need Tannie to be his eyes and ears, to make sure the club owners did good by him.

That thought was running through his mind as Tannie moved around the stage in the middle of her third show that evening. Just as she performed her signature move, where she raised her legs over her head and performed a handspring split from a vertical push up, Sebastiani pointed to her firm and curvaceous backside and announced to the band of boisterous customers next to him, "I've hit that ass."

He didn't realize Tannie heard him. But once her set was over, she stalked over to him and said that if she ever heard him refer to her that way again, "I will reach down into your pants and squeeze your nuts so hard your eyes will bulge out."

"Ouch, babe, it's just that I'm so proud of you," Sebastiani said, unfazed.

"Kiss my ass, Stu. The only person you're ever proud of is you."

"That's not true. As a matter of fact I have a proposition for you—"

"Stu, I don't want to hear it."

"You don't want to hear about an opportunity to make two grand for an hour or two of work?" Stu slowly swayed back and forth as he spoke.

"What's that you're doing?" she asked, moving her hands in the same swaying motion. "How many times do I have to tell you that I don't fuck for cash?" She punctuated her words by thrusting her hips toward him.

"I'm not asking you to fuck anyone. Why would I want anyone else to have what I can't get anymore?" he said with an exaggerated pout.

"Then what is it?"

"I need you to do your thing for a VIP guest." He started swaying again. "And by thing, I mean dance. Lynette and Curtis want to talk to someone about a little project and thought a little private show would be nice."

"Who's the VIP?"

"Don't worry about that. I asked Arty to invite you to the party because I know you'll be discreet."

Sebastiani leaned in a little closer and in a low voice said, "Remember I mentioned people with city hall connections were interested in working with us."

"Yeah, you've mentioned that a few times. Am I supposed to believe that the mayor's coming to JOLIE?"

"Nah. Not Sheridan, but close."

"Who? Someone from city council?"

Sebastiani gave Tannie a sly smile and a wink but refused to say more. He could tell she was trying to get him to name names.

"What's this city council person gonna do for JOLIE?"

"You better hope he saves your job."

"My job?"

"The tricks of your trade."

"What are you talking about? Why are you being so cryptic?"

"The lap dance, Tannie. We're on a campaign to save your lap dance from no-touch laws."

"From what?"

"You're asking a lot of questions."

"Why is the VIP coming here?"

"So you can demonstrate what his colleague is trying to take away from the good people of South Philly."

"Okay. I'll do it, as long as nobody expects me to *do* anyone. I mean it. Not for money. Not for you."

"Jesus, babe. What do I look like, a pimp?" He grabbed her hands and looked her in the eyes. "I just need you to let me know afterward, you know, what happened, what was said. Okay?"

As she nodded, Sebastiani's eyes dropped from her face to her breasts, still glistening with perspiration from her set. When Tannie turned to walk into the changing area, he followed behind her. *My, my, my...what a great ass*, he thought and extended his hand to cop a feel.

As if sensing him behind her, Tannie quickened her steps and moved just out of his reach.

As they passed through the dressing room doorway, Sebastiani's line of vision diverted from Tannie's backside to the others getting ready for their turn onstage, and he elected to drool over a dancer who didn't mind him admiring her assets.

Chapter 17

The following morning when she awoke, Kari checked her phone and saw that Tannie had sent a text at 2:00 a.m. The message read, *Councilman coming to club? Call me.*

She couldn't believe it. Of all nights to actually fall asleep and stay asleep, she had picked last night. Recently, she had been experiencing bouts of insomnia. During the middle of the night, she would get up and frost cupcakes for her son's soccer team or sew costumes for her daughters' school play. Keeping busy with her kids and work helped her cope with her mother's illness and the chaos of her regrets.

Fearing Kevin's rejection, last evening, she had resisted the urge to reach out for him and guarantee herself a restful night. After their big blow-up, Kevin had warned Kari he suspected she was using sex as an anxiety release.

"Go for a run, why don't you?" he had said. "You're confusing making love with a fitness routine." When she dismissed his diagnosis, Kevin had replied, "If I'm wrong, then why do I feel like a treadmill?"

That hurt. Because she knew he was right. She didn't deserve him. If he knew what she had done, he would never want to touch her again. She stuffed her feelings down deep and tried to concentrate on the problems she already had, instead of creating more.

Once she arrived at work, Kari sat staring at her office phone, waiting for Tannie to text or call her back. She was seldom out of bed before noon. How she managed to do that with a newborn at home, Kari had no clue, but she would have to wait until the magic hour to learn more about the meaning of Tannie's text message.

Around ten o'clock, she glanced around the squad room, searching for Everett, and figured he had already left for his biweekly visit with Bill Leone. At her insistence, Ev always took someone from the squad. Of course, he had no trouble finding guys to tag along with him to the strip club. Earlier, two agents had actually argued over whose turn it was. She made a mental note to emphasize again that all of Everett and Leone's meetings at Club Friskee II needed to be case related, corroborated by the presence of another agent, and meticulously documented.

***

Special Agent Everett Hildebrand entered Club Friskee II with squad mate Tommy Tanzola.

"Hi, Ev. How's it going, sweetie?" asked the club's hostess.

"Not bad, Honey." Everett led Tommy to the entertainment room and his usual table.

"Just so you know," Everett said to Tommy, "her name is Honey. I wasn't calling her, you know, honey."

The last thing he wanted was any problems. He knew some of the guys were jealous that he had been selected as Kari's co-case agent, but he didn't want to be relegated to carrying her briefcase. He was campaigning for an equal role, and so far he was pulling his weight. Kari had Tannie as her confidential source, and he had Bill Leone. The investigation had introduced him to a whole new world. He had never felt so confident, so self-assured.

Everett met with Leone on a regular basis once every other week around ten thirty in the morning, just before the dancers came in and an hour before the lunch crowd started to arrive. Morning made it easier to turn down the beers and lap dances Leone always offered.

Leone smiled and spread his arms to give Everett and Tommy welcoming bear hugs.

"What can I get you both? Some beers and wings?" As soon as Everett started to protest, Leone attempted to cajole them into accepting his offer. "Aw, come on, man. What are you, a candy-ass Boy Scout?" He turned to Tommy. "What about you, big guy? You look like you might need a lap dance. How about a lap dance?"

For the umpteenth time, Everett said he wasn't interested. Whenever they met, Leone tried to embarrass or shock him with one outrageous antic after another.

Today would be no different.

A leggy dancer glided over to their table. She was topless. Everett thought he should look away, but Tommy gazed directly at her with a grin from one ear to the other.

"Bill, ah...I'm sure it's illegal for her to be working topless." Everett tried for an authoritative tone, but he still sounded weak and defensive, as if he were tattling.

"Ev, what are you talking about? We aren't even open for business yet."

Leone shook his head.

"Even if we were, you'd only be right if she was really topless. That's what I wanted to show you. Come here, Lolly. Show my friends you're not topless." Leone grabbed the stripper's hand and pulled her in close. As if selecting a piece of candy, he removed a pastie from Lolly's left breast. The pastie looked like her real, now exposed, areola and nipple.

"See? It looks like a real nipple. I invested in the business. We're marketing them around the country and overseas too." Leone took the pastie from Lolly's other breast and placed one each in the agents' hands. "They come in all shades and colors. My Latina, Asian, and black girls can all wear them too."

Everett immediately handed the pink pastie back to Lolly. As she reapplied it to her breast, Leone continued with his pitch.

"They're made of a special polymer. The self-adhesive is similar to the tacky stuff on those yellow sticky notes."

Tommy was fascinated. He fingered and flicked the raised nipple and repeatedly applied then removed the pastie from the back of his hand. "Absolutely amazing," he said.

"Hey, check these out too." Leone directed their attention back to Lolly's breasts. "They're new. This is Lolly's first week back since her operation. What do you guys think?" Leone gave the woman a peck on her cheek. "I was happy to make it happen for her. She's a great girl."

"Congratulations." Tommy clapped his hands. "They're perfect."

Lolly beamed with pride. As she started to leave, Tommy called her back.

"Hey," he said, waving the pastie, "don't forget this."

Everett grew warm and imagined with embarrassment that a pink flush, the shade of the rubber nipple he had held in his hand, was moving up from his neck and across his face.

Everett endured Leone's games because he claimed to know about other city officials and their dirty dealings. What had been provided to date had potential but lacked names and details. He hoped when the Sebastiani investigation was over, Leone would help him work citywide public corruption cases for as long as he wanted. He'd stay on the squad for a few more years and earn a few Quality Step Increase awards, the FBI's equivalent of a merit bonus, then apply for a supervisor position at headquarters. It had taken his father nine years to become a section chief. Everett thought he could do it in seven, a major accomplishment.

But first he had to produce significant results for this case. Everett needed to convince Bill Leone to testify and wear a wire. To date, Leone had said no to both.

When Tommy excused himself to use the men's room, Everett tried again.

"Bill." Everett cleared his throat twice. "Have you given any more thought to letting me record you talking with Sebastiani?"

Leone studied Everett's face.

"I'm getting a new car tomorrow, a sweet little Aston Martin Vantage S Coupe. Come around tomorrow. *Alone.* I'll show it to you and we can talk," he said.

"Maybe you could install a microphone or camera in it, and you could take it over to show Stu and record him while you're riding around. What do you think about that?"

"Now that could work." Leone stroked his chin and smiled. "Yeah, I'd probably be willing to do that."

Everett practically beamed with accomplishment. He had done it. He had convinced Leone to take his cooperation to the next level.

"What made you change your mind?" Everett asked.

"I said I wouldn't wear a wire and I won't, but if you Feds want to put one in my car…that's on you guys."

"We'll still need your consent. You'll still need to testify."

"But it's not strapped *on* me. You get what I'm saying?"

"You won't feel like you're actively participating?"

"Yeah. That's it."

Leone glanced at Tommy, returning from the bathroom.

"Buddy," Leone said discreetly to Everett. "Don't forget. Come by yourself. These random dudes you keep bringing around are starting to creep me out."

"Sure," said Everett just as Tommy approached the table.

"Hey, what did I miss?"

Everett shrugged. "Nothing much."

Chapter 18

By the time Everett returned to the office, Kari had spoken to Tannie and learned all about the mystery VIP's upcoming visit to JOLIE.

"I've got great news," said Kari. She tapped on some forms she was filling out. "Sebastiani told Tannie someone connected with the city council is coming to JOLIE. She thinks the owners and Sebastiani plan to bribe him to vote against no-touch laws. I don't have the date of the meeting yet, but we need to plant a bug in the VIP lounge at JOLIE and…" She glanced up at Everett's vacant gaze and drooping shoulders. "You okay?"

"Yeah."

"How was your meeting? You have something to tell me?"

Everett shook his head. "Nah, you know Leone."

"Well, we have a strategy meeting scheduled for later. Juanita and Mitch are psyched that the Sebastiani investigation might be inching closer to the city council." Kari patted Everett on the arm. "This is why I love working this stuff. One simple allegation from a pissed off ex-girlfriend, and the next thing you know, a city councilman could be on his way to jail."

By four o'clock that afternoon, Kari, Everett, Juanita, and her boss, Assistant Special Agent in Charge Bob Dorsett, were all sitting around a large table at the United States Attorney's office with Whitmore and his boss, Jim Goldman, Chief of the Criminal Division.

Kari looked out at the spectacular twelfth-floor view of stately Independence Hall and wondered why the meeting wasn't getting underway. They sat around for several more minutes, making small talk, until the door to the conference room opened, and US Attorney Paul Crystal walked in and took a seat at the end of the table.

Kari had attended meetings with Crystal before. She found him to be an affable guy who was interested in the cases his office handled. He didn't need to attend a simple planning session. But then again, she was fully aware that if Crystal, a political appointee, was not convinced that the evidence was rock-solid, good enough to guarantee a public corruption conviction, he would be unwilling to indict. Kari had heard he had big plans after his term was up—maybe a run for the Senate or the governor's office. The last thing Crystal needed was an acquittal and a politically connected enemy out on the street to make things difficult for him.

It was the same in almost every FBI office around the country. The pressure to find the evidence required to nail down a guilty plea or verdict was always present and the question asked most often by the front office—"Are we there yet?"—had field agents comparing their bosses to impatient children out on a long car trip.

"Okay, what do we have here?" Crystal asked, looking around the room.

Mitch turned to Kari. "Why don't you bring us up-to-date on the Sebastiani investigation?"

All eyes focused on her.

"The investigation was predicated on a phone call from Tannie Colosi, the former mistress of Stuart Sebastiani, who is the current Director of Business Regulatory Enforcement for L and I. Tannie has told us"—Kari gestured toward Everett—"and we have been able to corroborate through other witnesses that, for several years, Sebastiani has been soliciting and accepting bribes for handling compliance issues and ignoring infractions occurring at his favored strip clubs. Tannie has also told us Sebastiani claims to know of other city government and elected officials on the take. Until recently, we hadn't been able to develop any further details regarding any high-level people other than Sebastiani. However, we hope to identify someone, possibly an elected official, later this week."

At that point, Crystal interrupted Kari. "Did your informant give you anything else?" asked Crystal. "Is it a man or woman?"

She realized why he was there. He didn't care about the case details. He was present because he wanted to know *who* the elected official was.

"I guess we can assume that it's not a woman coming in for a lap dance," Kari said. "But who really knows?"

"You gotta get me more than that. You think it's a council member?"

"Sebastiani hinted that the person worked inside city hall."

Crystal peered at Kari. She felt like he thought she was trying to keep something from him. She knew what he wanted to know: Was the person a political ally or a political foe? And would her investigation hurt or help his career aspirations?

"He didn't identify who it was," Kari said, "but he did say they wanted the person, whoever it is, to help them."

"Help them do what?"

"To vote against no-touch legislation. It's primarily about…lap dancing."

"What does this Tannie person do for a living?"

"She's a dancer at JOLIE."

"A stripper?" His tone made it clear to Kari that he was discounting the intelligence.

"I've been working with Tannie for several months, and she hasn't given any bogus information."

"As far as you know."

"Paul, this witness is pretty reliable," said Whitmore. "We couldn't have gotten where we are to date without her cooperation."

They tried to convince Crystal that the identity of the elected official didn't matter and they should go ahead with their plans to wire up Sebastiani's phone calls. To Kari and those in the conference room with no future political objectives, it was that clear and simple.

Crystal left the room unconvinced.

Chapter 19

As soon as the meeting was over, Everett hurried away from the US Attorney's office. No one had addressed any questions to him. Not once had they asked his opinion. Juanita Negron hadn't even looked in his direction, and Mitch Whitmore had turned "Witless" and ignored him too. He might as well have been invisible.

As he made his way across busy Market Street back to the federal building, his anger dissipated and more rational thoughts emerged. The Sebastiani case had upgraded his status in the office, but he could garner more respect if he didn't have to play second fiddle to Kari Wheeler. They were supposed to be partners, but she was still calling the shots. He needed to make something happen. He was glad he had waited to tell her about Leone's decision to let them wire his car. For now, her news trumped his. He would work out the details first, before he told her.

When he was young, his father used to motivate him with those words: *Make something happen.* Everett was never great at sports, but his father showed him that even if Everett didn't score the baskets or make the goals, if he could set up the right play or make the right pass, he could win respect from his teammates and coaches. He couldn't stand there and let the leaders do all the work. He had to contribute.

If Everett wanted to get the respect he deserved, Bill Leone had to come through for him.

***

The following morning, Everett strolled into his home office and logged on to his laptop. He had decided to go to Club Friskee II straight from home. He didn't want any of his squad mates tagging along. Bill Leone was right. Bringing a different agent every time he went to Club Friskee II was a distraction. How could he and Leone build any trust with a third wheel always hanging around? He left a voice message for the squad secretary that he was handling a case-related errand on his way into work and wouldn't be in until after lunch. He would work on a few reports until it was time to leave.

By the time Everett had finished typing his first 302, he was home alone. His daughter's science diorama of a poisonous puffer fish in its aquatic habitat was due that morning, and instead of making Claire navigate the school bus with the cumbersome project, Brenda had driven the kids to school.

As soon as he had heard the car backing down the driveway, Ev had minimized his report and accessed the Internet. As if on autopilot, he was soon peering at the portal page of his favorite porn site. Over the past few months, he had discovered hundreds of free sites that offered a never-ending library of videos featuring every possible sex act. Watching the clips relaxed him the same as when he was reading the newspaper or watching football. It was his time to unwind, to feel good.

He ignored the sales messages designed to entice him to enter his credit card info and create his own personal, all-access account. He didn't need all that. He was satisfied with choosing from the hundreds of brief clips featured. He was selective. Maintaining his own self-enforced set of rules, he only watched "normal stuff." That way he was not violating the high standards of decency and morality by which he was raised. Accordingly, he refused to watch any porn involving objects, animals, weird fetishes, and certainly no gay sex. Any site with even a hint of homosexuality was immediately rejected. As far as he was concerned, a man having sex with another man was morally reprehensible and it turned his stomach. But girl-on-girl acts? He enjoyed those.

As he clicked from one three-minute video to another, he told himself he'd check out one more clip and get back to work, but before he knew it, more than an hour and a half had passed in what had only seemed like minutes, and Brenda was walking back in through the kitchen. He was disoriented. Had he really been at the computer that long?

"Everett," Brenda called out, "can you help me bring in the groceries? I stopped by the supermarket."

He logged off and gathered up the soiled tissues.

"Coming. Be right there." He rushed through the living room to the powder room, where he flushed away the evidence of what he had been doing, then into the kitchen and out through the garage to the family van, where Brenda was already unloading grocery bags. He wiped beads of sweat from his forehead as he attempted to catch his breath.

"You're so sweet. You didn't have to drop everything and rush out here." She smiled at him and walked past with an armload of bags. "Slow down. I've got everything that needs to go in the freezer."

He couldn't answer because his heart was thumping in his throat. He leaned into the back of the van and retrieved four of the heavier bags. When Brenda came out for her second load, Everett glanced back as he squeezed by her. She was a good wife who deserved more from him than his juvenile behavior. She wouldn't understand that he wasn't attracted to any of those women. His actions were simply physiological responses. Compared to his beautiful Brenda, those women were unattractive, inside and out.

***

As he drove up the winding expressway to his meeting with Leone, Everett went over what he would say to win the man's full cooperation. He rolled down the car window and enjoyed the fresh air. It was a beautiful day. By the time he arrived at Club Friskee II, he had a plan.

He found an empty space along the curb right in front of the club's main door. Perhaps it was an omen that his visit would be successful. Just as he was congratulating himself for his flawless parallel-parking skills, Honey came out of the club and knocked on the passenger window.

She drew a wide circle with her finger and then pointed to the rear of the building. "Bill wants you to drive around to the private garage in the back," she said.

Reluctantly, Everett pulled away from his perfect spot.

As he turned the corner, Everett knew Leone would tease him about the late-model Pontiac Grand Prix he was driving. He attempted to position the car inconspicuously in the alley, but Leone spotted him and motioned Everett to the loading dock and large garage behind the building.

"What the hell are you driving?" Leone yelled out to Everett. "Don't park that piece of shit anywhere near my machine. Pull in over there."

Everett drove under the overhead door and maneuvered the Bureau car into an empty space at the opposite end of the garage. He hurried away from the vehicle as if it were contaminated.

Leone's salsa-red Aston Martin Vantage S Coupe was nothing short of spectacular, and Everett watched with envy as the owner preened about. The machine was a magnificent specimen of power. Leone opened the driver's side door and motioned for Everett to take a seat inside. The baby-soft caramel-colored leather seats and opulent burl walnut veneer console and dash overwhelmed Everett.

"Wow, Bill," he gushed. "This is a real man's car."

Leone walked around the car and pointed out all the expensive features before climbing into the passenger seat to show Everett all the swanky components. After several minutes, Leone got out of the vehicle, closed the door, and stepped back.

"Ev, you know why I love this car so much?" he said. "'Cause it's sleek, curvy, and well-built, like my ladies." Leone crouched in front of the grille and pretended to fondle the curved headlights. "What do these remind you of?"

Everett couldn't help but laugh. But his amusement was stifled when Leone shot off a challenge.

"Take it for a spin around the block."

Everett stammered, "I...I...I can't do that."

"Why not? You have a driver's license, don't you? You expect me to believe you prefer that crap-mobile over there?"

"That's not my personal car. It's a government car."

"I hope so. Look, dude, don't be a candy-ass. Take the Aston Martin out for a joyride."

Everett gripped the leather steering wheel. It was the most luxurious car he had ever been in. He inhaled and smelled wealth and prosperity. Did he dare imagine he could drive it? "No," he said. "I better not."

"What are you afraid of?" Leone asked. "If something happens, I'll take care of it."

Everett noticed the other luxury and sports cars parked in the garage. Leone leaned into the driver's side window.

"Drive it. I insist."

Everett believed Leone was extending a courtesy that few others received. He didn't want to insult Leone by refusing. So he palmed the gearshift nervously, placed the machine into reverse, and backed out of the garage, slowly.

"Take it out on the highway," Leone called out after him. "Push it hard. *Sixty miles per hour in four-point-five seconds, baby!*"

Everett's initial excitement soon turned into a sinking feeling in his gut as he lurched off in a car worth nearly twice as much as he made in a year. Once far enough away from the club, Everett turned down the radio so that he could concentrate on driving as defensively as possible. He rounded each corner carefully and robotically proceeded down the street. Leone had said each twenty-inch chrome wheel cost $9,500. Everett wasn't going anywhere near the interstate, but Manayunk, with its hilly and narrow streets, wasn't conducive for a safe road test either.

At first, Everett drove at a snail's pace, but that only made drivers tailgate. Better to drive at a normal speed and keep people from riding his bumper. He wanted to maintain a firm grip on the steering wheel but found it necessary to remove one hand at a time, for a split second, to wipe his clammy palms on his pants.

Everett knew he would lose all of Leone's respect if he returned too soon. He calculated he needed to stay out for at least ten, maybe twelve minutes. He thought about pulling into a parking lot and allowing the car to idle while the time ticked away but was afraid he would be spotted. So he drove around Manayunk in a $136,000 car at a speed usually reserved for seventy-five-year-old grandmothers. As soon as an acceptable amount of time had passed, he hightailed it back to the club.

Everett pulled into the garage and parked the Aston Martin in its spot. He looked around for Leone, but the garage was empty. Leone was nowhere to be seen.

Suddenly, shock swept over him. The Bureau car was gone.

Everett ran out of the garage, down the cobblestone alley, and out onto the street. *Why would Leone want to drive that clunker?* Only FBI employees were allowed to drive FBI cars. This was the most basic of Bureau violations—misuse of a government vehicle. Agents were jammed up every time they made an error of judgment involving a Bureau car. He only left the keys in the car because he thought they would be staying in the garage. He'd never imagined that anyone would want to drive off with it.

One minute went by, then another and another. Still no Leone. Everett imagined the worst.

What if Leone got into an accident? What if he ran over and killed someone? Oh my God. What if he hit a child?

Everett didn't know what to do. Should he take the coupe out again to look for Leone? Stay put and wait for him to come back? Call the office and report the car stolen? Just as Everett was reaching full meltdown mode, he spotted Leone speeding down the narrow roadway. Leone screeched to a halt and rolled down the window.

"How was it?" he said nonchalantly.

"*Get out! Get out of the car now!*" Everett tugged and pulled on the door handle. "*Open it!*"

"Pump your brakes, dude. What's your problem?"

Everett could feel the wetness of sweat or tears rolling down his face, but he didn't care.

"Are you fucking serious? You're having a fit because I drove off in this shit wagon?"

"*Get out!* Where were you? What did you do?"

"You were afraid I was going to fuck up this piece of junk?" Leone shook his head before gunning the engine and squealing off down the alleyway into the garage. Everett ran behind.

"This is a government-issued vehicle," Everett shouted, catching up to Leone as he climbed out of the old Pontiac.

"So what? I let you drive my car so you could see how I roll. I thought I'd experience how you get around. The car's a piece a shit, but I don't have a siren and lights in mine."

"Please tell me you didn't turn on the lights and siren." Everett's heart beat so fast he thought his chest was going to explode.

"Was that a bad move? How about keying the radio and giving a shout-out to the dispatcher? Would that have been wrong too?"

"*Are you trying to get me fired?*" Everett could feel his boiling blood pressure pounding in his ears. If anyone heard Leone on the radio or saw him driving the Bureau car, Everett would be censured and probably given a thirty-day suspension without pay.

Everett grabbed two fistfuls of his hair and bent over, hyperventilating.

"Chill out, dude. What's the big deal? Nobody saw me," Leone said. "I was teasing you. I didn't touch the bells and whistles." Leone pointed to the Aston Martin. "So, how did you like my ride?"

As Leone started walking toward the vehicle, Everett caught up to him and blocked his path. Leone couldn't walk any farther without pushing him out of the way.

"*Fuck you, Leone. Who gives a shit about your ride? This isn't a joke,*" Everett yelled, seething. "Didn't you hear what I said? Because of you, I could lose my job. You're nothing but a filthy smut peddler," he ranted. "You can't disrespect me like this and just walk away. I'm a law enforcement officer. I'm an FBI agent."

"Fuck you and the FBI. What are you gonna do, arrest me for kidnapping your goddamn government car?" Leone inched in closer. Everett stayed put.

The two men now stood eye to eye. Everett's height matched every inch of Leone's six-foot-three frame. The agent's chest rose up and down as he took deep, long breaths, his fists clenched. He was ready to defend himself. Leone returned Everett's chilly gaze. They both stood their ground, waiting for the other to make the next move. All of his life, people had disrespected him, compared him to his father, and made him feel less than. But no more. He refused to back down.

Leone caved in first.

"Hey, man, I shouldn't have taken the car," he said, holding his position. "I didn't know the rules about driving your precious Bureau Batmobile."

With Leone's weak apology, Everett allowed the tension to diminish. Finally, a faint grin replaced Leone's scowl. "Come on…how was I supposed to know it would be such a big deal? Jesus Christ, man, I came around the corner, and I thought you were going to throw yourself in front of the car to stop me."

Everett still couldn't bring himself to speak.

"Hey, did you tell me to go fuck myself?" Leone continued. "Did my Boy Scout, choirboy, teacher's pet, FBI pal just curse me out? Hell, man, I think I'm rubbing off on you. Way to go, dude."

Leone grabbed Everett's shoulders and gave him a big squeeze.

"And you were ready to take a swing at me too, weren't you? Now that's what I'm talking about."

Everett's mind raced with thoughts about being reprimanded. Juanita would love to suspend him or, in agent slang, give him "time on the beach" for another incident with a Bureau car. Everett raked his fingers through his hair and only then began to realize how physically spent he was. He could hear Leone talking and smiling at him and patting him on the back as if he had accomplished some rite of passage.

Everett took in a deep breath and became light-headed. He felt Leone take hold of his shoulders to guide him through the well-lit back entrance of the building and into the dimly lit club, which by now was open for business and nearly full with the early lunch crowd.

"Come on over here, buddy. Have a seat," Leone said as he directed the agent to an empty booth near the stage. "I'll get you something to drink." Before Everett could say anything, Leone clarified his offer. "I'll have them bring you a soda."

Everett lowered himself slowly into the booth and took several calming breaths. He loosened his tie and leaned back into the soft, comfortable cushion. Almost hypnotically, he looked up at the stage and watched the girls gyrating to the music's heavy beat. And that is where he remained for the rest of the afternoon, sitting in the near darkness of Club Friskee II with his new best friend Bill Leone, watching strippers shake their stuff.

Chapter 20

Kari was glad she had not waited for Everett yesterday. She had called his cell phone several times, but by the time he texted back hours later that he was at home sick with a stomach virus, she had already arranged everything. There was now an electronic eyeball staring at JOLIE. Dressed as electrical power workers, tech agents had climbed a street pole near JOLIE's back VIP entrance and mounted a camera. With it, they would record the arrival and departure of the mystery guest. Surveillance agents would follow him after he left the establishment. When it came to figuring out who the mystery guest was, they were good to go.

"Nice of you to show up today, Hildebrand," Kari called as soon as Everett walked into the squad area.

Everett slid his briefcase under his desk.

"I'm sorry. I think I had, uh, food poisoning. You didn't want to be around me yesterday." He placed a hand over his mouth and on his stomach. "I couldn't keep anything down."

"You missed a lot around here. I could have used your help."

"With the court order?"

"Nah. Whitmore and Juanita went along with Crystal. No hidden cameras or mics inside JOLIE."

"So what, then?"

"Pole camera directed at the parking area. Public space, no court order needed. We'll have to use Tannie and our own eyes to monitor what happens inside the club."

"When's the mystery man coming in?"

"Tonight."

"Oh, wow. We've got a lot to do today."

"It's all done."

"Done?"

"Yeah," Kari said, patting Everett on his back. "While you were home puking, I took care of it."

***

A few hours later, Kari slipped on her jacket.

"Ready?" she asked Everett. They were on their way to brief Tannie before the city hall mystery man's visit to JOLIE later that night.

"You want me to drive?"

"Sure." Kari tossed him the keys.

Everett guided the new model forest-green Ford Taurus through the maze of the federal building's underground parking garage, waited for the motorized steel security door to roll up, and sped up the incline ramp to the street above.

***

As soon as Kari and Everett pulled into the lot of a South Philly Target store, Tannie, parked her cute, little charcoal-gray convertible MX-5 Miata next to them.

In one swoop, Everett abandoned the Taurus to admire the tight, sleek body of Tannie's sports car. Kari watched with amusement as he inspected every inch, rubbing his hands along the curving metal frame.

"Nice ride," Ev said.

"Thanks, I really wanted a Porsche Boxster, but this will have to do. It fit the budget."

"The Miata has good horsepower." Everett took a closer look. "Oh, you got manual transmission. I hear the downshift is a breeze. What's the power-to-weight ratio?"

"You're into cars?" Kari asked. No wonder the incident with Juanita had hurt him so deeply.

"You bet." Everett walked around to capture a full 360-degree view. "It's a four cylinder, right?"

"I don't know. It was a baby shower gift from a friend," Tannie said.

"Sebastiani?" Everett asked.

"Hell no. I couldn't get bus fare from that asshole. No, this was from a customer who felt sorry for me when I got pregnant," said Tannie. "I think he thought I would go for a minivan or a station wagon."

"A customer bought you a car?"

Tannie ignored Everett's question and checked the time on her cell phone.

"Can we shop while we talk? I need to pick up some things for Dia."

Everett and Kari, with their conservative business suits, and Tannie—dressed like a young Hollywood movie star with dark shades, luxurious fur jacket, extra-short suede miniskirt, and over-the-knee boots—must have looked like a strange, mismatched set. As they strolled through the store pushing a shopping cart full of diapers and other baby supplies, every man and woman they passed admired Tannie. Used to the attention, she returned each look with a knowing smile. Kari had no doubts that Tannie had lots of special friends who wanted to buy her things.

As they neared the checkout lanes, Tannie turned to Kari and said, "You know, we can do more with your eyes."

"What?" With her eyes opened wide, Kari jutted her face toward Tannie. "See, I have on makeup."

Tannie smirked and then ducked down the cosmetic aisle. After a moment, she returned with lipstick, mascara, and eyeliner.

Kari stopped Tannie from laying the items on the counter.

"That's not for me, is it? I can't let you buy me makeup."

"Okay, you pay for it." Tannie pushed the small packages toward Kari. "And what are you laughing at?" the dancer said to Everett. "I don't even know where to start with you. What's with that haircut? I bet you've been wearing it the same way since grade school." Tannie ruffled the loose curls and limp curtain of too-short bangs framing his face.

Kari laughed but thought, *I must look like her assistant. And Ev could be her chauffeur.*

She handed the makeup to the cashier. She would toss the items in a drawer when she got home.

They made their purchases, and upon arriving back at their cars, Tannie asked Kari to climb into the back of the Bureau car so she could give her a quick beauty tutorial.

"No. I don't think so," Kari objected. "I have enough of that stuff on."

"You're going to an upscale gentlemen's club to conduct surveillance. Don't you want to look like you belong?"

Kari felt silly, but really, what was the harm? The offer meant Tannie considered her an ally. While Kari surrendered her face, she used the time to tell Tannie how she, Everett, and other agents would monitor the public areas of the club. Tannie would need to mentally record what was said and done outside of the agents' view. Tannie nodded and kept working.

As she applied the makeup to Kari's eyelashes, she touched Kari's face with one hand and wielded the tiny brush with the other. Each time their eyes met, Tannie smiled as if they shared a secret. It was difficult to avoid eye contact with someone applying color to her lips and liner to her eyelids, but Kari tried to focus her vision upward, refusing to allow Tannie to peer deep inside with those prying eyes of hers.

Two long, drawn-out minutes later, Tannie was done.

"Not bad, not bad. You're a hot momma," Tannie said. She then kissed her index finger and playfully tapped the tip of Kari's nose. Not sure how to respond, Kari touched the spot as if to verify the gesture had occurred but, otherwise, acted as if it had not.

"Thanks," she said. She hoped Everett hadn't witnessed the affectionate exchange between her and her informant.

"See you two later tonight." Tannie stepped out of the Bureau car and scooted into hers.

"I'll drive back to the office," Kari told Everett as she moved from the back to the front of the car. Sliding into the driver's seat, Kari adjusted the rearview mirror and took a peek at herself. *Wow.* She looked good.

"You clean up nice," Everett said.

She looked in the mirror again.

"I guess someone else was manipulated by Tannie," he went on. "What was that you said about me? That I let Tannie work her mojo on me?"

"What are you talking about?"

"Yes, Tannie, I want to be pretty like you," he teased.

"I let her do my face so she could feel like part of the team, to show her that I trust her."

"Oh, okay," Everett said, rolling his eyes. "Rapport building, right?"

Driving down the boulevard, Kari stole another glimpse in the rearview mirror. The only other time she had been talked in to wearing so much makeup was her wedding, but she had to admit, she looked good. Less than a block from the federal building, Kari caught her reflection in the mirror again and was mortified by her goofy smile. *Damn it, Kari. Get your head back in the game.*

Everett was right. She had been manipulated. Or was *seduced* the more appropriate word?

Chapter 21

The facade of the building resembled a stately English manor, and the sign at the entry portico read simply "JOLIE" in large, bronze letters. Kari and Everett pulled into the expansive parking lot at exactly nine o'clock, an hour earlier than their target was scheduled to arrive. They were positioned in a surveillance vehicle disguised as a suburban soccer-mom van with a Baby-on-Board decal on the rear window and a video monitor hidden inside. In the parking area with them were two other agents in their Bureau cars, standing by to follow the mystery guest after he left JOLIE. The pole camera provided a wide observation platform, and the zoom lens gave them a perfect view of the VIP entrance. The video feed was crystal clear, and they had photos of all the council members. Unless he was wearing a hat and fake mustache disguise, they should be able to identify their city hall visitor as soon as he emerged from his car.

Now, all they had to do was wait. Kari settled back into the wide bench installed in the back of the van, crossed her bare legs and closed her eyes.

"First time I've seen you in a dress."

"Just trying…" Kari placed a hand over her mouth and yawned. "Just trying not to look like law enforcement when we get inside."

"Humph. Well, you don't." He stared at her face before speaking again. "Even with that makeup Tannie slathered on your face, you still look kind of beat. Are you going to be able to stay awake?" asked Everett. "I went home and took a nap. I can't believe you went to a basketball game. I hope your team won."

"We did. Go Sparks." Kari mustered the energy to twirl her index finger in the air. "I am tired, but I didn't want to disappoint my kids. Plus, Kevin's been on my case about work." She swept her gaze across the parking lot and massaged her temples.

"So what's the deal with Mr. Wheeler?"

"Who?" she asked absently.

"Your husband, Kevin?"

"Oh. He's Mr. Jackson. Wheeler's my maiden name. I try to keep home and office separate."

Everett paused for a moment. His upper lip curled up slightly, as if he wanted to say something and thought better of it. Kari detected disapproval.

"We've been working some long hours. I can understand why he's upset."

"Yeah, but it's our job. Brenda supports me 100 percent. She's proud to be married to an FBI agent."

"I can't say the same for Kevin."

"Why not?"

"When I left home tonight, stuff needed to be done. The kids still had homework; the dog needed to be walked; it was trash day—"

"Are you sure it's that? He's not a 'window fogger,' is he?"

"A what?"

"That's what my dad calls them. People standing on the outside looking in, wishing they were FBI agents."

"Are you asking if Kevin's jealous of me?"

"Yeah. They make movies and write books about what we do, and he's home taking care of the kids."

"That's not it."

"How can you be so sure?"

"He likes being a teacher."

"Then it's the money. What do teachers make? Sixty, seventy thousand? With the number of years you have in the Bureau, you must be making almost twice that by now."

"It's not that either. He thinks I work too hard."

"I think he's jealous."

"He couldn't care less about the Bureau. He has no interest in hearing about my work."

"Yep, he's jealous. He's like a cuckolded spouse who can't bear to be reminded of his wife's infidelity."

Kari's body tensed and she closed her eyes in an attempt to control her rapidly escalating temper. She knew Everett had no idea about her cheating, but his remarks angered her anyway.

"Can I give you some advice?" he said.

As he leaned in closer to impart his words of wisdom, she jerked back and raised her hand to stop him. "No." She shook her head. "*For the love of God, stop talking.*"

Everett sat back in to his seat and stared out the window. She could tell she had hurt his feelings.

"Look, Ev, I'm sorry."

"I was only trying to help."

"Can we just sit here and watch?" She pointed to the video monitor. "Please."

They sat silently in the back of the surveillance van behind the dark tinted windows. It was only 9:17 p.m. They still had forty-three minutes to kill. As a sign of contrition, Kari invited the surveillance agents, who were sitting alone in their cars, to join her and Everett. They sat behind the dark-tinted windows of the van and made small talk until Everett directed their attention to the scene playing out in the parking lot.

The outfits worn by the dancers and female patrons going into JOLIE were outrageous. Their "street clothes," skimpy skirts and skintight tops, revealed mounds of cleavage and plenty of thigh.

A couple staggered outside of the club. For several minutes, Kari and the agents watched as the two, their libidos apparently stimulated from what they'd seen inside, went from groping each other to screwing on the hood of a car.

As they spied on the amorous couple, the guys grew quieter and Kari, feeling a warm wave of arousal winding through her body, decided it was time for her to vacate the scene. If she had been by herself, she would have continued to peep. But watching with the guys didn't feel right.

"Have fun, guys," she said. "Enjoy the show."

Kari moved to the front of the van, where she continued to watch the couple from the side-view mirror.

Movement at the back entrance of JOLIE yanked Kari's attention to the monitor streaming images of the club. JOLIE bouncers were physically escorting patrons out the side door, away from the main parking lot where she was parked, and around the corner from the VIP entrance. Typical club action Kari assumed. Of course the security staff would have to toss out a few of JOLIE's more boisterous clientele. But these patrons were ultimately led right back inside. *What's that about?*

***

Just before ten o'clock, Kari noted Sebastiani's arrival on the surveillance log. A few minutes later, a black Nissan Altima pulled into a reserved slot in the back of the building, where Tannie had told them the high rollers parked. As the driver stepped out of his car, he was warmly greeted by Lynette Hampton and Arty Sebastiani and escorted into the club.

"Who was that?" Kari asked as she zoomed in on the image frozen on the monitor. The mystery male was too young to be a city councilman and was not anyone she recognized.

"I have no clue," replied Everett. "I'll call in the tag."

"Six-one-three to Central," Everett announced his call sign into his handheld radio. The investigative specialist on duty at the office's twenty-four-hour communications center answered, and Everett recited the Altima's license plate numbers.

"Can you run that tag for me and let me know what you get back? Thanks."

In less than five minutes, Central was back on the radio. "Central to six-one-three."

"Six-one-three. Go," said Everett.

"That vehicle is registered to a Craig Snyder in the two-hundred block of South 24th Street."

"Thanks, Central." Everett turned towards Kari. "Who's Craig Snyder?"

Kari shrugged, took the handheld mic from Everett, and keyed the radio again.

"Hey, Central, this is six-oh-two. Get me a date of birth and whatever else you can find on that guy. And see if you can find out where this Craig Snyder person works. Try Facebook or LinkedIn," said Kari.

This time, they waited more than ten minutes.

"Central to six-oh-two," the voice from the handheld called out.

"Six-oh-two, go ahead."

"Okay, I ran his driver's license, and I have a photo for you. Check your phone. I just sent it to you," the investigative specialist reported back. "I also came up with five or six LinkedIn profiles with the same name, but I checked their ages and found your guy."

"Good work. So who is he?"

"Your Craig Snyder works for Philadelphia Councilman Yhost. His profile says he is the councilman's chief of staff."

"Bingo!" Kari high-fived Everett. "Thanks, Central. Route that info to my desk, please. Six-oh-two out."

"Ten-four," Central signed off.

Kari stared at the photo attachment opened on her iPhone. Chief of Staff Snyder was a good-looking blond in his late twenties.

"So, this is the person who's going to help Sebastiani save JOLIE and the strip club industry."

Now that Sebastiani's city council connection had been identified, they would need to find out how deep the connection went. Was Craig Snyder visiting JOLIE on his boss's behalf or his own?

Kari called Whitmore with the mystery VIP's identity.

"You say he works for Yhost?" asked Whitmore. "Do we know if he's there because the councilman sent him?"

"Not yet."

"Okay. We need an answer. That's got to be our number-one priority. Yhost is a friend of Crystal's. Shit, this could get sticky." Kari could hear his apprehension, but she needed to make a few things clear.

"Sorry, Mitch, but that's your problem. I don't work for Paul Crystal."

Kari looked over at Everett and rolled her eyes. *Small cases, small problems. Big cases, big problems*—the old agent's adage ran through her mind. If only she could keep everyone focused on the facts and not on what the higher-ups thought.

Once they were satisfied they knew who they were following, Kari and Everett joined Snyder inside JOLIE. Kari was impressed by the decor. The foyer, with wood-paneled walls, tapestries, and finely crafted Chippendale furnishings, was lit by an opulent crystal chandelier. The artwork mounted in ornate frames along the entry hall provided the first clue of JOLIE's offerings. A gallery of large sepia photographs featured beautiful nude women in sensual poses.

Unquestionably, JOLIE's theme was elegant eroticism.

The expansive main entertainment room had six bars, three stages, and private dining and entertainment balcony suites. Seating was arranged in intimate groupings, allowing for comfort and conversation, but also enabling the waitstaff and dancers to roam easily throughout the room.

Kari and Everett settled into a cozy grouping angled toward the main stage. There was no sign of Snyder or Tannie, although Kari thought she saw Sebastiani hanging around near the rear bar. About forty minutes after they arrived, Kari finally spotted Snyder coming out of one of the VIP suites to take a seat in the balcony overlooking the main stage. The MC had announced that the featured performers were up next.

As soon as Tannie hit the stage, she commanded the attention of every man and woman in the place. She was an entertainer, an artist. Kari sat dazed and delighted as a different part of Tannie's luscious body moved with each beat of the music. She was hypnotizing. Like an erotic gymnast, Tannie worked the stage. She climbed up the stripper pole and wrapped her long legs around the top and, using only her thighs to hold her, suspended her body on a vertical plane. *Unbelievable.* She hung upside down and moved her torso slowly, then fast and slowly again, sliding down the pole and catching herself at the bottom before crawling across the floor like a panther. *Mesmerizing.* She gripped the pole with her hands and swirled around with speed and grace. *Amazing.* Sexual tension pulsed with every core-controlled movement. Her performance, with ballet-like movements, was deliciously exotic and powerfully athletic. Tannie was like caged heat. Kari couldn't take her eyes off of her. She felt like Tannie was looking directly at her. She didn't want to miss a move. She was captivated, infatuated, and self-conscious that others might be able to tell.

When the music ended, the audience rose as one, pumping fists in the air and barking approval. Arty Sebastiani escorted Tannie back to the VIP room.

Kari turned to Everett. Her partner was flushed. "Are you all right?"

"Yeah. That was surreal," he said. "Didn't it seem like she was looking right at me?"

***

Two and a half hours later, the agents stationed outside signaled that security personnel were carrying Snyder to his car. Kari and Everett hurried out to the van and caught sight of the burly attendants stuffing Snyder into the passenger seat. One of the two women with them climbed into the driver's seat and the other got into an ice-blue BMW parked nearby. Ten minutes later, the surveillance agents radioed to Kari and Everett that the two-car caravan had arrived at a high-rise residential building along the waterfront.

The mission had been accomplished. Snyder, the unmasked mystery guest, appeared to have been charmed, coaxed, and compromised.

Chapter 22

Kari heard her phone chime once. The text message was from Tannie. *I'm home. Where r u? Come over?*

She frowned. It was after two in the morning. They had broken off from the surveillance, and Everett had just dropped Kari at her car.

Kari texted back. *What's up?*

Even though Tannie's response—*Don't you want to know what went down tonight?*—didn't reveal an exigency, Kari was wide-awake and wired. If she went straight home, she would probably spend wasted hours lying awake in bed wondering what Tannie had to say. The plan had been to debrief Tannie later in the afternoon, but what harm would there be in dropping by Tannie's now? At the next light, Kari texted back. *Okay. B there in 10.* She made a quick U-turn.

Kari circled the block twice before snagging a parking space a block away from Tannie's building. The evening air was cool, and Kari pulled her jacket close as she ran up the steep brick steps.

When Tannie opened her condo door, Kari was taken aback. Every other time they had met, Tannie had been dressed provocatively and lacquered with makeup. Kari had expected to find her at home wearing a similar costume, but standing in the doorway motioning her to enter was a woman she almost didn't recognize. Tannie's face was scrubbed clean, and she wore fitted yoga pants and a tank top with racer-back straps that highlighted her muscular shoulders and arms. Time spent at the gym was chiseled into her well-defined cuts and curves. She looked more like a gymnast, certainly not a stripper.

Kari wondered which image was the real Tannie. Other than her overplucked eyebrows, her face—devoid of lined and painted lips, contoured cheeks, heavy black mascara, and false eyelashes—could be described as "fresh."

Something else was different too. Tannie seemed almost vulnerable. Only the sturdy metal pole bolted to the center of the living room ceiling provided a glimpse into her exotic profession.

"So how'd it go tonight?" Kari asked, giving Tannie a chaste embrace.

They each took a seat on opposite ends of the sofa.

"They showed that guy Snyder a real good time," Tannie said. "He was a hot mess."

"I guess that means the evening was a success."

"According to Arty, in college, Snyder was the guy who had everything going for him—intelligence, good looks, and the promise of a bright future. But…in less than an hour, he was wild, drunk, and out of control. I heard him mumbling a thank-you to Kincaid for offering to pay off his debts."

"He said that?"

"He was so smashed, everything was slurred." Tannie laughed. "But I'm used to deciphering the mutterings of drunk people."

"I bet."

"If he hadn't been an invited guest, he would have been thrown out of the club. He tried to grope me, so I shanked him in the foot with my Jimmy Choos." Tannie grounded her heel into the floor to demonstrate. "He was so wasted he barely felt it."

Tannie told Kari that the two dancers he left with must have assumed he was a wealthy young entrepreneur or the beneficiary of a big trust fund. They offered to make sure he got home safely.

"Wait until those bitches find out he doesn't have any money," Tannie said, laughing. "If he hadn't been Arty's guest, he would have ended up out back with security."

Kari stopped taking notes. She remembered the curious side-door activity she'd witnessed earlier that night. "What happens out back?"

"He would've been persuaded to pay up like all the other JOLIE customers whose eyes and appetites are bigger than their wallets."

"Persuaded to pay up? What does that mean?"

"You know, if the customers refuse to pay their tabs"—Tannie made a back handed slap in the air—"security scares the crap out of them."

"So, if customers complain about their bill, they're threatened or beaten up?" Kari was incredulous. "Why didn't you mention this before?"

"This kind of stuff goes on all the time. I thought I was supposed to keep you posted on what Stu's up to."

"I need to understand what you're talking about," Kari said. "Tell me how it works."

"You know the dancers pay JOLIE to work there, right? We collect money from our clients and give JOLIE 15 percent."

"Right, you explained that to me before."

"Well, if the clients refuse to pay or start to argue about the charges, we tell the shift manager, and depending on the customer and other circumstances, the shift manager calls security to help out."

Such persuasion had to be utilized at JOLIE most nights, Tannie explained. When customers mistakenly believed JOLIE should offer discounts or be willing to negotiate, club bouncers "encouraged" them to pay up. Given the size of the bouncers, no one disputed charges or questioned management for long. If necessary, the security guys threatened to telephone spouses and employers, or bang heads and twist arms. Any one of the intimidation methods worked.

"Do Lynette Hampton and Curtis Kincaid know what the bouncers are doing?"

"Absolutely. They're directing the action. And if the customer is really drunk, they might even add some extras onto his tab."

"They're overcharging? And what about Arty? Does he know what's going on?"

"I don't know. He's supposed to be a partner, but he's working the main room. They don't let him deal directly with the finances."

"So what's his job?"

"Pushing the staff and dancers to sell more drinks, services, and lap dances. The goal is to get patrons to spend as much as possible."

Tannie explained that she had heard that, although JOLIE was taking in nearly a million dollars each month, the club's expenses were massive. The well-appointed bars stocked with top-shelf liquor, the four-star food, and the luxury private suites were there to bring in the big players and their big bucks.

"But your average Joes get carried away too sometimes. So…security has to be called to speak with disinclined customers about their options." Tannie shrugged. "Dire times called for drastic measures."

"It would seem to me that if JOLIE keeps robbing their customers, they'll end up in a bigger mess. Why would anyone return to the club after that kind of treatment?"

"Because the regulars think they're in real relationships with us dancers. They'll put up with just about anything to be with the ones they love."

"And your customers, have they roughed up your customers to get them to pay you?"

"Nah. I try my best to make sure my clients know exactly what it's going to cost them to be entertained by me," Tannie said. "I don't like to get the staff involved."

Nodding sympathetically, she assumed Tannie was looking out for her clients' well-being.

"The bouncers get an hourly wage," Tannie went on blithely, "and if you have to call them in to help, you have to give them a bigger tip at the end of your shift."

Kari raised her eyebrows and changed the topic. "By the way, your set was fantastic. You're really talented."

"Thanks. Did you notice what I was doing?" Tannie giggled.

"What?"

"I dedicated my set to Agent Hildebrand."

"You did?" Kari tried not to show her disappointment. How silly she was to have thought Tannie had been zeroing on her. And why would she want her to?

"Yeah. Whenever I dance, I search the crowd for that one poor slob who knows he's too fat or too poor…" Tannie paused and winked. "Or too goofy to ever get a woman like me, and I direct every thrust of my pelvis, each rotation of my hips, at him. I lock my eyes on my victim until he's ready to pop." She laughed heartily, bumping her fists together. "Onstage, I'm the bomb. Never doubt my superpowers."

"Your flexibility is amazing."

"That's the key to pole dancing, Kari. Keeping loose, letting go. You can't move if you're too controlled and holding on tight."

"How'd you start dancing?"

Tannie gave a world-weary shrug. "I was a pudgy kid, and my dad used to tease me a lot. Who knows? Maybe that's why I'm a stripper. He didn't mean any harm. He thought he was being funny. His favorite nickname for me was 'Snack Queen.' Even now, when I wear low riders, he'll tell whoever's in earshot how the fat used to spill over my belt when I was little. His other name for me was 'little muffin top.' No matter how many times I say, 'But look at me now,' he'll say, 'Yeah I know, sweetheart, but you used to be chubby.'

Tannie stared down at her hands. After several moments of silence, she slowly raised her eyes up to meet Kari's.

"I don't know why I told you all that."

"I hope it means you trust me." Kari reached across the sofa and patted Tannie's hand. "It's okay."

"So. Anyway," Tannie said, extracting her hand from Kari's. "You enjoyed my set."

"Yes, I did. Your routine was breathtaking."

"Breathtaking?"

"I don't know what it was, but during your routine, I felt like I was flying around that pole with you. It was exhilarating."

"Exhilarating?" Tannie raised her eyebrows.

"I mean, you were so captivating. I couldn't take my eyes off of you."

Tannie leaned in close. "Agent Wheeler, are you flirting with me?"

"No. No," said Kari and waved her hands in front of her. "I didn't mean it like that."

"It's okay if you are. I've been with women before."

"That's none of my business."

"I'm just saying…my motto is 'It's all good, if it feels good.'" Tannie closed her eyes, inhaled and exhaled a deep breath. "You only have to lie back and enjoy the experience."

"So do you have female customers? The women in the audience, were they hoping to hook up with a stripper?" Kari had never thought about the women before.

"I doubt if it really matters who they hook up with. Women go to strip clubs for the same reason men do. They're looking for a cheap thrill, a zipless fuck. We all need to wave our freak flags once in a while." Tannie touched her hand to her throat and gave Kari a wry smile. "When's the last time you waved yours, Agent Kari Wheeler?"

Kari laughed uncomfortably. "I don't recall. But if not for this case, I can assure you I wouldn't be hanging out in strip clubs."

"Really? How many clubs have you been to since you met me?"

"Does it matter? Every visit was work related."

"But you enjoyed the experience."

"Maybe."

Tannie furrowed her eyebrows and smirked. Kari wondered if she could somehow detect her past indiscretions.

"Okay," she said. "For an old, married woman like me, I'll admit the strip club scene is…interesting. But my point is that the only reason I'm going to strip clubs is because—"

Tannie raised her palms high. "Hey, no need to get defensive."

"Bottom line," said Kari, "I'm not one of those female customers trying to make a love connection."

"Keep hanging out in strip clubs, and you might change your mind."

Kari waved her hand dismissively and shook her head. For a few uneasy seconds, Tannie stared back in silence, a hint of a smile on her lips. Kari grew uncomfortable again. Could Tannie sense something about her?

Tannie scooted closer and rubbed her hand against the silky fabric of Kari's dress. "I like your dress," she said. And then, with her hand still resting on Kari's thigh, Tannie cocked her head to the side and smiled.

"Have you ever been with a woman, Kari Wheeler?"

Kari stumbled for the appropriate response. "No. Never. Plus, I, I would never have a relationship with an FBI source," she said. "It's against the rules."

With a twinkle in her eyes, Tannie leaned in closer, "Who said I was talking about me and you?"

Had she misread Tannie's intentions? Kari couldn't deny that, deep inside her, carnal cravings pulsed. She felt the familiar quickening of her heartbeat. The novelty, of what she imagined would occur if she let their playful banter continue, made her shiver. She was intrigued, but this was more than a moral decision. Many an agent had succumbed to the ethical pitfall of an improper personal relationship with a source. A slip-up with Tannie would ruin her career. Kari knew if she stayed just one minute longer, she wouldn't be able to control what happened next.

"Look," Kari began, gathering up her things. "It's time for me to get out of here."

"Wait, you just got here. I was going to open a bottle of wine."

"It's late. Unlike you, I have work in the morning."

"Are you sure you not running away from me?" Tannie asked.

Shaking her head unconvincingly, Kari placed a firm hand on Tannie's shoulder and immediately felt ambushed by confusion. "We need to keep our debriefings on track and on topic."

"Sure. Of course," Tannie said. Her voice was composed, but her eyes were unreadable.

***

When Kari reached the lobby, she paused to collect her thoughts. She had made a rational decision to leave Tannie's condo, but her imprudent thoughts returned as she turned away from the Society Hill Towers and headed back to her car. Across the street was the Sheraton, and during the short walk along cobblestoned Dock Street, Kari felt the hotel beckoning to her. *What day of the week is it? Wednesday?* No. It was now early Thursday morning. Maybe salesman Joe Wilson was in town and at the bar? Kari smiled. She would drop by to buy him a drink.

Chapter 23

The spacious lobby of the hotel was eerily vacant. She had forgotten what time it was. Of course, the bar was closed. Kari approached the front desk.

"Hello," Kari said. "Could you check to see if a Joe Wilson is registered and, if he is, call up to his room and let him know he has a visitor?"

"Is he expecting you?" The registration clerk was probably close to Kari's age but looked worn down and at least ten years older. Her bland beige uniform matched her dull complexion.

"Tell him someone wants to sell him health insurance." Kari gave her a conspiratorial smile.

"At two thirty-two in the morning?" Wearily, the woman gestured to the clock mounted on the wall behind the counter. Her name tag identified her as Gloria. Her unsmiling face displayed her disapproval.

"I would appreciate it if you would pick up that phone and let him know I'm down here." Kari glared at the woman. She didn't like being judged. The clerk grudgingly reached for the phone. Kari could not make out what was being discussed, and when the call ended, the woman's flat expression revealed nothing.

"So?" Kari asked. "Is he in?"

"Room 859," she said, moving to the opposite end of the registration counter and turning her attention to other matters.

In the elevator, Kari rummaged through her sturdy leather purse, running a comb through her hair, reapplying lipstick, and fishing out a breath mint.

At the last minute, she remembered under her jacket she had her gun holstered on her belt. "Oh shit," she said, and pushed the elevator button for the top floor. The ride up and back down to the eighth floor gave her enough time to slide the weapon into the hidden zippered compartment of her Galco handbag. She didn't like carrying her gun off her body, but what was she to do, keep it strapped on while visiting Wilson? Kari laughed, intoxicated with anticipation.

When she stepped off the elevator, she was surprised to see Wilson standing in the doorway of his hotel room, hair rumpled, bare chested, and with a sheet wrapped around him.

"Wow. It's really you, my favorite insurance agent." Wilson grinned broadly. He was as cute and sexy as she had remembered. He held out his hand as she glided down the hall. "Get in here, beautiful," he said, and pulled her into the room's narrow entryway. He pressed her body up against the interior wall.

"What a wonderful surprise. You have no idea how much I've been pining over you and your soft, brown skin."

Wilson's hands slid under her clothes. One caressed her left breast as the other slid urgently up her dress, his fingers exploring the warmness between her thighs. He kissed her passionately while adeptly removing her panties. "I bet you taste sweet like chocolate."

The encounter was exactly what Kari craved. She ran her hand up his bare back and gripped his shoulders, moving her body in rhythm with his.

Wilson pulled at her sleeve and whispered, "Take off your clothes."

She abandoned all qualms and pushed her jacket over her shoulder to free her left arm. She had kicked off one shoe when she heard a female voice call out from the bedroom.

"Hey, did you forget about me?"

Kari jolted back to reality and squirmed from Wilson's embrace. Her chest tightened. "Who's that?"

Wilson released his hold and gestured down the short entryway toward the bed, where a disheveled blond in her early twenties lay naked. She waved at them.

"That's, uh, Daphne."

Kari slowly assessed the sobering reality of what she had walked into. She had never considered that he wouldn't be alone.

Wilson, allowing his sheet to drop to the floor, flopped onto the bed next to Daphne. He held his hands out to Kari.

"She doesn't mind," said Wilson. "I told her all about our last hookup. She felt left out."

Daphne beamed her acceptance. "You're pretty."

"This is so fucked up" was all Kari could say.

"What do you want me to do?" Wilson looked as if he was truly apologetic. "It's not like we ever imagined you would be dropping by tonight."

"Yeah. What the hell was I thinking?" Kari held her head in her hands and massaged her temples, trying to gather her thoughts. Thank God, Daphne's presence enabled her to come to her senses in time.

He pointed to the nightstand, where several brightly colored condom packets were tossed about. "Look, we're all set and…" He tugged at the nightstand's drawer and tossed out a clear plastic container of pills. "We got skittles. Oxy, 'ludes whatever you want. Daphne, you got any coke left?"

Daphne held up her hands and pouted. "All gone."

Wilson shrugged. "You should have come earlier."

Kari shook her head. "I'm sorry," she said. "I don't do drugs. You two have fun, but I'm out of here." With trembling hands, she adjusted her jacket back over her shoulders.

"What's the problem? The more the merrier," said Wilson.

"This is not my thing."

He put his arm around Daphne. "I'm not kicking her out."

"I'm not asking you to."

Wilson started to get up from the bed, but Kari signaled for him to remain where he was.

"Aw, come on." Wilson's facial expression hardened. "All of a sudden you're a good girl?"

"I changed my mind."

"Is this some kind of game you're playing?" Wilson's stare narrowed, and he glared at her.

"Look, you're some guy I met at a bar. I don't owe you anything. This," Kari said, pointing at her body, "isn't going to happen tonight. Not ever again."

"Sweetheart, you came up here and disturbed us. Interrupted our evening. You can't go around pulling shit like this."

"Joe," said Daphne. "Just let her go. We were having fun without her."

"She thinks she's special, parading around like she'd got something magical down there." He grabbed his crotch.

Kari picked up her purse as Wilson stepped off the bed and sauntered toward her, full monty on display.

"*Stop*. Don't come near me." Kari took a defensive stance and watched as a confounded Wilson considered his next move.

He chuckled. "Come on, now. You know you want it."

Kari glanced down to grab her shoe and before she knew what was happening, Wilson pounced and pinned her against the wall, smashing his mouth against hers, using his thigh to spread her legs apart.

"No, Joe. Don't." Over Wilson's shoulder Kari could see Daphne standing up on the bed. "*Stop. We don't need any trouble.*"

Wilson turned his head toward Daphne. In one instinctive move, Kari twice propelled her right knee into his groin, and when he released her, she grasped her hands together and gave him a double elbow thrust in the back, thanks to years of FBI defensive tactics training.

Wilson withered to the floor in agony and rolled himself into a ball. Rocking back and forth, he moaned, "Oh my God, oh my God."

For a brief moment, Daphne's look of horror made Kari regret what she had done to the spluttering, muttering man. But then Wilson looked up from the floor with vengeance flashing in his eyes.

"*What the fuck did you do that for?*"

Daphne jumped off the bed and knelt down at Wilson's side. Tears streamed down her face. "It's okay, baby. You're gonna be all right."

Before he could attempt to struggle to his feet, Kari snatched her shoe from the floor, held her purse tight, and hobbled toward the door.

"*You fucking bitch!*" he screamed.

Kari slammed the door, leaving her dignity and panties behind.

***

Kari scurried down eight flights of stairs. Once at the lobby level, she paused to catch her breath, adjusting her clothes, running her fingers through her hair, and contemplating what had just taken place. It was something more than fate that on this night she'd be presented two nefarious opportunities—a lesbian affair with her informant and a ménage à trois. She was being tested.

Trapped in solitude within the confines of the fireproof-steel stairway landing, the recklessness of what she had done—had been doing—hit her like a blow to the stomach. By the time she exited from the cramped quarters into the lobby and encountered the condemnatory glare of the night-desk clerk, fear and humiliation caused her to stumble forward.

"Are you all right?" Gloria the desk clerk called. "Do you need me to call someone?"

"No. No. I'm okay. I'm all right." Kari gripped a lobby chair to steady her frame. Despite Kari's declarations of well-being, Gloria abandoned the front desk post and came over to check on her.

"I ran down the stairs," Kari offered, as an explanation for her obvious distress.

In the dim light of the deserted lobby, the woman's harsh convictions softened. "He's a regular here. Once or twice a month I see him on my shift."

It took Kari a moment to realize she was talking about Wilson.

"He's a lying, cheating, nasty dog, just like my ex-husband." Her lip curled up in an angry sneer. "And her. I wish I knew what was up with that one, all that sneaking around. One day they're going to get caught."

Gloria rubbed Kari's back and brushed a lock of hair from Kari's face.

"They're up to no good," said Gloria, with a sympathetic smile. "You don't need to be up there with them."

Kari nodded sheepishly.

***

By the time Kari arrived home, it was almost four o'clock. She took off her clothes and attempted to slip into bed without disturbing Kevin, but he was awake. She had warned him she would be out late, but he glared at her and then the bedside clock. The red glow of the digital time read 3:47 a.m. Kevin tugged at the blankets and turned his back on her.

A short time later, she could tell from the steady rhythm of his breathing that he had fallen to sleep again. She closed her eyes, but tears flooded behind her shuttered eyelids. So with eyes wide-open, Kari lay silently next to her husband, her every brain wave agitated and every nerve cell activated. Sleep refused to come.

Thank God she hadn't actually had sex with anyone tonight, but no moral victory could be claimed. She was out of control. By definition, this time she hadn't been unfaithful, but that was just a technicality. If Tannie wasn't her confidential FBI source or if Daphne hadn't already marked territory in Wilson's bed, she would have. Who the hell was she? What the hell did she think she was doing? Throughout the night, the sickening feeling in her gut grew more pronounced, and just before dawn, she was forced to scramble out of bed to vomit up her shame. The guilt was unbearable.

Kevin had been right all along. Tannie had warned her too. Hanging out in strip clubs wasn't working for her. Whatever made her think someone with her history could handle the temptation? She had been asking for trouble when she decided to take on the case. And now she had exactly what she had asked for. Trouble. From now on, she and Everett would interview witnesses only in a neutral setting.

No more going to strip clubs. No more meeting with Tannie alone. Kari was surrendering her freak flag.

Chapter 24

"Stu! Stu! Over here."

Sebastiani figured he would call Tannie later in the day to find out about Snyder's night out at JOLIE, but as luck would have it, he ran into Snyder and his boss, Councilman Yhost, outside council chambers while dropping off documents at city hall.

"Councilman. How are you?"

"Couldn't be better. This is Craig Snyder, my chief of staff. He looks like a teenager, but he is *freaking brilliant*."

Sebastiani shook Snyder's hand and sized up what he was wearing—a skinny suit and a disinterested gaze. *This punk can't be the guy Arty thinks is going to help rescue JOLIE.*

"Craig, I want to introduce you to one of the luckiest bastards I know, Stuart Sebastiani."

Sebastiani expected to see some sign of name recognition on Snyder's part, but nothing registered. Perhaps, after his late night, he was too hungover.

Yhost continued his introduction. "Stu's the business regulatory director at L and I. The city actually pays Sebastiani to hang out in strip joints."

This time, Snyder's eyes widened, and Sebastiani could tell that the name had clicked. Snyder murmured something about having to go inside to set up, but Yhost reached out and yanked on his sleeve as he started to leave.

"No, no don't go yet," Yhost insisted. "Stu has some of the best stories. You got to hear some of the wild things this guy has seen and done."

Yhost, as was his routine, began to pump Sebastiani for juicy details about his latest escapades. Sebastiani obliged but continued to observe Snyder. *Why's this guy so damn nervous?* Even if Snyder believed Sebastiani knew about the deal, did he really think Sebastiani would say something and implicate himself?

Sebastiani enlightened them with a few salacious tales before he grew bored with tormenting Snyder and turned the tables on Yhost.

"So, what's happening with you, Barry? A powerful man like yourself has to be offered a good piece of tail every once in a while." Sebastiani was curious if Yhost would tell him about meeting Natalia. Only a couple of weeks had passed since the failed rendezvous attempts.

"Maybe, if I looked like you. Craig, look at us," Yhost said as he stood side by side with Sebastiani. "We're around the same age, but Stu's got two things going for him that I don't: a pretty face and a dick that works."

"I know lots of women who are as attracted to power as they are to looks," Sebastiani said.

"Stu, my friend, those days are long gone." Yhost, with a sober expression, confided, "Prostate cancer a few years ago, before they knew how to treat it without aggressive surgery. They saved my life, but…" His voice trailed off as he looked down toward his crotch, blocked from view by his protruding paunch.

"Shit, I didn't know," Sebastiani said, surprised Yhost would reveal such intimate details. "Is everything okay now?"

"Yeah, I'm fine, other than, you know," he said. "That's why I have to live vicariously through you." Playfully, Yhost patted Stu's face. "I'm sure Craig has some great stories too, but he won't share his."

"A handsome, young guy like him, I'm sure he does." Sebastiani smiled cunningly at Snyder. "In fact, I'd bet on that."

"Stu, I'd buy you a cup of coffee so you could recap some more of your conquests, but we got to go in there and listen to Frances Finney." Yhost reached for the door handle.

"I understand she wants to clean up all the titty bars in South Philly," Sebastiani said, pleased that Yhost had brought up the subject. "She had me prepare a brief for her on the current zoning codes and regulations."

"Yes, she is a very determined woman. She wants to return to the days of old-fashioned burlesque clubs with no full nudity and absolutely no touching."

"Barry, I think they're about to start," Snyder interrupted, opening the heavy, wooden chamber door. "We better go inside."

Sebastiani stared at Snyder. *What is wrong with this guy? He looks like he's about to have a coronary. Does he really think I'm going tell Yhost he's agreed to take a bribe to influence his vote?*

"Finney seems to have strong support among the council members," said Sebastiani, pushing the topic further. "Club owners in South Philly are scared to death."

"How'd they hear about it? It's supposed to be hush-hush."

Sebastiani shrugged. "Is anything ever secret around here?"

"Well…" said Yhost. "I think a police officer's time is better used patrolling neighborhoods than monitoring strip joints. I'm not voting for that damn bill."

"You already know how you're voting?" Sebastiani asked Yhost, but his attention was focused on Snyder. *If that's the case, what the hell are we going to pay you for?*

"Keep that to yourself. We haven't figured out how I'm going to introduce my opposition," Yhost replied. "For now, I'm trying to delay the vote."

"What about councilmanic prerogative?"

"Yeah, I know." He gave a loud sigh. "Everybody assumes I'm with Frannie. She's my girl, but I can't vote for her rezoning project." Yhost held a finger to his lips and walked into council chambers, leaving Sebastiani and Snyder in the hallway.

Sebastiani was livid. *Snyder's running a scam.*

Catching Sebastiani's glare, Snyder tried to scoot into the room behind Yhost, but Sebastiani grabbed him by the arm before he could escape.

"I need you to call me. *Today.*" Sebastiani handed Snyder his card.

"I don't know why I agreed to take the money when I already knew Yhost was gonna vote no," Snyder pleaded. "I'll call Arty and tell him the truth."

"Whoa, not so fast, buddy. I got a better idea."

Chapter 25

"We took a good look at the video this morning," said Kari.

She was with Everett at the US Attorney's office briefing Mitch Whitmore on what had been captured on the surveillance camera aimed at JOLIE's back door. She had worked with many AUSAs. The ones who were lazy, superslow, screamers, or excessive worriers she avoided. She thought no-nonsense Whitmore, a former marine judge advocate, was the right prosecutor for this case.

"It's seems dragging slow-to-pay customers out back is a regular practice at JOLIE." She had already explained that Tannie told her the broad-shouldered bouncers often threatened and intimidated patrons who questioned the padded bills they had been handed.

"I read something about that," said Whitmore. "A man at a New York strip club disputed an outrageous tab for a bachelor's party—the story graced the front pages of the tabloids for weeks."

Whitmore turned toward his computer, and after a few minutes surfing the web, shouted, "Aha, found it!" He printed out the article and handed copies to Kari and Everett.

Kari scanned over the newspaper story. The bill was for a single evening of drinks, food, and private lap dances for the man, his future brother-in-law, and a few friends. The man claimed to be drunk when he signed the charge card receipt and had later refused to pay the $241,000 tab. The stink he raised eventually resulted in the club owners being charged with extortion and his bill being cleared. The article also featured a sidebar story about other club owners using force or threats to compel customers to pay exorbitant bills.

"This is exactly what Tannie told me is happening at JOLIE," said Kari.

"If that's true, in addition to public corruption and bribery charges against Sebastiani," Whitmore said, "I think we can also charge Lynette Hampton and Curtis Kincaid, under the Hobbs Act, with theft and robbery by extortionate means."

"Cool. This is turning into a kitchen-sink case," Kari said. "Let's throw everything we can at these guys and see what sticks."

"If this is a billing scam, we'll need to dig up some victims," said Whitmore. "I want you to round them up and get their stories."

Kari bristled. "Whoa there. You know our rules."

"How could I forget?" Whitmore chuckled. "You run the investigative side, and I focus on the prosecution."

She often had to remind Whitmore that, unlike local prosecutors, who have investigators assigned to work for them, FBI agents usually worked independently and then presented their packaged investigations to an assistant US attorney for prosecution. She didn't need a lawyer telling her how to work a case.

"If you don't mind, I'd like to sit in on a few interviews," he said with a fake put-upon tone and reproving glance toward Kari. "This is a hot case. Why should I always have to hear about all the juicy tales secondhand?"

"Sure. That's not a problem," said Everett.

Kari smiled weakly at her partner. She wasn't sure what had made the difference, but now Everett was more at ease with the investigation, and she was the jumpy one, frightened that she would lose control again.

They reviewed the status of the investigation well into the evening. Before they left, Whitmore suggested they begin putting their witnesses before the federal grand jury to lock in their testimony.

"Bill Leone will be the perfect witness to give the jurors a broad view of the strip club industry," he said. "Ev, why don't you get Leone in here sometime next week, so we can prep him for his appearance? Frankly, after all you've told me about him, I can't wait to meet the guy."

***

The following day, as Everett sat in his office cubicle, typing yet another interview report, he wondered how he could prevent Whitmore and Leone from meeting. When Whitmore had asked him to schedule an appointment with Leone, Everett had nodded. But he could never risk that. Neither Kari nor Whitmore knew about his friendship with the club owner and that he spent many undocumented evenings at Club Friskee II. He wasn't doing anything wrong. He continued to refuse lap dances and any contact with the girls, but Kari and Whitmore wouldn't understand. There was no way he would allow Bill Leone to talk to the prosecutor or appear before the grand jury.

Recently, Kari had forbidden him to step foot inside any strip clubs and insisted that they no longer interview any of their witnesses there. He wondered if she'd heard rumors of his solo visits to Club Friskee II. When he prodded her for an explanation, she refused to give one. He couldn't tell if she was being cautious or if she had real suspicions. But she wasn't his boss; she couldn't tell him what to do. Perhaps, she was simply done in by comparisons of her body to those of the strippers. Could it be that she felt inadequate among the dancers with their high, rounded breasts and tight, firm buttocks?

From across the squad area, he watched her. Capturing her image in his mind, he closed his eyes and pictured his co-case agent with no clothes on. Everett concluded with a nod of endorsement. For a woman her age, Kari Wheeler probably looked good naked.

***

Later that evening, Everett sat in front of his home computer. Before logging on to his favorite site, he leaned over in his chair and looked down the hallway to make sure Brenda had gone upstairs to bed. Although he told her he would be up shortly, lately, his usual hour on the computer before bed had morphed into an extra two or three. Whenever she called down to ask when he was coming up or complained the follow morning, he reminded her that he was working on one of the biggest cases in the office and he needed to catch up on work.

In reality, surfing porn sites had developed into a routine, perhaps an obsession. Everett even enjoyed logging on a few times throughout the day. Watching the adult videos stream across his monitor blunted his conflicted emotions. The more he watched, the less wicked it felt. It was like taking a cigarette break or having a drink, except, he told himself, his habit didn't cost anything and didn't cause any harm.

Once more, Everett craned his neck to check for Brenda. She was still upstairs. Alone in the stillness of his home office, he bypassed the pop-up ads for the raw, hardcore XXX sites and clicked on one that promised in flashing neon, "Exotic Horny Slut Pictures and Videos." Just a few minutes more, and then he would go up to bed.

Chapter 26

As instructed, Snyder had called Sebastiani immediately after their fortuitous meeting in city hall.

"Keep taking the money," Sebastiani had told Snyder. "Who's gonna know?" Snyder only had to tell Arty, Hampton, and Kincaid he was making progress with Yhost and pocket the cash.

After giving half to Sebastiani.

At first, Snyder went along with the plan and split the initial payments. But a month into their arrangement, problems began to surface.

"It seems to me I'm taking all the risk," Snyder complained. "Tell me again why I'm splitting the money with you?"

"Because this charade was my idea." He wanted to be fair, but that didn't mean letting Snyder take advantage of him. "I could possibly concede to a sixty-forty split," said Sebastiani. "Let me think about."

But then, Snyder made a wrong move—a stupid move.

"No. I'm done," Snyder had said. "Leave me alone, or I'll tell Arty the truth."

Who the fuck does he think he is? Sebastiani knew it was just an idle threat. Snyder wouldn't say shit. But he would have to teach Snyder a lesson, wrangle him under control. And a compromising sex tape was the way to do it.

***

"Arty, you can't let that greedy bastard take your money and walk away with no results," said Sebastiani when Arty told him Snyder wanted out. "Council's voting on Finney's rezoning at the end of the month. Snyder needs to keep working on Yhost until he votes."

"I told you, Snyder called and said Yhost has already decided he's voting against it. We don't need Snyder anymore."

"Oh yes you do. What if Yhost changes his mind?" said Sebastiani. "You need Snyder in your corner until the very end."

"What more do you want me to do, Dad? We can't force him to cooperate."

"Oh yes we can." Sebastiani smiled at his son. "Back to plan B."

"Plan B?"

"Don't tell me you forgot about the sex tape. You guys are gonna need it to secure Snyder's continued cooperation." Truth be told, Sebastiani needed it more—to secure Snyder's silence.

Natalia was incredulous. "Stu, you can't be serious." Her earlier attempts to lure Yhost and make a sex tape had failed miserably.

"This guy is going to take the bait," Sebastiani insisted.

"That's what you said the last time, when you had me hanging out in parking lots trying to pick up some creepy, old guy."

"That's because Yhost can't get it up anymore. This guy will get a hard-on as soon as he sees you."

"You're full of shit, Stu."

"No, really. He's cute and young. If I liked guys, I'd do him myself," said Sebastiani. "Plus, they're gonna give you five grand."

"Why only five thousand? The last time they offered me ten."

"I know, but this time we'll make the introductions and set everything up."

"I don't know."

"How about we get you two a room at the Ritz Carlton?"

"I swear, this time there better not be any problems. I'm not a prostitute. I'm only doing this because you asked."

"So you'll do it for nothing?"

"Fuck you."

"Ah, babe, don't be mean."

After he and Natalia worked out all the details, Sebastiani hung up and made another call.

"She's all set," said Sebastiani as soon as Arty answered. "She wants ten grand and insists we put her up at the Ritz Carlton. You'll need to get your security guys to install the equipment. Call me after you talk to Snyder and book the room."

Arty called back in less than thirty minutes.

"Dad, we're good to go. Snyder's in. He assumed the invite is just another tactic to entice him to stay attached to the plan. Everything's coming together beautifully."

"I told you that greedy prick couldn't resist a freebie. What time did you tell him to get there?"

"He's meeting Natalia at seven o'clock."

"When are your security guys setting up the video camera?"

"They're leaving as soon as they load the stuff in the car. Hotel check-in is one o'clock."

"Good. The Ritz Carlton is around the corner from my office. I'll walk over and get the key card from your guys when they're done in the room. That way, they won't have to hang around waiting for Natalia."

"Okay, sure. That makes sense."

"You trust your guys with the cash?"

"Yeah, of course."

"Then give that to them too, and I'll give it to Natalia," offered Sebastiani.

"Before she hooks up with Snyder?"

"Arty, Natalia's a good girl. She won't cheat you."

"Okay, if you say so."

"Oh, and, Arty? Call your mother. She says she hasn't heard from you in three days."

Sebastiani called Gina next. He was tired of them sneaking behind the shed in the backyard or messing around in his car.

"Hey, Stu," she answered.

"You up yet?"

"Nah, I don't have to be at work till six thirty."

"I want to see you."

"I want to see you too. Drive me to work, and we can mess around in the car like last time."

"No. I want you to get your sweet, lazy ass up and meet me at the Ritz Carlton. I got us a suite."

"The Ritz Carlton?"

"Yeah you heard me: the Ritz Carlton."

"You shitting me?"

"Come on, babe, stop wasting time. Meet me in the lobby in an hour."

"But, Stu, I haven't eaten. I haven't showered."

"It's the Ritz Carlton. You've heard of room service, right? And they have showers too."

"How did you—"

"Gina, stop asking questions. The room is ours for only a few hours. Get your sweet ass over there."

***

As soon as Gina entered the hotel suite, Sebastiani's anticipation was replaced with uneasiness. Perhaps it was the way she bounced up and down on the king-size bed or *oohed* and *aahed* over the impressive menu but only ordered a cheeseburger and a chocolate shake.

He didn't find her behavior adorable or endearing. In the sophisticated setting, Gina, who still wore her brown hair pulled back in a ponytail, seemed different. Something didn't feel right. Sebastiani froze with fear when he realized why. Gina may have been twenty, but now all he could see was the neighbor girl begging for his attention.

"What ya doing standing in the middle of the floor, Stu?" Gina tugged off her jeans, pulled her T-shirt over her head, and shimmied out of her bra and panties. "Come over here." She giggled. "We've never done it in a bed."

Sebastiani remained glued to the floor. Usually, he would have been the one to remove her panties—with his teeth. But now his mind was saying, *No, don't move.* But his body responded to her lithe and nubile nakedness. Maybe he was doing nothing wrong.

***

Several hours later, after Gina had left for work and housekeeping had been called in to freshen up the room, Sebastiani followed the instructions left by JOLIE's security guys and turned on the hidden video equipment. When Natalia arrived, he handed over the key card and half of the $10,000 he had been given to pay for her services. He left her to her task. Walking to the elevator, he patted the sides of his pants, double-checking his pocketed share of the cash.

Chapter 27

Oh crap, she's here again. Sebastiani walked through his front door and immediately recognized Gina's voice coming from the kitchen. He could have kicked himself. What was he thinking, screwing around with the girl next door? He had been avoiding her since their tryst at the Ritz Carlton two weeks earlier. He was so glad Mia would return to school in another week. She had been home from college all summer, but recently, Gina kept finding excuses to come over and hang out with her. His entire family was perplexed as to why she kept showing up at their door. Although the girls had been friends when they were little, they hadn't socialized in years. Now, all of a sudden, Gina was dropping by the house to "chill." Ironically, he felt the same way as Mia did—Gina needed to get a life.

He knew Gina was worried. Stalking his daughter was her desperate attempt to hold on to him. It wasn't working. Gina was starting to creep him out. If his wife and kids found out what he had been doing, he'd be in big trouble. He needed to get rid of her.

"Hi, Mr. Stu. How was work?" Gina greeted him before his family members even noticed he had entered the room.

Ignoring her, he went over to his wife and kissed her on the cheek. He glanced about the small kitchen filled with savory smells and one person too many.

"So what's going on here?" He hoped his smile looked sincere, relaxed.

"The girls wanted to learn how to make my ricotta cheese pie," said Anna Sebastiani, smiling proudly.

"I didn't want to learn," Mia said. "Gina did. I like to eat cheese pie. I don't need to know how to bake it. And anyway, isn't it supposed to be like a secret family recipe?"

"Mia, don't be rude," scolded Anna. "Gina is like family. We've known her most of her life."

Sebastiani hoped no one saw him wince.

"That's okay, Mrs. Sebastiani," Gina said, coming to Mia's defense. "She's right. It was my idea. I can't wait to see how it tastes."

"I'll tell you what." Sebastiani placed his hands firmly on Gina's shoulders and guided her toward the back door. "When it's ready, we'll bring over two big slices."

***

"Thank you, Daddy." Mia gave Sebastiani a hug after he returned from escorting Gina outside. "I tried all afternoon to get rid of her. She has serious problems."

"She likes being with our crazy family," Anna said. "She's just a little lonely. We should all try to be nice to her."

"You're going to have to take that pie you promised over to her." Mia declared to her father. "That girl's obsessed with me."

Sebastiani wished he had not volunteered to venture next door with pie. Maybe he would send Anna instead. He stretched his neck and shoulders to ease some of the tension from his upper torso. He needed to fix this. He needed to find some way to jettison Gina. Perhaps someone could find her a job and a place to stay at the shore. The summer college help would be leaving soon to return to school. Surely, workers were still needed as long as the weather stayed warm? How could she turn that down? He could tell her he'd come down to see her and never go. He began to think of people he knew in Atlantic City, Wildwood, and Ocean City. One of them must need something from him. He would swap favors.

For God's sake, didn't he have enough to worry about? His name kept coming up in some big federal investigation. Last week the zoning bill had finally been voted down. JOLIE and lap dances were safe. But Sebastiani suspected Snyder was running his mouth. It was time to use the sex tape he had recorded of Snyder and Natalia.

If Snyder was talking or even thinking about talking, that should shut him up.

Chapter 28

Kari was pleased. Tannie had done an excellent job identifying victims of JOLIE's overzealous collection efforts. After being cautioned that it was illegal for her to look at any JOLIE files or records she didn't routinely have access to, Tannie simply engaged in the old-fashioned method of gathering information—eavesdropping. At the end of their shifts, when the bouncers bragged about their encounters with reluctant patrons, she listened in.

That's how Pastor Richardson, a youth minister at a large church in Northeast Philly, came to be interviewed in a windowless room in the William Green Federal Building.

"We're not here to judge you, Pastor," said Kari. "We just need to know how you got hurt. Can we talk about that incident?"

"It was my fault. I didn't keep track of the lap dances," Richardson replied.

"You said the bill came to $3,130? That's a lot of lap dances. Could you even walk after all that?" Whitmore's tone and sarcasm warranted a soft kick from Kari.

"I really didn't think I ran up the bill that much."

"Do you think they padded the bill?" asked Kari. "That they overcharged you?"

"They did it before, but this time I told them I couldn't pay it." Richardson drummed his hands on his thighs.

"You didn't have a credit or debit card with you?" Ev asked.

"I did, but I told them I didn't. The bill was so high, and I knew we couldn't afford all the money I was spending at JOLIE. So I said I couldn't pay."

"Had you complained about the amount of the bill before?" asked Whitmore.

Richardson's bottom lip trembled. "Yeah, but they threatened to tell my bishop, so I always came up with the money."

"But this time you couldn't?" Everett spoke slowly, sympathetically.

"I guess I could have." Richardson looked down at his clasped hands. "It was more like I wanted to push them to see what they would do if I didn't pay. I was hoping if the consequences were bad enough, I would finally stop."

"And the broken ribs, did that work for you?" asked Whitmore.

"Not really, I guess."

The agents both shot a disapproving look at Whitmore. Kari touched Richardson's arm, purposely redirecting his attention away from the prosecutor.

"We understand you've been back several times since," Kari said.

Richardson nodded.

Kari flipped to the next page of her steno pad. "Why don't we go over what happened during those visits?"

Richardson told them about being coerced into signing excessive credit card receipts and being tricked into paying for services that he had been told were included in his club membership fee. He claimed to have been deceived into signing a credit card receipt for itemized amounts he thought ranged from $14 to $25, but which were actually $140 to $250. He was once even escorted to an on-site ATM and ordered to make a withdrawal.

As the interview drew to an end, Kari made a quick review of her notes. "I have one last question I need to ask you," she said. "And I need you to be especially careful to answer this one honestly."

"I've answered all of your questions honestly." Tears welled in the corners of his eyes.

"And we appreciate that." Kari looked around the room at her colleagues, and they all nodded. "But I need to know if you've used any of the church's money to pay for your visits to JOLIE or any other strip club?"

Richardson's head jerked forward, his eyes practically begging her to believe him. "No, I charged it all on my personal card."

"That credit card—is it under your name or the church's name?" Everett asked.

"My name but the church's address." Richardson added, "I didn't want my wife to see the bill."

"We don't want to discover any surprises later," said Kari. "We can't have the defense damage your credibility by telling the jurors that you lied to us about something."

"Jurors? You're gonna make me testify?"

"Why else would we be talking to you?" Whitmore asked. "We're going to take a look at that account and any other account connected with you and the church. If you're *screwing* around with church money, you could face charges."

Alarmed by Whitmore's tone, Richardson lost all his composure. He slumped in his chair and cradled his face in his hands. "If my wife and parishioners find out about my visits to JOLIE, I'm ruined."

Whitmore looked at the weeping figure with unveiled disgust. While Kari understood how difficult this interview must be for Richardson, she too wished that he had cut out all the waterworks.

Everett was the only one to display any compassion. He patted Richardson's shoulder.

"Everything will be okay," he told Richardson. "What you did doesn't make you a bad person. It's all going to work out fine."

Kari knew Everett was speaking to the pastor, but his kind words were reassuring to her too.

***

When Kari and Everett left Whitmore's office, Kari caught sight of a face in the lobby she hadn't expected to see. Her heart clutched. She'd never expected to see him again. Never. Certainly not here, not now.

He was in deep conversation with two other men. She had to get away before he saw her. She hurried through the waiting room, swinging open the heavy, glass door. With her back to the reception area, she pushed the button to summon the elevator.

"Kari, wait."

Everett caught up with her just as she slipped inside the first elevator to arrive. He reached for her elbow to pull her back. "It's going up."

"I don't care." She shrugged off his hand and burrowed into the back corner of the elevator. "Just get on."

Only after the elevator began to ascend did she start to breathe again.

"What was that about?" Everett asked.

"What do you mean?"

"What do you mean, what do I mean?" He stared her down. "Something happened back there."

"I don't know what you're talking about."

"You saw someone who knows you. Someone you didn't want to talk to."

"No. That's not it." Kari's simple response was more like a half-truth than a lie. The person in the waiting area didn't know her. He didn't even know her name.

She had fled from him once before at the Sheraton.

Joe Wilson.

Chapter 29

"I have to admit, this is a great case."

Juanita Negron patted the thick folder on her desk. Investigative reports spilled out of the six-inch case file. Papers not yet serialized lay stacked next to it.

"You've done a stellar job."

"Thanks. Hildebrand's been a great help."

"Is that your way of saying I told you so?"

"Ev and I have our moments, but it's a good partnership. He's a hard worker."

"I'm seldom wrong about people. But perhaps, in this case, you're right and I'm wrong." Juanita shrugged. "I guess even an entitled brat has to grow up eventually."

Everett was a changed man. He wasn't arguing for a bigger role anymore, and he was pulling his weight and suggesting key actions to move the investigation forward. He was more confident, even sporting a fresh, hip haircut.

"I can tell you it's one of the most talked-about cases during the weekly management meetings. What's the status of the T-3?" Juanita asked.

Here it comes again. Ever since they recorded Councilman Yhost's chief of staff, Craig Snyder, hanging out at JOLIE, Special Agent in Charge Jack Roeder and US Attorney Paul Crystal were in a power struggle over the next step of the investigation. They had found nothing concrete to indicate Yhost had been corrupted. Should they initiate a Title III wiretap, also known as a T-3, on the telephones of Councilman Barry Yhost and Craig Snyder? Crystal was against it. He insisted they first exhaust all less-intrusive investigative methods before dragging Yhost into the case.

SAC Roeder, a practical man with a no-nonsense attitude, was 100 percent for a wiretap. Wiretaps made a good impression at FBI headquarters. Yeah, maybe Roeder and supervisor Juanita Negron's primary motivation was to rid the city of corruption, but a secondary incentive had to be checking off that goal on their executive management performance plan. The FBI was a competitive culture. Kari was used to the power plays.

"Snyder's financial records show he's been recently receiving large sums of cash from an undocumented source," said Kari. "But there's still no evidence that a dime is going to Yhost." She took a moment to visually connect with Juanita. "We know Snyder's been meeting with Arty Sebastiani, Stu's son, but other than the fact that Snyder works for him, nothing ties Yhost into the mix. To convince a judge to authorize a wiretap, we'll need much more than that."

"Okay. So what's your plan?" Juanita asked.

"We're going to start putting witnesses before the grand jury soon. Closer to indictment, we'll approach Snyder. If he agrees to cooperate and Yhost is a part of the scheme, we'll wire Snyder up and make a consensual recording. If Yhost has nothing to do with any of this, we'll just have Snyder make a few calls to Stuart and Arty Sebastiani and call it a day."

Juanita took a moment to digest the game plan. "And if Snyder doesn't want to cooperate?" she asked.

"We'll proceed straight to indictment and execute search warrants at Sebastiani's office and JOLIE."

"It appears that you have everything under control." Juanita leaned across her desk to shake Kari's hand. "This case is worthy of a code name. Any thoughts?"

Kari smiled and nodded her head. "As a matter of fact I do." She paused for added effect. "Operation G-String Sting."

"Kind of risqué," said Juanita, arching her eyebrows. "I'm not sure it's going to fly with the suits at FBI headquarters. I like it, but how about we go with just G-Sting."

"That kind of changes the whole point."

"Karolina, you know HQ. Any case title with 'G-string' in it is never gonna pass."

There she goes again using my full name like I'm a child.

"Okay. G-Sting. That works too." Kari dropped it. She didn't feel like being lectured.

"One more thing. I need to take a few days off," Kari said. "My mother's ill. I've gone down with the family for several quick weekend visits, but we want to spend more time with her and my dad."

"Sorry to hear that. Sure take some time off, if you need to."

"Everett can take care of getting the witnesses before the federal grand jury while I'm away."

"Sounds like all he'll need to do is pick up the phone. Certainly even he can handle that." Juanita gave an off-kilter smile and returned to conducting her file reviews.

* * *

After leaving Juanita's office, Kari went back to her desk, settled into her seat, and took a moment to gather her thoughts. Shame still gnawed in her gut. Like a plastic lid melted by the heat of the dishwasher, Kari felt distorted, like she didn't fit in her own skin. She was accidently-left-the-baby-in-the-backseat-of-the-minivan exhausted. She was happy the whole family was driving down to visit her parents for a week. It would be a good time for them all to regroup, for Kari to work on fixing and forgiving herself.

Her ringing phone interrupted her thoughts.

"Agent Wheeler," she answered.

"Who did you say?" asked the male on the other end of the call.

"This is Special Agent Kari Wheeler. Who are you trying to reach?"

Silence.

"Who is this?"

The caller hung up.

She was uneasy for a fraction of a moment, but with so much going on and too much to do, she quickly forgot all about the call.

"I saw you were in with Juanita. Is everything okay?"

Kari looked up to see Everett standing before her. She had been so immersed in self-reflection—or was it self-pity? —she hadn't heard him approaching. She gave him a smile and double thumbs-up.

"Code name G-Sting," she said.

"What happened to the G-string part?"

"She cut it." Kari smirked and made a scissor motion with her fingers.

"Figures. She's so by the book."

"Look who's talking."

"What else did she say?"

"Actually, she complimented you on the great work you've done on the case."

Everett, with an exaggerated look of surprise on his face, shuffled back a step or two. "She did?"

Kari nodded.

"I told her I was taking a few days off, and she said she has full confidence you can handle everything while I'm away."

"Great. And I'll be stuck having to deal with Whitmore. He's insisting that Leone appear before the federal grand jury next week."

"So? Whitmore's been asking you to bring in Leone since…forever." Kari refused to referee the disagreement. "What's the problem? Just get him in."

Chapter 30

Kari searched her mother's face and, after several seconds, found the softness that had been missing. Cancer had made her skin gaunt and tight. Her cheeks were hollow. Her teeth protruded from thin, dry lips, and although she smiled at Kari, her eyes were vacant. The last time Kari was home, her mother had looked more like herself, although a bit jaundiced and tired. She had been strong enough to direct Kari and her father on how to prepare dinner, had enjoyed her grandchildren running around the house, and hadn't minded when they pestered her with questions.

This time it was different. Carter recoiled with fear when they stepped into her bedroom to see her. The twins, Casey and Morgan, cried. The woman lying before them was dying. Kevin gathered the kids in his arms and led them out of the room. If Kari and Kevin had known what to expect, they would have prepared their children better. They would have prepared themselves better. The suddenness of her deterioration was frightening. They had visited just a couple of weeks ago. Kari looked over at her father and wanted to ask him what had happened, but she knew the answer already. Her mother had given up. She was through with cancer—she had had enough. After two years of lopped-off breasts, pin-cushioned skin, and poisoned insides, she was ready. It was only a matter of time.

Kari spent the next few days doting on her mother, bringing her food she was unable to keep down, and attempting the impossible task of making her comfortable. Kevin and the kids floated around the house, numb with grief, tiptoeing with uncertainty and dreading the inevitable.

"I wanted to show Grandma my drawings." Carter held out the sketchbook his grandmother had given him for Christmas.

"You can go sit with her," said Kari. "I'm sure she would like to see how good you've gotten."

He peered anxiously into his grandmother's room. "I'm afraid."

"It's okay. She's still your grandmother and she loves you very much." Gently, Kari rubbed his shoulders.

"Are you afraid?" Carter asked.

"Yes, I am sweetie. I'm afraid to let her go."

"Is Mom-Mom afraid?"

Kari held him close, and through her tears, she answered, "I don't know. I guess we should ask her."

Even as she spoke the words, Kari knew she wouldn't get the chance. Either the cancer or the chemo had caused canker sores to form in Bernice Wheeler's mouth and talking had become painful. So, Kari talked instead. What was not said weighed down the room.

This was how it had often been, Kari talking and her mother listening. Kari watched her mother. *What is Mom feeling? Is she afraid to face death, or is she at peace knowing that she had a good life?* Kari wanted to know, wanted to ask, but it was too late. In the last few months, Kari had realized that she knew very little about this woman who had raised her and loved her. She was sad, almost ashamed, that she had never pressed her mother to open up and share more. And Kari was heartbroken that there wasn't time to remedy having been so self-absorbed.

As a young girl who thought the world revolved around her, Kari never noticed that her mother seldom spoke about herself. She had more than adequately managed the thankless job of uprooting her family from place to place and creating a new home for them. She had done the best she could to make the transfer fluid. She was a good mother who loved her children and cared well for her family. But Kari now realized with regret and sorrow that without the title of "homemaker," few words were available to define her mother. How did that happen? How come Kari hadn't noticed that before?

Her mother was always intrigued that she was such an adventurous woman. But Kari never shared with her mother what had made her so tough—at least on the outside—and so determined to prove her place in the world. She had never confessed that the rumors slung around about her with the neighborhood boys were mostly true. Kari wept to realize she had never asked about her mother's dreams and hopes beyond her maternal role. Temporarily removed from her own personal universe, Kari knew this was her chance to focus her energy on her mother—her last chance.

As soon as she told Kevin she was staying, Kari felt instant relief. They both agreed that he could handle everything at home if she stayed on with her parents a few more weeks—until the end. The hospice nurse estimated that was probably all the time Kari's mother had left.

Kari called Juanita, who offered to arrange for Kari to work out of the Charlotte FBI office. Kari thanked her, but said she wanted to stay close to her mother's bedside. As soon as she finished speaking with Juanita, Kari made one more call, to Everett.

"Hey, don't even think about the case. I have it all under control," he said.

"I know. Do me a favor and don't start any fights with Mitch or Juanita while I'm gone."

"Don't worry. Assistant US Attorney Witless, uh...I mean Whitmore and I will be fine," said Everett. "As for Juanita, I'm planning to do what I always do—stay out of her way."

Kari laughed. "Good plan. And, Ev, thank you. Really. Knowing that you have everything under control at work will allow me to focus on everything I have to do here."

"No problem. Just take care of your mother. Call me if you need anything."

By the time she ended her phone conversations, Kari felt comforted. With her husband and kids on their way home and Juanita and Everett taking care of things at work, she could devote all her energy to making her mother comfortable and preparing her father for his loss.

She had accounted for everything.

***

Two weeks later, still in North Carolina, Kari and her father barely left her mother's bedside. They had increased the dosage of her medications, so that, heavily sedated, she was pain free but barely conscious of her surroundings. Her breathing was labored and her heart rate dangerously low. They had called the rest of the family to let them know it was days if not hours. Her sisters and Kevin and the kids were on their way.

When Kari checked her messages, she discovered one from Brenda Hildebrand. What did she want? Kari barely listened as she played it back, but when she heard panic and urgency in Brenda's voice, she tapped the callback button, worried that something had happened to Everett.

"When are you coming back? I'm sorry to hear about your mother, really. I know you want to be there for as long as you're needed." Brenda spurted out as soon as she heard Kari's voice. "It's just that with you gone, Everett is out or up late into the night."

Kari had no idea what Brenda was talking about.

"Ev's working long hours?" Kari asked.

"With you away taking care of your mom, he's trying to meet all the case deadlines," she said. "I mean he is gone almost every evening doing interviews, and if he's not out, he's at home working on the computer late into the night."

Kari didn't know what to say. It didn't make any sense. There were no case deadlines. Everett told her he was working with Whitmore prepping witnesses for the grand jury or in the office reviewing L&I business-licensing records subpoenaed before she left town. Working late? Kari didn't know what was going on, so she said nothing.

After Brenda rambled on incoherently for almost a minute, Kari finally interrupted her.

"I don't want to be rude, but what do you want me to do? Why did you call me?"

After a long silence, Brenda blurted words Kari never expected to hear.

"He's looking at porn. Last night, I caught Everett looking at porn. When the strange ads started popping up on our computer I thought my son was the one looking at those filthy, disgusting sites. So I said something to Everett, and he said he would have a talk with our son, but I never heard any yelling, and when Everett disciplines our son, it's usually loud. So…"

Kari could feel her blood pressure beginning to climb. "Brenda, Brenda," she said, "I understand that this must be hard for you, but you do know that I'm down here because my mother's dying. Right?"

"Yes. I'm sorry to bother you, but I didn't know who else to call." She continued to cry and blabber about her husband's nocturnal computer habits.

"Why me? Why are you calling me?"

"It's that case he's working on. It's partly your fault."

"What are you talking about?" Kari wanted to blast Brenda for her insensitivity but held off. "Look, Brenda, lots of men and even women watch porn."

"Not my Everett. Every night, after I go to bed, he's up late looking at that filth. Last night I came downstairs and he thought I couldn't tell what he was doing, but I could see what was on the screen," she wailed. "He kept talking to me about working on some report when the whole time I could see exactly what he was doing."

"My mother is dying," Kari repeated slowly.

"In a way, my husband's dying too."

"That's a tad melodramatic, isn't it?" Kari's icy tone at last revealed her anger.

"Oh my God," Brenda sobbed. "I'm so sorry, but he's changed. He's not acting like my Everett."

"Can't his family help you?"

"His parents would be horrified if they knew what he was doing."

"Look, Brenda, things aren't so good here right now. I can't deal with this, but I'll…I'll get someone to talk to him."

"Who?"

"Someone from the squad, someone we can trust." Kari did feel somewhat responsible. She had taken him on his first visit to a strip club.

Satisfied that something would be done, Brenda asked Kari not to tell Everett she had called. "The humiliation would kill him," she said.

Kari agreed and, ignoring Brenda's questions about when she would be returning, quickly hung up the phone.

Not knowing when her mother would take her last breath, Kari resented every second she wasted talking to her squad mate Shawn Lakewood.

"What do you mean you already know he's looking at porn?" Kari asked when Shawn admitted he knew about Everett's new habit.

"First of all, what's the big deal? Who doesn't look at porn? But…yeah. A few of us have caught him."

"You mean at work? Hildebrand's looking at porn on his Bureau computer? What the hell, Shawn? You didn't think I needed to know that?"

"To tell you the truth, no I didn't. Who are you, his mother? And it wasn't his desktop; it was his laptop."

"That's not okay either. It's still Bureau property. What if he's caught misusing a government computer? Did you ever think of that?"

"I thought he was just fooling around. You think he has a problem?" said Shawn. "Wait, how'd you hear about it?"

"That's a whole other story." Kari dodged his question. "Does Juanita know?"

"I doubt it."

"Shawn, I need you to talk to him."

"What am I supposed to say to him? 'Dude, stop looking at porn'?"

"Why don't you give him one of those quarterly Office of Professional Responsibility reports—an OPR that lists what happens to employees who get jammed up for weird behavior and bad conduct? There are always a few cases involving someone checking out porn on FBI computers. Print out one of those for him and highlight those sections."

"I guess I can do that," he said. "You want me to tell him to check in with the Employee Assistance Program? You know…if he thinks he has a serious problem."

"Yeah, that's a good idea. Tell him that too."

"So, when are you coming back?"

"As pissed off as I am at Hildebrand right now, I'd like to say never."

"Damn it. Sorry I forgot to ask. How's your mom?"

Pain and sadness threatened to erupt. "I've got to get off this phone. Take care of that for me. Okay?"

Chapter 31

It was Wednesday, federal grand jury day, and he was bored. All morning long, Everett had been stuck in the waiting area, playing host while Whitmore was inside, leading witnesses through their testimony. He felt like Whitmore's clerk and resented the assignment. If Kari were back from her death watch, would she be expected to just sit out there, twiddling her thumbs?

Everett's jaw clenched as he recalled what had happened earlier that morning. He knew grand jury proceedings were secret. He had signed the 6(e) letter establishing the rules of procedure but assumed he could sit in the back of the room and listen as Whitmore questioned their first witness. When the witness arrived, Whitmore went in to first speak to the jurors and then popped his head out the door to motion for the witness. When Everett attempted to follow behind them, Whitmore laughed and barred him from the room.

"Hey, buddy, you can't come in here. Witnesses only."

"I've been allowed in before."

"You must have been testifying." Whitmore pointed to a chair. "Go sit down. I'll explain it to you when I'm done."

He protested, but Whitmore placed an index finger to his lips and then pushed Everett away from the doorway.

Everett's anger rose. He had not appreciated being shushed and shooed. While the prosecutor and the witness were with the grand jurors, Everett spent ten minutes calling other agents and attorneys to prove Whitmore was wrong.

He wasn't.

Angry at himself for not knowing the rules, Everett seethed for the rest of the morning.

He was alone in the anteroom now. The last witness of the day, a JOLIE extortion victim, was in the next room, recounting his story to the twenty or so ordinary citizens inside. Everett pulled out his cell phone to check his office voice mail. The only message was from that Joe Wilson guy who kept calling for Kari. Her away-message referred all case-related calls to Everett, but Wilson would only say he needed to speak directly to her. He had passed on the message, but Kari told him not to tell him where she was or when she would return.

Suddenly, the door opened and the witness exited. He looked as if he had been crying. Everett handed him the reimbursement forms and showed him where to mail in his parking and any other receipts. At last, he could get out of there. But Whitmore remained inside. What was he doing in there? Everett put his ear to the door of the jury room and realized he could hear everything Whitmore was saying on the other side.

"You've heard from a number of witnesses, and I hope you're seeing a pattern develop here. What you're learning about is a culture of fraud and abuse, promoted by frat-boy indulgences and motivated by greed," said Whitmore. "Now I won't attempt to impeach the entire gentlemen's club and strip club industry, but I will continue to present you with the evidence we've discovered regarding Stuart Sebastiani, the public official who is profiting from bribery and fraud, and Lynette Hampton and Curtis Kincaid, who are responsible for the extortionate operation of JOLIE. Next Thursday, you'll hear from someone who will give you an inside view."

Everett scrambled away from the door just as Whitmore excused the jurors until the following Thursday and they filed out of the room. Whitmore stood in the doorway and grinned. He even winked. Everett wondered why the prosecutor was so giddy. He soon found out.

"Okay, we are ready for the big guns." Whitmore placed his hand on Everett's shoulder. "Call up your boy Leone and tell him he's up next week."

"Ahhh . . ." Everett couldn't think of what to say, what excuse to make about why Leone couldn't testify next week. He instead just stared at Whitmore, fixing his gaze on Whitmore's severe crew cut. He assumed it was a remnant of Whitmore's time in uniform.

"What is up with you?" Whitmore's tone refocused Everett's attention. "I've been telling you for weeks that we were going to need Leone to testify. But first we need to prep him. If you're not gonna call him, I will."

"No, don't do that. I told you, he said he doesn't want to testify." Everett's voice was barely audible.

"So what? Who gives a shit what he doesn't want to do? You get him and his lawyer in my office."

"I'll try again."

"Try? He's been subpoenaed." Whitmore peered suspiciously at him. "You keep bragging about this great rapport you've developed with him. So get him in here. *Now!*"

As he left the room, Everett overheard Whitmore grumble, "That guy's worthless."

***

Everett showed up at Club Friskee II less than an hour after leaving the grand jury room. He nodded to Bill Leone as he settled into his usual booth.

Since Kari had been out of town, Everett had been finding numerous excuses to drop by the club almost daily, convincing himself that he was still conducting case-related informant debriefings. Today was his fourth visit that week. Everett enjoyed his visits with Leone, who teased him unmercifully about his ability to pull off a by-the-book image while gawking at tits and ass.

Just the other day, Everett had overheard Leone bragging to some of his high-profile customers and associates about him. "See that guy there?" he goaded them. "He's an FBI agent friend of mine, and if you try to screw with me, I'll get him to look at your business records." When they asked why Everett was there, Leone recited his favorite response: "I'd tell you, but then he'll have to kill you." He followed it up with a thigh slap and a laugh. His covert presence was busted, but Everett wasn't worried.

Tonight, Everett had a legitimate purpose, and as soon as Leone came over to greet him, he said, "I need to speak with you, in private."

"Sure."

Instead of taking Everett to his office, Leone opened a small door off the main room and escorted him up to a VIP suite on the mezzanine level. As many times as Everett had been in the club, he had never realized that the mirrors that lined the upper sections of the high walls hid a secret room.

He blinked twice in the dim light coming from the wide opening overlooking the room below. Above the window, a neon sign flashed the words "For Your Viewing Pleasure."

Turning his attention to the room's interior and the retro purple-and-gold disco decor, Everett noticed the most prominent feature—the all-glass shower conspicuously placed in the corner of the intimate space. Why hadn't Leone ever offered to bring him up here before, where he wouldn't have to feel so exposed among the regulars?

"Concerned about something?" Leone motioned for them to take a seat on the purple velvet sofa. "What's on your mind, my friend?"

"I have something I need to ask you."

"Sure. What's up?"

"I need you to meet with the prosecutor."

"What the fuck? Not that again." Leone stood and frowned at Everett. "I thought you were handling that. You were supposed to tell him I said fuck the subpoena. I'm taking the fifth."

"He won't take no for an answer. You have to at least meet with him in his office."

"I don't have to do shit."

"Yeah, you do, or else he could compel you to appear before the grand jury and have the judge throw you in jail for contempt of court for the remainder of the grand jury's term."

"Tell him I said go screw himself."

"I can't tell him that."

"Why not? You're always telling me what a know-it-all asshole he is. Now, why would I want to talk to him? Answer me that."

"As a favor...to me?"

"The best thing I can do for you is to stay away. What am I supposed to say if your prosecutor asks me about your visits here?" Leone pressed his face close to Everett's. "You don't want me to lie. Do you?"

Everett withdrew from Leone and knew his friend could see the panic in his eyes.

Leone placed his hand on Everett's shoulder. "Take it easy. Let me get you something to help you chill out." Leone headed toward the door. "Sit and make yourself comfortable."

Everett waited and tried to steady his nerves. From the observation skylight, he gazed down on the floor beneath. He watched the girls work the room, climbing onto laps and tabletops to provide one-on-one entertainment to their customers. He could see the nearly naked dancers performing onstage and appreciated the advantageous angle the higher elevation permitted. He experienced calm in the comfort and seclusion of his clandestine roost.

By the time the door opened and Honey entered carrying a tray of food and sodas, Everett was feeling much better.

Honey smiled sweetly at him as she placed the serving dish down next to the couch.

"Bill got pulled away for a moment. He told me you were having a bad day. Why don't I sit with you while you have something to eat?"

Everett looked up at the beautiful, young hostess and nodded. She was always so kind to him, but they had never had a chance to talk alone.

"Thanks. Everything's all messed up. I need Bill's help to make things right." Everett eyed the food. He had rushed over from the grand jury and hadn't eaten. He took a big bite out of the turkey sandwich she had brought him. He hadn't realized how hungry he was.

"Bill likes you," Honey assured him. "I'm sure if he can help you out, he will."

They chatted as Everett ate. He learned that Honey was her real name. He had always assumed it was a stage name. She told him she had worked as a stripper at another club in Northeast Philly for a few years, but now that she was enrolled in community college and taking business management courses, she preferred to help Bill run the floor.

"With your ambition and brains, being a hostess suits you better," Everett said.

"You think? I am a good dancer too, you know." Honey tossed her long, blond locks from side to side in time with the music of the dance floor below. "Even now, if one of the girls doesn't show up for her shift, I don't mind filling in." She rubbed her fingers through Everett's hair and gave him another one of her sweet smiles. "Can I show you?"

He blushed. Before he could answer, she pushed herself up from the couch and slid the tray across to the end of the table. Maintaining eye contact with Everett, Honey crawled onto the low table that now doubled as a stage and began to dance.

Everett didn't say a word, even as she deftly disrobed from her minidress and knelt before him in only a push-up bra and tiny thong. Honey took his silence as a sign to continue, and she mounted his lap and rubbed against him. She braced herself against the back of the couch and used it to support her movements. He could feel her lovely body as she rotated her pelvis against his, grinding and humping to a sexy, rhythmic pulse. Everett had always adamantly refused the many lap dances offered to him, but this time he was comatose, frozen with indecision. He closed his eyes and allowed her to continue.

It felt good, euphoric, intoxicating, as if her fruity fragrance was a drug floating up into his nostrils and activating all his pleasure cells. And her so-soft skin against his was a sensation he couldn't resist. *I should tell her to stop.*

Soon, Honey was whispering something in his ear, but he didn't understand what she was saying. His mind was only able to decipher what "I want to be nice to you" meant when she repeated the words as she reached for his crotch and began to unzip his pants.

He didn't stop her.

There was no way for him to calculate how much time went by before a low animal-like grunting brought him back to reality.

"Umph, umph, umph, ummph."

Could those primal noises be coming from him?

Opening his eyes, he was shocked to discover Honey was completely nude. And from the waist down, so was he. She straddled his lap and he was holding on to her midriff with one hand and her butt with the other, thrusting her up and down. And he was inside her.

When...how did that happen?

Everett catapulted forward. He jumped up so violently Honey had to wrap her legs around his hips, press tightly against his torso, and hug his neck and shoulders to keep from being thrown backward onto the hard coffee table. Everett, in panic mode, began to run wildly around the room, a dangerous move with his pants down around his ankles. He wanted to pull them up, but he didn't quite know how to perform the maneuver. He knew she was holding on to him. But he was too afraid to pry her off and risk touching her naked body.

Just as he reached for the doorknob and was on the verge of running out of the room and down the narrow staircase, Honey freed one hand from her death grip and stretched forward to slam the door shut.

"Stop. Stop! What are you doing?"

She loosened her legs from around his waist, uncoupled their bodies, and lowered herself to the floor. She punched her fists against his chest, barring him from exiting the room.

"*You can't go out of here like that!*" she yelled. He looked down. She was right. He yanked up his pants and clumsily buttoned his shirt.

As Everett stared down at the naked woman in front of him, his panic vanished and was replaced by disgust and humiliation. His bottom lip quivered, and he burst into tears.

"Oh my God, what have I done?"

"It's okay. It's okay," said an alarmed Honey.

His whole body shook with shame.

"Please don't cry. It's okay," she repeated softly, leading him to the couch. He allowed her to push him down onto the cushions and raise his legs up so that he could stretch out.

"Let me help you," she said, stroking his damp hair.

They stayed in the room together with Honey kneeling beside him for at least a half hour more, as he waited to regain the strength his shame and self-loathing had drained away.

When he was finally able to pull himself together, he sat up and smoothed out his disheveled clothes. Barely acknowledging her presence other than to ask that she put her clothes on, Everett brushed by Honey and out the door. Once downstairs, he avoided eye contact with anyone as he rushed across the floor of the crowded club and out onto the street.

The subtle breeze of the warm June evening was enough to reactivate his numbed thoughts and feelings. Again, despair took hold of him. Everything had gone awry. Everett unlocked the car and climbed in behind the wheel. Reaching for the key, he noticed his trembling hands. He felt so foolish, so pathetic. As he pulled the car away from the curb, he didn't bother to glance in the rearview mirror at Club Friskee II, even though he knew it would be the last time he would ever see his old hangout and Bill Leone again.

Chapter 32

Kari attempted to reply to e-mails and return voice messages accumulated while she had been away in North Carolina. She had thought returning to the office would be a welcome distraction from the rawness of her grief, but each kind word of condolences from coworkers revived all of the sadness and emptiness she was desperately trying to deaden. Several times during her first day back, she had to slip into the bathroom and hide in a stall to pull herself together. She'd return to her desk, only to be forced to retreat again to the safe haven of the ladies' room by yet another, "I'm so sorry to hear about your mother." Kari wished they would all just send a card.

What a privilege it had been to focus for three and a half weeks on the needs of her mother and father and the funeral arrangements. Now, she had been sucked back into a world where she was responsible for making sure a multitude of people were happy and content. At home, she tended to the family she had temporarily deserted as Kevin, Carter, Casey, and Morgan jockeyed for her attention. At work, it was no different. Both Everett and Whitmore wanted her attention too. They had not played well together while she was away.

But she found another development far more disturbing. Everett had let her know Joe Wilson had been trying to reach her. Within days of her return to the office, her desk phone rang. She picked up but didn't announce herself.

"Agent Wheeler?" asked the caller.

Kari froze. This time she recognized his voice.

"Special Agent Kari Wheeler." He said her title and name slowly, with a touch of mockery. "I'm just calling to wish you a happy Wednesday. It's Joe Wilson. Remember me?"

"What do you want?" Kari craned her neck to peek out above her cubicle. Several squad mates peered in her direction. She waved them off with a gesture of indifference, before ducking down and burrowing into the confined space. Whispering into the phone she asked, "Why have you been calling me?"

"I missed you. As a matter of fact, I thought I would never see you again, and there you were, coming out of the federal prosecutor's office. I recognized you right away. My, my, my. What a surprise it was for me to find out that my mystery insurance agent is really an FBI agent."

"How did you find out who I was? Who did you ask? What did you tell them?"

"Nothing. I just asked who that gorgeous black woman was. My public defender told me. No one knows anything. Yet."

"What do you want?"

"To see you again. We have some unfinished business."

"You're kidding, right?"

"You hurt me. Remember that?"

"Go to hell."

"But you owe me—"

Speaking slowly, Kari overenunciated her words. "I. Don't. Owe. You. Anything."

"You're wrong, sistah. You got to pay to play."

When Kari didn't respond, he asked, "What's your boss's name? Does your supervisor know you pick up guys in strip joints?"

"Are you threatening me?"

"I'm the one who needs to be afraid of you."

"I was defending myself."

"Can we meet somewhere? You want to get together at the Sheraton tonight?"

"Are you crazy?" Kari gripped the phone receiver like a club capable of smashing Wilson and his disingenuous words into bloody little pieces. "If I ever see you again, I'm going to kick your ass a second time."

"Whoa, now who's threatening who?"

"Do you really think you're going to get away with calling into the FBI office to threaten a special agent? Around here, we call what you're doing blackmail. That's a crime, you know."

"I'm so scared," Wilson said, his tone darkening.

"Really? Did you know incoming calls are recorded? All calls can be traced. You're not calling from your personal cell phone, are you?" It was more a challenge than a question.

Wilson was silent for a second or two. Then he hung up.

Kari leaned back in her chair, frozen with fear. She hadn't asked him why he was at the USAO with his lawyer. She would have to do her due diligence and run his name through NCIC to find out who and what she was up against. She knew it wouldn't be the last time she heard from Joe Wilson.

Kari did her best to compose herself. She checked the time. It was grand jury day and Adrianne Myers, the stripper from Sugar Lips, was scheduled to testify that morning. Kari left her cluttered desk to walk over to 9th and Market, where the federal proceedings were held. She would have to deal with Wilson later.

***

Adrianne greeted Kari cheerfully as she entered the waiting area.

"Hey there, Kari. They told me you were out of town. How's your mother?"

"She died," Kari replied flatly.

"Oh, I'm sorry to hear that." Adrianne's words seemed misplaced with her ever-present smile.

"Thanks."

She pointed toward the closed door of the grand jury room. "So, what am I in for today?"

"Nothing to sweat about. Just go in and tell your story. I think you'll have a good time."

For many of the grand jurors, Adrianne would probably be the first stripper they had ever met. They were in for a special treat. She looked the part, unsuitably dressed in low-rise pants and the tiniest of T-shirts with "I Just Did It" under the familiar swoosh logo. Her taut, tanned midriff was exposed and her belly button was bedazzled with a shiny diamond.

Kari looked around the small room and out into the hallway. "Where is everyone?" she asked.

"The lawyer guy, Mitch, is in there talking, warming them up for me." Adrianne pointed at the entrance to the grand jury room. "And that agent friend of yours ran out of here right before you came in. I think he's afraid of me or something."

"Oh, I doubt that," Kari said, laughing.

"He looked different."

"It's his new haircut."

"That's not what I meant. He looked scared. He wouldn't even talk to me."

Shortly after Whitmore had escorted Adrianne inside to testify, Everett returned. While the agents sat in the waiting area, laughter and chuckles filtered out from the adjoining room. The jurors were enjoying the scandalous witness before them.

"Who's next?" Kari knew Whitmore liked to fill the day with as many witnesses as the schedule would allow.

"No one."

"No one? What happened to Bill Leone? I thought Mitch said he wanted him to come in today?"

"Nah. I tried, but he won't come in. I told Whitmore to just drop it." Everett turned away and straightened papers on the sign-in desk.

"Just drop it?"

"Not you too?" Everett sighed deeply. "Please, you have to trust my judgment on this. Leone is my source. I'll keep talking to him, but for now, we need to move on." Everett acted as if crossing Leone off the witness list was a done deal.

Adrianne was right. Everett was scared, but about what? Kari had been so self-absorbed that she had paid little attention to how the case was affecting Everett. What was the deal with him and Leone?

***

Later that afternoon, when Kari informed Whitmore that Everett still hadn't scheduled Bill Leone to appear before the grand jurors, they decided to take matters into their own hands. Kari called Leone.

"Of course I remember you," said Leone as soon as she identified herself. "Where have you been? You calling 'cuz you miss me?" He chuckled, but when she didn't respond he added, "Is my buddy okay?"

"If you mean Agent Hildebrand, he's fine." Kari steadied her tone. *What a sleaze.* She knew if she wanted his cooperation, she had to be civil. "Did he give you the grand jury subpoena?"

"Yeah."

"And did he let you know that the prosecutor wants to set up a time to run through the questions with you?"

"Yeah."

"Look, we don't have time for games."

"Who's playing games? I'll come in. When and where do you want me?"

What? She hesitated for a beat before saying, "Hold on." She placed her hand over the receiver and whispered, "Tomorrow at ten?" Whitmore nodded.

Leone agreed to bring his attorney with him to the United States Attorney's office the following day. Everett was not invited.

***

The next day, when she and Whitmore met with Bill Leone and his attorney, Kari was blindsided by what he told them. At first, she didn't believe a word of it. But when he bragged that he had sent Everett to his stylist and paid for his fancy new haircut, she knew there was some truth to what he was saying. Kari wished she could stuff into a box everything Leone was telling them about Everett, seal it up tight, and bury it someplace until she could speak with her co-agent. Instead, at Whitmore's insistence, she reluctantly stopped the interview long enough to notify Juanita Negron, who ran over to sit in on the debriefing.

Once everyone was settled at the conference table, Juanita took over before Whitmore could resume the interview.

"I understand you've implicated Agent Hildebrand in prohibited behavior." Juanita smiled at Leone, making no attempt to mask her pleasure. Kari felt her stomach flip.

"Is that what I did?" Leone glanced around the room. "I only mentioned that Ev's been popping into Club Friskee II four or five nights a week."

"To debrief you?" asked Whitmore.

"What do you think?" Leone glared at the prosecutor. "He's checking out the strippers, of course."

Whitmore folded his arms across his body and returned Leone's gaze.

Kari, suspecting that Everett had shared his feelings about Whitmore with Leone, reached out to touch the prosecutor's arm, her signal for him to pull back. Everett was in enough trouble. They didn't need to make it worse with a good cop, bad prosecutor routine.

"But he also comes in to see you about official business," said Kari.

Leone shook his head. "We ran out of official stuff to talk about months ago."

"But you're his informant," Kari said.

"I don't like that term. I consider Agent Hildebrand…Everett, a friend."

"So what has Hildebrand gotten out of this friendship?" Whitmore asked, continuing to push hard.

Juanita added, "I understand you comped him admission, food, drinks—"

Kari corrected Juanita. "Everett doesn't drink alcohol."

"She's right. He doesn't." Leone smiled slyly. "But that's about the only thing he turned down. If you know what I mean."

"No, we don't." Whitmore made a dismissive gesture. "Why don't you tell us?"

Leone rubbed his chin and smiled. "Let's just say Everett's like a big, old bumblebee. He loves Honey." Leone flicked out his tongue.

"Ew. Stop that." Kari was in no mood to put up with Leone's crude antics. "What exactly are you accusing Everett of doing?"

"Honey, my assistant—he's screwing her. Agent Wheeler, you've met Honey. Can you blame him?"

"He's having sex with one of your strippers?" Juanita turned to Kari. "Did you know anything about this?"

Kari answered no. If she had known, she wasn't sure what she would have done. She would be the last person to point an accusatory finger at Everett.

"Is that why he wouldn't schedule you for grand jury?" Whitmore pounded the table, startling them all. "Did you threaten to expose him?"

"I was looking out for him. I didn't want to get him in trouble."

"Kiss my ass, Leone," said Whitmore.

"I see why Everett doesn't like you." Leone wagged his finger at the prosecutor. "But anyway, under the circumstances, I'm not so sure it's a good idea for me to appear before the grand jury."

Whitmore looked as if he wanted to grab Leone and choke him.

"Was this your plan from the beginning?" asked Kari. "To set up Agent Hildebrand so you wouldn't have to testify against Sebastiani?"

"What?" Leone sat back in his chair and clasped his hands together behind his neck. "You think I did this on purpose?"

Leone had beaten them at their own game. He had succeeded in ratting out his friend without anybody ever finding out. Stuart Sebastiani would continue believing slimy, conniving Leone was a stand-up guy.

Kari glared at Leone. *Well played, shithead.*

Chapter 33

All weekend long, Everett had had a feeling of foreboding. Driving into the office on Monday morning, he fought the relentless urge to turn the Grande Prix around and return home. When he finally arrived at the FBI office and walked up to his cubicle, he knew his premonition had been valid. The first thing he noticed was that his computer had been removed and case documents he had left on his desk were missing. He felt a cold prickle up and down his spine.

The next thing he knew, Juanita Negron and Peter McPherson, the supervisor of the FBI's Regional Computer Forensics Laboratory, were standing next to him. Placing his hand firmly on Everett's elbow, McPherson directed him to follow them.

Everett was then escorted to the office of Assistant Special Agent in Charge Robert Dorsett, who was responsible for all administrative matters in the division. Supervisors Negron and McPherson reported directly to ASAC Dorsett. Everett's heart pounded and sweat flowed from his pores as he learned from the three administrators that, based on the allegations of Bill Leone, they were initiating an administrative inquiry against him.

"Agent Hildebrand, in that this is an administrative inquiry, you understand that you do not have the right to refuse to answer our questions?" Dorsett gave him a sidelong glance.

Everett swallowed hard and nodded.

"You can consult with an attorney, but he or she cannot be with you in the room when we take your official statement—close by if you want to step out to speak with him, but he can't represent you during—"

"I guess I should talk to my father too." As soon as he said the words, the gravity of the situation struck him hard and he audibly gasped. *Oh God! My father. I can't tell my father.*

He could feel all eyes on him. They knew his father would not take the news of his humiliating downfall well. He avoided their scrutiny and glanced down at his hands.

"Yes, of course." Dorsett laid his hand gently on Everett's shoulder. "You should definitely discuss this with him."

The allegations included misuse of his official position, misuse of a government vehicle, improper relationship with an informant, acceptance of gifts from a prohibited source, unprofessional behavior, and sexual misconduct. "That's a lie!" *Oh my God! Brenda. If she learns the truth, it will kill her.* "I haven't had sex with anyone other than my wife. That's a lie."

"Agent Hildebrand," said Juanita. "Let me warn you not to try to deceive us. You have enough to worry about. Here's your chance to avoid a lack of candor charge."

"I'm being charged?"

"We told you. This is an administrative inquiry." Dorsett sighed. "The Office of Professional Responsibility investigation will determine what integrity guidelines you violated."

"OPR is involved?" OPR was the FBI's version of Internal Affairs.

When they made him turn over his weapon, credentials, access badge, laptop and Bureau car keys, Everett almost fainted.

"Am I being suspended?" His heart skipped a beat or two. He knew it was a stupid question, but he asked anyway. He needed to hear it out loud before he could begin to process what was happening, what he had done.

"Yes, you are suspended. You are not allowed back in this building until we contact you to come in and provide your sworn statement."

Everett blinked back tears but regained his composure before he spoke. "Can I get Kari Wheeler to drive me home?"

"Absolutely not," ASAC Dorsett groaned and shook his head. "And unless you want us to add an obstruction of OPR process to your troubles, I strongly advise you not to contact Agent Wheeler or anyone

one else connected, even remotely, to G-Sting. Are we clear on that?"

"Yes, sir," he said sheepishly.

"So, can we give you a ride home or did you want to call your wife?" Dorsett asked.

"I need a ride." Everett added, "Thank you, sir."

***

Arriving in the squad area shortly after Everett had been escorted to the front office, Kari learned he was with Juanita and Pete McPherson. This was not a promising development. When she saw his personal items had been cleared from his workstation, her throat tightened. She stayed close to her desk throughout the morning, but neither Everett nor Juanita returned.

Kari's worry reached maximum level when she logged on to her computer and read the e-mail sent from the SAC's office to the entire division. With the subject line "Security Message," the message simply read, "On this date, Special Agent Everett S. Hildebrand was suspended from the rolls of the FBI and no longer has security access to FBI space."

That's all it said, nothing more.

Why hadn't she seen the signs that he had lost control? Of all people, she should have been able to recognize what was going on. How much trouble was he in? How would it all affect the investigation? Would they find out about her transgressions? Joe Wilson had already threatened to expose her. Was she next? When Kari called Whitmore to tell him about the message, he expressed little concern.

"Don't worry," Whitmore assured her. "Hildebrand's lack of restraint is not about to derail this investigation. But you know what this means, don't you?"

Whitmore explained they wouldn't be able to use any evidence obtained solely by Everett, not just what Leone had told him. All of Everett's work was tainted.

"The first thing a good defense attorney does is to attack the investigation and those responsible for it. The defense would love to hear about Everett's strip club hanky-panky bullshit."

"But we don't even know if any of what Leone said is true. Shouldn't we wait to hear from Everett?"

"The law is clear, Kari." Whitmore cleared his throat. "*Giglio v United States*. The court ruled even if allegations of misconduct are part of a pending disciplinary review, if the information is serious and could impact the credibility of law enforcement personnel, I have to disclose it."

"But who's to say Everett didn't do whatever he did because he was trying to get Leone to testify?"

"Come on. Be real," Whitmore said. "We can't expect a jury to believe that Ev can pleasure himself at strip clubs and then investigate the industry with no cost to his effectiveness, his integrity."

"Is that similar to the pleasure you're getting out of all this?" Kari's words came out more harshly than she intended.

"Excuse me? Where did that come from?" asked Whitmore. "I'm just being practical."

"I'm sorry. I know that." Kari sighed. "But we haven't heard Everett's side yet. You shouldn't judge him." What she really meant was she didn't want Whitmore to judge her.

"We both know there's at least some truth to all this. Why else did Everett refuse to bring Leone in to testify?"

"I should have kept a better eye on him."

"Now don't start with the guilt trip," counseled Whitmore. "This is not your fault, nor is it mine."

Kari and Whitmore would have to spend the next two weeks reading through all the interview reports and memos prepared by Everett and isolating evidence that only he could introduce. If he wasn't called to testify, they wouldn't have to divulge his associations with Leone and Honey. But Kari realized she would have to recontact witnesses and write up new reports, invalidating and expunging Everett's contributions to the investigation.

Initially, she resented the file-purging work until she came across the license tag report she had had run on Joe Wilson the night she followed him to the Sheraton. There it was, pointing an accusatory finger back at her. She found the paradox jarring. She had wrestled with the same carnal temptations as Everett. And now, his failures threatened their investigation and his career. Why him and not her?

Chapter 34

Everett Hildebrand hadn't looked at porn since his suspension a week earlier. What used to calm him and give him pleasure was now the source of his torment. He wallowed in a black hole of self-loathing, submerged in inescapable guilt.

"Ev? Everett?"

He looked up from the couch at Brenda. He had been languishing in the same spot since the kids had left for school. The effort required to keep up the charade of normalcy when they were around zapped him of energy.

"Why don't you get up and come with me to the store?" Brenda's face revealed the concern behind her upbeat tone. "We can pick up a few things and maybe go around to that new eat-in deli for a sandwich. Wouldn't that be nice?"

"Brenda, I can't." He tried but was unable to flash her even a weak smile. "I'm not ready." How could he go out in public? He couldn't even move off the couch.

Brenda dropped her keys in her purse and placed it on the table. "Okay. I'll go when the kids get home."

"*Just go.*" He flung his hands in the air. "You don't need to be afraid to leave me alone."

She stood next to the couch and looked down at him. "We can't just do nothing. You need to get help."

The lost look on her face was enough to set him off again. The sadness didn't waft over him. It erupted. And for the umpteenth time since he learned he had been suspended, he sobbed so violently his whole body shook. Brenda sat beside him and stroked his damp hair away from his face. He didn't deserve her. She had believed him when he said he "did not have sex with that stripper." And she forgave him when he finally admitted he had.

Just like all the other times before, he eventually calmed himself and wiped his clammy face with the back of his trembling hand.

"See why I can't leave the house yet? The deli clerk would have asked if I wanted mayo or oil and kaboom! Off I go again." This time, he managed to squeeze her hand and form his lips into an unconvincing smile. "I'll be okay. I promise you I'll be right here"—he patted the cushion—"when you get back."

She picked up her purse, backed up slowly, and blew him a kiss over her shoulder as she turned and headed toward the garage door. He began to cry again as soon as he heard the car start down the driveway.

He cried when he thought about Brenda and the kids. He cried when he thought about his FBI career. And he cried when he thought about his dad. The proudest he had ever made Assistant Director Hildebrand was at his FBI Academy graduation, when his father had handed him his special agent credentials. Everett had accepted long ago that his father was a reserved man who didn't know how to celebrate a person's character and individuality, only their deeds. That's what made it impossible for him to face and accept what he had done.

His cell phone buzzed. It was his brother, J. T. It was the second time he had called that day. Everett let it go to voice mail.

During the eight days since his suspension, he had avoided no less than five calls from his brother and three from his mother. He hadn't spoken with anyone from his family and begged Brenda not to answer any of their calls either. But since the FBI network surged from office to office and extended to the Society of Retired Agents, Everett knew he wouldn't be able to hide his mess from his brother and his father for long.

A real possibility that he would be forever stripped of the title of Special Agent existed and his sense of self had collapsed completely, like the violent implosion of a high-rise building. He had wanted to be an FBI agent since he was a child. And now that the Bureau had abandoned him, he didn't know who he was.

The moment when Juanita had demanded his FBI credentials and gun replayed in his head again and again, along with one thought: *I'm nobody now.*

His phone buzzed again, and this time it was a text from J. T.: BEEN TRYING TO CALL YOU GUYS. MOM TOO. WORRIED. ABOUT TO DRIVE DOWN AFTER WORK. *Oh crap.* What if J. T. was serious about coming by to check on them? He had to stop him.

It took every ounce of strength left in his drained and damaged spirit to return the call.

"Hey, where you been?" said J. T. as soon as the call connected. Everett felt guilty when he heard the relief and excitement in his brother's voice. "What? You're too busy to talk to your family?"

He cleared his throat and hoped he could disguise his depression enough that his brother wouldn't detect that something was off.

"The kids had games, helping with homework. You know, life happens." He tried not to sound dismissive, just busy.

"You'd better call Mom. She's the one who was worried about you. She was going to send Dad over."

"Can you call 'em and let them know we're fine?"

"Ahhh...no. It's your turn to play twenty questions."

"About what?"

"About why you guys weren't answering your phones."

"Like I said, just busy." His head throbbed.

"Dad was also asking about some agent in the Philly office? What's going on down there?"

"What?" He let out a gasp as his stomach clenched tight, as if someone had reached in and squeezed his guts.

"If the rumor made its way to dad, you must have heard too."

"I haven't heard anything," he said with a cautious tone.

"Some pervert in the Philly office was caught looking at kiddie porn at work on his office computer. You know the guy?"

Everett let out the breath he hadn't realized he was holding. The rumors weren't about him. He wasn't the pervert. "No. I don't know what you're talking about."

"That's strange. Dad didn't get a name. You at work? Ask somebody." J. T. paused for a beat, but when Everett didn't respond, he continued. "I thought you'd know who I was talking about."

"Why would I?" He wished he hadn't returned J. T.'s call. He didn't need to hear about some agent's deviant acts. He had problems of his own to worry about. He was exhausted and jittery and he needed to rest.

"Because he's in Philly and it sounds like he was working on the same case you were. They say he was also having sex with the witnesses, dancers in the strip clubs under investigation."

He froze with confusion. "They're saying the kiddie-porn guy was also the strip-club agent?"

"Yeah. I thought you said you hadn't heard anything."

Everett's mind was racing. Sidetracked by his thoughts, he didn't reply. He was further distracted by Brenda returning home. He pointed to his cell and mouthed to her that J. T. was on the line. He was about to raise a finger to his lips when she shouted out hello.

"Is that Brenda?" Everett could hear the confusion in J. T.'s voice. "Are you home? I thought you said you were at work?"

"Hhhhold on." His throat felt raw and tight.

"Ev, wait. What's going on?"

He croaked out his words. "Let me ccccall you back."

"No, no. Don't hang up. Are you in trouble?"

Panic flooded him. He was drenched with sweat.

"Everett, what's going on? Everett?"

"It wasn't child pornography. Why are they saying that?" He was speaking haltingly now. He tried to catch his breath, but he couldn't take in air. His heart pounded as adrenaline surged through his body and he was overtaken with immobilizing fear. He grabbed his chest. He felt as if he was going to die. Brenda snatched the phone from him.

"J. T. *Oh my God.* I think Ev's having a heart attack."

Chapter 35

With Everett's suspension, everyone on the corruption squad had been helping out when they could, but as the G-Sting investigation progressed toward indictment, the workload demanded another dedicated agent. Kari chose Becca Benner. She didn't usually work with women, but she didn't need to have another partner ensnared by the temptations of a nudie bar. Even though she knew Becca was a lesbian, she hoped strippers weren't her thing.

They were hanging out in the squad area, making plans to hit the streets and conduct a few key interviews. Kari looked up from her desk just as Shawn peeked inside the plastic grocery bag lying on the file cabinet and plucked out a large cucumber.

"Who brought these in?"

"I did," said Kari. "Compliments of the gardens of the Wheeler-Jackson estate."

"Sliced up with vinegar and oil." Shawn made a cutting motion with his finger. "Mmmmm. Thanks."

"Do you seriously want your wife to see that one?" Becca asked from across the room. "You might want to downsize your selection."

Shawn eyed the cucumber with mock amazement. "Good call. You're single. Why don't you take this one home?" He tossed the cucumber to Becca, who caught it with one hand. She laid it down gently and backed away with mock trepidation.

"Oh, I'm sorry." Shawn pressed his hand against his mouth and raised his eyebrows. "I forgot that's not your thing."

"No harm, no foul," said Becca.

Kari appreciated the lightheartedness and joking. She was deep into the grind of witness prep and grand jury testimony and welcomed the respite.

Rebecca "Becca" Benner had even less time in the Bureau than Everett, but she had already proven to be an excellent investigator. A pretty brunette in her midtwenties, she had graduated from college with a dual degree in international studies and Dari, the Persian dialect spoken in Afghanistan. At only twenty-four, she had been the youngest recruit in her academy class. Upon completing the twenty-week training course, she assumed she'd be assigned to investigate federal and private-sector funds earmarked to rebuild Afghanistan, which had been instead diverted to support the Taliban. But when she arrived in Philadelphia, instead of the Joint Terrorism Task Force, she was assigned to fight fraud on the public corruption squad. A true team player, she accepted her assignment but helped out the JTTF whenever they needed her expertise.

"Someone's calling you." Becca pointed to the phone shimmying on Kari's desk.

"Hello?" She placed her hand over the mouthpiece and whispered to Becca and Shawn, "Its Juanita."

"That can't be good," Becca mouthed back with a vigorous shake of her head.

Kari shrugged. After only a fraction of a second on the call, she hung up.

"What did our supervisor want?" Becca asked. "You two BFFs now? Was she calling to give you fashion tips?"

"Uh, not exactly. I've been summoned to the SAC's office. Juanita didn't sound happy." Kari gathered her reading glasses, a notepad, and a pen. Glancing back woefully at her colleagues, she began a hasty trudge to "mahogany row"—the enclave of the SAC and his front-office staff.

Kari wiped her palms on her blazer and proceeded into the room, half expecting Joe Wilson to be on the other side of the door. Instead, she was greeted with awkward glances from SAC Roeder, Juanita, and Brenda Hildebrand. *What's Everett's wife doing here?* She quickly answered her own question. No doubt Everett's father had something to do with Brenda's special audience with the special agent in charge.

"Come in, Agent Wheeler. Have a seat." SAC Roeder motioned to a place on the couch next to Brenda. "You know Mrs. Hildebrand, don't you?"

"Yes, of course. We've met a few times when I have been working with Ev. How's he doing?"

Brenda stared at Kari with cold, glassy eyes. "You mean other than his almost daily panic attacks?"

"Kari, Mrs. Hildebrand says she called you and told you Everett needed help, and you did nothing," said SAC Roeder. "Is that correct?"

"When?" She sat near the edge of the cushion with rigid posture. "I'm not sure what you're referring to. I haven't spoken to Everett since—"

"She tells us she called you when you were out of town visiting your parents."

"I wasn't visiting them," Kari said tightly. "I was caring for my dying mother." She explained she hadn't known Everett was having trouble adjusting to the case assignment until Brenda called. "I did what I could, but at the time, I was in no position to help. My mother died later that day."

"You should have called me," said Juanita. "I could have gotten him some assistance."

"That's a joke," Brenda snapped at Juanita. "You've always hated Everett." She turned to Kari. "But she was his partner. If she had gotten him some real help, he wouldn't be in trouble now."

"What was it you wanted Agent Wheeler to do?" asked Roeder.

"I told her I thought Everett was addicted to porn. And all she did was sneak around and take his flash drive collection of smut out of his desk drawer. How was that supposed to stop him? He told me he just downloaded more."

Juanita jerked around to face Kari. "Agent Hildebrand was looking at porn in the office and you knew about it?"

"Wait a minute, wait a minute," Kari said. The meeting was turning into a witch hunt. "I don't know anything about anybody removing porn from Everett's desk."

"I want to know what's going on here." Juanita pointed her finger at Kari. "If you're lying, you're in as much trouble as Hildebrand."

"My husband is not the bad guy!" Brenda yelled. "He's the victim here. All of you should be ashamed!"

With a raised fist to punctuate her words, Brenda lashed out. "You were the ones pressuring him to go to strip clubs and talk to whores and whoremongers, and now you want to punish *him* because *he's* dirty and soiled." She shook her head. "I don't think so. If he's polluted, you polluted him."

"It was part of his assignment," Juanita attempted to explain, "to interview witnesses at gentlemen's clubs—"

"Strip clubs. Don't you dare use that banal terminology. They're strip clubs!"

"Other agents conducted interviews in those clubs too, including Agent Wheeler," SAC Roeder said, trying to explain the situation to Brenda Hildebrand.

"Everett isn't like them." With contempt, Brenda tilted her head toward Kari. "Those clubs were unfamiliar environments to him. He didn't belong there. It was like sending him out on an undercover assignment with no support."

"I'm not following you," said Roeder.

"When an agent goes undercover, don't you assign someone to make sure he stays connected to his true identity?" asked Brenda. "What happened to my husband's handling agent, his psychological prop, his lifeline to the real world?"

SAC Roeder hesitated before nodding his head. "There's some truth to what you're saying."

"What?" Juanita said. "That's nonsense. This wasn't some kind of dangerous assignment."

Brenda rose from the couch. "*You* have no idea what you have done to him. You've destroyed him and everything he stood for. *You ruined him!*"

As Brenda screamed the words, Kari pictured an emasculated Everett sitting in a dark room, staring into space.

"You're not getting away with this. If the Bureau continues to persecute my husband for falling into a pit of pornography and smut, I swear I'll make sure the whole world knows who led him right up to the edge of that pit and did nothing as he fell in and slipped under."

"If it's really not his fault," Juanita said, standing up to face Brenda, "your husband will have his chance to explain that to the OPR investigators." Juanita placed a hand on her hip and mimicked Brenda's intonation. "He can let them know that the devil made him do it."

"How dare you! I'll go to the media. I'll tell them the whole story."

"Who do you think you are? Coming in here and threatening—" Before Juanita could finish her sentence, SAC Roeder cut her off.

"Supervisor Negron, *sit down*! I don't believe Mrs. Hildebrand was threatening anyone. She's expressing her opinion."

Juanita plopped down heavily in her chair. Her tight face signaled she was furious, but Roeder had declared Brenda Hildebrand off-limits. Juanita glared at Kari, who decided to become almost invisible in the battle room. She kept her mouth shut and tried not to get hit by shrapnel.

"I must add, Mrs. Hildebrand, that I really don't believe the media would be interested in reporting about this situation." Kari understood his comment to be a warning and not a simple observation. The FBI doesn't like to hang out their dirty laundry. They leave that to the Secret Service.

Once Brenda had her say, SAC Roeder thanked her for coming in, told her that someone from OPR would be in touch, and called in his administrative assistant to escort her out.

As soon as Brenda left the room, Roeder cautioned Kari and Juanita, "This situation is going to be problematic. I've already received a call that the director has been briefed."

"The director?" Juanita repeated with disbelief.

"It appears Everett's father still has friends in high places," said Roeder.

"But Everett abused his position." Juanita sputtered out a list of his sins. "He engaged in sexual misconduct while on duty, and he—"

Roeder raised his hand to cut her off. "He took the new Bureau car before *you* had a chance to assign it," he said. "Yes, I heard about that. Get over it."

***

Once dismissed, Juanita vacated the front office several paces ahead of Kari. The squeaky sounds of her sensible OrthoWalker shoes bounced off the walls. With each pounding step, Kari could feel her fury. Then, Juanita stopped suddenly and, arms folded across her chest, waited until Kari caught up.

"I think you know exactly what Brenda Hildebrand was talking about. Hiding evidence is obstruction of justice. If you were involved in taking stuff out of Everett's desk, I'll find out." Juanita leaned in close to Kari. "This isn't over."

Chapter 36

Bribery and kickback cases required witnesses who were willing to testify. Signed receipts and promissory notes did not exist. Lately, wherever Kari ventured out to conduct interviews, telltale signs— the cautious demeanor of the witnesses, their guarded responses to questions—indicated that Sebastiani had gotten to them first. Obstruction of justice would be yet another count in the indictment.

When Kari and Becca visited Dollar Express and Loan, a West Philly pawn store, they met Lawrence Wright, one of the people prepared to fib for his friend.

According to L&I records, Wright, the owner of the shop, needed to make a code violation go away, and Sebastiani had intervened on his behalf. A three-thousand-dollar diamond necklace was rumored to be involved in the deal. Driving through the West Philly neighborhood, Kari easily spotted the cramped little storefront located off Market Street near the El tracks. A huge, orange-and-red neon sign depicting winged dollar bills circling a chubby little cartoon bald man advertised the pawn, check cashing, and short-term "payday" loan services of the storefront.

Becca parked the Bureau car in the closest open space. A young man leaning against the front of the building watched as they approached him and slipped into the pawnshop just ahead of them. Once inside, they were greeted by a short, overweight, and balding fellow in his late sixties who unbolted the inner door that kept the public on one side of the bulletproof glass of the service counter.

"Can I help you young ladies?" he said, standing in the doorway.

"Are you Lawrence Wright?" Becca asked.

"That's me. Come on in. We can talk back here."

Kari glanced at Becca and smirked. Sebastiani must have already gotten to him. Wright hadn't asked them who they were or to display credentials? What safety-conscious check casher invites complete strangers to splinter his security defenses?

Once in his office, Kari and Becca identified themselves and held out their badges for inspection.

"We're here to check out a rumor about a gift you gave to Stuart Sebastiani," Kari said, jumping right in. Wright knew why they were there. Why play games?

"A gift? I don't think so. I don't know him like that."

"We heard that Mr. Sebastiani often brags about a diamond necklace he received from you in exchange for helping you with a compliance issue concerning that oversized sign you have in front of your business."

"Some of the other shops in the area gave me a ration of shit about getting my sign approved." Wright reacted to his choice of words. "Oh, I'm sorry, ladies. Please excuse my French."

"No problem." Kari smiled. "We speak French too."

"L and I said the sign was an accessory or something like that. It was too bright, too big, but I went through the proper channels, filled out all the required paperwork to get a variance."

"And the diamond necklace?" asked Becca. "You didn't give Mr. Sebastiani a necklace for assisting you with the paperwork?"

"No."

"Do you have any of the paperwork available to show us?" Kari scanned the cluttered office.

"Sure, I keep it in here," he said, patting the only file cabinet in the room. "I just need to find my glasses."

The agents waited as Wright sifted through the stacks of papers on his desk and lifted folders stuffed with forms and documents.

"I have more glasses than I have eyes," he confided. "I got four or five pairs, but I can never find them—the glasses, that is," he rambled, touching his eyes as if to signify that he did indeed know where they were.

When he finally rescued two pairs tangled together beneath a pile of sports magazines, he smiled and turned away from the untidy desk to open the middle drawer of the file cabinet. Wright thumbed through the surprisingly neat files and, reaching into one simply labeled "Invoices," retrieved from the otherwise empty folder a handwritten receipt. He proudly handed it to Kari.

"What's this?" She had been expecting him to hand them a messy file full of L&I forms and documents. She shared the document with Becca.

"The receipt. See right there? It shows Sebastiani paid me for that necklace. I didn't *give* him nothing."

How convenient that the receipt was so easy to find. The date on the form indicated that the alleged transaction had occurred more than two years earlier and that Sebastiani had given him $250 in cash for the expensive piece of jewelry.

Becca, her voice oozing doubt, asked, "He gave you $250 for a three-thousand-dollar diamond necklace?"

"Who said it was worth that? I never had it appraised."

"So how much did you think it was worth?"

"The guy who brought it in said it was worth a grand. I gave him a hundred and Sebastiani gave me $250 for it." Wright rubbed his palms together and grinned. "I made money, so what do I care."

"Can we have this?" Kari waved the receipt.

"Yeah, sure."

"And the other paperwork?" Becca looked at the file cabinet.

"What other paperwork?" Wright answered slowly, as if he thought they might know more. "That's the only thing I sold him."

"What about the paperwork pertaining to the zoning variance Sebastiani helped you with?" Becca tapped her fingers on the top of the steel cabinet. "Are those records neatly filed away in here too?"

"Uh, can you come back next week?" Wright mumbled. "I'm gonna need some time to look for 'em."

Neither agent was surprised. It was obvious Wright had been

coached. After asking him a few more questions, the agents, annoyed by Sebastiani's obvious influence and interference, walked to their car.

Kari handed the receipt to Becca. "Perhaps we should ask Mrs. Sebastiani about that diamond necklace."

Chapter 37

Kari assumed he would attempt to contact her again, but when she spotted Joe Wilson in the lobby of the Federal Building hanging back a bit from the workers heading out to lunch, it spooked her. Now that she knew who he was and what he was into, she didn't want any of her colleagues to see them together.

She motioned for him to follow her into the elevator and down one level into the basement parking garage. Two IRS employees stood in the elevator with them. Kari smiled pleasantly in their direction and, when the doors opened, let them exit first. She then walked out in front of Joe Wilson, talking to him under her breath.

"Don't say anything to me. Don't even look in my direction until we're out of the vestibule and around the corner."

She hurried, never looking back to see if he had heard what she had said or if he was keeping up with her.

"Surveillance cameras are all around here. I know where there's a black-out area."

"That sounds good to me." He let out a naughty chuckle.

"Shut up."

They walked in silence until Kari reached the location and turned to face Wilson.

"I ran your name in FBI indices," she said, leaning on a Bureau car. There had been forty-two references for Joe Wilson, but she was able to narrow the hits down by using his DOB from the license plate registration she had queried after they had left Bustle & Booty so many months ago. She had read the opening serials in his electronic FBI file.

"I know you were working with Saul Prescott. I know that you, Prescott, and the other members of your crew have been charged with conspiracy to traffic and distribute illegal pharmaceuticals imported from India and Mexico. You and Prescott met while in pharmacy school. What a waste of good education."

"You did your homework."

"I know your fate is sealed. Undercover agents and informants purchased hundreds of painkillers from the dirty pharmacies you supplied."

"That's where you come in," said Wilson.

"I've got no stay-out-of-jail cards to hand out."

"You wouldn't do me a small favor? Now that we're friends—"

"We are not friends," she said.

"Don't be so cold. I'm a nice guy. Even you thought so once."

"That was a major mistake."

"I disagree." His eyes swept over her body. "But I need something more important from you now."

"I'm not doing anything for you."

"I need you to retrieve something for me," he said, placing his hand on her shoulder.

She smacked it off.

"I need you to get back a key for me."

"From where?"

"Your colleagues seized it with a bunch of other stuff when they searched our warehouse last month. It was in my partner's office. I need that back."

"You want me to steal evidence? No way."

"You might want to hear me out first."

She shook her head vigorously. "There's nothing you can say."

He crossed his arms. "Really?"

"Don't threaten me."

"Prescott's the violent one. I consider myself to be a lover not a fighter." He grabbed Kari by the waist, but a car entered the garage and drove down the parallel aisle, and he released her. Kari didn't back away but stood so as to block him from view. She couldn't risk having someone driving past recognizing him. They both tried to look inconspicuous until the car was out of sight.

"I don't like being here either." Wilson glanced in the direction of a car pulling into a space several aisles away. "It would be a lot easier if you just gave me your cell phone number."

"Are you nuts? Why would I do that?"

"We wouldn't have to meet in person. Cell calls aren't recorded."

"No, but they can be traced."

He reached under his jacket and pulled out a bright-blue flip phone. "I went out and got me one of these disposal minutes-only phones, a burner."

"Don't waste your time using that to call me."

"Then maybe I'll use it to call your boss?"

"Go ahead. Call my boss. Then they can tack a blackmail charge on your rap sheet."

"How about instead I tell your husband and your kids about your skanky ways?"

Kari went rigid. Her hands curled into tight fists. Her anger choked the silence. She waited until she could control her words before she spoke.

"Don't ever mention my family again."

She had had enough of Joe Wilson and his threats. She turned and headed toward her parking space, her quick footsteps echoing in the dense, underground lot.

"*Hey!*" Wilson called after her. "I'm not finished."

She could feel him catching up to her. "Leave me alone." Her chest rose and fell with each deep breath.

"I can tell you exactly where to find the key. I need you to get it. I have the property receipt from the search."

"Good. Stick it up your ass. I'm done talking to you."

"Before you go, I have something I want to ask." Once more, he reached out and grabbed her around the waist. He thrust his other hand between her legs. "When you gonna let me get some again?"

In a flash, Kari dropped out of his hold and stomped on his ankle. She then rammed him in the nose with her fist. Wilson cried out and brought his hands to his face, staggering a few steps away from her.

"You need to learn to keep your dirty hands off me."

Kari sprinted to her bu-car, jumped inside, and sped away, never bothering to look back at her pursuer. He had infected the only pure part of her life.

How dare he speak about her family!

***

Two days later, on Saturday morning, the soccer fields near Kari's home swarmed with kids in multicolored uniforms. With Kevin, Casey, and Morgan camped out in their portable chairs alongside the manicured turf, Kari cheered Carter's team to victory. Only two minutes inside the first half and she was already up on her feet.

"Watch your angles. Anticipate. *Anticipate.*"

She pointed to another thirteen-year-old crouching low and hopping from one cleat to the other, waiting to take off down the field.

Cupping her hands around her mouth, she cautioned, "Cover the man on your left."

The ball bounced directly in front of Carter. He maneuvered his legs and back to block the other boy and dribbled the ball down the field, passing and receiving until within a yard of the opponent's goal.

Kari held her breath. But the goalie came forward at the last instant and kicked the ball out of bounds.

"*Corner.*"

The referee tossed the ball to Carter, who jogged to the left side of the field to take the corner kick. Kari remained standing, ready to will her boy's foot to send the ball whizzing between the goalposts.

Then she saw him. Right there, standing in the parking lot directly behind Carter. Even with his dark sunglasses, she could feel Joe Wilson staring straight at her. Fury engulfed her. *What was he doing? How dare he show up here!*

"I'm going to the bathroom."

Kevin looked at her as if she was crazy. "Now? We're about to score. Can't you wait until the end of the half?"

"No. I gotta pee."

Kevin shrugged and returned to the play at hand.

Kari hastened toward the snack stand and restrooms. When she reached the building, she glanced toward the field before sneaking around the back, where the dumpsters would hide them from view.

She waited, her heart pounding furiously, knowing Wilson would follow her.

"Good grief, Agent Wheeler." He sniffed the foul air and pinched his bandaged nose as he slipped around the corner and stood by her side. "Couldn't you have chosen a nicer place to chat?"

"What the hell are you doing here?"

"I told you I wasn't finished talking to you."

"And I told you to leave my family out of this." She spoke softly, but her voice was trembling and her stare pierced Wilson's face. She wanted him to feel her fury.

She held her hand over her mouth and nostrils. She hadn't noticed the smell before he'd arrived.

"Do you really think I'm afraid of you?" he said in a heated whisper. "What are you gonna do, throw another sucker punch?"

She was about to tell him she wasn't afraid of him either when she heard Casey and Morgan calling her from the other side of the building.

How would she explain what she was doing behind the dumpster with a strange man? She turned toward their voices with mounting panic. At the same time, Wilson made his move, pinning her from behind. She didn't struggle. He must have known she wouldn't, couldn't fight back as he forced her down to the ground, the fabric of her jeans the only barrier between her knees and the filthy concrete pad on which the dumpsters were parked.

She heard him unzip his pants and her fear and alarm soared. And when he grabbed her hair and yanked her face in front of his crotch, she did what he wanted her to do.

"Mom, where are you?" Casey called. "*Mommmmyyyyyy.*"

"Come on, Casey," said Morgan. "Let's go back to the swing set."

"No. I saw her walk over here. Let's wait until we find her."

Afraid that her daughters would, at any moment, discover them together, Kari made sure her face was shielded by Wilson's open jacket.

Please don't come back here. Please don't find me like this.

Wilson let out a moan, and Kari froze, praying that the twins had not heard him. She could hear the soccer parents cheering in the distance, but she couldn't tell if the girls were still close by.

When Wilson whacked her on the head with his fist, she continued her task in earnest, working fast and hard trying to bring him to climax as quickly as possible, to get it over and done with. How quickly he had summed her up. He knew she cared more about her daughters than she did herself. This momentary humiliation she could endure, but the twins finding her there, on her knees, would be unbearable.

She sucked and pulled with her mouth as noiselessly as she could. The metal teeth of his zipper raked her cheek. She kept her eyes closed and tried not to think about what she was doing. But the situation overwhelmed her and she gagged—not from the stench of the rotting garbage and foul, fermenting spills, but from the mortifying possibility of exposing Casey and Morgan to the pornographic scene occurring right around the corner from where they waited for her. She gagged again.

Wilson bent down low and whispered in her ear, "Don't you dare." He yanked her hair again and smashed her face into his grinding pelvis.

And then it was over.

He glanced down at her and laughed. "Was that good for you too? Did you swallow?"

Kari looked up at him with angry eyes and spit in his face.

"No. I didn't." She wiped her mouth with the back of her hand.

The gunk landed in his left eye, slid down his cheek, and dangled off his chin. She steadied herself as he towered over her. She expected him to whack her in the head again. But instead he lifted his T-shirt to wipe his face.

Then he held out his hand and shook it in her face.

"Give me your phone."

She handed it to him. He dialed his phone, securing her number, and then tossed hers back.

"It would have been easier if you had just given it to me when I asked for it the other day. Then I wouldn't have had to follow you all the way out here to Pleasantville."

Right there with her husband, kids, and neighbors nearby wasn't the place or the time to fight back. "I'm not going to let you get away with this." She glared at him and turned away.

"Oh really?" He nudged her with his knee. "Look at me."

When she raised her head, he took a picture with his phone, her face only inches from his exposed penis. He then placed his palm on her forehead and pushed her backward onto the grimy pavement.

"I'm going to call you later," he said zipping up his pants, "and tell you exactly what I need you to do for me."

He peeked from behind the dumpster and spoke to her over his shoulder. "You might want to slip into the bathroom to clean yourself up. If I see your daughters, I'll send them to the playground to look for you."

"Don't," she hissed. "Don't you go near them."

"I'm not a perv. I won't harm your little girls."

He left her sprawled out on the ground, flicking stale crumbs and dirty bits of paper off her clothes and hair. She was already plotting her revenge.

Chapter 38

She dreamed of killing him.

Each time Kari thought about the incident at the park, she replayed it in her mind differently. In her version, as soon as she spied Wilson standing near the soccer field, she pulled out her gun and shot him. Dead. Just for coming near her family.

Wilson's degrading attack had sent memories bubbling up to the surface, and she had begun to reflect on her past, painful to dredge up since she'd stuffed them down so deep. But the fresh mental picture of her on her knees released it all.

She was only fourteen years old. Her family had moved again, this time to a small army base in Germany. The girls at the new school ignored her. But she and that boy had become fast friends. He let her sit with him and his friends at lunch and she had thought he was kinda cute. She had no qualms about going home with him after school.

When she knelt in front of him with her back to his bedroom door, she heard the others snickering in the hallway.

"You told them?" She looked up at him, tears flooding into her eyes. A tremble ran through her body.

"No." He didn't bother to deny it with conviction. They both knew he was lying. "Can you do them too?"

"How many?" Her voice squeaked out in a frightened whisper.

"It's just the guys. They won't tell anyone."

When he opened the door to the hallway and let them in the room, she didn't believe she had a choice. She didn't believe she could say no.

Afterward, she lay on the shag carpet with her back against the lower bunk and shook so violently the boys were scared that she would tell on them, and so they never told anyone. It was their secret.

She could vividly recall the room's blue-plaid comforter and matching curtains. But she couldn't recall his name anymore. She didn't remember what any of them looked like.

She always thought she deserved what had happened that afternoon. No matter how great her accomplishments, she would always think of herself as a slut. From that point on, her relationships had been purely physical. She had even picked up Kevin in a bar, but he had managed to convince her that theirs was more than a fleeting carnal connection. But she had been faithful their entire marriage—until Wilson. So confident and pulled together on the outside, but inside she was still that scared little girl.

But now, she was dreaming about revenge, about murder. She had always heard that addicts couldn't get sober until they hit rock bottom. If being sexually assaulted while her kids were only yards away wasn't the basement floor of her dark pit, she feared to know what was.

She waited for Wilson to call.

***

She was in the car heading to work when she heard her phone. Her heart raced when she saw his number. She pulled into a parking lot to take the call.

"Hey, Agent Kari Wheeler." He started the conversation as if the other day had not happened.

"Don't you dare act like we're friends, like you didn't just rape me."

"Rape? I was only trying to get your attention."

"Whacking me on the head with a ball-peen would have done the job, but you chose to pull out a sledgehammer."

"You weren't listening to me."

"I'm dreaming about you now."

"Really?"

"Yeah. Fifteen plus one."

"What's that supposed to mean?"

"That's how much I want to shoot you dead." Her right hand

caressed her holstered Glock 23. "I dream of emptying all fifteen rounds from the magazine of my automatic, plus the one in the chamber into your center mass."

"Ouch. You're FBI. You're not a killer."

"Come anywhere near my family again," she warned him, "and I'm *your* killer."

"It was your fault."

"No. No, I didn't deserve that."

"Now you know I'm serious. I need you to get that key back. The log says it's in evidence box D-3. I take it you know what that means. While you're at it, take a look at my FBI file and tell me who's talking and what they're saying."

"I'm not doing that."

"Agent Wheeler. Kari." He said her name with a creepy intonation. "It's all about self-preservation. It's either me or you."

She didn't respond.

"I'm gonna give you some time to think, to reconsider. But I'll be back."

He hung up. But a few moments later, she received a text from him. She shrieked when she saw the photo he had sent her. It was the one he had taken of her kneeling at his feet. She hit delete.

Chapter 39

"I can't believe you talked me into this." Kari swept a wide gaze around the room.

"Had to," said Becca. "It was downright embarrassing working a case about corruption and fraud in the strip club industry and my partner wouldn't let me go inside a strip joint."

"Believe me, you weren't missing anything."

The agents were at Slippery Tales, a strip club in Northeast Philly. The owner, Johnny Bell, had ignored their attempts to connect with him away from the club. Each time they called him, he made excuses about why he was unavailable to meet. And now that they had surprised him with an in-person visit, he claimed to have a pressing matter to take care of before he could speak with them. He asked them to wait a few minutes and escorted them to a table in the front of the room, exactly where Kari did not want to be. She purposely sat with her back to the stage but found it almost impossible to divert her eyes away from the private performances taking place all around her. Since she had nowhere safe to focus her eyes, she focused her thoughts, tapping her foot and drumming her fingers on the tabletop.

It was less than a week after Wilson had viciously assaulted her. Kari had told no one. She had convinced herself she could carry on as if nothing had happened. But like a TV left on in another room, the ugly memories were always playing in the background of her mind, haunting her every thought.

Since Kari refused to watch the dancers, Becca, who didn't seem to mind the wait, provided play-by-play commentary.

"Kari, check her out. She's humping the floor. Okay, now she's bouncing and jiggling her butt cheeks. Oh yeah, make that booty pop, girl."

Becca's effusive review of the dancer helped Kari mask her uneasiness.

"How long do you think she can keep going like that?" Becca asked.

"I don't care."

"Come on. Look. Oh my God, you got to see her back that thing up."

Kari took a sideways glance.

"Do you think I should slip a fiver in her G-string?" asked Becca.

"Don't you dare!"

"You're no fun."

Kari relented and turned to watch the dancer for a beat.

"Her pole dancing skills suck. You and I could do better than that. You know, one day, I'm going to ask Tannie to teach me," said Kari, turning away.

Becca snapped her fingers and moved her head and shoulders to the beat and sang along with the music playing. *"Shake, shake, shimmy, shimmy. Hold up now. Listen to what your daddy say—"*

"Could you at least pretend you're having a terrible time?" Kari said with a humorless smile. "That owner may never come back over to us."

After a several more songs and raunchy routines, Kari checked the time. They had been sitting in Slippery Tales for twenty-seven minutes.

"Where is he?" Kari scanned the room. "Damn it." Although she'd been investigating him for more than seven months, she'd never seen him in person. She tilted her head in the direction of the front door. "Look who just showed up."

With wide eyes, Becca whispered, "Sebastiani?"

She kept her eyes on him as the club owner approached and shook his hand. "That asshole told him we were here."

"So what do you want to do?"

Instinctively, Kari patted the gun holstered at her hip. "Let it play out."

She rejected Sebastiani's nodded greeting and kept her gaze on him as he strutted over to their table. He was as handsome as everyone had said. His eyes were a startling, mesmerizing gray green. His square jaw held his arrogance well.

"Ladies, I'm going to have to ask to see your business privilege licenses." Sebastiani stood over them. He was dressed in a business suit, but his shirt collar was unbuttoned and his tie loosened. "You're dancers, aren't you?"

"You know who we are, Mr. Sebastiani." Kari's eyes met his. She had never met a person with eyes that color before. Then she remembered Tannie's daughter, their daughter, Dia. She was definitely Sebastiani's baby girl.

"Stu. Call me Stu."

"Agent Kari Wheeler," Kari said. "And this is my partner, Special Agent Becca Benner."

He nodded and placed his hand on an unoccupied chair. "Do you mind if I sit?"

Kari shrugged.

"I hear you've been asking about me." He smiled. "Here I am. Under the bright lights." He pointed to a spotlight near the stage. "What do you want to know?"

"Do you have an attorney?"

"Yeah."

"Well, that's the end of this interrogation." Kari pantomimed closing a notebook.

"So what will we talk about?" Sebastiani peered down the neckline gap of Becca's blouse.

"Is there anything you want to ask us?" Becca shifted in her chair.

"Yeah…" Sebastiani's grin was sly and knowing. "How did I get to be so lucky to have two beautiful FBI agents investigating me?"

"Agent Benner, is he hitting on us?" Kari's mouth gaped open with exaggerated bewilderment.

"Agent Wheeler, I think he is."

Kari clasped her hands together, rested her chin on her knuckles, and scowled. "Mr. Sebastiani, if luck's involved, it's bad luck."

"Whoa, I didn't mean anything. I just thought we could try to resolve this misunderstanding."

Sebastiani reached out and touched Kari's arm. She couldn't believe it. How dare he be so familiar with her?

"Misunderstanding? You're the target of a federal investigation." Kari slapped his hand away and began to gather her things. "You got the letter from the United States Attorney's office. Tell your attorney to call us."

Sebastiani shoved his hands in his pockets and retreated a step as Kari abruptly left the table. Becca followed.

"You're leaving?" He looked surprised. "Was it something I said?"

Neither agent responded.

"Hey, I was just playing around. I meant no disrespect."

Kari swung around to face him. "You disgust me."

She watched Sebastiani hesitate momentarily, speechless. Even she was surprised by the vitriol in her tone.

"Are you serious? What did I do to you?" he asked, finding his voice.

"Maybe I'm pissed that my city wage tax pays your salary," Kari said. "Let's go, Benner."

As they neared the front of the club, Kari walked over to the club owner. "You and I, Mr. Bell," she said, wagging her finger at him, "are not done yet."

"I...I...I didn't know he was coming."

"Tell it to the grand jury." She handed him the subpoena she had planned to give him after their interview. "What an asshole," Kari mumbled as she and Becca crossed the club's threshold out into the cool, early evening air.

"Holy cow, Wheeler," said Becca. "What got into you back there?"

"Sebastiani reminds me of someone I used to know. Someone always on the prowl—"

Before she could finish her sentence, Kari felt an unexpected presence, spun, and banged straight into a drunken patron who had staggered out behind them. He wobbled from the impact but managed to remain upright.

"I saw you two watchin' the action in there." His words were slurred. He struggled to focus on the agents with one squinty eye, while he rubbed the bulge in his pants. "How much?"

"How much for what?" Kari asked, slowly enunciating her words. The anger she had felt for Sebastiani was back. Waves of rage were coursing through her veins.

"For the two of you?" He bobbed forward and bumped against her again. He was close enough for Kari to smell liquor and cigarettes on his sour breath.

"Are you grabbing your junk?" Kari used her shoulder to nudge him off her. "Step back. Let me see what we have to work with."

He looked down at his crotch.

"I promise you, if you show me yours," said Kari, "I will definitely show you mine."

The man grinned, unzipped his pants, and reached inside his boxer briefs to free his erection.

"You obviously didn't understand what I meant." Kari pulled her jacket aside and drew her weapon, aiming it at the ground between his legs. Her eyes centered on his crotch.

"Kari." Becca move next to her and spoke softly but firmly into her ear. "This is not funny. Put your gun away."

"Now, listen up. If you don't get away from me," she said, ignoring her partner, "I'll shoot it off. I swear I will."

This time, he received her message loud and clear and, shielding his crotch with his hands, he hastily backed away, stumbled hard, and lost his footing. He fell onto the hard asphalt. With bloodshot eyes, he looked up at Kari and then to Becca. "What's wrong with her?" Suddenly sober, he scrambled to his feet, brushed the gravel off his palms, and stuffed himself back into his pants. "I should call the police," he said.

"Go ahead, shithead. Oh, hell. Let me call for you. 'Cuz I'm wondering if, in your condition, you're going to try and drive home."

"I'm walking.

"Good. Go ahead, then. Walk."

Kari waited for him to cross the parking lot to the sidewalk before she holstered and turned to Becca. "I scared the piss out of that sick bastard."

"What the hell, Wheeler? That wasn't funny." Becca's face was contorted in a look full of fear and shock. "What if your gun had accidentally gone off? You can't play around with a loaded weapon."

"He was. Why can't I?" Kari laughed, but seeing Becca's grim expression, added, "I didn't even have my finger on the trigger." She let out an exaggerated sigh and stared at the artificial-colored lights of the Slippery Tales marquee. "I told you I didn't want to come here."

"I had no idea one visit to a strip club would end up like this."

Kari lowered her head and took in several deep breaths, trying to hold on to her composure, her sanity. She was afraid that she would lose it and crumble in shame.

"It's inevitable," she said quietly, fighting back tears. "You start hanging out in strip clubs, and next thing you know…you're thinking with your genitals and not your brain. Tannie calls it waving your freak flag."

"Who are you talking about? Sebastiani or that guy?" Becca pointed to the man now staggering down the street.

"Maybe I'm talking about me."

"What'd you do?"

"No one's immune."

In that moment, Kari wanted more than anything to tell Becca, to tell anyone, to unburden herself about Wilson. But she couldn't.

"All I'm going to say is from now on, my own freak flag is safely tucked away in my underwear drawer, only to be taken out and unfurled for my husband on special occasions, like his birthday or Christmas." Her lips formed a weak smile.

They both relaxed a little.

As they climbed into Becca's Bureau car, Kari said, "I'm sorry. That was really stupid of me."

"You told me you didn't want to come."

"I can't put myself in this type of situation again. I can't be sure I'll be able to control myself."

"I understand. It's all about this," Becca said and waved high an imaginary flag of her own.

"Girl." Kari took a fleeting and surreptitious look about the lot and lowered Becca's arm. "You better put that away around here."

Chapter 40

"You won't believe who we just bumped into," Kari said as soon as Tannie, wearing a sports bra and short shorts, opened the door to her condo. The agents had called and gone straight there from the Slippery Tales. Kari wanted to tell her in person about their encounter with Sebastiani.

"Stu. He just called and told me."

Becca hesitated in the doorway. "Is he coming over here?"

"Nah. He'd only come here for a booty call. And he knows that's not happening."

"What did he say?" asked Kari.

"He said two hot FBI agents were flirting with him and they—you—might start investigating him because he rejected you. He called it retaliation."

"That's half-right. We do want to get together with him"—Kari raised her eyebrows—"and his attorney. I guess he forgot that part."

"Why did he call you?" asked Becca.

"He said if you came by to see me, I shouldn't talk to you."

Kari held up three fingers. "That's three counts of witness tampering we can prove."

"The fact that two female agents are investigating him is blowing his mind. He's used to women letting him get away with murder." Tannie smiled. "That's just a figure of speech. But Stu does think he's irresistible to all women. I guess I'm the only dummy to fall for his shit."

"Nah! He's right. I want him too." Kari laughed and put her arm around Tannie. "Just not in that way."

Tannie wiped her brow with a hand towel. Kari noticed she was sweating.

"I'm sorry. Did we interrupt your workout?"

"I was almost done." Tannie motioned to the corner of the room.

"Oh, you have a stripper pole." Becca had met Tannie several times before but had never been to her condo. She strolled over and touched the shiny steel. "I heard this is great exercise for the core."

"It's more than that for me." Tannie grabbed on to the pole and spun around. "It's a stress release, powerful, renewing." She looked over at Kari and Becca. "There's this…strength I get from it."

"I believe you," said Kari weakly.

"I'm not sure you do." Tannie climbed up to the top and slid halfway down into an inverted knee hold. "It's like vertical meditation. It's tantric. When I'm pole dancing, I shut out the world, and it's all about me."

Tannie hung upside down, her eyes closed. Her chest and taut belly moved with each deep, rhythmic breath. After a couple of seconds, she slithered down the pole and onto the floor.

"Who wants to try it?"

Becca waved her hand, but Kari shook her head.

"But at the club you said you wanted to learn."

"We can't risk having Sebastiani's defense attorney discover Tannie taught us to work a stripper pole. How would you like to be up on the witness stand describing that?"

"Are you sure, Kari?" Tannie's face displayed her disappointment. "You seem frazzled. If anyone needs a turn spinning on this pole, it's you."

"Maybe later. But right now, me up on that pole would be like Joan of Arc at the stake." Kari stared at the pole and spoke softly. "I look at that thing, and all I can see is Kari Wheeler going up in flames."

***

Back at the office, Kari was about to call Whitmore about the surprise rendezvous with Sebastiani when the phone rang. She almost jumped out of her skin until she realized it was her desk phone and not her cell.

"Agent Wheeler?" the caller asked. "This is Sam Shiffler from the *Philadelphia Inquirer*."

"Did you say the *Inquirer*?" Kari stalled for a few seconds to think. She knew of Shiffler, a thorough reporter who covered the federal courts.

"Yes. Sam Shiffler. I'm a reporter."

"What can I do for you?"

"I understand you're about to indict Stuart Sebastiani on corruption charges. I was hoping to get a comment from you before we go to print with the story."

"I can't talk to you, Sam." Kari wondered who had clued him in about the case.

"That quote is all I need for the article. Consider this a courtesy call. With or without your cooperation, the story's going to run."

If Shiffler only had the Stu Sebastiani part of the investigation, the potential harm was minimal. Their subject knew they were after him, and he couldn't destroy any L&I compliance records. They already had them.

But did Shiffler know about Tannie, the attempts to influence Snyder, or the JOLIE extortion counts? Those aspects of the investigation were still covert. Shiffler needed to be convinced to hold his story. If they didn't want the case splattered on the front page of the paper before they had a chance to indict, Whitmore would have to make a deal.

"Before you file your story, why don't you speak with Mitch Whitmore over at the US Attorney's office. Let me give you his number."

Chapter 41

"I think it's time to pay either Snyder or Yhost a visit," Kari said.

Even though incriminating testimony and evidence had been presented to the grand jury, US Attorney Paul Crystal didn't think they were ready. He had refused to sign-off on the forty-three-page draft indictment until all questions about Councilman Yhost's culpability were answered

"Okay. Which one first?" asked Whitmore.

Kari considered the options. "I vote for Snyder."

"Then Snyder it is."

After several unsuccessful attempts to surprise Snyder at home, Kari resorted to picking up the phone and placing a call to his municipal office.

"Mr. Snyder, we need to sit and chat about your connection to Stuart and Arty Sebastiani," said Kari after identifying herself.

Snyder hesitated a moment before he responded. "Do I need an attorney?"

"You're the only one who can answer that question." Kari was under no obligation to provide him legal advice. She preferred to speak with him before he lawyered up.

They set up an appointment to meet at a local bar, but then Snyder called back. He had retained a lawyer after all. His new attorney recommended a formal proffer session, during which the information Snyder provided could be used against him only if the agents later discovered he had lied.

On the day of the proffer, Whitmore presented Snyder and his attorney with an official letter denoting the conditions of the agreement, including the statement that the government was not offering a plea bargain or immunity.

"My client is prepared to discuss his current predicament with you," Snyder's defense attorney said. "However, Mr. Snyder is not here because he believes he has engaged in any criminally prosecutable actions. He believes he is the victim of an extortion attempt by Stuart Sebastiani and the owners of club JOLIE."

"Really?" said Kari.

"Yes, my client was asked to participate in a scheme to bribe an elected official, and when he refused, he became the subject of a conspiracy to malign his reputation."

"I'm not sure we know what you're talking about." Whitmore glanced at Kari and Becca.

"My attorney is referring to these." Snyder took out a large manila envelope from his briefcase and tossed it onto the table. "There's a video too."

As Kari reached for the envelope, the defense attorney cautioned her.

"I'm not sure if you ladies want to view the photos. They're very racy, very raw. You might find them offensive. Perhaps Mr. Whitmore should look at them first." Before he could push the envelope toward Whitmore, Kari grabbed the packet and held it tightly.

"Over the past year, *this* lady has visited nearly every strip joint in Philadelphia. I think I can handle whatever's in this envelope." Kari opened the envelope and spread the photos out on the table.

The stills captured Snyder and a woman, naked and intimately enjoying each other's company. The two of them, both blond, beautiful, and fit, were pictured in graphic sexual positions. Kari and Becca examined each photo before passing them one at a time to Whitmore to view.

"Impressive." Kari tapped her finger on one particular photo, before sliding it over to Becca. "So, where did these come from?" she asked Snyder.

"Arty set up the date." Snyder rose up in his chair to see which of the photos Kari had admired. "But Stu was the one who gave the envelope to me a few weeks ago. He said if I was the one talking, I should stop, or he would paper the walls of city hall with the photos."

"Talking to who?"

"You guys, I guess."

Craig Snyder told them how Arty Sebastiani, Lynette Hampton, and Curtis Kincaid had recruited and bribed him to persuade Yhost to vote against Finney's no-touch rezoning proposal. He recalled what he could about his visit to JOLIE, although it was "a bit of a blur."

"They paid me to convince Yhost to vote against the legislation. But I knew all along Yhost was voting no, and I would never have to do anything or say anything to him. I saw no harm in scamming them. When Sebastiani caught on, I wanted to come clean, but he demanded a cut of the bribe. Those pictures were taken at the Ritz Carlton. The Sebastianis arranged everything. They set me up."

"When were they taken?" Kari said.

"More than a month ago."

"And when did you get them from Stu?"

"A few weeks ago. Were you following him? Is that how you found me?"

She didn't answer. Kari preferred Snyder to believe they were watching from every street corner and behind every window.

"When the city council voted on the rezoning and it was killed, I thought the deal was over and done, but then, out of the blue, Stu showed up and handed me these photos. I have the video at home. You can watch it if you need to, but it's really—"

"We'll need to get that from you," said Whitmore. "It's evidence."

Before the proffer continued, Snyder's attorney made a persuasive pitch. He asked Whitmore to grant his client immunity in exchange for his testimony, telling them that Snyder would turn in a letter of resignation to Yhost. He argued that although Snyder's actions represented a conflict of interest, they were not criminal.

"How can you charge him with bribery?" the defense attorney debated. "He never attempted to nor intended to influence Councilman Yhost to vote against the no-touch zoning."

Kari sat back in her chair and laced her hands behind her head. "What else can he tell us that might help us out?"

Before his attorney could answer, Snyder interrupted. "I can run down the whole plan, what JOLIE's owners said and what they wanted me to do."

Kari glanced in Whitmore's and Becca's direction. They both nodded. "Okay. Let's start from the very beginning..."

***

The proffer continued for another hour, and when Craig Snyder and his attorney were done, they left the photos behind as evidence. As soon as Whitmore escorted the men down the hall, Kari removed the images from the envelope to take another peek. Suddenly, she looked up from the photos. *She forgot to have him ID the woman.* She bolted from her chair and trotted down the hallway.

She caught up to Snyder and the others waiting at the elevator.

Kari waved a photo of Snyder and his female companion. "Who is she?"

Snyder hiked a shoulder. "I assume she works at JOLIE. We didn't talk a lot."

"She didn't tell you her name?"

He shook his head. "And I never asked."

"What?" Kari chided. "Was that information too personal?"

With a sheepish grin, Snyder reached for the photo and pointed out a delicate chain the woman wore around her neck.

"Look there. Can you see that?" he said.

Kari noticed the thin platinum chain.

"Her diamond pendant spelled out Natalia," Snyder recalled. "That's the best I can do."

Kari returned to the conference room to show Becca the necklace. They dialed Tannie's cell.

"I remember Sebastiani bragging about Natalia. But she doesn't work at JOLIE," said Tannie. "According to Stu, several years ago, Natalia dumped him and married some filthy rich guy she met while working at Club Friskee. It was like a real-life version of *Pretty Woman*, you know, where Julia Roberts meets Richard what's-his-face. Stu once showed me her wedding photos. He took his wife to the reception. It was over-the-top glam and glitz. You think Stu arranged for her to have sex with Snyder?" she said with disbelief. "I gotta see those photos."

"Where are you?" asked Kari.

"In Olde City. At my Pilates instructor's studio on 3rd Street."

"Becca and I are only a few blocks away. Wait there, we'll walk over and meet you on Market Street."

It was a warm late summer day but raining heavily. The agents opted to jump on the Blue Line and ride underground to 2nd Street. When the doors of the subway car glided open, Kari and Becca quickly slipped inside and stood in the doorway. As they sped through the tunnel, Kari discreetly looked around at the characters assembled in the well-lit car. Most noticeable was the kooky couple standing opposite them. He had a huge tattoo of the name Joann prominently inked on his neck. She had purple hair and her own collection of body art and piercings. Kari studied the man and woman closely. *She doesn't look like a Joann. What if that isn't Miss Purple Hair's name? How do you reconcile being with a man who has another woman's name tattooed on his neck?* Kari quietly pointed out the pair and she and Becca shared a chuckle.

At their stop, the agents exited the train and climbed the stairs from the lower concourse level. They found Tannie waiting inside the station shelter.

"Follow me," she said. They giggled like schoolgirls as they ran half a block in the pouring rain and ducked into a small coffee shop where Kari pulled out the photos. Tannie took a good look.

"I can't really see her full face, but yeah, that's Natalia," said Tannie. She stared at the images. "But why? Stu told me she had married that rich guy, had a child, and moved away."

***

Later, when they returned to the office, a driver's license check led them to Natalia Hall's photo and home address across the Delaware River in Moorestown, New Jersey.

"I know this neighborhood. Natalia's more likely to be hosting garden parties and GOP fundraisers," said Kari. "Why would she agree to meet up with Snyder?"

"You want to take a ride over to visit her now or wait until tomorrow?"

"Let's hold off until the morning." She waved her phone in the air. "I just got a desperate text from Carter. He needs help with tomorrow's math quiz."

"What's the test on?"

Kari squinted to read the small font of her cell phone. "The relation of nonlinear functions to geometric contexts of length, area, and volume."

"Wow. You know how to do that?"

"No, he just needs me for moral support."

"That's nice. Everybody needs that."

"Yep. Why do you think I keep you around?"

Chapter 42

Kari flashed her credentials at the security guard manning the sentry gazebo of the gated community, told him where they were headed, and drove through the neighborhood of large, imposing homes on the way to Natalia's.

The agents parked along the curb and climbed the beautifully landscaped flagstone walkway, passing by a koi pond and flowing fountain. They waited less than a second at the front door before a housekeeper ushered them inside. Security must have called ahead to announce them.

A chic blond met them in the grand foyer. The platinum pendant in the photo was visible from the open neckline of her elegant satin blouse.

"Can I see some identification?" she asked.

The agents took out their credential cases and allowed her to examine them.

"When they said FBI agents were here to see me, I certainly wasn't expecting the two of you to show up at my door." With a smile, she indicated her admiration. "You sure you want to speak to me?"

The agents were led into a lavishly decorated parlor that resembled a vignette of a Luxe Home furniture showroom. The room was dripping in classic feminine charm with luxurious, white leather tufted sofas placed opposite each other, crystal chandeliers, and ornate mirrored consoles. Kari watched their host admire her own lovely surroundings as she guided them to have a seat on one of the couches, while she sat on a silk brocade divan opposite the exquisite Italian-tiled fireplace. It was obvious that material things were important to Natalia.

"This is a beautiful room," Kari said.

"Thanks," Natalia replied. "But I don't think that's what you came here to tell me."

"We have a few questions about Stuart Sebastiani."

"Oh. Do you know Stu?" Natalia asked. "He's a sweetheart, isn't he?"

"We've heard a lot about him." Kari chose her words carefully.

"How do you know him?" Becca asked.

"He's a good friend." Natalia crossed her legs and placed her hands in her lap. She no longer seemed at ease. "What's this all about?"

"We're not sure if you can help us—" Kari began, but Natalia interrupted her.

"I owe practically everything I have to Stu." Her tone was cool with a hint of defiance. "If this is about him, I seriously doubt I can help you."

"Can you talk about that? The reason you're so loyal to him."

"Sure. That's one question I'll be happy to answer," said Natalia. She kicked off her shoes and curled up on the divan.

"I was new to the business, and, I swear Stu didn't know at the time, I was actually underage when he and his inspectors raided the club where I was dancing. Stu came up to me and asked to check my license, and I didn't have one. Boy was I frightened." Natalia became animated with wide arm gestures and enthusiastic hand movements as if she was acting out a scene from a play about her life.

"I thought he was going to haul my ass off to jail. But Stu could see I was scared to death and he was like, 'You shouldn't be working in a dump like this.' So he hands me his business card and tells me to call him, and he'll help me find a better job. And…"—her eyes widened with amazement, her sophisticated demeanor slipping away—"he lets me go, lets me walk right out of the place. The police are handcuffing the other girls, accusing them of doing stuff in the booths in the back rooms. But I was told I could leave."

"It sounds like he came to your rescue," Kari said.

"He practically saved my life. Many of the other girls working at that place ended up into drugs and prostitution."

Had she already forgotten about Snyder? Sex with a stranger as a favor to Sebastiani wasn't prostitution? Kari kept her opinions to herself.

"I called him a few days later," Natalia continued, "and he gave me the name and address of a better club, and I started working there that same evening."

"What club was that?" Becca asked.

"Club Friskee," she replied. "I worked at Bill's place for three or four years, before I met my husband. My ex-husband."

Natalia went on to explain that she had stopped working after meeting a rich Philadelphia investment banker who offered to take care of her. He left his wife when she found out about the affair and married Natalia. But after three years of marriage and the birth of their son, he unjustly accused her of cheating on him and divorced her.

"While it lasted, I was in heaven. That man really loved me, and I loved him too." Natalia's eyes misted, and she took in a deep breath to regain her composure. "I never thought we'd get divorced. That's why I signed that stingy prenup. Next thing I knew, I was a single mother struggling to get by on child-support payments."

Kari scanned the expensive furnishings in the room.

"I earned all of this myself," she said. Natalia told them how, during her courtship and too-short marriage, she had met many prosperous associates of her rich husband.

"After the divorce, I put together a selective list of self-made men, boyfriends, gentlemen friends, however you want to refer to them, and I go out on dates whenever one of them needs a companion. They love my rags-to-riches story. Many of them are self-made millionaires who can relate." She shared her story without a fragment of fear about exposing her lifestyle to the agents.

"Fascinating. You should write a book," said Becca. "Or a screenplay. It would make a great movie."

"Wouldn't it?"

"Do you get to travel?" Kari wanted to keep Natalia talking.

"I do. It's the perfect situation for me. My clients, uh, companions allow me to support my son, my mom, and myself. Mother takes care of Trey when I'm out of town on business trips. I travel around the world on private jets and yachts, and they give me nice jewelry, expensive clothes, and spending money," Natalia boasted. "Everything a girl needs." She explained that her livelihood enabled her to spend quality time with her son and fund an investment portfolio that would comfortably support them for the rest of their lives.

"So, basically," Natalia addressed the agents, "Stu's kindness was what started my success. I doubt there's anything I can tell you about him that would be helpful to your investigation."

"You make him sound so heroic and virtuous," Kari said. "That's not what we've been hearing." Kari regretted her words as soon as she had spoken them.

Natalia's posture went rigid. "Excuse me? Stu Sebastiani is a good man."

Kari needed more time with Natalia Hall to discover her vulnerabilities. It was probably too soon to address the subject that had brought them there in the first place. But if Kari didn't broach the topic now, they might never get another opportunity. If they were going to persuade her to tell them about Sebastiani arranging her "date" with Craig Snyder, it was now or never.

"Can I show you a couple of photos?" Kari asked as she pulled out the candid shots of Natalia with Snyder. "Is this you?"

Natalia shuffled the photos, taking only a brief look at each.

"I don't know. You think she looks like me?" She stared at the agents and was visibly upset. "Where did you get these? Who took them?"

"Didn't Sebastiani ask you to go out on a date with this guy?" Kari said. "I guess he didn't mention that he would be recording everything. There's a video too."

"I don't want to answer any more of your questions." Natalia returned the photos to Kari and stood.

Damn it. We need her to talk to us.

"Mother," Natalia called, "can you come show the ladies to the door please?"

The woman Kari had mistaken for the housekeeper walked into the room. Following directly behind her was a beautiful little boy about five or six years old, a handsome child with lovely, gray-green eyes that appeared to radiate from his deep-olive complexion—a boy who was the spitting image of Stuart Sebastiani.

"He is adorable," Kari said, before whispering, "Sebastiani's son?"

"No." Natalia offered a weak denial.

The resemblance was unmistakable. The only thing that could have made the tot's parentage more obvious was if the Sebastiani name had been tattooed somewhere on his little body. He was Sebastiani's kid.

"Never mind, Mom. Take Trey outside to play. I'll show our guests out." Natalia struggled to keep a smile on her face until the little boy was led out of the room. The child and his grandmother had barely crossed the threshold before Natalia turned to Kari and Becca, her expression pinched with anger.

"I was married when I had him. He's not Stu's son." Natalia said the words slowly, as if saying them made them true.

"You said that your husband accused you of being unfaithful. I see why." Kari spoke gently, without judgment. "He knew you had been with Sebastiani."

"I didn't say that."

"You didn't have to. I saw the boy and the likeness, and I'm sure your husband did too." Pointing to the doorway where her son had just stood, Kari said to Natalia, "That's Stuart Sebastiani's kid."

While Natalia continued to deny Sebastiani's paternity, Kari glanced over at Becca.

"Another one?" Becca said to Kari. "I wonder just how many of these Sebastiani mini-me's are out there running around."

"What did you say?" Natalia's forehead wrinkled.

Kari's gaze darted to her partner and Becca raised her eyebrows, signaling that she understood. They may have just found Natalia's kryptonite.

"You said something about Sebastiani mini-me's. You're talking about Arty and Mia. Right?"

Neither agent responded. *Bingo*. They had hit a hot button. Natalia didn't know about Tannie and baby Dia.

"Are you saying he has another kid?"

"Stu didn't tell you about his new daughter?" Kari's voice was soft but deliberate. The disclosure could be their ticket to getting Natalia to cooperate.

"What? No." Natalia, her anguish palpable, shook her head. "Are you sure? Stu's never said a word."

"We're really sorry," Kari lied.

"We assumed you knew," Becca added.

"How old is the baby? Did you say it's a girl?"

"Yes. A girl, less than a year old," said Kari.

"Who's the mother?"

"We can't give up the identities of the people we talk to," Kari said. "We have confidentiality rules."

Knowing that they were closing in on their goal—full cooperation—Kari stood and pretended to be ready to leave.

"Wait!" Natalia raised her hands. "You can't come in here and drop a bomb like that and think you're just gonna walk away."

"I think we have to," Kari said. "Nobody would ever talk to us again if they thought we would divulge all their secrets."

"You don't have to tell me her name. Call her and see if she knows about me. You have my permission. I don't care."

Kari glanced over at Becca, who shrugged. "What's the harm in that?"

"I guess we can ask her about you," said Kari. "We'll let you know what she says."

"Wait. Can't you call her now, from here?"

Natalia offered to step out of the room so the agents could discuss the matter privately. It was a no-brainer. Kari had to tell Tannie that Sebastiani had fathered another child. The disclosure was what the agents needed to convince Natalia to work with them. Unfortunately, in the government's case against Sebastiani, Tannie and Natalia—like civilians caught in the crossfire of battle—were about to become collateral damage.

Kari looked at Becca and then turned back to Natalia. "We'll call and see if she's willing to talk to you."

They called Tannie and spoke with her privately, before calling Natalia back into the room, placing the call on speaker and introducing her to Tannie. Both women were bruised by Sebastiani's betrayal and deception. By the time his former lovers ended their phone conversation, his duplicity was exposed and Natalia was ready to answer all of the agents' questions.

Natalia admitted that her son was nearly three years old by the time the genetics connecting Sebastiani and Trey were undeniable. But during her nasty divorce, she was relieved when the judge, citing legal precedence called marital presumption of paternity, had ordered her husband to pay child support.

Consequently, Natalia had always publicly maintained that the boy was her husband's child and allowed herself to believe Stu's refusal to acknowledge his son was due to her divorce settlement. But now she knew the truth. At least twice, he had fathered a child and walked away from his obligations.

Natalia, bitter and disgusted, was primed to tell the agents everything they wanted to know. She described how she had occasionally accepted Sebastiani's requests for her to "date" his associates. She made him pay for her services. Since he never paid her a cent of child support, taking his side jobs had allowed Natalia to convince herself he was contributing to Trey's care. Her conversation with Tannie helped her recognize that Sebastiani was just another deadbeat dad. But she certainly hadn't known that when he'd paid her to sleep with Yhost and Snyder.

Kari took out her pad to take notes as Natalia admitted that it was she in the photos with Snyder and then told them about her encounters with a much older man.

"I tried on two separate occasions to seduce him. Both times I arranged to bump into him in the parking lot of a diner near his home. Stu told me…Do you know who I'm talking about?

"Councilman Barry Yhost," Kari said.

"Councilman?" Natalia grimaced and shook her head. "Stu said he went to the diner every Sunday morning while his wife was at church. The first time, I was in the parking lot when he came out of the place. I told him I had accidently locked my keys in my car."

Natalia told the story robotically, as if she couldn't believe she had ever stooped so low for Sebastiani.

"I asked him if he could give me a ride back to my hotel room, so I could pick up my spare set of keys. I remember him looking around the parking lot, wondering why I had chosen to ask him for a ride. I poured on the innocent act and convinced him I was a true damsel in distress."

She explained how after he agreed to give her a ride, she slid into the passenger seat of his old Volvo sedan, exposing a generous view of her long legs. She had introduced herself as Natalie from New Jersey.

"I said, 'Oh, Barry, you're my hero and savior. I don't know how I can ever thank you.' I could tell he was excited. But when we got to the hotel, and I asked him to come up to my room to help me look for the extra key, he said no. He waited outside in his car until I came out with the key and then drove me back to mine. I couldn't believe he turned me down."

She gave Yhost her cell phone number and told him that she came into the area frequently on business. She suggested that they get together the following Sunday. When he didn't call, Sebastiani pressured her to go back to the diner. This time, she'd arrived early and purposely sat in the booth she had seen him sitting in the first time. When he came in for his usual Sunday morning meal, he seemed confused to see her sitting in his favorite spot but recognized her once she smiled and motioned for him to join her. She explained that the least she could do was buy him breakfast for coming to her rescue. They sat together, eating and talking for over an hour.

Yhost, like a raunchy frat boy, had eventually moved the conversation to her love life. Natalia flirted back, teasingly calling him a dirty old man. This time, everything was going along just as Stu had told her it would, but when she invited Yhost back to the hotel room where the video camera was waiting, he turned her down again. For a second time, she had failed to lure Yhost into the sack. Worse, she received only $2,500 for her efforts instead of the $10,000 promised if she had been successful.

The more Natalia spoke about the Yhost encounters, the angrier she became. Stu had told her it was about gambling debts. How dare he ask her to take part in a plot to blackmail an elected official?

"That pig. Those two wasted weekends cost me more than they were worth," Natalia said. "I turned down a trip to Prague for that bullshit."

***

Later in the week, when Kari and Becca met with Councilman Yhost to verify what Natalia had told them, he was beyond thrilled. After his first encounter with Natalia, he had called his wife to tell her everything that had happened.

"I told her, you won't believe what just happened to me, and guess what? She didn't believe me," the overweight councilman confided. "My wife thought I was making up the whole thing, especially when I told her about the second time that girl appeared."

Now that he had proof a beautiful woman had tried to seduce him, he was more tickled than disturbed that he was a victim of an attempted blackmail plot. Yhost dialed his wife and put the agents on speakerphone with her.

He had FBI verification. This time she would have to believe him.

Chapter 43

Kari looked up from applying her makeup just as Carter stepped through the bathroom door. He wore a worried expression and she instantly knew why he was there. She still hadn't purchased his ticket for the first school dance of the year. Lately she was distracted, barely able to hold it all together. Joe Wilson still lurked in the shadows, ready to pounce at any moment to ruin her nearly perfect life.

"Mom, you promised yesterday you would do it on your way home from work."

"Tell me again why you can't buy a ticket at school?"

"'Cause the dance is at the youth center. You gotta get 'em at parks and rec."

She must have seemed flustered because Carter said, "Don't worry, Mom. I'll ask Dad to do it. It's all right."

"No, I'll do it tonight. Look." Kari reached for her bag. "I'll put it in my phone to remind me. The rec center is open until seven."

"And can you still take me to the mall on Saturday to get a new shirt to wear?"

"Absolutely. You're very excited about this dance. Any particular reason why? Or perhaps a particular person?"

Carter grinned and let Kari give him a quick squeeze and peck on his forehead before pulling away.

"What? You're not going to answer me?"

"I gotta go." His grin widened. "You don't want me to miss the school bus."

"Okay. But you can't avoid me forever," Kari called as Carter fled the room. "I'll hold the dance ticket hostage until you tell me her name."

Within ten minutes, everyone had left and the house was empty. Kari finished dressing, gathered her things, and locked up. Once at her car, she opened the trunk, took out her gun and strapped it on. It was against policy to store it there, but Kevin didn't want her to bring the weapon into the house. She'd rather be reprimanded by the Bureau than have something unspeakable happen to her kids or their friends. She tossed her suit jacket, purse, and tote bag onto the passenger seat and slid into the car. She was backing out of the driveway when her phone rang.

It was Carter.

"Yes, I remembered to put it in my phone," answered Kari. Although she hadn't yet made a calendar entry to pick up the ticket, she would do so as soon as she hung up.

"That's not what I want. I left my science homework on the kitchen counter. Can you bring it to me? Please?"

"Carter, I told you last night to put it in your backpack."

"I know, but if I turn it in late, Mrs. Grieber will take points off."

Kari glanced at the dashboard clock. "Okay, but now you're making me late."

Kari threw the car in park and ran back into the house to retrieve the paper, which was not on the counter but instead lying on the dining room table. She drove less than a mile—thank goodness for neighborhood schools—and pulled in front of the building. Waving the rescued homework assignment in her hand, Kari was buzzed in by a mom serving as the main door sentry.

The parent volunteer in her flowery top and apple-green capris greeted Kari cheerfully and pushed the sign-in sheet forward but turned speechless as Kari approached the table.

"Just dropping this off at the office," Kari said. She noticed the woman's smile had been replaced by a look of concern as she disregarded the warning notice for all visitors to show ID and jogged down the hall, bypassing the woman and her clipboard.

"Stop! Wait!" the woman frantically yelled after her.

Kari ignored her. *Someone is taking her little post a bit too seriously.* "I'll sign-in on my way back," she said without looking back. "I don't need a name tag. I'll only be a minute."

As Kari continued down the hall, a shrill alarm sounded, and an authoritative voice announced over the public address system, "Code red, corridor A. Code red, corridor A. Code red, corridor A."

Kari glanced back and saw the woman and a uniformed guard gesturing in her direction. *There must be a problem in the main office.* She approached the glass-fronted space cautiously but saw nothing that indicated a disturbance. When she entered the room, she smiled at Carter who was there waiting for her.

"What's going on? What's that alarm about?" she asked.

Carter didn't seem to know either, but when the office staff ducked down behind the counter, and three school police officers crouched low in the hallway prepared to make a tactical entry, he pointed at Kari.

"Mom, it's you."

Kari's eyes dropped to her waistline where her semiautomatic Glock 23 was snapped in its holster. She instinctively raised her hands high, gazed up toward the ceiling, and whispered, "Oh shit."

***

Kari slinked into the squad area and went directly to her cubicle. When Becca looked up from her desk, Kari motioned for her to come over.

"Morning, partner." Becca pushed some papers aside and leaned against the edge of Kari's desk. "You look weird."

"You need to buy me a coffee."

"What's up?"

"I just did something so ridiculously harebrained, so moronic, I can't believe it really happened."

"Oh, this I gotta hear."

"I'll tell you all about it when we get downstairs."

They took the elevator down to the second-floor cafeteria, where Becca filled two containers of coffee while Kari selected a huge cinnamon bun.

"Sugar bomb? What happened to the healthy fruit and fiber routine?" Becca said.

"It has nuts and raisins on it."

During the three minutes it took Kari to confess her embarrassing tale, Becca laughed heartily, especially when Kari mentioned she had left her credentials and badge in the car and had to have her thirteen-year-old son vouch that she was an FBI agent authorized to carry.

"I'm a mess. My boy may never talk to me again."

Becca snorted. "It's not that bad," she said. "Carter probably thinks it's cool. He's probably telling his pals all about it."

"Thanks. That makes me feel so much better."

"I bet this kind of thing happens all the time."

"Oh sure. Tonight at six, Mom threatens innocent children with her awesome display of firepower." Kari looked down at her hands and played with her wedding ring, turning it around and around on her finger. Thinking about the incident sent her emotions spiraling downward. "Honestly," she said, "sometimes I wonder if I even deserve to have such a great husband and kids."

"Whoa. Where did that come from? You're not talking about the thing with Carter anymore, are you?"

Kari shook her head. "There's stuff you don't know about."

At that moment, she contemplated telling Becca about her shameful past. Ever since they'd met with Natalia, Kari had endured tortured thoughts about how her fairy-tale marriage had been destroyed by infidelity. Kari felt ready to surrender to true friendship, ready to release her own guilt and confess she wasn't who Becca thought she was.

"I've screwed things up so badly," Kari said.

"What are you talking about? What's wrong?"

In her head, Kari shouted, *Everything! My marriage, my family, my career. All of which could explode with one word from Wilson.* He was out there. Somewhere. When she realized she was holding her breath, she exhaled and gulped in air. She knew she didn't have the guts to share her truth. She had never trusted anyone, never opened up to anyone before. She couldn't start now.

"Hildebrand? Is that what's this is about?" Becca shook her head.

"How were you supposed to know what he was up to? You weren't his babysitter."

Kari nodded in agreement and pretended Everett was the source of her distress.

"What's going on with him?"

"I don't know." Kari hitched a shoulder. "The OPR is still active. I'm not allowed to ask or have anything to do with him." That much was true. She was grateful she didn't have to face him and be reminded of the transgressions they had in common.

Becca's eyes locked on hers. "If there's something else you want to talk to me about, anything that's troubling you, you know I'm here for you. Right?"

"What? My 'mom brings weapon to school' confession isn't enough for you?"

"Don't be so hard on yourself."

"I'm fine," said Kari. "I promise."

"Really? 'Cuz you look like crap." Becca reached out for Kari's hands and held them tight. "Seriously, I'm not saying this to make you feel better, although I hope it does. You're a great mom, wife, and agent, regardless of whatever shortcomings you think you have."

"I'm starting to believe I can fix this." Kari pulled back a hand and pointed at herself. "That I can change."

"Don't change too much," said Becca. "I was thinking I want to be just like you when I grow up."

Kari shook her head. "You are so fickle. Last week you said you wanted to be just like Judy what's-her-name on the drug squad."

"Oh yeah, the vampire hunter."

"No, we're vampire hunters. They're ghost busters."

"How does it go again?"

"White-collar suspects are like vampires. We know who these troubled souls are, and we gather evidence to bring them into the light."

"And the ghost busters?"

"They have unknown subjects, masked bank robbers and unsolved murderers. They're searching for phantoms with no identities—ghosts."

Becca squinted at Kari and cocked her head.

"Don't hurt yourself trying to figure it out," said Kari. "It's just a metaphor."

Becca sighed and drummed her fingers on the table. "I was planning to conduct some interviews today, collect some silver bullets, wooden stakes, whatever. What about you?"

"Okay, okay," Kari said. She used her fingers to make the sign of a cross and held it up like a shield between them. "I'm done whining. Let's get to work."

Chapter 44

A few weeks later, when Kari walked into the digital duplication and recording room to make copies of surveillance videos, she wasn't expecting Everett Hildebrand to be standing in front of her. Earlier in the week, she had learned he had been reinstated. But seeing him for the first time, Kari wasn't sure what to say.

"Hey, Kari. I'm back," Everett said awkwardly.

"So I see." She studied him. He looked thinner. And just beneath the facade of his wide grin, she detected suppressed sadness.

When he reached out to hug her, she embraced him weakly and let go quickly. Their reunion was uncomfortable. She needed to hear what he had to say before she could decide how to receive him.

"You look good. Did you lose weight?" asked Everett.

Kari shook her head.

"Uh, I understand you're about to indict. Congratulations. I'm glad everything worked out in spite of my stuff."

"I wasn't allowed to check up on you directly. You know, because of the OPR. But Brenda mentioned that you had a rough time."

Kari waited in uneasy silence for him to say more.

"Kari, I'm sorry." He finally said, his voice cracking. "I am truly sorry I was so weak." He pressed his palms together. "I'm asking for your forgiveness. I didn't mean for any of that to happen."

Kari was just about to say she had already forgiven him—of course she would; she had been weak too—but before she could say anything, he added, "You can't possibly understand what I was going through. I was trying to fit in, to be one of the guys."

"*What?* I'm a black female FBI agent," she said. "What makes you think it's easier for me? Next time, how about aiming to be one of the team, instead of one of the guys?" Surprised by her own passion, her own frustrations, Kari slammed the disks she was holding down on the nearby shelf. One of the cases shattered, and parts fell to the floor.

"I thought I had everything under control." Everett stooped to pick up the plastic pieces and looked up at Kari. "I was wrong."

In the isolation of the cramped ten-by-ten tech room, among the monitors, recorders, and DVD duplication equipment, they stood side by side in silence for a beat.

"I made some really poor decisions." His gaze was fixated on the little piece of plastic he twirled around with his fingers. "It was hell sitting at home, waiting to find out if I would be allowed to keep my job."

He explained that the OPR investigators had cited him for unprofessional conduct, misuse of a government vehicle and computer, and violation of the guidelines on how to operate sources. None of the charges were deemed criminal. Everett's penalty was the sixty-day suspension without pay he had already served while waiting for OPR to adjudicate the matter. He had been reinstated, with his top-secret security clearance intact.

"I know people are saying that the only reason I wasn't fired was because of my father's intervention."

"Well," said Kari, "is that true?"

"In addition to the suspension," Everett said, ignoring her question, "I also received a formal censure. That letter is gonna be in my personnel file for the rest of my career, affecting future assignments and promotions."

"It's a piece of paper." She wasn't sure why she was being so insensitive. Was she trying to make herself feel better at his expense?

"You know it's more than that. That letter can be used to impeach my credibility," Everett confided. "Kari, anyone who thinks I got off easy doesn't understand how much this hurts."

"You're still an agent."

"Yeah. But I wanted to be a lead case agent, and for the rest of my career, I'm watching from the sidelines. The mark on my personnel record makes me a liability to the FBI. I'm never going to be able to testify in a trial."

"So what do they have you doing?"

"I've been reassigned to the tech squad." Everett drummed his fingers on a small monitor, one of many electronic devices stacked around the room.

"What makes you qualified to handle this techie stuff? Do you have any idea what to do?"

"Not yet. I've got to pass a technical interview before I can go for training. There's no guarantee. In the meantime, I'm a glorified stock boy, conducting equipment inventory." He took a narrow box off the shelf. "Can I offer you a case of blank CDs?" he asked with a dry, bitter tone.

Kari looked around the room and realized that Everett was now in a position to help her when Wilson returned to torment her again. As a member of the tech squad, he would be able to tell her what wiretaps and consensual communications were being monitored. All of the agents in the division eventually ended up in the duplication room to download their digital recording. If anyone was cooperating in Wilson and his codefendant Saul Prescott's case, Everett would have access to that information. Kari knew he would do almost anything to help her. She only needed to decide if she was desperate enough to exploit his friendship. And then it hit her, the hypocrisy of her attitude toward him. Who was she to judge him so harshly?

"Are you okay?" Kari stood in front of him and really looked at her former partner. Witnessed his remorse. Felt his shame. Recognized his desperate need to be understood. "Are you getting...help?"

He nodded. "I'm still having some trouble dealing with what happened." Everett maneuvered his hand as if it were a plane in a nosedive. "Everything turned to shit so fast. I thought I could handle it all, but I was in over my head."

"Are you sure you didn't come back too soon?" she asked.

"Not soon enough. Juanita's still fighting my reinstatement. She believes that by assigning"—Everett formed air quotes—"'disgraced agents' like me to the tech or surveillance squad, the FBI's creating liar squads full of agents unable to investigate cases or testify."

"Who cares what she thinks?"

"If it had been up to her, I would have been fired and jailed." He smiled slightly. "After the tarring and feathering."

"Like I said, don't worry about Juanita," Kari said. "You're back, aren't you?"

Everett smiled weakly. "I thought you would be angry with me."

"I was at first."

"But not anymore?"

"Disappointed perhaps, but not angry. You have to deal with your moral issues. That's your struggle."

"I was referring to Juanita's campaign against you."

"I'm not thinking about her."

"Wow, so you don't care that Juanita convinced headquarters to initiate an OPR inquiry on Shawn, Tommy, and you for going through my desk and not turning me in when you found out I was watching porn on my Bureau computer?"

Kari was speechless. Had she heard him correctly?

"You're kidding me, right? Tell me you're kidding."

***

Kari barged into her supervisor's office. "Juanita, I just heard you initiated an OPR on me?"

"I advised headquarters of your misconduct. The fact that an investigation was ordered indicates to me that others also find it unacceptable that you took those porn videos out of Hildebrand's desk and hid the evidence."

"I did not! I've done nothing wrong." Kari stared at Juanita but found no empathy. "There was no cover-up."

"I warned you this wasn't over yet." Juanita let the *T* sound vibrate off her teeth, then motioned for Kari to leave. "I'm a witness. I've been instructed not to discuss this matter with anyone involved."

Kari rushed out of the office and hurried toward the bathroom, where she sequestered herself in the same stall she'd found sanctuary in when healing from her mother's death. She couldn't believe it. In addition to waiting for Wilson to make his next move, she was now the target of an OPR, an administrative inquiry that could end up sabotaging everything she had worked so hard to build. How could all this be happening to her at the same time?

***

Kari raised her right hand and repeated the preamble Assistant Special Agent in Charge Bob Dorsey dictated to her. Supervisor McPherson was there to witness her sworn statement. She had already been interviewed and had approved the text transcribed in the statement.

"I, Karolina Wheeler, having been duly sworn, hereby make the following statement. I am willing to take a voluntary polygraph examination concerning the truthfulness of the information I am about to provide…" Her heart beat so fast she could feel her pulse throbbing in her eardrum. After signing the document, Kari launched an inarticulate appeal.

"This is B. S."

"Kari, it may seem unfair to you," said Dorsett, "but the director's Bright Line policy states—"

"So bright that it's blinding you to what's really going on here." Kari knew she should stop talking. Nothing would put a halt to the process that was underway.

"The boss tried to squash this," McPherson said, "but he was overruled by HQ."

"What did you expect? The way Juanita wrote up the referral, you would've thought the whole squad was engaged in wild sex orgies." Kari made the argument she had made many times before. "Everett was looking at porn. We did what we thought was right and tried to handle it without making a big deal about it. And I know nothing about a flash drive containing porn taken from his desk."

"But it was a big deal. What business allows employees to sit around and view pornography all day?" Dorsett refused to minimize the significance of Everett's behavior. "They don't allow that stuff at the accounting firm or the bus company down the street. This is the FBI. We're certainly not allowing it here."

"Everett already paid the price for what he did. I'm about to start the Sebastiani trial. If I'm called to testify, the prosecutor has to tell the defense about the OPR."

"Kari, let's just get through this and move forward," offered Dorsett. "Perhaps we can get everything cleared up before the trial begins."

Frustrated, Kari got up to leave. "Are we done?"

"Wait," McPherson called after her. "We all need to steer clear of ethical pitfalls. I hope you understand we're just making sure the rules are being followed."

"Sure. I get it." Kari paused in the doorway. "Don't hate the player. Hate the game."

Chapter 45

The alarm had already buzzed a couple of times. Each time it sounded, Kari hit the snooze button. She wasn't ready to leave the comfort of her bed. To prepare herself to toss the covers aside and get up, she stretched her legs and arms out to the cool areas of the sheets, and like an auto mechanic conducting a diagnostic engine check, she made a mental list of her stress indicators: head—painful pressure right behind the eyes; neck and shoulders—muscles tight and tender; torso—slab of belly fat from sternum to pelvic bone; arms and legs—as heavy as lead weights; heart and nerves—surging with overloaded current.

Her examination verified what she already knew. She felt like shit.

Wilson was torturing her in absentia. She hadn't heard from him in weeks, but she knew he would be back. He kept popping in and out of her life, like a serial killer in a horror movie terrorizing his victims as he picked them off one by one.

She had suffered through another sleepless night. Awakened by her restlessness at 2:30 a.m., Kevin had assumed she was worried about the pending OPR investigation and had offered his drowsy opinion.

"I told you so," he mumbled. "You're just a body to those bastards."

"Just because you're right doesn't mean I'm wrong."

Kevin had rubbed his eyes and stared at her with heavy lids. "What does that mean?"

"It means I still love being an agent, and I still have a case I need to work."

"You're thinking just like an abused woman. 'If I just do better, he won't need to beat me anymore.' Don't you see how warped that is?"

"You're not helping. Please go back to sleep."

Kevin rubbed her shoulders and kissed her cheek. Within seconds, he had drifted back to sleep, leaving Kari alone in the dark to endure the anxiety idling in her veins. He was useless in these situations, but she loved him. She lived in fear, wondering what he would do if Wilson scattered her dirty deeds about for all to see.

***

She fell asleep for a short moment. The next time the snooze alarm buzzed, she could smell the fresh coffee Kevin had climbed out of bed to brew. While muscle-numbing fatigue threatened to bind her to her bed, Kari wrestled her legs to the floor and propelled herself out from under the consoling warmth of the covers. Sitting on the edge of the mattress, she touched the left side of her face and added another symptom to the list: jaw—sore. She must have been grinding her teeth.

Despite her sluggish start, Kari showered and quickly dressed for work. Indicting the subjects of G-Sting was enough motivation to push aside her self-pity. Today, Kari would be the last fact witness going before the grand jury to wrap up the case. Immediately after her testimony, Whitmore would ask the jurors to decide if probable cause existed to return a "true bill," a decision that would allow the investigation to proceed to trial.

By the end of the day, after a nine-month-long covert investigation, Kari and Becca would unwrap all the evidence they had discreetly packaged together and expose it for the entire city to examine.

The case was solid, even if Kari was a wreck.

***

Kari was scheduled to testify before the grand jury at 9:30 a.m. By the time the jurors certified their vote before the magistrate judge, it would be close to noon. But the indictment would not be made public until after the agent teams on standby were dispatched to Sebastiani's office and JOLIE to execute the search and arrest warrants. Kari and Becca had prepared a detailed list of documents and records they were hoping to find at each location. As soon as the evidence was secured,

AUSA Whitmore would unseal the indictment.

For Kari, the highlight of the task-packed day would be putting cuffs on Sebastiani. The day's events would throw him for a loop. Typically, in public corruption cases, the agents would provide the court the evidence or probable cause to conduct searches first, after which the agents would mine the seized documents for additional evidence to support an indictment. But based on Sebastiani's blatant disregard for his position and his sloppy efforts to sabotage the case, they had enough probable cause to indict, search, and arrest Sebastiani, Kincaid, and Hampton in one huge tsunami. Whitmore was holding off charging Arty Sebastiani until after they had a chance to meticulously review JOLIE's files and records. If they found information directly implicating Sebastiani's son, Whitmore was set to prepare a superseding indictment. Until that time, Arty would be considered an unindicted co-conspirator.

When all the formal papers had been signed and filed and the go-ahead given for the agents to execute, Special Agents Karolina Wheeler and Rebecca Benner were almost giddy with anticipation. Although it might have been unprofessional for her to admit it, during the investigation, she had acquired an intense loathing for Stuart Sebastiani. She especially begrudged the way he had treated Tannie and Natalia and their children.

Before leaving the office, Kari instructed members of the search teams to wear their vests and raid jackets.

"Jeez, Kari," Shawn complained. "Why the body armor? Is that really necessary?"

"Who knows? Maybe one of the city bean counters has a serious rap sheet and thinks we're coming for him." Kari slipped on her navy nylon jacket with FBI in gold letters across the back, chest, and sleeves. "You can take it off once we've secured the room. But yeah, I need you to follow procedures."

"He's missing his adrenaline rush." Becca rested her hand on her holstered weapon. "I hope the mailroom kid doesn't make any sudden moves."

At exactly 11:56 a.m., Kari and Becca, with warrants in hand, walked into the Department of Licenses and Inspections offices located in the city's Municipal Services Building. As the search team spread out into the room and announced their presence, two pretty, young clerical workers on opposite sides of the large room ran toward an office located in the rear of the large space. The agents instinctively followed behind the women as they made a beeline to Sebastiani's office. It was comical to watch the women eye each other suspiciously as they approached his door at the same time. Sebastiani wore a bewildered expression as he observed the rival girlfriends barging through his office door, with Kari and Becca closing in right behind them. Kari, focused on the mission, pushed ahead of the pack.

"Stuart Sebastiani"—Kari handed him the warrants authorizing his arrest and the search of his office—"you're under arrest."

Sebastiani stumbled a step backward. "What? Wait."

"Mr. Sebastiani, I need you to step out of the office and put your hands behind you," Kari said, after directing his confused love interests to their cubicles.

"But my attorney told me he would arrange for me to self-surrender."

"Well, he didn't. Last warning: step out of the office and put your hands behind your back."

Kari double locked the handcuffs securing Sebastiani's wrists.

A member of the search team frisked him.

Kari tapped the agent on the shoulder. "I got this," she said.

Cautiously, she patted down Sebastiani, examining and emptying the contents of his suit jacket and pants pockets. Kari removed a wad of dollar bills secured with a thick rubber band, some change, a couple of sticks of gum, and a small glassine bag containing three golden, teardrop-shaped pills. Although she could clearly read the brand name imprinted on the pills, Kari relished the opportunity to have him confirm it.

"What are these?" she asked.

"They're prescribed."

"Okay, but what are they?"

"Cialis," he said, almost whispering.

"Log that in for me, please." Kari spoke loud enough for Becca and anyone within fifteen feet to hear. "List Mr. Sebastiani's personal effects at the time of his arrest as $166.55 in coins and cash, three pieces of spearmint gum, and three Cialis pills."

Becca jotted down the dictated items and then stepped behind their prisoner. Making eye contact with Kari, she smiled and mouthed the words, "You bitch."

Kari suppressed the urge to snicker.

As they led Sebastiani out in front of all of his subordinates, one of the agents pulled Kari aside to show her images contained on a digital camera found in Sebastiani's desk drawer.

Most of photos were of nude and partially dressed women and the background revealed they had been taken right there in his office. Kari scrutinized the photos closely and, among the many women featured, recognized the two L&I workers who had tried to warn Sebastiani of the agents' arrival. Kari elbowed an agent rummaging through the papers on Sebastiani's desk and pointed at the young women standing among the small crowd that had gathered.

"Make sure you interview those two."

***

The next morning when she came downstairs for coffee, Kari found a note from Kevin with the letters "ISPOU," their code for "I'm so proud of you," attached to the *Inquirer*. Featured on the front page was a photo of Becca and Kari, leading Sebastiani out of the Municipal Services Building in handcuffs, and a comprehensive story outlining the investigation and all the players. Reporter Sam Shiffler must have devoured the forty-three-page indictment as soon as it was unsealed. Along with the key interviews with Whitmore and US Attorney Crystal he had been asked to embargo, Shiffler had managed to conduct a number of pertinent phone interviews before his late-evening deadline. Kari was impressed.

An attention-grabbing headline, "From Boobgate to Bribegate: G-String Sting case exposes sex & $$$ perks," shouted from the printed page. Kari smiled. The editors at the paper had unknowingly used the original code name for the case. They probably were quite pleased with their clever caption. The article included juicy quotes from strip club owners and city government officials who, prior to Sebastiani being indicted, would have been reluctant to make any negative comments about the revered compliance enforcer. Now, they were more than happy to accuse him of being a slimy shakedown swindler.

Kari knew the details of her case inside and out, but reading the newspaper narrative still gave her a buzz. Seeing the facts of the investigation spread across the front page made the explicit details seem all the more juicy. The story noted the federal bribery, corruption, and "extortion under color of official right" counts could result in a possible sentence of up to twenty years in jail and a $250,000 fine for Sebastiani.

A breakdown of the charges filed against Lynette Hampton and Curtis Kincaid was also included. Unnamed sources described the reactions of the JOLIE owners when the FBI walked into the exclusive club and presented a warrant to search the premises and haul them away to jail. A shaken Lynette Hampton was quoted as excusing any "unpleasant confrontations" that occurred at the club as the unfortunate result of overzealous bouncers and security staffers, and an ill-advised involvement with minority investor Arty Sebastiani and his father, Stuart Sebastiani.

Kincaid and Hampton were facing ten to fifteen years in prison, in addition to the seizure and forfeiture of more than $3.5 million in JOLIE assets linked to their unlawful debt-collection tricks and threats.

They had all been released on bail. Kari wondered what Sebastiani, Hampton, and Kincaid were doing at that very moment. Were they at home reading the article and enjoying a cup of coffee? She leaned back in her chair and, full of self-satisfaction, took another sip of hers.

Chapter 46

"What did you guys do, run over here?" asked Tannie. She stood to the side as Kari and Becca entered the condo. Both were dressed in spandex and running shoes.

"Yeah," said Kari. "We started off talking about the case, and before I knew it, we were passing through Society Hill."

"I don't have much choice, Tannie. Running flushes out all the surplus adrenaline in her system." Becca shook her arms spastically to illustrate. "Otherwise she'd be driving me crazy."

"I guess things are going well for you two since your big indictment last month," Tannie said, her tone oddly resentful.

"Is something wrong?" asked Kari.

"Yeah. It sucks that I might have to give up the best job I've ever had."

"Are Hampton and Kincaid still trying to sell JOLIE?"

"If they wait to dump the club and they're convicted of even one felony count, they could lose the liquor license." Tannie made a paper-tearing motion with her hands. "Without a liquor license, JOLIE will be impossible to unload."

"Someone will come along and buy the business. You wait and see."

"Who? Some royal asshole who'll buy JOLIE and run it into the ground." Sadness passed over her face. "And what about Arty? He's the one operating JOLIE now. When he finds out I'm on the prosecution's witness list, don't you think he's gonna fire me?"

"If that happens," said Kari, "you'll find another job, I'm sure."

"Not like JOLIE. That place is different. Management's respectful and the girls are professional. Yeah, there's competition among us performers, but JOLIE is like a sports team: the biggest earners are the starters. If you aren't bringing your A game, someone else can earn your spot. Unlike other places I've worked, no one has tried to sabotage my act by stealing or damaging my costumes or trying to entice away my regulars by offering them a blow job in the parking lot."

"Sounds like a great place to work," said Kari.

"It's one of the best things that ever happened for me. The hours were good, and the money was great. I'm pulling in $1,500 a night on average."

"Make sure you're keeping accurate records," Kari warned. "We certainly don't need Sebastiani's lawyer accusing you of tax fraud."

"Hey, I always fill out a 1099 tax form for the tips. I used a new preparer this year. He was very interested in my list of deductible work-related expenses."

"Such as?" said Becca.

"Such as my crystal-studded G-strings, sequined nipple tassels, and tear-away satin pants."

They all laughed.

The conversation stalled after Tannie asked, "But who knows if I'll have any income to deduct this year?"

"Have you talked to Natalia lately?" said Kari, changing the subject.

She and Becca still felt guilty for using Tannie to persuade Natalia to cooperate. Tannie had been full of piss and pity since learning Sebastiani was the father of Natalia's little boy. Since their initial telephone conversation when they learned Sebastiani had deceived them both, Tannie and Natalia had become fast friends.

"Yeah, Stu's ears must be on fire when Natalia, the kids, and I are together. We spend a lot of time talking about him. It's like therapy for us."

"That's good," said Kari.

"We were both fools, but I think I'm going to pay the bigger price."

"Tannie, you've known for a long time Stu is a pig. You told me that the first time I met you," Kari said.

"I know, but I thought he would eventually do right by Dia, be a good father. I've given up hope of finding someone to love me right."

"What are you talking about?" Becca draped her arm around Tannie. "You're a beautiful woman. Everyone in the club wants to be with you."

"Yeah, they like my parts," Tannie replied, exposing a vulnerability that Kari and Becca had never seen before. "They don't give a damn that these parts are attached to me. So…great. Everybody wants to fuck me. I'm looking for the guy who wants to kiss me."

Chapter 47

Sebastiani had said and done everything he could think of to discourage Anna from attending the trial. He had seen disgraced men facing the public with their wives standing dutifully by their sides and had wondered why those men made their wives share their shame. But Anna asked to costar in his humiliating exhibition, and in turn, he had absolutely no luck with persuading Arty and Mia to stay away. Having them in the courtroom would be both comforting and disheartening. But they would all be there together, as a family.

That morning, before leaving the house on the way to the federal courthouse, Sebastiani asked his family to sit down at the kitchen table, where he began the most heartbreaking conversation he'd ever had.

"Today and during the rest of the trial, you're going to hear some awful things about me. Things I'm not proud of."

He looked around the table and saw tears welling in their eyes and had no ability to stop his own.

"I screwed up." Sebastiani lowered his head in self-reproach and would have continued crying if he hadn't caught the look of horror on Mia's and Arty's faces. His children had never seen him cry before. What was he saying to them with his wimpy behavior? He ordered himself to man up and show his kids he had the gonads to handle the trial. He smeared away his tears with the back of his hand. "In my business, I have to deal with scumbags and liars all the time, and they'll be in court trying to bring me down." He nodded toward his son. "Arty knows what I'm talking about. You're going to hear some stuff—some of it true, some of it bold-faced lies."

"Dad, do you think they're going to send you to jail?" Mia asked, her tone hesitant.

"I don't know what's going to happen." He reached across the table and patted her hand. "Let's hope not."

Anna placed her hand on theirs and motioned Arty to join them. "No matter what happens or is said in that courtroom, we have to remember that we are in this together. I'm not stupid. I'm not going to like some of what I may hear." She smiled tenuously at her husband. "But you've always been a good provider for your family, and we'll be there for you."

He drew strength from her words and her loving touch.

"Okay, let's go get 'em." Sebastiani stood and marched the family out to the driveway. As they climbed into Arty's Escalade, Anna ran into the house to retrieve something she had left behind. While waiting, Mia pointed to the house next door.

"Daddy, did you hear about Gina? She tried to off herself." Mia made a slicing motion across her throat.

The news knocked the air out of him. He felt light-headed. He could barely breathe.

"*What?*"

"She took pills."

He turned away and placed both hands on the hood of the car. "Gina's dead?"

"No. No. Not dead." Mia rubbed his back. "They found her alive, but barely, at her place down the shore. They said she did it because her boyfriend dumped her. I heard he's married."

"Does your mother know?"

Mia shook her head. "No, I forgot to tell her."

Sebastiani turned and grabbed her hands tightly. He didn't care if she could see the tears swelling in his eyes.

"Please don't say anything to Mom," he pleaded. He felt a wave of nausea pulsing through his gut. "She's got enough to worry about." Then, slapping both hands over his mouth, he held back his breakfast long enough to bolt away from the car. Anna discovered him propped up along the side of the garage and helped him inside the house to change into a fresh shirt and tie. He told her he was nervous about the trial, and he was grateful that she dotingly helped him clean up.

But Anna had no idea how soiled he was.

***

Sebastiani and his family valiantly filed into the federal district courthouse together. Sebastiani took his place at the defense table next to Brian Crawley, his attorney, and to the left of the prosecution's table, where Whitmore, Kari, and Becca sat. He did not acknowledge their presence.

With the first row reserved for staff associated with the trial, Anna, Arty, and Mia were positioned in the second row, directly behind Sebastiani, sitting stoically side by side as the prosecutor attacked him during opening arguments.

"The Department of Licenses and Inspections is involved in almost every facet of the enforcement and regulation of businesses operating in the City of Philadelphia. And ladies and gentlemen, this man here," Mitch Whitmore said, pointing at Sebastiani, "had the power to shut down every one of those businesses. All he had to do was write them up for noncompliance, and just like that"—Whitmore snapped his fingers—"the businesses would be closed. This case is not about strip clubs. This case is not about lap dances. It's about the rule of law and whether or not we want maliciously motivated public officials such as Stuart Sebastiani determining when and by whom those laws should be followed."

The courtroom spectators listened attentively. With the start of the trial, all the sensational G-Sting allegations were now being addressed in the proper forum.

"For years, Mr. Sebastiani's lack of ethical leadership has fueled a system run on greed, disregard, and indifference, where L and I inspections were accomplished with a wink and a nod. As the Chief of Business Regulatory Enforcement, Mr. Sebastiani extorted in excess of $1.3 million in free drinks, food, and *services*. Those kickbacks were offered in exchange for his help." Whitmore's mocking tone demonstrated his disapproval. "A government official should never violate the public trust by accepting a bribe. And with this investigation and trial, we're going to make sure Mr. Sebastiani, and others like him, fully understand that."

AUSA Whitmore had strategically placed himself right in front of the defense table, and when he concluded, he was pointing his finger directly in Stuart Sebastiani's face.

Sebastiani didn't flinch, but he glared at Whitmore for the briefest of moments in spite of his attorney's warning not to display any animosity toward the other side. His reaction was automatic. He had been taught that no one should disrespect a man in front of his family. In South Philly, the derogatory comments Whitmore had just made would have been fighting words. Stu turned slightly, but he couldn't see his wife's face to gauge her reaction. He worried about her. He wished he could have convinced her not to come. He would have to swivel his chair to catch a glimpse of her. During the first break, he would ask her to slide over a bit.

Sebastiani's attorney's opening statement was next.

"Good morning, ladies and gentlemen. My name is Brian Crawley, and I'm Mr. Sebastiani's attorney. As you recall, during the juror selection process, one of the questions we asked was about your views, your condemnation of adultery. I'm sure you wondered why. Well, the reason that topic was on the questionnaire was because Mr. Sebastiani is a philanderer. And although being a cheating husband is a serious matter for which he must ask his wife for forgiveness"—Crawley turned for a moment to acknowledge Anna Sebastiani with hands pressed together and a bowed head—"it is not a federal crime. But in my opinion, that's what this trial is all about.

"Mr. Sebastiani has worked for the Philadelphia Licenses and Inspection Division for nearly thirty years. He knows a lot of people and has a lot of friends in this town. His duties include inspecting strip clubs, so it makes sense that some of his associates are club owners, dancers, and strippers. But that doesn't mean he should be dragged in here to explain those relationships to us.

"What would you do for a good friend? What have your friends done for you?" Crawley stood before the jurors with one hand on his waist. "The government is throwing words around like 'bribes' and 'kickbacks.' Is that what you call it when your neighbor watches your dog while you're on vacation and you bring him back a souvenir? When your car breaks down and your coworker offers you a ride to work—is that gas money you give her a bribe? No, it's not. They are simply gifts exchanged between friends for kindnesses and favors. For your sake, I hope your friends are not as fickle as Mr. Sebastiani's. It's my understanding that some of his close acquaintances will be strolling in here in the next couple of weeks with a reinterpretation of what their friendship with him meant to them." Crawley bowed his head and tsked. "What a shame. In the words of Martin Luther King, Jr., 'In the end, we will remember not the words of our enemies, but the silence of our friends.' And because of the capricious status of his so-called friendships, I need to remind you all that it is Mr. Sebastiani's constitutional right not to present any witnesses, and doing so should not affect his presumption of innocence. Our case will be primarily established through the cross-examination of the prosecution's witnesses."

With a commiserating glance toward Sebastiani, Crawley completed his remarks. Sebastiani appreciated when his attorney made a point to pat him on the shoulder as he took his seat.

***

From a list of thirty-four witnesses scheduled to take the stand, the first days of the trial saw a succession of business and strip club owners, managers, and dancers provide testimony. At times, it seemed to Kari as if L&I was on trial too. Witnesses complained about being nickeled-and-dimed by the agency, and some even confessed a preference for making a payoff to an inspector in lieu of supporting a nuisance revenue stream of fees and fines created by a cash-strapped administration.

Through testimony, the jurors and spectators were introduced to the adult entertainment industry or, as one of the club owners bluntly labeled it, "the flesh business." By the second week of trial, the courtroom was packed to capacity. The observers wanted to hear for themselves the salacious testimony transcribed in glorious detail in their morning paper and by newscasters reporting live from the courthouse steps each evening.

Those lucky enough to secure a spot inside the courtroom were not disappointed when Adrianne Meyers, the stripper from Sugar Lips, was called to take the witness stand. As she teetered forward on six-inch stilettos, the courtroom grew curiously quiet, but only for a moment. Laughter erupted when Adrianne, always the bubbly type, waved hello to the judge and jurors before scooting into the witness box. Even Sebastiani grinned.

Once she was seated, only the top portion of her outfit was still visible, but it was impossible to forget the unique version of a business suit she had chosen to wear that day. Kari had asked her to dress professionally, and Adrianne had picked out a shiny, pink satin skirt and matching jacket. The hem of the skirt stopped, as the *Daily News* noted in the paper the following day, "several miles above her knees" and the neckline of the jacket plunged dramatically toward her navel. Kari rebuked herself for not clarifying which profession she had in mind.

"Ms. Meyers," Whitmore said, "what do you do for a living? Where do you work?"

"I'm a performer, and I work at Sugar Lips. It's an entertainment venue in South Philly."

"Is that like a strip club?"

"Yes. But it's really nice." She turned to look at the jurors. "Have any of you been there?" The entire courtroom erupted in laughter. Even Sebastiani and his family chuckled.

"Adrianne, you need to address your questions to me or the court." Whitmore pointed to Judge Jeffrey Jiles.

"Oh, I'm not gonna ask him if he's been to Sugar Lips," she said with a cute giggle that disappeared as soon as she saw the judge's scowl.

Judge Jiles surveyed the audience. His sternness warned them that he would not tolerate another outburst. "Mr. Whitmore, please continue," he said.

"How and when did you meet the defendant, Mr. Sebastiani?" asked

Whitmore. He folded his arms across his chest.

"You mean Stu?" Adrianne glanced over at him. She was suddenly noticeably subdued. "I don't really remember the date, but we met when I went to the municipal building to apply for a business privilege license. I was trying to figure out what I was supposed to fill in on the form, and Stu walked by and saw I was confused."

"Did he offer to get someone to help you?"

"We started talking and I told him I was applying for a license to be an exotic dancer, and he filled out the application for me. It was easy for him. He's really good at his job."

"He filled it out for you?" Whitmore ignored the compliment she had given Sebastiani.

"Yes. He also showed me which answers to choose to avoid unnecessary, uh, scrutiny when it was reviewed in the clerk's office."

"Did he tell you who he was?"

"No, but I figured it out when we were in his office."

"He took you to his office?"

"That's where we were when he was helping me fill out the application."

"Oh, I see." Whitmore glanced at Sebastiani. "Did you have any other opportunities to visit Mr. Sebastiani at his office?"

"Yes."

"Tell us about those visits."

"What do you want to know?"

"When did you go to Mr. Sebastiani's office, how often, and what did you do while you were there?"

"I told you already, at the grand jury thingy."

"I know, Adrianne—Ms. Meyers, but these jurors here haven't heard what you told me. You need to tell them too."

"What did you want to know again? What we did in his office?"

"We can start there."

"We did it...on his desk."

"You had sex?"

"Yes."

Sebastiani lowered his head and rubbed his forehead. He had

warned his family that they would hear embarrassing testimony.

"And was this after hours, when everybody in the department was gone?"

"Sometimes. Sometimes not."

"And what was your relationship with Mr. Sebastiani? Were you two having an affair?"

"No, I was just thanking him, uh, returning a favor."

"You had sex with him in his office as a favor. What exactly did he do for you that you needed to, as you said, return a favor?"

"A couple of times he did me a favor, but most of the time, he did something for my boss."

"Let me make sure the jury understands. When you had sex with Mr. Sebastiani in his office, on his desk, it was because you were returning a favor for your boss? Did I get that right?"

Adrianne squirmed in her chair, played with one of her dangling earrings, and nodded.

"I don't mean to make you uncomfortable, but I need you to answer out loud, so the transcriber can record your response." He added, "I'm going to ask you a few more questions. We're almost done."

Adrianne smiled weakly.

"What else did your boss have you do for Mr. Sebastiani?"

"You mean when I gave him cash? That's the real reason I was sent over there by my boss, to bring Stu money. And I know you're going to ask how much. So...let's see, it was usually around a thousand or two thousand dollars."

"And what was the money for?"

"I don't really know."

"Did he give you a receipt or ask you for any forms or paperwork?"

"No."

"You just gave him cash?"

"It was in an envelope."

"May I have a minute, Your Honor?" Whitmore asked as he walked over to the prosecution table and conferred with Kari and Becca.

"Did I forget anything?" he whispered, but Sebastiani could make out what he said.

"Ask about the business card," said Kari.

Returning to the podium, Whitmore had Adrianne address two more questions.

"Did you ever get that license, the one Mr. Sebastiani helped you apply for?"

"Yes, but when it later expired, Stu told me I didn't need to get it renewed."

"Why not?"

"He gave me something even better—his business card with the words 'Don't even think about it' written on the back."

"And how did that work?"

"Oh, the card was magical. If I was working at a club and it was raided, all I had to do was show Stu's card to the inspectors, and no one bothered me." Adrianne giggled. "I called it my get-out-of-jail-free card."

Sebastiani looked over at his attorney to gauge the damage done by Adrianne's testimony. Crawley discreetly shook his head and pretended to brush something off his shoulder, their code that everything was fine. When it was the defense's turn to question her, Crawley approached the lectern and took a moment to scribble notes on a pad he had brought with him.

"Ms. Meyers," he said when he looked up from the podium, "what's the penalty for not having a business privilege license?"

"I think you have to pay a fine."

"How much?"

Adrianne gazed forward intently.

"How much is the fine for dancing without a license?"

"Oh, I think it's three hundred dollars. I've never had to pay it."

"So, let me make sure we all understand you. The penalty is just a fine. So, Mr. Sebastiani's card didn't save you from doing time in jail, like you just told the jurors."

"I was joking about that."

"I see. Has Mr. Sebastiani done anything to help you stay out of jail?"

"No."

"Let me ask you one more question, Ms. Myers, since you brought up the subject. Have you ever been to jail?"

"Objection," said Whitmore.

"Overruled," said Judge Jiles. "The witness opened the door. Please answer the question, Ms. Meyers."

"Have you ever been to jail?" Crawley stood directly in front of Adrianne with a knowing smile.

Adrianne scrunched her face as if trying to recall and, with a single nod, said, "Yes."

"And the charge that resulted in you going to jail? What crime was that?"

"Drugs and prostitution."

"Drugs *and* prostitution," Crawley echoed. He paused and stroked his chin. "When was the last time you were arrested for having sex for money?"

"A long time ago." Adrianne tossed a stray bleached curl off her face. "What does that have to do with anything?"

"I'm just checking to make sure you're not engaging in your old profession."

"What are you trying to say?" Adrianne leaned forward in the witness stand. "That I was paid to have sex with Stu? Not true."

"So you didn't receive any money. Is that what you're telling the jurors?" Crawley flicked a finger at his witness. "Think before you answer."

"My boss gave me a few bucks for going over to Stu's office—"

"Oh, like a tip for your troubles, because visiting Mr. Sebastiani was such a discommodious assignment?"

Adrianne's face went blank as she appeared to struggle to make sense of his words. She raised her voice and pointed toward Sebastiani. "I wasn't paid to have sex with Stu."

Crawley followed her gesture over to the defense table and then down to his notepad resting on the podium. He reviewed it, flipping back and forth between two pages.

"Forgive me. I didn't mean to insinuate that *you* were paid to have sex with Mr. Sebastiani. Your testimony is right here in my notes."

Crawley smiled and tapped his notepad. "You would like us to believe you had sexual intercourse with Mr. Sebastiani in his office and then...you paid *him*." Crawley cocked his head at an angle, and when Adrianne opened her mouth to speak, he held his hand up to silence her.

"Thank you, Ms. Meyers," he said with a calculating smirk. "I have no further questions for you."

***

Natalia Hall, tactically chosen by the prosecutive team to follow Adrianne Meyers, was the next witness. Sebastiani's eyes followed her from the gallery to the witness stand. In stark contrast to Adrianne, Natalia's attire befitted the chic and sophisticated persona she had adopted during her brief but socially advantageous marriage. She was outfitted head to toe in designer clothes and expensive jewelry.

"Mrs. Hall, could you tell the jurors what you do for a living."

"I am a successful entrepreneur. I own my own business."

"And what type of business do you operate?"

"I'm a social consultant. I travel around the world with my clients and provide them companionship."

Sebastiani was impressed with the way Whitmore continued with his questioning, until the illusion of respectability gradually evaporated, and he gently and delicately helped Natalia concede she was an escort, a call girl, albeit one with an exclusive registry of wealthy clients.

After the bumpy start, her testimony flowed easily, especially when asked to tell the jurors how and when she met Sebastiani. She appeared to be pleased to share her *Pretty Woman* story with her largest audience yet. Whitmore let her narrate her fairy tale and then had her concentrate her testimony on her relationship with Sebastiani. She told the jurors she and Sebastiani had been lovers and mentioned he had once given her a diamond necklace, which she sold because it wasn't her taste.

Sebastiani didn't dare look behind him to assess Anna's reaction. He never wanted to hurt her, to humiliate her this way. He waited for Natalia to reach the main focus of her testimony. She had been called to corroborate the conspiracy to blackmail Councilman Barry Yhost and Craig Snyder. Sebastiani regretted involving her in the convoluted schemes. As Natalia answered Whitmore's questions, he watched the way she handled her words and actions. She demonstrated such self-confidence and self-reliance, he couldn't help but be proud of all she had accomplished. Financially, she had rebounded from her failed marriage and made a good life for herself and the boy.

Sebastiani wondered if his wife would remember meeting Natalia at her lavish Main Line wedding a few years ago. He turned to look at Anna, but he was still unable to make eye contact with her. She kept sitting directly behind him, hidden from his view.

He recalled how Anna had remarked that Natalia was one of the most beautiful brides she had ever seen. The wedding reception was certainly one of the most extravagant. His thoughts continued to wander, but the audible reaction of the courtroom brought him back. *What had Natalia just said?*

"So you believe Mr. Sebastiani was responsible for the failure of your marriage?" Whitmore asked Natalia.

"Absolutely, my marriage ended very badly soon after the birth of my son."

"And why was that?"

"No matter how much I denied it, it was obvious Stu is my baby's father. All of his kids look just like him, like little clones." Natalia spoke calmly and deliberately. She appeared satisfied to finally acknowledge the true paternity of her son in such a public forum.

Sebastiani heard Anna gasp. This time, he didn't hesitate to turn around to look at her. She glowered at him. His heart sank.

"Not only does our son, Trey, look exactly like Stu, but so do his kids Arty and Mia and his new baby daughter, Dia. She looks just like her daddy too." Natalia spit the words out while she locked her eyes on Sebastiani.

He froze and then glared at the agents sitting at the prosecution table. They were purposely trying to humiliate him in front of his wife. How many kids he fathered had nothing to do with why he was on trial. He elbowed his attorney and whispered, "Can't you object?"

Crawley waved him off.

"Are you saying that Mr. Sebastiani has two more children other than the two sitting here in the courtroom?" Whitmore continued.

"My little boy and his new baby are the only extra kids I know of. There certainly could be more. He gets around."

Sebastiani pivoted all the way around, his concentration now focused on his wife. Initially, he wasn't sure she fully comprehended what she was hearing. But he could tell that Natalia's admission registered, and he watched as tears brimmed in Anna's eyes. She had sat behind him for three days as one person after another provided testimony that he was a liar, a thief, and a cheat. But what was being said about him now was the worst.

He knew Natalia's testimony would be too much for her to bear and that Anna could not casually accept that he, the father of her children, was a deadbeat capable of hiding from her the existence of his illegitimate offspring. For the rest of the hour, as Natalia was questioned and cross examined about Snyder and Yhost, Sebastiani's and the courtroom spectators' attention were divided. They listened and watched as Natalia testified about the blackmail plot from the witness stand and stole glances at Anna Sebastiani as she struggled to stifle her tears.

Sebastiani was devastated that Anna's resolve to remain stoic had been shattered.

Chapter 48

When court recessed for the day and the jurors and audience were exiting the room, Kari noticed Everett waiting in the back. *What is he doing here?*

"That was something else," Everett gushed when Kari approached him. "Did you know that witness was going to say that stuff about her and Tannie having Sebastiani's kids?"

"I thought it might come up."

"Sebastiani's wife looked like she was ready to cut his thing off. I doubt if she'll be here tomorrow."

"She'll be back. They always come back."

Kari looked over at the electronics cart next to him. "What are you doing here?"

"Did you forget? I'm on the tech squad now. I'm setting up the flat screens and video equipment."

"Of course, tomorrow's movie day. The jurors get to view the evidence captured from inside Sebastiani's car."

"It should be another fun day in court," said Everett, "though not for Sebastiani's wife."

"And not for me." Kari rubbed a hand through her hair. "I'm the only one who can authenticate the videos. I'm testifying in the morning."

Everett's demeanor grew somber. "Does the defense know about the OPR, the fact that you're under investigation?"

"Of course. Whitmore had to disclose it. Sebastiani's attorney will try to make the jurors question my credibility." Kari let out a long sigh. "It won't be pretty."

Kari waved to Whitmore and Becca, who were waiting for her near the double courtroom doors. Everett timidly raised his hand to greet Whitmore. Whitmore did not acknowledge the gesture.

"I better go," said Kari. "We still have to prep for tomorrow."

"Wait. A stack of overhear sheets showed up on my desk this morning. I guess my name is still listed on the case file."

"What? Did you look at them?" Kari was immediately concerned. Title III wiretap rules require that everyone intercepted during court-ordered electronic surveillance be identified and listed on overhear sheets. Kari knew of agents who were sanctioned by the court and suspended for thirty to sixty days for not properly notifying anyone on the overhear sheets.

"Yes," Everett answered. "I flipped through them."

"Please tell me all the notifications were made."

"Whoa, whoa. Don't have a conniption." Everett rested his hand on Kari's shoulder. "Everyone captured on tape was notified."

Kari breathed a sigh of relief. Remembering that Becca and Whitmore were waiting for her, she gestured to them to go on without her and mouthed, *I'll meet you in the war room* before continuing her conversation with Everett.

"Damn it, Hildebrand. You almost gave me a heart attack."

"I just thought that you would want to know that one of the women recorded having sex with Sebastiani wasn't a stripper. She was ID'd as his twenty-year-old next-door neighbor, Gina somebody. I forgot her last name."

"I'm not sure how useful that information is at this point." Kari stared at her former partner and shrugged. "Look, Ev, you need to set up this equipment, and I need to go catch up with Mitch and Becca. I'll see you tomorrow."

"Okay. Sure."

As Kari turned to walk away, Everett called after her. "Kari, I forgot one more thing. There was a guy here asking about you. He left this envelope."

Kari froze. It was Wednesday. She had no doubt who had been there to see her. She took the manila envelope, peeled back the flap, and peered inside. Her body stiffened.

"He was here in the courthouse?" Kari's eyes darted around the room as she attempted to contain the rising wave of panic building inside her.

"He said he's been following the case in the paper. He asked if you would be testifying."

"What else did he tell you? What did you tell him?" Her words barely squeaked past her lips. She hoped Everett couldn't detect the fright that gripped her by the throat.

"I told him you'd be on the stand tomorrow. What's wrong?" His eyes widened. "Is he the one who was calling you when you were caring for your mother? Joe Wilson?"

He looked down at her trembling hands clutching the envelope. "Who is this guy?"

Her hands groped her forearms, her shoulders, kneaded her thighs. She let out several long breaths.

"What's in the envelope?"

She shook her head. No way would she show him the panties she had left behind in Wilson's room so many months ago.

"What does he want?"

"Oh my God, Hildebrand. I can't testify tomorrow."

"But you have to authenticate the videos."

Kari held her head in her hands and tried to gather her thoughts. She sighed deeply before looking up at Everett. "I know, but—"

"This Wilson guy," said Everett. "Does he know something about you that you don't want to get out?"

"Yes."

She knew Everett recognized her fear and desperation. He'd probably felt the same when confronted by Juanita about his improper association with Bill Leone.

"I really messed up this time," she said.

"Don't worry." He placed his hand on her shoulder. "We'll figure something out."

"You don't understand. Wilson can ruin everything, my career...my marriage." She felt like a hypocrite, saying this to Everett, but his compassionate expression remained.

"Come to court tomorrow," Ev said. "I won't let anything happen to you. I'll think of something."

"Like what?"

"I'll make sure everything is set. I'll personally take care of the videos."

"That's not what I'm worried about."

"You'll see." He stood firm, his broad shoulders pulled back.

He made her smile, even if only for a millisecond. "Why are you being nice to me?"

"What do you mean?" Everett seemed startled. "You're my friend."

"Hildebrand..." Kari couldn't finish her sentence.

"Don't worry. I'll take care of everything. I mean it."

"Please don't do anything that could get you into trouble. I don't want that." She looked sadly around the empty courtroom. "I should go."

Everett called out as she moved across the room. "Kari, I'm glad you're not angry with me anymore."

She paused and felt engulfed by a deep sadness. "Truth be told, I never had the right to be angry with you," she said before slipping through the courtroom's doors.

Chapter 49

As soon as she had retrieved her weapon from the lockbox and her cell phone from the courthouse security desk on the main floor, Kari received a call from an unfamiliar number. Wilson. It had to be. She rushed to the sidewalk before answering.

"*What* do you want?"

"I think you know what I want. You didn't think I had given up, did you? Did you get the envelope I left you?"

"Are you still near the courthouse?" Her eyes darted up and down the street.

"Why? You got that key?"

"That's an impossible task. I can't walk into the evidence room and start going through boxes."

"You better figure something out."

"What does the key open that's so important?"

"I guess you could say it opens a treasure chest."

"You're lost then. I can't help you."

"Really? I was reading the paper this morning, and there you were in a photo, walking out of the courthouse behind the prosecutor. I read all about the case in the paper. The article mentioned strip clubs. What a coincidence. Isn't that where we met?"

"Screw you."

"Really? So you're okay with me telling your husband and boss about our little escapades? Maybe I should think about exposing you to a larger audience. Maybe that will get you to change your mind."

"I'm not sneaking into the evidence room for you."

"Yes, you are, and I want you to come by tonight with the key."

"Are you crazy?"

"How about you take a moment to consider your options and then get your sweet cheeks over here."

"Or what?"

"If I don't see you tonight, be prepared to answer some difficult questions after your turn on the witness stand tomorrow."

"What are you going to do?"

"How about I slip a note to that reporter who's been following the trial? I'm sure he would love to write about how, during the course of your investigation, you were picking up guys in the same strip clubs where you were interviewing witnesses. How many others? I'm sure I wasn't the only one."

She suddenly grew cold and a shiver snaked down her spine. "Stop threatening me, or I swear—"

"What? Come by the Sheraton tonight, or I promise, you'll see me in court tomorrow."

Kari punched the end call button. She could give Wilson what he wanted or risk losing everything that mattered to her most, her family and her career. The choice was hers. She had to make a decision. She couldn't allow him to torture her anytime he wanted. Either she would pilfer the key he said was locked up in the evidence room, or she would consider ways to eliminate him from her life. Whatever it took.

She decided to pull his FBI file and see if she could find anything in his dossier that would placate him until the trial was over. She wouldn't be able to look at the more recent volumes of the file. They were stored on the drug squad, but the older volumes and sub-files would be maintained in the closed-files storage area. She had no business thumbing through any of the drug investigation documents, open or closed. If anyone were to see her, she wasn't sure how she would explain the intrusion.

***

Back at the office, she punched the file number into the automated system, and the vertical shelving began to separate and slide together like a giant accordion. The aisle containing the files she sought opened wide for her to enter. Kari flipped haphazardly through the sections of the multivolume file. Interview reports laid out details about the callous street-corner pharmacy business Wilson and Prescott had operated. Documents in the file revealed that at least three people had died from abusing the unregulated OxyContin and Percocet they imported from India and Mexico. Prescott was especially ruthless. Transcripts revealed that during wiretapped conversations, he had been recorded threatening to kill anyone who got in the way of their illegal enterprise.

Kari pulled another one of the thick files and flipped through it, watching with one eye for the clerk in charge of closed files. She wasn't sure what she was looking for—certainly not anything that would actually compromise the investigation. Even if she wanted to obtain the identities of those cooperating with the investigation, those files weren't available to her. They were kept under lock and key within the Human Intelligence Unit and could only be signed out by the official case agent. But perhaps she could find an innocuous photo or memo that would prove to Wilson that she had accessed the file and attempted to get the information he sought. Kari opened the large evidence envelope at the rear of the file and sifted through a stack of surveillance photos. Most were miscellaneous images of Wilson and Prescott entering and exiting the small-time storefronts they supplied, but one was extremely interesting. It was a photo of Prescott and the woman who had been with Wilson at the Sheraton.

What was her name again? Daphne?

Kari turned the photo over and read the back: "Saul Prescott and Rochelle Prescott" and the location, date, and time it had been taken. *Rochelle Prescott?*

Kari delved inside another evidence envelope and pulled out more photos. One was labeled "Saul Prescott with wife, Rochelle Prescott."

Wilson was having an affair with his codefendant's pretty, young trophy wife.

Chapter 50

The next morning, Kari was present and prepared to testify. If Hildebrand couldn't follow through on his promise and Wilson did follow through on his, she would have no opportunity to make use of the clandestine revelation she had just unearthed and the whole world would learn about her own secret life.

Still, she knew one thing for sure—she was done being a victim.

Everett approached her as soon as she entered the courtroom. "I have it all worked out," he said. "You won't have to testify."

"Thanks, but so what? As long as this trial continues, Wilson will be a threat. I'm telling Whitmore. He needs to know what's going on."

"No. Don't." Everett had never looked more confident, more determined. "Trust me," he said. "This trial ends today."

Kari stared at Everett. *How could he promise that?* She was conflicted, but when she reached the prosecutor's table, she said nothing to Whitmore about Wilson.

"I had to allow them to review your personnel file," said Whitmore. He pointed in the direction of Sebastiani and his attorney. "Crawley will try to use the pending OPR cover-up inquiry against you. But otherwise, you have an exemplary record."

Kari looked over at Everett making last-minute adjustments to the video equipment. He gave her an assuring nod.

"It's okay. I'm ready," she said to Whitmore, but for what, she didn't know.

"I'll show the videos first, and then call you up to testify about how and when they were recorded."

At that moment, Kari spied Joe Wilson slipping into the last row. Her heart stopped. He had chosen a seat right next to Shiffler, the *Inquirer* reporter and regular trial attendee. Wilson caught her gaze and gave her a discreet finger wave. She turned away and bumped into Whitmore.

"Don't worry," he assured her. "I'll protect you as best as I can."

Kari rested her right hand on her chest.

"Forget about me. Protect the case."

***

As Kari had predicted, Anna Sebastiani was in court for another day of heartache. Surely, her husband had encouraged her to stay away, but there she was, about to view videos of her husband frolicking with strippers.

Whitmore warned the jurors and the gallery that they were about to view sexual activity that most would find offensive. He signaled for Everett to start the video. In no time, everyone was on the edges of their seats, watching Sebastiani's insatiable greed.

The graphic black-and-white scenes of Sebastiani pocketing cash, accepting hand jobs, blow jobs, and engaging in acrobatically flexible sex in the front and backseat of his car played on several large, digital monitors positioned around the room. Kari scooted her chair sideways to view the closest flat screen. From her peripheral vision, she could see Anna, and she knew the only method Anna could use to shield herself from the images would be to close her eyes. Anna chose instead to face the humiliation head-on. She sat with her hands in her lap and a blank look on her face. Kari wished she could say something to her to make her feel better, but it wouldn't be appropriate. Plus, what could she say to woman who had just learned all the dirty details about her husband's betrayal?

And then, Kari thought about Kevin. He too might soon be forced to face the ugly, sordid truth about his spouse.

Sebastiani, the judge, and the jurors were darting their eyes between the monitors and Anna, waiting to see how she would react. Just as she had the day before, Anna began to weep. The courtroom was eerily hushed except for the moaning sounds of her husband's liaisons and Anna's sobs.

During the screening, Kari snuck a look at the rear of the courtroom. Spotting her, Wilson raised two fingers to his lips and flicked his tongue out between them. She turned away quickly and hoped no one else, especially Shiffler, had witnessed his crude gesture.

The videos continued for several long minutes more.

"Mr. Whitmore, I think we've all seen enough." Judge Jiles spoke haltingly from the bench.

"Your Honor, each, uh, encounter is a bribery count."

"Can't you and Mr. Crawley agree to stipulate?" Jiles peered over his glasses. "Is it really necessary for us to watch each and every one of these clips?"

"The defense agrees to stipulate to the existence of the surveillance videos," Crawley said.

"Excellent. Mr. Whitmore your audiovisual person may stop the recordings."

Whitmore nodded to Everett. Kari was not disappointed. She never really thought Everett could do anything to stop the inevitable. What had he possibly had in mind?

Slowly, Kari rotated to view the back of the room once again. Wilson mouthed the words, *You're next.* What did he mean by that? There was no way that he would be allowed to take the stand to introduce unsubstantiated evidence about her.

When she turned to face the front of the courtroom, she was surprised to see the video still playing. Everett, displaying blundering ineptitude, was pushing buttons on the remote. The video fast-forwarded, speeding from one image to another. Kari understood he was new to the tech squad, but, *Damn, Hildebrand, who doesn't know how to operate a DVR?*

Finally, he found the pause button and the video frame froze. Displayed on screens around the room was the image of a pretty, young brunette with her hair pulled back in a ponytail performing oral sex on Stuart Sebastiani.

Anna Sebastiani shrieked and howled, sounding like a wounded animal. She jumped up from her seat and glared at her husband with frightening intensity. He was motionless. His eyes, full of dread, were fixated on the closest video monitor.

"How could you? How could you?" Anna yelled at Sebastiani, but he didn't seem to hear her. Since the front pew prevented her from leaning forward to pummel him, she ripped off her shoes and flung them violently at his head.

One shoe struck him in the face. Tiny drops of blood fell from cuts above his left eye and right cheek, and dripped onto his fresh white shirt. The entire courtroom erupted. It all happened so suddenly that the marshals assigned to the courtroom took several seconds before reacting. Fearing the worst, they scrambled to the front and quickly escorted Judge Jiles and the jurors out of the room to safety.

At the same time, Anna Sebastiani, having momentarily forgotten that her husband was on trial for graft and not his moral failures, screamed out in earshot of the jurors, "He's guilty! He's guilty!" as her children led her out into the hall.

While chaos swirled around him, Sebastiani remained immobile, staring at the monitor and lightly dabbing at his injuries. For most of his life, he had been rewarded for being a philandering pig, and now he had to pay the price. And it was going to cost him everything.

"What just happened?" Whitmore asked Kari and Becca.

Becca's eyes bounced around the room, but Kari was calm. She knew exactly what had happened. The clip was not one of the counts she had selected for the jurors to view.

Everett smiled disarmingly at her.

"Gina?" Kari half whispered.

Everett shrugged. But when Kari started to walk toward him, he discreetly shook his head, warning her not to approach, not to say anything. He tilted his head to the back of the courtroom. Wilson was nowhere to be seen.

After the notion of threat was cleared, Judge Jiles returned to the bench and banged his gavel. "Order, order in the court."

With one more bang of his wooden gavel, the judge announced court was in recess. Defense Attorney Crawley wasted no time using

Anna Sebastiani's angry outburst as grounds for a mistrial. The judge could deny the motion and choose instead to instruct the jury to disregard Anna's spontaneous waiver of her spousal right not to testify against her husband. But who could ignore her anguished shrieks upon discovering his betrayal with the young girl next door? Kari knew what was supposed to be a three- to four-week trial had just come to a screeching halt.

Chapter 51

It came as no surprise to Kari when Whitmore called to tell her Sebastiani had entered a guilty plea. She assumed he wasn't willing to put his wife through another humiliating trial. As part of the deal, the prosecutor agreed not to pursue criminal charges against Arty, and Stu agreed to testify at Lynette Hampton and Curtis Kincaid's extortion trial. When the JOLIE owners also agreed to plead out their charges, the prosecuting phase of the G-Sting investigation came to an unceremonious conclusion.

But Kari wasn't able to enjoy the successful end to the case. The OPR inquiry was still active and Joe Wilson, who had slipped away from the courtroom during the chaos, had not resurfaced. She knew he would be back. She had told Everett enough about her predicament to garner his assistance and now, with Everett's help, she had a plan in place to neutralize Wilson, a plan that had been ripped from the pages of Sebastiani's playbook.

***

Even if Kari wasn't ready to rejoice, Tannie and Natalia were. Halfheartedly, Kari went with Becca to a barbecue at Natalia's for a post-trial celebration.

"Here's to Stu, may he rot in jail." Tannie lifted her wineglass for an impromptu toast.

"Tannie, we're not sure yet what's happening with JOLIE," Kari said, raising her glass high. "But please know that we are willing to do whatever we can to make sure you land safely on your feet."

"Don't worry about me," said Tannie. "Natalia has some great news, big news."

Kari and Becca both turned to look at Natalia, who grinned broadly.

"You know how Hampton and Kincaid were ordered to sell JOLIE prior to the acceptance of their plea agreement, so the proceeds could be used for restitution and forfeiture purposes?" Tannie asked.

"Yeah?" Kari's curiosity was piqued.

"I bought JOLIE." Natalia couldn't keep the secret any longer. "I'm the new owner of the best gentlemen's club in town, on the whole East Coast." She did a little dance around the room.

"Wow. This is unbelievable." Kari reached out and pulled Natalia in for a hug. "How'd that happen?"

"During some serious pillow talk."

"You need to know people with major capital to strap on a business like JOLIE," said Tannie.

Natalia explained that she had been able to persuade a few of her generous gentlemen friends to become investors. With their considerable net worth and discretionary income, they had agreed to fund her business venture. In a few short weeks, Natalia Hall would be JOLIE's principal executive. Tannie, Dia, and Trey would each hold a 5 percent minority ownership.

"I'm hoping to invest in a bigger slice of the business eventually, possibly ten percent," Tannie said proudly. "I'll be the featured performer. You two are welcome at JOLIE anytime you want."

Becca pumped her fist. "I'm there."

"Uh, don't take this personally," said Kari, "but I'm done with strip clubs."

"Oh, I'll get you to change your mind," said Tannie.

Kari shook her head. She was thrilled everything was working out for Natalia and Tannie, but felt she should raise the obvious question.

"I don't want to be a Debbie Downer, but do either of you know anything about running a business?" Kari asked. "Hampton and Kincaid had trouble making the numbers add up for JOLIE."

"That's the other big surprise." Natalia could barely contain her excitement. "Arty's going to remain the operations manager. He's been running the club since the indictment, and he's already started to cut expenses and balance the books."

"Wow, you guys are like one big happy extended family now," said Becca.

"And you know what's so freaking weird? We have to thank Stu for all this." Natalia looked over to where Trey and Dia played nearby. "Who would have guessed that their deadbeat dad would make it possible for all of his kids to build a secure future together?"

Kari smirked. "Nice. But I suggest you hold off sending his name in for Father of the Year."

Chapter 52

When her phone finally lit up with his number, Kari was more energized than anxious.

"Is this really you, Joe Wilson, ringing my damn phone again?" she answered with a deceptively pleasant tone.

Wilson may have thought a couple of weeks of silent treatment would unnerve her or provide false hope that he had abandoned pursuit, but since his appearance at the courthouse, she had used the time wisely.

"I bet you thought you scared me off with all that commotion in the courtroom." Wilson snorted, but then his tone darkened. "Did you get what I asked you for?"

"Not exactly," said Kari. "But I found something in your FBI file."

"What do you got for me?"

"You're staying at the Sheraton?"

"Yeah."

"I'll bring it over. I'm on my way."

"You coming here?"

"Yeah."

"You coming alone?"

"Yeah. Just me…and the SWAT team." Kari laughed.

"What's going on?"

"It was a joke, Joe. Don't go getting all paranoid."

"Is this some kind of setup?"

"You have things backward, don't you? You have me dangling by the short hairs, not the other way around."

"So, you're really coming over?"

"Sure. Why not? If I don't, aren't you still threatening to send a note to my boss, or the director of FBI, or even the president? Oh wait, you switched that to blasting out my dirty deeds for the masses to read in the newspaper."

"If you don't have what I asked you for, why do you want to see me?"

"Isn't there anything else..." Kari paused for effect, "...I can do for you?"

Wilson was quiet for several seconds.

In the momentary silence, Kari could visualize his face, lit up with a shit-eating grin, and his freak flag fluttering and flapping in the wind. And sure enough, his kinky predilections overruled his misgivings.

"Room 809."

"Whoa. Not so fast," said Kari. "You need to buy a girl a drink first. I'll meet you in the bar."

***

Wilson stood to greet her as soon as she approached. He met her eyes and then scanned the area behind her.

"I'm not alone." Kari motioned to Everett sitting at the bar. "He's here with me."

"What kind of bullshit is this?" Wilson sized up Everett and sat anyway.

She slid into the opposite side of the booth.

"Every Wednesday since the trial ended, I've been expecting your call." She passed him two manila envelopes, playing the same hand Sebastiani had dealt Snyder, knowing that compromising photos would work this time.

"What's this?"

"Open it."

The first set of photos that slid out of the envelope captured him and Rochelle naked and in various sexual positions and embraces.

"What's this?" he repeated. "These were taken in this hotel. How did you get 'em?"

"Don't worry about that. There's a video too. My guarantee that you will never, ever bother me again."

He picked up a photo and shoved it in her face. "Big fucking deal. I don't care who sees these. Put them up on a billboard on the Walt Whitman Bridge for all I care."

"Really?" She motioned with her head for him to pick up the second envelope. "There's another photo I want you to see."

He reached into the envelope. It was a copy of the photo from the case file—the photo of Rochelle and Saul Prescott.

He slapped the photos facedown on the table with the palm of his hand. A bright red streak of anger flashed across his cheeks.

"*What the fuck?*"

"Her name's not Daphne. It's Rochelle. Rochelle Prescott. You're having an affair with your codefendant's wife," Kari said smugly. "So why do you meet on Wednesdays? Is that when he goes out of town?

Wilson didn't respond.

"I guess I got that right?"

Wilson gathered up the photos of him and Rochelle and held them in his hands. "What are you going to do with them?"

"I was thinking of sending them to Prescott."

"That's not funny."

"I'm not joking."

"He'd have me killed."

She hiked her shoulders and waved the photo in his face.

"You don't have it in you."

"Maybe I can't pull the trigger to kill you."

Wilson leaned against the high back of the banquette and studied her. "But you'd let Prescott do it for you?"

She nodded and knew at that moment she had just regained control of the situation.

Wilson stabbed a finger at Everett, who still stood guard nearby. "What about him? Doesn't he know what a sadistic guy like Prescott will do if he finds out I'm doing his wife?"

"No clue. He thinks I'm threatening to tell *your* wife."

"I don't have a wife."

She shrugged. "But he doesn't know that." She drummed her fingers on the compromising photos. "But you know. All you have to do is agree to never call me, never come near me, never put your dirty hands on me again. And Prescott never *needs* to see these photos."

"You wouldn't do it."

"And there lies your dilemma. You're not sure how much I hate you, how far I would go to stop you from destroying my marriage and my career. Enough to get you killed?" She held out her hands, palms up, and hunched her shoulders.

"This is my life you're fucking around with."

"And you're not fucking with mine? You think I've forgotten what you did to me? Plus, I sat in that courtroom a week ago and watched a woman get her heart torn out when she heard her husband was a cheater. That was a preview of my life. I'm not putting my husband through that."

Kari took one of the comprising photos and placed it next to one of Rochelle and Prescott. She glowered at Wilson.

"You wouldn't be able to live with yourself if you showed Prescott these photos, and he—"

Kari tilted her head. "I'd have to try my best to forgive myself."

Wilson balled his hand into a fist. His face twitched. "You wouldn't get away with it, you know."

"Eventually, we all pay for the mistakes we make. I understand that getting you out of my life will come at a price."

"I don't believe you have the balls do it." Wilson huffed and jerked his head toward Everett. "Why don't you get rid of him and come upstairs to suck my dick again?"

He reached across the table and touched her arm, but she recoiled as if he had taken a blowtorch to her skin. She focused on the spot where his fingers had been, where the loathing she felt toward him seemed to smolder and throb. Kari's hatred was all-consuming. At that moment, he represented each of the boys who had stolen her innocence so many years ago.

She ground out the words deliberately: "You. Must. Be. Crazy. Just try me."

His eyes darted away from her piercing gaze for a beat, and she rapped on the table to make sure he was paying attention.

"One thing I have to ask you. Why me?"

His answer came quickly. "I just want to stay out of jail. If we could get into that safe deposit box, we would be on the other side of the world before anybody realized it."

Kari now understood the importance of the key.

"Good luck with that," she said and smiled benignly as she slid out of the booth. "By the way, is Rochelle upstairs?"

He nodded slowly.

"Tell her I said hello."

Kari whirled on her heels and, without a look back, walked across the lobby to the hotel registration desk.

"Excuse me," she said to the young male working the counter. "Could you do me a favor? I'm Kari. Could you tell Gloria that the presentation she helped me put together turned out beautifully."

"Gloria works the overnight shift. Is there something I can help you with?"

"No. I'm good. But could you leave her a note that I'll be by in the morning to pick up the items she's been keeping safe for me."

"If we're holding luggage or a package in the storeroom for you, I can get it."

"Thanks, but Gloria's the best. She's already taken care of everything."

**

Everett joined her outside. She gave him a thumbs-up.

"So, we're done here?" he asked.

"We can come by in the morning, pick up the camera equipment, and get everything back to the office." She reached out and placed her hand in his. "Everett. Thank you."

"I told you I would help you get that guy off your back. We all make mistakes. God knows I'm not perfect."

She felt awful that she had not told him the full story. She had only told him she and Wilson had had an affair and now that she wanted to end it, he was threatening to tell Kevin. Everett had helped her install cameras in Wilson's hotel room to capture the images of him and Rochelle together and Gloria, the desk clerk, had helped them get into Wilson's room and had removed the equipment before housekeeping went in to clean the following day. Everett had insisted that Gloria provide him with the Sheraton registration info, so he had Wilson and Rochelle Prescott's true names. But Kari wasn't worried. She knew he wouldn't dare violate office policy by running their names through indices or NCIC.

Everett placed his hand on her shoulder.

"Kari, have you thought about just telling your husband? Confessing so that Wilson won't have this threat over you?"

Her eyes widened. "Please don't ask me to do that.

"But Brenda forgave me."

"No. Let's stick to the plan. This way no one gets hurt."

Chapter 53

Early the following morning, when they arrived at the Sheraton, a column of guests stood along the curved driveway, waiting for rides to their destinations. When a departing car allowed room for another to enter, the hotel valet flagged over the next taxi in line at the stand across Dock Street.

"Just pull into the loading zone," Kari said. "Gloria should be getting off of work any minute now. She said she would walk the equipment out to us."

Everett parked illegally at the curb directly across the street from the hotel.

"Kari. Look." With a tilt of his chin, Everett directed her attention to the front of the Sheraton, where, among the people in the queue, Joe Wilson and an attractive blond snuggled together in a passionate embrace. Kari recognized the woman immediately. Rochelle Prescott.

"There's your guy and that woman we filmed in the hotel room together," said Everett.

The agents watched as Wilson brushed his hand softly across Rochelle's cheek and placed two delicate kisses just above her eyelids.

"I can't tell from way over here." Kari squinted as if she were almost blind, hoping she could make Everett distrust his eyesight too.

"Sure it is." Everett nodded. "They're practically begging for their spouses to catch them, carrying on like that in public."

Kari watched as Rochelle giggled at something Wilson whispered in her ear. He then caressed her tenderly, their bodies swaying in unison to a silent love tune.

Suddenly, an abrupt feeling of doom and dread came over Kari. Something inexplicable told Kari to stop Gloria from going outside.

"I'm going in to get the equipment." Kari grabbed the door handle, but Everett pulled her back before she could slip away.

"What are you doing? He'll see you. You don't need that drama." He leaned across the console and touched her shoulder, as if to transmit common sense.

He was right. She tried to ignore her pangs of uneasiness and stared silently ahead, trying to come up with a logical way to sequester Gloria, when a black sedan backed out of one of the spaces next to them, slowly inching onto Dock Street. Something about the driver's fixed and enraged scowl drew Kari's attention. At first, she didn't recognize him. She had only seen him in photos. But when he double-parked in the driveway of the Sheraton and bolted from the car, she knew it was Saul Prescott and that something terrible was about to happen. She sprang from the car and pointed in Prescott's direction. She was too far away to do anything but yell.

"*Nooooooo!*"

Prescott marched up to his wife, raised a pistol, and fired one shot into her chest. Rochelle's primal scream pierced straight through Kari's being. She sprinted across the street and took a position behind a parked car just as Wilson pulled a small revolver from his waistband, firing several times at Prescott before he could take another shot. It happened so fast, and Kari was still not close enough to safely get off a round to stop him. Wilson's bullets slammed into Prescott. The rounds shot at close range drove him off his feet and against the wall. The blood soaking the front of his clothes matched the deep red of the Sheraton's brick facade. Wilson scrambled to Rochelle and howled when he discovered her slumped on the ground, blood trickling from her mouth. In a futile attempt to save her, he lifted Rochelle onto her feet and held her inert body in his arms. He shook her and called her name. It was too late.

Wilson searched the crowd and screamed for help. But hotel guests and bystanders were too occupied with fear. They cried out in horror from prone positions and crawled on hands and knees to escape the mayhem.

And then he saw her crouching toward him.

"*Put down the gun,*" Kari called. She uttered in alarmed spurts to Everett. "Careful. Bystanders. Crossfire."

Wilson, with an absent look in his eyes and his weapon at his side, stared at them. His gaze zeroed in on Kari.

"You bitch," he growled as he lowered Rochelle's body to the ground.

"*Put the gun down,*" she warned again. This time she had a clear shot.

He raised the barrel. She fired. After years of training, she instinctually aimed for center mass and kept shooting. The barrage of bullets struck Wilson in the torso and leveled him backward.

And then it was over.

Her heart raced. Everett stood next to her with his gun still aimed at Wilson's lifeless body. He stared at the man with a dazed look in his eyes.

"Everett, are you okay?"

He nodded slowly and holstered his gun. She did the same.

They approached the Sheraton's blood-splattered sidewalk, Wilson, Rochelle, and Prescott were dead. Wilson's body was riddled with multiple gunshot wounds. Kari secured Prescott's and Wilson's weapons, rendered the pistol safe, and opened the cylinder of the revolver. All of the shell casings were spent. Wilson, most likely, had no idea that his gun was empty when he'd pointed it at them.

Everett stood beside her, dazed and numb.

"We had no choice," she said. "We had to shoot."

Everett just stared at her.

She grabbed his shoulder and blurted, "Ev, it wasn't supposed to go down like this. I'm sorry. I'm sorry—"

"No, wait." He was ashy gray, and a stricken look was plastered across his face. "I think I'm the cause of all this."

"What? How?"

"I thought I was helping. I went back to the office last night and ran an Internet search. I was trying to contact Wilson's wife to tell her about his affairs, but when I couldn't find her, I tracked down Rochelle

Prescott's husband instead. He thanked me for the information. I had no idea he would do anything like this."

Kari reached out to console him. She issued no recriminations.

"It's not your fault. I got you involved in this." He quivered and let out an uncontrolled sob that had been stuck in his throat.

"This time, I really messed things up. This time, they'll throw me out of the Bureau for sure." He pounded his fists against his forehead.

She couldn't let him take the blame. Although she could have never made the call to intentionally create this chaos, isn't it what she said she wanted? She grabbed Everett by the shoulders and shook him until she knew he was focused and listening to her.

"No. It was a love triangle that resulted in two murders and a suicide by cop. Got it?"

His eyes searched hers for understanding and his hands covered his mouth. She pulled them away from his face and gazed into his eyes.

"We'll figure out a reason why we happened to be here. But it was definitely self-defense. That's not a lie. He pointed that gun right at us. Got it?"

"Yes." He nodded and took in a deep breath. "Kari, you just saved my life, and now you're saving my career."

"Saved your life? What are you talking about?"

"I froze. I only got off one shot."

Only then did she glance at her holstered gun and notice the slide locked back. She had emptied all her rounds into Wilson.

Fifteen plus one, just as she had promised him.

Chapter 54

SAC Roeder's door was open. Kari stuck her head inside.

"Agent Wheeler, come in, please. Shut the door."

It had been a week since the violent episode at the Sheraton, and she knew whatever Roeder had to say to her didn't matter anymore. She had already saved what mattered most—her marriage. She stood with her hands clasped behind her back, her feet planted firmly on the FBI seal area rug in front of his desk.

"Please sit down."

Kari didn't move. "Whatever this is, I'd rather stand," she said.

"I have news about the internal inquiry, but I also wanted to check on how you were doing. I spoke to Agent Hildebrand earlier. You both were true heroes that day at the Sheraton. It was a miracle you were in the area to visit your former source and able to stop the threat and take control of the crime scene before the locals arrived."

She and Everett had agreed to tell the fact-finding team from headquarters that they were in the vicinity of the Sheraton to make an unannounced stopover at Tannie's. Kari had given up on trying to redirect undeserved commendations. When Roeder extended his hand, she shook it.

"Right place, right time," she said.

"You must be still processing what happened that day. I hope you're taking advantage of the employee assistance program."

"Absolutely. The Bureau shrinks are helping me deal with the shooting and some other issues stirred up by the Sebastiani case."

Roeder raised an eyebrow, obviously curious about what she meant.

But she knew he wouldn't ask for details. "Use the EAP services as long as you feel they're useful," he said.

"I plan to."

"The review team's official report is not in yet," he said, changing the subject. "But I'm told it's been deemed a good shooting. Clearly self-defense."

Kari finally sat down and felt the relief that his pronouncement provided. *Clearly self-defense.* Even the shooting review team agreed she and Everett were not getting away with murder. "And the OPR?"

"I won't prolong this for you. You're cleared of all charges. They determined that you had no knowledge of efforts to cover up for Agent Hildebrand's unethical behavior."

"No censure letter? No suspension?"

"No. It's all over."

She took in a deep breath and let it out slowly. "Thank you."

She stood to leave but remembered her squad mates.

"What about Shawn and Tommy?"

"They're going to have to take a hit."

"That's not right. They weren't trying to cover up anything either."

"Wheeler, they black-bagged Hildebrand's desk. They admitted to removing and destroying a flash drive that they said you knew nothing about.

"What's gonna happen to them?"

"Five-day suspension each for violation of miscellaneous rules and regulations. It could've been worse. The charges were mitigated because they were trying to help."

"And Juanita? By pushing for the OPR, she's alienated more than half the agents on the squad."

Roeder nodded. "We realize she's no longer an effective manager. She's on her way back to headquarters."

"That's a reprimand? Smells like a promotion to me."

"Juanita has her flaws, but don't we all?" The way he looked at her made her wonder if he knew hers. "But agents like Juanita, with their rigid expectations, help to maintain the top standards of the Bureau."

Kari gave Roeder a puzzled stare.

"She demands that everyone around her maintain the highest principles possible," he explained. "And when they don't, like a critical parent, she expects them to be disciplined."

"No. Destroyed," Kari corrected. "She tried to destroy Hildebrand. He didn't deserve that. I'll never be able to repay him for everything he's done for me."

"My guess is, sometime during her career, someone told her she wasn't good enough, that she didn't have what it takes to be a successful agent." Kari noticed Roeder had given the subject some thought. "As minority and female agents, you both must have felt, at times, that you have something to prove."

Kari made no response—not because she quarreled with his assessment, but because she grudgingly agreed.

"To prove her critics wrong, Juanita's excessively demanding, of herself and those who work for her." He placed his elbows on his desk, clasped his hands together, and continued. "There are agents like her throughout the Bureau. They push themselves hard and sacrifice for the cause. Juanita's an extreme case, but I call people like her 'mission martyrs.' I suspect you might be one too."

Kari stiffened. That "martyr" word again. Kevin had called her that. Was it possible? In spite of her transgressions, was she a mission martyr too?

***

Kari left Roeder's office, returned to her desk, and sat contemplating what he had said. After only a couple of sessions of therapy, she had begun to ask herself if she'd been attempting to prove she was worthy at too great a price. Self-sabotage? Caused by doubts that she deserved to be a member of the greatest law enforcement agency in the world.

It all made sense now. It was all related. She had been playing the role of the new kid in school, still desperately wanting the others to like her, to be her friends, but at the same time only being capable of remote connections. She had been both punishing herself and seeking validation, even from strangers—especially strangers. Now that she understood why, she was done blaming herself for things that were never her fault. Thank God she was finally getting help. Perhaps it was time to forgive herself.

Kari glanced around the squad area. Everyone was gone. She wasn't sure how long she had been sitting alone at her desk. In the course of investigating Sebastiani, with her mother's death and her own struggles to keep from being seduced by the sleaze, the past eleven months had been tough. She would spend the rest of her life justifying all that she had sacrificed, especially the mortal offerings, to finally be free of her self-loathing and inner doubts. Kari took in a deep breath, held it for a count of three, and let it out slowly. Strange? She actually felt like some part of her had become unblocked, unlocked.

Kari called home.

When Kevin answered, all Kari could say was, "You were right."

"About what? What's wrong?" His voice was filled with concern. "Did something happen?"

"Like, did I shoot somebody today?" Kari said.

"Don't joke about that."

"Sorry. I'm calling to tell you that the OPR is over. I've been cleared."

"You don't sound happy about it. That's what you wanted. Right?"

"Yeah."

"Where are you? Are you okay?"

"At work. I'm fine."

"You sure?"

"I'll explain when I get home. Did the kids do their homework?"

"Yeah. They're good."

"If you don't mind, I'd like to work out first, maybe go for a run."

"Why don't you go out to celebrate? Where's Becca?"

"She's already gone. I just need to chill a little. I won't be too late."

"Kari, I love you."

"I know and I love you too."

And even though she knew he would never find out about her betrayal, she planned to dedicate the rest of her life to being the wife he deserved. Her heart ached when she thought about the secrets she was keeping from him.

She hung up and reached for her gym bag and running shoes. Then she changed her mind and made another phone call.

Chapter 55

Before Tannie could say anything more than hello, Kari walked into the condo and over to the vertical pole in the middle of the living room.

"I have a confession," Kari said, swirling amateurishly around the pole. "Since the first time I saw you dance at JOLIE, I've wanted you to show me how to do this."

"I offered to teach you before. You said it wouldn't be appropriate."

"The trial's over." Kari shrugged. "And you're no longer my informant."

"So the rules no longer apply."

"Not the ones about pole dancing." Kari stroked the metal pole, alternating hand over fist. "I remembered you said that you find inner peace and power when you work the pole."

"Is that what you want? Inner peace?"

"I think so."

"You want me to show you some basic moves?"

"You go first," said Kari. "I want to watch you again."

Tannie, dressed in her usual home attire of sports bra and shorts, turned up the music, and grasped the pole with both hands, swinging her long, lean legs around the narrow metal shaft. She climbed, spun, flew, and propelled her body to the thumping bass beat. She arched her back, scooped her chest forward, and thrust her hips in sensual and flexible motion. Tannie, rotating her torso like a serpent, fluidly transitioned from the pole to the floor and back to the pole again.

While Tannie danced, Kari watched silently and waited for her lesson. She could feel the stress seeping from her pores. When the music ended, Kari unstrapped her gun belt and holster, and placed them on top of the bookcase. Then, she discarded her shoes and suit jacket, along with her inhibitions.

"You have to take those off too." Tannie tugged at Kari's pants.

Kari hesitated.

"Friction." Tannie patted her bare thighs. "You won't be able to grip the pole with those on. You have to take them off."

Kari unzipped and stepped out of her suit trousers. As she stood awkwardly in the middle of the room, her purple pinstriped dress shirt just about covered her panties. Tannie strolled over casually and took the pants from her.

"I'll put them over here so they won't get wrinkled." She draped the pants across the back of a dining room chair. "Did you want to take that off too?" Tannie pantomimed removing an imaginary shirt.

"No."

"That's fine, but you'll want to at least roll up those sleeves. Okay?"

Kari unbuttoned the cuffs and pushed the fabric up and over her elbows.

"That's better. Now, come over here." Tannie held her hand out to lead Kari over, but Kari ignored the gesture and walked unaided toward the pole.

"What do I do?" she asked.

"Press up against it as close as you can get. Introduce yourself."

Kari scrunched up her face. "What?"

"You and that pole are about to enter into an intimate relationship. You should get to know it better."

When Kari hesitated, Tannie placed her hand on the small of Kari's back and gently pushed her closer, so her forehead, nose, and lips kissed the cool metal shaft. Tannie stood close behind her. When she spoke, Kari could feel her moist breath on the nape of her neck.

"Shut your eyes," Tannie whispered. "Keep them closed and listen to your breathing."

Kari tried, but she could only feel her heartbeat quickening.

"Relax. Slow it down like mine." Tannie moved in even closer and Kari could feel the gentle rise and release of Tannie's chest as she slowly breathed in. Out. In. Out.

"Now, grab the pole with your hands."

Kari touched the pole at chest height.

"No. Higher, up above your head," said Tannie.

Kari did as instructed.

"Good."

With deep and measured breaths, her eyes still closed, Kari could feel the tender stretch of the muscles in her neck and spine.

"You'll be using your arms." Tannie's hands traced the outline of Kari's arms from her shoulders to her hands and up again. Her fingertips lightly brushed Kari's skin. "But remember, the real control comes from here." Tannie reached under Kari's shirt and stroked her stomach. Kari gasped and opened her eyes.

"Are you ready?" said Tannie.

Kari searched Tannie's face for meaning and released the pole, wiggling out of her close hold. "No," she said. "No, I'm not."

"What's wrong?"

Reality jolted Kari like a third rail energy surge. She finally recognized what she was feeling when she was around Tannie. She didn't want to *be with* Tannie; she wanted to *be like* Tannie. She wanted to be someone who was comfortable in her own skin, someone who didn't seek approval. That's what her attraction to Tannie had been about. This time Kari recognized the difference.

"I think I may have given you the wrong impression." Kari smiled apologetically. "I just want to learn how to pole dance."

A sly little smirk zipped across Tannie's face. "You think I'm trying to seduce you?"

"Yes, I definitely do," Kari said. "You're sweet and I'm flattered. But I'm not interested."

"How can you be so sure?"

The two women stood facing each other in silence for a beat, until Kari smiled and eased the tension.

"I'm a happily married woman who wants to do something special for her often-neglected husband by learning a few pole dance moves. Will you show me?" Kari stepped forward again. "Please."

Tannie eyed Kari warily but motioned for her to take hold of the pole.

Kari grasped the metal shaft with both hands. "Okay. Now what do I do?"

"The key to pole dancing is keeping loose and knowing when to grip, ease up, grab, and release again," she said, demonstrating her words by closing and opening her hands. "You can't spin if you're too controlled and clutching on too tight."

Kari thought about Tannie's words for a moment and repeated the phrase out loud. "You can't spin if you're too controlled and clutching on too tight." Kari smiled. "Pole dancing sounds a lot like life."

"I told you this is way deeper than it seems."

Tannie placed one hand on Kari's shoulder and the other on her hip. "Okay. The first thing I want to show you is a side-spin leg extension. Take your right hand, and with a reverse hold, grab on like this." Tannie stared into her eyes. "Ready?"

Kari nodded. She wrapped her fingers around the pole and then loosened her hold, just a little. "Ready," she said.

Thank you!

I hope you enjoyed Pay To Play.

Please take a moment to write a short review and post it on the online sales page of the retailer where you purchased Pay To Play. Reviews help readers find good books.

Visit: jerriwilliams.com

Join my Reader Team and I'll send you the FBI Reading Resource— books about the FBI written by FBI agents, the FBI Reality Checklist, and my monthly email digest to make it easy for you to keep up to date on the FBI in books, TV, and movies and more!

Also check out Jerri's other books in this Philadelphia corruption squad series featuring Special Agent Kari Wheeler:

Greedy Givers

Spoiled Spenders (Coming Soon)

And her non-fiction book about FBI clichés and misconceptions in books, TV, and movies:

FBI Myths and Misconceptions: A Manual for Armchair Detectives

Acknowledgements

Many people have played important roles in my author journey from the first draft to publication. John Shiffman, a journalist who has been employed at several major newspapers, was the first "writing industry professional" to read the original manuscript of *Pay To Play*. John provided a list of must-read craft books and then introduced me to the second person I must acknowledge, Avery Rome, his editor at the Philadelphia Inquirer. Avery was an excellent coach who taught me how to write fiction, encouraging me to improve my skills and, in turn, my novel. My hard work paid off when my literary agent Steve Kasdin of Curtis Brown, Ltd. made "the call" offering me representation and industry validation. He also offered invaluable suggestions to get the novel ready for submission. I am extremely grateful for Steve's assistance in getting *Pay To Play* published.

I must also express love and gratitude to my husband Keith Wert and my children Chase, Shawna, and Dana for allowing me to sequester in my home office for hours and hours during countless evenings and weekends to get the words down on paper.

I'm also grateful to my beta readers—my sisters, Janine and Lisa Williams; Carol Sydnor, Sue McCullough, Wendy Stein, Bill Iezzi, and Barbara Allen, and appreciative of all my FBI and SEPTA former co-workers— Joe Connolly, Fran Kelly, Maxine Dobbins, Rochelle Culbreath, Kathy McAfee, Vicki Humphreys, Judy Tyler, Bob

Wittman, Pam Stratton— to name a few, who never failed to ask, "How's the book?"

This novel is dedicated to my parents, Buford and Odessa Williams. I'm so blessed to have grown up in a loving home where books were valued, and reading was encouraged.

Thank you all for your support!

Jerri

About the Author

 **Jerri Williams**, a retired FBI special agent, jokes that she writes crime fiction in an attempt to relive her glory days. After 26 years with the Bureau specializing in major economic fraud and corruption investigations, she calls on her professional encounters with scams and schemers to write crime fiction inspired by real FBI cases. Jerri is also the host and producer of FBI Retired Case File Review, a true crime podcast. She resides with her husband in South Jersey, just across the river from Philadelphia. You can find out more about Jerri at www.jerriwilliams.com. You can also connect with her on Twitter @jerriwilliams1 and Facebook at Jerri Williams Author.